BOOK TWO

THE MORTAL KNIGHT

MICHAEL CRONK

To Anna - for the inspiration.
Everyone's going to think I'm so clever and I literally just copied your advice, so thanks for that.

Contents

Chapter 1	1
Chapter 2	13
Chapter 3	25
Chapter 4	37
Chapter 5	56
Chapter 6	67
Chapter 7	79
Chapter 8	91
Chapter 9	105
Chapter 10	115
Chapter 11	129
Chapter 12	142
Chapter 13	151
Chapter 14	162
Chapter 15	173
Chapter 16	191
Chapter 17	197
Chapter 18	207
Chapter 19	222
Chapter 20	245
Chapter 21	264
Chapter 22	280
Chapter 23	294
Chapter 24	312

Chapter 25 326

Chapter 26 343

Chapter 27 361

Chapter 28 377

Chapter 29 394

Chapter 30 406

Chapter 31 414

Chapter 32 429

Chapter 33 439

Chapter 34 454

Epilogue 464

Acknowledgements 466

Chapter 1

"Good news, Rookie."

Jason looked up from his single page report. It was another slow day at the precinct, and he'd been trying to stretch out the paperwork to last the whole shift.

He saw the detectives approaching his desk. Lynch and Cole were the only two detectives at Plymouth station, but there was still barely enough work for them most days. Lynch was a tall, dark-skinned man in his late thirties, with a broad chest and lean waist. He was the 'bad cop' of the two, and Jason vividly remembered just how good Lynch was in that role. His partner Cole was a short woman in her forties, with blonde hair that barely reached her chin and a fringe that was cut short. She wasn't the good cop, so much as she was the professional, calm and distant.

"Hey detectives. What's the news?" Jason asked.

"Your wildest dreams are coming true," Cole answered with a grin.

Lynch nodded seriously. "We're having a tea party and you're invited. Hope you like cucumber sandwiches."

Jason stared back at him, unblinking. Lynch was always taking the piss. The only way to beat him was to not react.

"Ok I'll admit. You weren't our first choice. But we need someone to bring the scones and you seem like the right—"

"Lynch," Cole drawled.

"Alright, Cole," Lynch mimicked her tone back. He faced Jason levelly. "We're starting a new case next week and we want you to tag along as our assistant."

Jason jolted upright. "Wait…do you mean…as an investigator? To learn detective work?"

Lynch blinked. "I see we have our work cut out for us. *Yes*, rookie, to learn detective work."

But Lynch's mockery did nothing to stop the thrill running through Jason. This was it! His chance to do real detective work and learn from the experts. This is what he'd been dreaming of since he was a child, watching crime shows with his mum and fantasizing about catching the bad guys and saving the day. Jason had to work very hard to keep his professional demeanour and not jump around the room shouting and punching the air in triumph. *It's finally happening!*

"We figured it's about time," Cole said. "You more than proved yourself capable with all that business at your girlfriend's mansion six months ago and catching the murderer, Erikson. But we had to see if you could handle desk duty. Too many rookies think detective work is all Sherlock and Poirot. They don't understand it's a lot of hard work."

"And a whole lot of boring," Lynch said flatly.

"The captain says you're always on top of your work," Cole went on.

Jason shrugged. "To be fair, there's just not that much work."

"Doesn't help your old pal Dingus," Lynch said.

"It's Douglas." Jason turned around. His partner, Douglas, a large chubby man and one of the nicest human beings Jason had ever met, was chuckling at a video on his phone. He played it with the volume on max as he sipped a coke before laughing so hard he burped. Jason couldn't help noticing the stack of manila folders across multiple trays. He'd clearly stacked the trays on top of each other in an attempt to make his desk seem neater. "Point taken," Jason sighed. "What's the case?"

"Oh it's a good one!" Lynch cried, while Cole rolled her eyes. "It's the type of case every detective dreams of getting."

"In their good dreams?" Jason asked.

"Their wet ones! You ready for this, rookie? You won't believe your luck when you find out—"

"Tax fraud," Cole interjected.

"*Tax fraud!*" Lynch cried as if he hadn't heard her. "How good is that?"

Jason only stared back again. He tapped his finger on his desk and raised an eyebrow.

"It's boring as shit," Cole said. "He thinks he's going to *bore* you into changing your mind."

"Oh, how could it not? It's all number crunching and techno babble. It's as boring as it gets."

Jason held up his paperwork. "I'm filling out a drunk and disorderly form. Happened today at two o'clock. I've filled out this form twenty times this week alone. It's eighty percent of what I do here." He stared levelly at Lynch. "You're not going to bore me with tax fraud."

Lynch scowled, and Cole couldn't hide her smirk.

"You still working on that secret project?" Lynch asked, gesturing to Jason's computer.

"It's not that secret. I've been trying to get you to read it. We could do with your report as well."

"What are you calling it these days? The Magic Files?"

Jason winced. "The Immortal Investigations."

Lynch snickered. "Oh right, that's *so* much better."

"The Captain ordered me to keep a record of all supernatural occurrences in my experience. That includes everything the three of us saw at Silvana's mansion six months ago. Shapeshifters, vampires, wizards. You were all there."

"Exactly. That's why I know there was nothing supernatural about it." Lynch steeled himself. "I had a psychotic episode, brought on by the extreme stress of a life and death situation."

"A telepath was planting thoughts in your mind, Lynch. You're perfectly sane."

"Hey, don't minimise my work. I've spent a lot of time with my shrink to make sure I'm cleared for duty. Don't try to tell me 'the devil made me do it.'"

"But it's not your fault. It happened to the captain too."

"*She* didn't open fire on her squad!"

Lynch's voice had suddenly raised into a sharp snap. Several officers turned around to stare. "Everything alright over there, buddy?" Douglas called out. Jason gave him a thumbs up, and Douglas went back to his video, immediately laughing again. Meanwhile, Lynch was staring at the floor, his lips pressed together in frustration.

"I'm seeing Silvana after work," Jason said. "We're going to some big event tonight. A kind of gathering among the Immortals. Apparently there'll be dancing." The detectives didn't look impressed. "The point is, I'm learning more and more about this secret world of supernatural peoples. It will all be in my report. You both really should read it."

Neither acknowledged his suggestion as Cole changed the topic, "How long you two been together now?"

"Just over six months," Jason said. He couldn't keep the broad smile off his face.

"God, you're young," Lynch shook his head.

"Ease up, you old love grinch," Cole said. "The kid's happy. Let him have this."

Lynch crossed his arms, and the muscly sinews in his forearms flexed. "She still think she's a vampire?"

"She *is* a vampire. We're not hiding it."

"And does she drink your blood?"

Yeah. Once a month. But there's no way I'm telling you that. Jason felt a twinge of itching on his inner left elbow. He knew his long sleeves hid the scabs, but he had to resist the urge to double check. The detectives were sharp enough to notice if he so much as glanced in that direction.

"I could answer that, but the answer is not suitable for the workplace."

"Oh, please," Lynch scoffed. "I've told you plenty of times what my boyfriend and I get up to."

"I know. And I've asked you to stop many times."

Lynch only chuckled. "You know what we tried the other night?"

"Every goddamn day," Cole said and started walking away towards the precinct exit.

Lynch pointed his thumb at her back. "See the homophobia I have to work with?"

"Don't even fucking start," Cole called out.

Lynch chuckled again and moved to follow her, grabbing his bag from his desk as he left.

"Monday at nine, rookie," Lynch said. "You get your first taste of the real detective experience." He paused. "And that's not a euphemism. This is a workplace, you know." He gave Jason a wink before striding across the bull pen to follow Cole.

Jason finished his single page form and looked up from his empty desk. It was 3:30pm on a Friday afternoon and the station was nearly empty. Plymouth police had been losing funding for several years now, so the large building built for forty officers now housed only four, leaving a ton of floor space. A small handful of desks took up the centre of the room. One wall had a holding cell that was currently unoccupied, while the other wall housed a small kitchen area.

The other three officers had already started relaxing in preparation for the weekend. Martin and Wilson had struck up a conversation in the kitchen, something about kids' birthday parties. Douglas was at his desk, still on his phone and scrolling silently now.

With no one watching and not much else to do till knock-off time, Jason opened up a file on his computer, titled *The Immortal Investigations* and resumed typing.

I've had five months of combat training now. Subjects Phillip Windsor and Nicholas Romanov are excellent teachers, though I confess a bias towards Nicholas' friendlier attitude. I've now mastered all basic hand-to-hand combat moves and basic sword forms, though I'm still struggling to apply them in combat.

The court mannerisms are far more difficult to grasp. The customs within the Immortal Imperium are extensive, complicated, and most of all, rigid. The slightest breech can cause instant offense, which is extremely serious when dealing with wizards capable of mass destruction. As a mortal member of an Immortal family, I have a very specific role to fill. The role of a Knight Templar. Tonight, my teachings will be tested at the gathering of Immortal Houses.

Most dangerous of all, Silvana and I are still not married. This is the highest sin within the Imperium. A vampire must be married before they can take the blood of their husband or wife. We've been doing so for six months without marriage. I still believe it is vital for Silvana to remain unmarried. Her state of mind has improved significantly with this layer of freedom and independence. But we take an awful risk. If the Vigiles – the enforcers of the magical community – ever find out, they can execute us both on the spot without trial.

And no one can challenge a Vigile. They are masters of combat magic.

Each one is equal to the military might of a major nation.

It is my hope that my performance tonight causes no offence. I also hope I don't witness any crimes, or I'll be forced to choose where my duty lies.

Jason closed the document again. A moment later, he saw the double tick icon on the screen. His superior, Captain Aisha Kader, had seen his most recent update. She was reading it now. Without waiting to be summoned, he went to the captain's office and knocked on her door. He entered before she gave permission.

Kader sat at her desk, eyes glued to the screen, and absently gestured towards the chair opposite. Jason sat without a word. Kader was twirling her thick curly hair with one finger and squinting her dark eyes. She had lightly tanned skin, and was anywhere between early forties and late fifties. Jason still didn't have a good sense of her age.

"This…event," she asked, still reading.

"Sort of a gala. I don't know what to call it."

"Why is it happening?"

Jason shrugged. "I don't know. Some sort of annual end-of-year event. Maybe it's a Christmas thing? It's invite only, so it's rather prestigious."

"So you can expect to meet the VIPs of the Immortal community."

"Well…more like see them from a distance. I've been told not to expect any one-on-one time."

Kader looked up, staring down her long nose as her eyes settled on him. Jason remembered anew just how sharp her mind was. "Take it slow, tonight. Don't draw attention to yourself. Just do the bare minimum to get by without upsetting anyone."

"That was my plan exactly."

"Good. And if you come across an opportunity to learn more information on this world…" she sighed. "Let it pass. There's too much risk tonight as it is."

Jason had to supress the urge to argue. He was desperate to know more about Immortal society. But Kader was a lot smarter than him, so he simply nodded in agreement.

"You haven't said where it is. Surely not in Plymouth? Not when it's a massive annual event of the major Immortal Houses."

"They haven't told me where."

Kader squinted her eyes. "This is far riskier than I'm comfortable with. You told me that wizards can teleport. If that's true, then you could be anywhere in the world tonight."

"Not necessarily. Wizards are top of the food chain. I think it's unlikely they'll be performing a taxi service." He offered a smile, but Kader remained tense and worried. In fact, she was tenser than he could remember seeing her in six months. Something about this event was unsettling her. She'd commented twice on how risky it was. And she had never advised him to be cautious with his investigation so far. She was usually the one pressing for more information. So what was different now?

Maybe it had something to do with...that fear of hers. He remembered that night in the mansion, when a telepath had been planting thoughts in people's minds. Lynch had turned on the others, while under the influence. But it had affected Kader very differently. Something had caused her so much trauma and horror that she had held a gun to her own head and come close to pulling the trigger. Kader had refused to speak of it later, saying it was a question for another time. Jason had to consider the possibility that whatever darkness lay in her past may share something in common with this mission.

"I'll be ok," he said gently. "I'll play it very safe. I won't draw any attention to myself. I promise." Kader seemed to relax a little. Even offering him a rare smile.

"Don't promise," she said. "Don't commit to a course of action before you get a feel for the situation. Use your judgement in the moment. Just try to be safe, if it's possible."

"I will."

She nodded, then her eyes twinkled with humour. "You can go home early, Cinderella. You could use the extra time to get into your ball gown."

Jason stared back. "Please don't start calling me Cinderella. Cop nicknames can last for their entire careers."

She grinned even wider. "Then don't give me cause."

* * *

Jason's home these days was a moderately affluent house on the north side of town. It had a lawn, multiple bedrooms, and even a full-sized kitchen. Jason had been extremely lucky to find this place. Especially since his rental credit had plummeted after a wizard burnt down his last apartment. That had been a tiny, miserable apartment anyway. This home was comfortable, affordable, and located exactly halfway between his work, and Silvana's mansion.

However, there was one complication.

He could hear thumping music playing even before he'd opened the front door. A strange scent assaulted his senses as he entered, smelling like a mix between wood, herbs, and diesel. Inside, a male voice could be heard shouting in Korean.

Jason dropped his shoes and bag by the door and let his feet sink into the soft carpet. *It's the little luxuries that make life sweet.* He walked down the hallway to the room where the music was blasting, and rapped on the door.

Someone shouted what were probably Korean swear words and the music cut off. A moment later, the door opened and a rich herbal smell rushed out. A lean, shirtless young man stood in the doorway.

Freddie Je was a twenty-two year old university student, shorter than average with glasses and messy dark hair. Like an Asian Harry Potter. He smiled broadly as if to reassure Jason that what he smelled couldn't possibly be related to the giant glass bong with decorative green leaves that sat in the middle of Freddie's gaming desk. Still, he looked even cuter than normal. Maybe it was the shirtless part. *Focus, Jason,* he scolded himself. *Damn it, why are my roommates always attractive?*

"Hey sorry man. Didn't realise what time it was."

"I would have thought you knew exactly what time it was," Jason said. "It's nearly four thirty, after all."

Freddie chuckled. "Ha. Four twenty. I get it." Then he stuttered and glanced back at the bong on his desk. "I mean, no I don't get it. I have no idea what that smell is. Someone broke into our house."

"Uh huh."

"Shit, sorry man. Please don't arrest me. I need this, I swear."

"Freddie, it's legal."

"Oh yeah. Why do I always assume it isn't?"

Jason let out a sigh. "Can you please just open a window?"

Freddie's smile made him look goofy. "Thanks man. You're the best." Then he disappeared back into his room. Jason sighed again. Freddie was a good guy. He'd saved Jason's life, when Jason had been attacked by a shapeshifter and was bleeding to death. He had been Freddie's enemy for all intents, yet Freddie still saved him. And when Jason's apartment had been burnt down, Freddie was so quick to offer his spare room. So his character was honourable. It was just that Freddie was so…undisciplined. *Or maybe I'm just such a tight ass.*

"Oh hey, how was work?" Freddie called out.

"Super boring. But Monday should be good. The detectives are finally going to take me out on a case."

'Oh sweet!" Freddie appeared in the doorway, pulling a somewhat clean t-shirt over his head. "And any news on the...." he whispered, "Immortals."

Jason smirked. "Yeah man. I have that ball tonight."

"That's tonight?" Freddie cried. "That's awesome. Man, you're going to see so much cool stuff. If I were you, I'd be trying to learn all I could about the Immortals."

Jason chuckled as he took a beer out of the fridge and popped the lid. "Didn't you use to hate all that stuff?"

Freddie groaned. "Don't remind me. I was an idiot when I joined those Monster Hunters. Now I see that magic is pretty damn awesome." He gestured to Jason. "So what are you gonna do? Make friends with a dragon? Make out with hot vampires?"

"My captain advised me to play it safe."

"Then you should take me! I'll be like your bodyguard. I'll make out with the hot vampires for you."

Jason chuckled again. "It's going to be dangerous enough for me, and I was invited by name." *Silvana's name, but that still counts.*

Freddie sat up on the kitchen bench, his feet dangling above the ground. "Come on, man. I've got to do something to help you. I've been trying to help you for six months, but so far all I've done is be here to talk. I'm not your therapist."

"Freddie, that's a huge help. Besides, I was homeless when you took me in. And I could never afford this place without you." *Or your parents, more accurately, since they're the ones who own it.* "You help me live that much closer to Silvana."

"What about tonight? Do you need a lift?"

Jason smiled. "No, thank you."

"What about fashion advice?"

"I've already got a suit."

"Ok then. I'll do your hair."

Jason blinked. "What? You want to do my hair?"

"Hey girlfriend," Freddie put one hand on a hip and held up a sassy finger. "Don't you be doubting my magic." He dropped the pose and chuckled. Jason didn't laugh like he was supposed to.

"As long as that's *all* the magic you can do," Jason drawled.

"I also do The Gathering." Jason stared at him until he got it. "Oh right. Actual magic. My bad."

"Sorry if I'm oversensitive. My last roommate could do actual magic and tried to kill me…"

"Alright, my bad. I definitely don't do magic." Freddie said, then he smiled again. "Come on, dude. Let me do your hair. It's what all the straight guys do for their friends."

Jason laughed. "Alright fine." Though he noted that Freddie said 'straight'. *Just you remember that. Now look your best for Silvana. She's the one you want to impress.*

Chapter 2

Silvana took a long, deep breath. *Ok. Here I go.* She smoothed down the creases of her dress, readjusted the waistline slightly, and pulled the neckline up higher. It was already higher than she wished, but lower than her aunts would approve anyway. Maybe she should change into one of her older, more modest dresses. *No. I can't back down.* She looked at herself in the mirror, and grinned. Besides. She liked the blue and silver clothes. It matched her sapphire eyes and pale skin.

She gathered up the pile of documents on her desk and held them in a tight stack. She took one more deep breath to settle her nerves then stepped outside her bedroom.

The old family mansion was still in one piece. Barely. The beauty of the lush red carpets and majestic stone walls was undermined by the scratches of bullet marks on the walls and chips in stone. Worse was the entire collapsed wall that still left rubble in the central hallway. The pile of broken debris had only been pushed to the side to create a walkway, but no serious attempt had been made to fix it. The scars from the attack by the wizard and his allies seemed to be here to stay.

The dust had gotten worse since Silvana stopped cleaning so much. *Typical. If I don't clean it, no one does.* She tightened her grip on the papers and employed just a touch of vampiric speed. Not enough to use her supply but enough so she could feel the warmth of Jason's blood flowing through her, reminding herself of his support.

Her aunts were waiting at the dining table. *Well, so much for getting here first.*

Aunt Lisbeth wore a bright dress of white silk and silver gems, which sparkled like starlight in the flickering orange glow of the candelabras lining the table. Her long blonde hair was tied up at the very top of her head, the sides hanging down to the middle of her back in wavy curls. A silver diadem with a blue gem in the crest had been carefully positioned in the centre of her hair. Yet with all this décor, the woman herself was still the most beautiful part of the display. Lisbeth's face was perfectly symmetrical, porcelain, and delicate. Her blue eyes were brighter than the diadem's gem. Lisbeth was the kinder of the two aunts, yet she had a way of being critical and expecting Silvana to be grateful for it.

Aunt Emberline was a different story. Her dress was a mixture of red and black fabric woven in layered frills. Her matching diadem was framed in gold with a ruby in the crest. Her short bob of black hair was unadorned in any way. And her eyes had none of the gentleness that made Lisbeth's so welcoming. Emberline was like cold fire, and Silvana already felt like her aunt was judging her most private thoughts.

God help me.

"Silvana," Emberline said by way of greeting. "We expected your report hours ago. It's nearly time to leave."

Silvana's heart started pounding and her breathing grew rushed. *I'm already anxious? Fuck.* She clenched her fist tighter around her documents. "The report is ready now. I have copies for each of you." She handed a folder to each aunt, and noticed the sour upturn to Emberline's lip. "Please turn to the front page, and we'll get started."

She stood opposite them, hands clasped over her notes, and the front page of her report staring up at her. It had a logo, title, and photo.

"Is this going to take long, dear?" Lisbeth asked.

"No, I…" she stopped making excuses and chose to be bold instead. "I've been very thorough, aunty. My presentation will be brief, though I recommend reading the report for more details afterwards." There was a pause, and Silvana began before any more questions could cut in.

"The attacks on our home six months ago have proven one thing beyond a doubt. Our House is at risk of collapse."

It was an ambitious opening, cutting straight to the point and confronting the reality of the situation. Predictably, her aunts opened their mouths to interrupt, so Silvana powered on.

"We have been unable to repair any of the damage suffered in the battle with the wizard. If we cannot even fix this house, then our financial situation has clearly become so desperate that we are one more disaster away from total ruin. If this House fails, we will be reduced to mere holders of titles and nothing more. We may easily become as poor as our former enemy, Peter Erikson, who lived among mortals and desired what little we have. We cannot become like that. House Romanov must survive."

Silvana couldn't hide her smug smile. Her aunts were stunned into silence. It had been six months since the disaster and no one had even spoken about their inability to rebuild. This was the first time someone had called them out for their denial. Silvana went on.

"The Clarke family assets are very limited. Most of our wealth is tied up in Maristow House and its contents. We have very little money in circulation right now. In short, in order to improve our financial standings and ensure our House's continuation, we need to diversify our assets and put our money into action." Silvana allowed herself a brief smile. *That delivery was perfect. Great introduction.*

"I'm sorry," Emberline cut in, not sounding sorry at all. "Is this whole presentation going to be about taking financial risks?"

Silvana stammered, "I…well, no. Not exactly."

Emberline gave an exasperated sigh. "Silvana," she said in that patronising tone of hers, and Silvana clenched her hands into tight fists. "The money of this family is thousands of years old. We are but the most recent stewards in a long line. This money must remain for the next generation, else this family fall into disgrace like so many before us."

"But we'll fall into disgrace if we continue as we are," Silvana said.

The room went quiet. Silvana nearly gasped in surprise at herself. *Holy Father, did I just contradict her?* Yet her aunts were silent in shock, so she launched back into her talk as she shuffled papers around.

"Immortals who do not adapt to the times will become obsolete and fall into poverty and destitution. Therefore, I have several options to modernise our assets. Of course, I understand it is of the uttermost importance to preserve the integrity of our home and heirlooms. As such, I have no intention of selling anything. What I propose is a loan, using our property and materials as leverage. We can obtain a cash loan up to the value of this mansion without having to sell it. Then we can invest that money and get it working for us. Active money is growing money." Silvana smiled. "You can see this information on pages three to six of my report."

Lisbeth hurried to those pages and began to scan. Emberline continued staring at the front page.

"So you want to borrow money, just to spend money," Emberline said.

"Invest it," Silvana corrected. "The rate of investment growth will always outperform the rate of loan fees, if we find the right deal. Then in a few short years we'll earn enough to pay off the loan entirely, leaving us with pure profit."

"And just where will you be investing it, my dear?"

Silvana had to quiet down another flutter of anxiety. "If you turn to pages eight, through to page fourteen, you'll see several proposals for options of investment."

She was most proud of this. She had not one, but six investment options, and any single of them would be enough to save her family's fortune. She'd even created a graph at the top of each page for easy comprehension. They only had to pick one.

This is going to work. I can convince them.

"Option one is property," Silvana said. "In my ninety two years of life, the value of property has gone up by over a thousand percent. Mortals have dramatically increased their population, which has led to greater demand and inflation. For the value of this mansion, we could buy a dozen houses. Or build entire complexes of townhouses. This has minimal risk, and one of the greatest potentials of growth."

Silvana turned the page. "Option two is—"

"Property?" Emberline said. "What happens if they're destroyed by fire or malicious tenants?"

"That's what insurance is for," Silvana said. "Fun fact, it's actually *more* profitable if they are destroyed—"

"You don't understand the risks!" Emberline snapped, snatching up the report and shaking it at Silvana. "Do you realise that if something happens to any of our investments, that money is gone?"

"But…but insurance. That's *why* it exists."

"Those loan sharks can seize our property. Do you comprehend that? If our investments fail, the bankers will claim our debt and take everything from us. It'll be worse than selling, because we won't make anything off the loss. Then we'll be left with nothing. We'll become vagabonds and outcasts from Immortal society."

"We're already heading that way," Silvana said, stepping up to the table's edge and leaning towards her aunts. "And the banks won't sieze our properties as long as we make our repayments. There are legal clauses that protect us from that sort of thing."

"But you're not considering other Immortals," Lisbeth said. Silvana winced to see both aunts unified against her, as usual. She was hoping Lisbeth would at least be open-minded. "If we expose ourselves to risk, you can bet our enemies will find out about it and take this opportunity to ruin us absolutely. There is no mercy within Immortal society."

"What enemies?" Silvana cried and threw her hands up. "Our House is on good terms with everyone. Why do you think we got invited to tonight's event?"

"Because the sharks smell blood in the water." Emberline stood up, her voice rising. "The wizard's attack nearly destroyed us. Now others know we are vulnerable, if only four youths at the beginnings of their power could threaten our lives. You can bet tonight is about testing us for weaknesses."

"We got invited because we won that battle. Jason killed a wizard. We've impressed people."

"No, daughter. We've only caught the curiosity of the powerful. Tonight is about survival."

"But who, aunty? Who would want to destroy us?"

"Everyone!" Emberline shrieked, slamming her fists on the mahogany table. She lowered her voice to a soft hiss, "And *anyone*."

Silvana lost her voice. All she felt was a blind terror, and any counter argument slipped from her panicked mind. She folded her report closed and lowered her gaze.

I'm an idiot. I never should have tried this. They were never going to listen to me.

"You need to listen to me, Silvana," Lisbeth said in a softer voice, her eyes narrowing in her sister's direction. Silvana took note of that. "Any House will remove us from existence if they stand to gain from it. If there is profit in being our enemy, then that's what they'll become. Therefore, no," she closed the report. "This idea is impractical."

Emberline dropped the report on the table before her and stood up. "We won't be taking any loan, or risking this home in any way. We're already taking enough risk with you and your *boyfriend* bedding each other without shame. Any Immortal could have you killed if you are discovered."

"Is that what this is about?" Silvana snapped. "You won't approve my financial plan, just to coerce me into getting married?"

"You're risking all of our lives, just to let that mortal boy touch you. I didn't raise you to be a *slut.* I raised you to—"

"I wish you never raised me."

Silvana stopped, her face flushed and burning hot. The words had burst out of her before she thought them through, and even as she said them, she knew she had gone too far. Emberline's eyes had gone blank. Not cold or angry. Just…empty.

"Your aunt is right," Lisbeth said, cutting in with a calm voice and directing all attention to herself. "Any Immortal House would destroy us if they learnt about a loan. In the past they would send armies, Silvana. Now they would raise their businesses against us, undermine the market, and do whatever it took to end us for no other reason than to build their own power base. That's how serious you should view this risk. You've had a good idea, sweetie, but it comes with too much risk."

Silvana couldn't speak. She couldn't trust herself to do it without snapping and screaming. So, instead, she bowed her head and left the room without looking back.

She marched back to her bedroom, staring only at the floor. She calmly shut her door behind her and took a long deep breath.

Then she let blood surge within her hands and ripped the entire report in half.

* * *

An hour had passed when she heard the car pull up. That engine, that crunching of dirt on the forest floor could only mean one thing. *Jason.*

She left the bedroom with superhuman silence and moved to the mansion's huge double doors, where the heavy wood swung on its hinges as she pushed them open. The fresh aroma of fallen tree leaves wafted through the doorway. Already, she could smell him. Cleaner than normal, less of that musky sweat he was usually covered with. And something else foreign. Hair products? Surely not.

A few seconds later, Jason appeared in the doorway. He was already in his full tuxedo, complete with jacket, black bowtie, and golden cufflinks. It was a cheap suit, made of polyester that gave a plastic shimmer on the surface, yet it was shaped to fit him perfectly, tightened around the middle to hint at his flat core. His shoulders already broader than most now had pads in the jackets lining that made them seem even larger. He seemed to loom over Silvana, all masculine firmness and strength.

Except, his cheeks were red. *Is he embarrassed? The poor fool doesn't realise how good he looks.*

"Is this ok?" Jason asked, giving himself a once over. "Freddie did the hair." The fringe was artfully tucked to one side and accentuated his eyes. "I'm not sure about the bow tie. That's why I came early, in case you wanted to change anything." He trailed off when he saw her staring silently. "I mean, you look great, Silvana. Really beautiful." He blushed again. "Sorry. I'm just nervous. I've never dressed up—"

Silvana took his hand and all but dragged him inside, shutting the door behind him without a noise. Then she dragged him upstairs towards her bedroom.

The mansion was silent. Her aunts and uncles were probably still getting ready themselves, doing final touches even though they had looked ready an hour ago. *Uptight snobs.* She stepped into her room, locked the bedroom door and turned to face Jason.

At her feet were the discarded sheets of her financial report, now shredded into tiny little pieces and laying in a pile.

"So," he said, grinning like a boy and reaching for his bow tie. "What did you…"

She threw herself at him.

It was the exact kind of action that would have shamed her just months ago. Her aunts would never let her act with such abandon. And Arthur – her late husband – would never have elicited such a response from her. But Jason was different. It was his strong gentleness that always made her feel safe enough to be herself.

She kissed him with a rough franticness that surprised even her. Her fingers folded into his hair and pulled him down towards her. She wanted to feel the press of his body against hers, the heat of his chest, the touch of his chiselled muscles gripping her soft curves. Jason's hands were already on her waist. She pushed them lower, onto her ass, where he didn't hesitate to squeeze firmly.

Yes. That's what I want.

"Wait," he whispered, already breathless. "You're fully dressed. Won't this ruin your hair and—"

"I don't care."

"Oh. Right. Well, I don't care either. I don't know why I asked."

He reached for his top button but instead, Silvana reached for his pants. She let speed surge into her hands and had his buckle out of the way in a second. Her hand reached straight down towards her goal and clasped him tightly. She felt him shudder against her. She loved that such a strong man could be brought to his knees so easily at her touch. Silvana began to move her hand in slow, rhythmic motions. Her fingers pressed down, rubbing against him, and she felt him swell beneath her touch. She smiled in satisfaction. As he hardened, she pulled his cock out and began to tug, eliciting a small moan as she did. It was enough to send Jason pawing at the curves of her ass.

"God, Silvana," he gasped in her ear, his breath sending shivers down her neck.

She kept going, and as she did, she could hear Emberline's voice in her head. *I didn't raise you to be a slut.* Silvana snarled at the memory and moved her hand faster. Jason's breathing grew louder as another moan slipped out. But it didn't silence the thoughts that kept pushing their way to the front of her mind. *You put us all at risk to bed that boy. Shameless.*

I'm happy, Aunty. I'm happy for the first time in my life.

But Emberline's voice kept saying over and over.

Slut. Slut. Slut.

Jason gripped her shoulders, his fingers digging into her skin. "I want…" he panted, unable to speak. "I want you."

Silvana set her jaw firmly. This beautiful man wanted her, and no one was going to ruin it for her. She let him turn her around and press her face against the wall as she started pulling her gown all the way up over her hips. Jason was helping a half-second later. He kicked aside the pile of paper on the ground. The dress was clear. Silvana slipped her underwear down to her knees. Then she reached behind her to clutch him and guide him, arching her back.

The moment he entered her, she heard the word again, shrieking in her mind. That filthy word, filled with the shame and guilt Emberline wanted her to feel. She ground her teeth together, squeezing her eyes closed and focused on the pleasure building inside her.

I don't care what you think of me. I'm happy. I'm fucking happy!

Jason began thrusting his hips faster, rougher than normal. He was clearly too excited to think straight. He was pounding awkwardly into her internal wall. She changed her angle until he was sliding more smoothly. Then she braced her forearms and elbows on the wall and widened her legs.

"Is this ok?" Jason gasped.

"It's perfect," she whispered back.

She wasn't going to climax. But that was never the goal, not now. All she wanted was to feel in control of herself. To feel proud of herself. And to know this man desired her with an absolute, undeniable desperation.

"Darling, I'm…" he gasped.

"Do it, Jason. I want you to do it. Come for me…"

That was all the encouragement he needed.

He folded against her back, his fingers digging hard into her hips, before he laced an arm around her middle and pulled her up against him. He held her close with such tenderness that it sent a wave of pleasure through Silvana. She pressed her head back into his chest and let out a pleased sigh.

It was some time before the throes of ecstasy seemed to leave him. They both panted softly as the sweat began to trickle down Silvana's back between the fabric of her tight corset and skin. Just when the position became uncomfortable, Jason withdrew and stood back, letting her stand up straight. He looked bashful.

"I'm sorry if I was too rough," he whispered.

"It's was perfect."

"And sorry I didn't get you to…"

"Jason," she cut him off with a hand on his chest. "That was exactly what I wanted."

"Ok. Good." He looked down, and she followed his gaze to see his junk poking out from under his shirt and jacket. It looked a tad ridiculous, and, if she were being honest, somewhat unflattering. "Uh…excuse me," he stammered and waddled awkwardly towards her ensuite with his pants still bunched around his ankles.

She looked down at the torn-up report. Jason had brushed it aside without conscious thought. Silvana smiled to herself. The voice in her head had fallen silent.

Chapter 3

Jason tucked his shirt back in and straightened his belt. *What the hell was that?* He checked himself in the mirror and sighed at his ruined hair, ruffled and all out of place.

Or maybe, the hair served its purpose.

He wandered out into the bedroom and found Silvana by the dresser, adjusting her chest and how it sat in her corset. She already looked just as perfect as before. "So, um," he started. "Is everything ok?"

"Oh yeah," she said gently. "Just changing underwear." She sat down on her bed and started lifting her dress again.

Jason kept a respectful distance. "Right. But what just happened?"

She turned around with a coy grin. "Has no one ever explained it to you?"

"No, actually. Between my dead mum and the foster system, I never got the talk."

He stopped. A pained expression crossed Silvana's face as she said, "I'm sorry. I shouldn't have…"

"No, I'm sorry," he insisted, holding his hands up in surrender. "I thought that would be funny, for some reason? But that was just dumb." He shook his head. "I'm concerned for you. I know I'm not showing it well."

"Jason, I'm fine," she said, smiling. "Truly. You just looked really handsome."

He nodded. "Uh-huh. And what's that pile of paper over there?"

"Oh. Nothing." Silvana abruptly finished fixing her clothes and raced across the room to collect the discarded shreds of paper. She scooped them up into a ball and dumped them in her metal trash can, before turning and smiling innocently.

Jason raised an eyebrow. "Nothing?"

"I was attempting a drawing. It was really bad. I wanted to start again." She pointed to the posters on the wall, depicting superheroes in various costumes and several anime characters. "I'm trying to copy this art style, but I'm not very good at it yet."

Jason opened his mouth, but stopped himself. He had the urge to start cross-referencing like a detective on an investigation, but even with his little experience in relationships, he knew that wasn't the way to help. Silvana was holding something back, and she didn't want to talk about it. He needed to accept that and move on. *What if she's dumping me?* He pushed the thought aside. She wouldn't do that. She'd just had sex with him. *Unless it was a pity fuck.*

"Jason?" she asked.

He forced himself to smile. "You'll have to show me your drawings, next time. I'd love to see them. I bet they're really good."

"You're sweet," she said simply.

Something flickered in her eyes. Was it guilt? Even so, Jason made a mental note to ask her about it later.

"We should go. My family will be waiting. We need to get you ready before we leave."

He followed her to the door. "What do you mean get me ready? I'm dressed. And Phillip and Nicholas have already been teaching me Immortal customs for months."

"It's not that," she said, but volunteered no other information.

Jason followed her out to the hallway. He stared at the back of her dress, noticing the way it swished with the slightest movement of her hips. He thought of how that dress had looked all scrunched up on her back. How it felt to have her ass perched on his stomach…then he let the thought go. Silvana was bothered by something. He needed to be on watch tonight for her emotional needs. *Like a detective, but for emotions.* He grinned. That made it sound badass.

He took her hand and held it as they walked.

The central hallway still had broken stones piled along one wall. They had at least been shifted to the side, but no one had made any serious effort to move them in the last six months. The hole in the wall had only gotten wider as more stones fell out of place over time. *When are they going to fix that? Maybe they can't afford to.* Jason didn't stare.

The parlour room was decorated with several large oil paintings in golden frames. Lounge chairs made from red velvet filled the space. But no one sat in them now. Two women and two men stood in the room, waiting.

The women wore elaborate gowns of silver and blue, red and black. They had thick coats of makeup, making their skin appear even whiter than normal. Jason didn't understand all the rings, necklaces and diadems the women wore, but noted the details like a detective writing a report. They might have symbolic significance.

The two men were adorned in old military uniforms, like the ones Jason had seen in history books from the late eighteenth century. They wore blue vests and jackets lined with golden pads on each shoulder and a golden sash that ran diagonally across their chest. Their forearms had more golden embroidery. Their breast were ornamented with rows of medals. At their waist was a long, thin sabre. And they held a flowery white hat in their hands.

"Jason," said Nicholas the Third – the older man in his eighties –

as he nodded his head in greeting.

"Sir," Jason replied with a lower bow.

"Silvana," Emberline said in a flat tone. "You've finally...*finished*."

Jason looked between them, and saw Emberline's steel gaze mirrored in Silvana's rigid stance. Had something happened between them? Jason knew their relationship had grown increasingly tense since Silvana's refusal to marry, but the mood here suggested something more had occurred recently.

"We're almost out of time, Silvana," said the other man, Phillip the Second. "Your carelessness has put us at great risk."

"I'm sor—" Silvana cut herself off. Then she swallowed and spoke in a clear tone, "I regret any inconvenience caused." She offered no other explanation.

Jason gave her a full smile. She hadn't apologised in subservience. She was standing up for herself.

"Well, let's begin," Lisbeth said, her voice laced with strain. "We will be leaving in less than five minutes, and timing is of the essence. Nicholas?" Jason wanted to ask why the lack of time, but decided not to waste it with questions.

Nicholas took a step forward. "Jason Turner. Come forth."

Jason obeyed without thinking. He'd spent months under Nicholas's instruction and training, so obedience was drilled into him. He stood before Nicholas with his hands at his side and head high. "Sir," he said.

"Kneel."

He didn't hesitate. He bent a knee before Nicholas and lowered his head slightly.

"I, Nicholas the Third of House Romanov, as the head of my House and patriarch of my family, officially recognise Jason Turner as my son."

Jason looked up in shock.

Did he just say son?

Nicholas beamed back at him. He whispered, "Watch your head, son." He held his sword in his hand and lifted it above him. Jason bowed his head again, just as his eyes began to sting. *Son. He sees me as his son.*

"I acknowledge him as the Mortal Knight of our House, and as my heir and successor."

What? Jason nearly looked up again. But Nicholas shifted, and he felt the soft weight of the old Knight's sword on his shoulder. He dubbed Jason on both sides.

"May he defend this House, its interests, its members, and most of all my dear Silvana, long after I am gone."

Nicholas stepped back and rested his sword at his side. "Rise, Sir Jason Turner, Knight Templar."

Jason stood. His mind was racing with questions, yet his discipline held long enough for him to remain quiet. He even resisted the urge to wipe the tear that rested on his lower eyelash.

"Sir Phillip," Nicholas said. "Present."

Phillip moved forward, his face a calm mask with an edge of steel. He drew out something from behind him, a long black sheath with golden dragons etched into the sides and a handle with a golden brace around the grip.

"This sword," began Phillip, "is an heirloom of our family. It belongs to you, yet even now you are merely a steward, holding it until it passes to the next owner. Let it remind you that you are a guardian of this House, and this family. Leave it in better condition than you found it." He offered the sword on two outstretched palms.

Jason merely stared at it. He whispered, "Do I need to say anything?"

"Take the damn sword, zounderkite," Phillip whispered back.

He did. The sheath was cold metal and had a strange weight to it.

Jason couldn't tell if it weighed one kilo, or ten. The sheath had a leather strap which Jason wrapped around his waist, under his suit jacket and over the top of his hips, so that the sword hung on his left side with the handle in easy reach. The weight felt strange on his hip. It would throw off his balance while he walked, as it already threw off his posture. But he would grow used to it in time.

Phillip stood back in line. "Welcome to House Romanov, Sir Jason Turner." There was only a hint of distaste in his tone, but Nicholas repeated the phrase in a much lighter voice, closely followed by Lisbeth and Emberline. Last, spoke Silvana. Tears rimmed her beautiful blue eyes, glistening like sapphires in firelight.

Jason stood a little awkwardly. He waited. "Is that everything?" he asked nervously. Emberline made a huffing sound.

"Almost, son," Nicholas said warmly. "Give me your hand." Jason moved to his side and held out his right hand. "No, the other one." Nicholas took Jason's young hand between his two wrinkled hands with spotted skin. He reached into his breast pocket and pulled out a ring.

It was a pure gold ring, the band plain and unadorned. However, the centrepiece had a broad flat surface with something carved into the signet. Jason noted a red coiled dragon that held a sword in its four legs. The sword looked very similar to the one now strapped to his side.

"This marks you as my heir," Nicholas said. "And this one," he pulled out a simple gold band, "will mark you as Silvana's husband."

"What?" Jason said. "Wait, is that what just happened?"

"No, son!" Nicholas chuckled. "The wedding ring is just for tonight's ball, to keep up appearances."

"Oh." He heard Phillip muttering under his breath. Jason could guess the gist of what was said.

"But this ring," Nicholas went on, finally sliding the heirloom ring on Jason's index finger. "This is real. You are ready and worthy to be my heir. There's nothing fake about it." As an afterthought, Nicholas also put the wedding band on Jason's ring finger and patted his hand firmly. Yet, he seemed dissatisfied with so small a gesture. Suddenly, Nicholas fell on Jason and embraced him, his old arms squeezing him tight with a firm grip. Jason stood rigid for a moment. *Relax, Jason. He's being affectionate. This is normal. Act normal.* He relaxed into the old man's embrace and hugged him back.

Phillip came forward and shook Jason's hand amicably and without crushing his grip. There was no warmth, but there was a certain respect in the gesture. Lisbeth gave him a gentle hug and a kiss on the cheek. Emberline came forward last. She hesitated a long moment. Jason waited without fidgeting. Finally she leaned forward to kiss him on the cheek.

"You stink of semen," she hissed in his ear, before she leaned back and offered him the perfect impression of a genuine smile.

Oh yeah, she and Silvana definitely just had a fight about me. That's just great.

"Alright. Who wants champagne?" Nicholas said cheerfully.

"Nicholas," Emberline said. "Surely we're going to drink enough tonight."

"This is a special occasion. We have welcomed someone to the family. I doubt I will ever see this happen again in my lifetime." He spoke the words with a boldness, like stating a fact. "I will not miss this chance to toast my new son. My love?"

"Yes, dear," Lisbeth said and crossed the room to the fridge, disguised within a cabinet. She took out a bottle, collected a tray of goblets, and placed them down on the benches near the group. She leaned back dramatically and pointed the bottle high. It popped with a loud crack. Lisbeth let out a high-pitch whoop at the same volume and poured drinks, before she handed them out so everyone had one.

Jason smelled his. The scent was bitter.

"To Jason Turner," Nicholas said. "And to our darling Silvana. We love you both. And we couldn't be prouder."

The sting of tears welled up in Jason's eyes again. *God, he just said he loved us both. Both! What the hell...* Silvana must have noticed. She put her arm around him. He had to breathe through his nose, else his lips would start trembling.

Is this what it's like? To have a father who loves you? To have... a family?

"To Jason and Silvana," Nicholas finished. The others all echoed him in a cheer and raised their goblets. Jason struggled to swallow his champagne over the lump in his throat.

Afterward they stood in silence as Jason felt his emotions somewhat settle. He wanted to say something to show his gratitude, but he didn't know what. How do families speak to each other? Should he say he loved them too or would that be too forward? It wasn't perfect, since Emberline was clearly furious at him. He was surprised to find he didn't mind that. A family member being angry at him felt strangely familiar, even comforting in a sick way. Her disapproval seemed more like family to him than Nicholas's kindness. *Maybe it's all part of family.*

"Thank you," he said, his voice soft. "Thank you all."

It felt insufficient. But they nodded in understanding.

"Do you know what that ceremony was?" Emberline asked. She looked directly at Jason.

"Em?" Lisbeth said, a tone of reproach in her voice.

Jason shrugged. "Induction into the family?"

Emberline raised her chin. "It's the final stage of a wedding ceremony. Performed after the marriage is finalised." She offered a smile. "We had to perform it out of order."

Silvana stiffened and blew air from her nose in a sharp breath. Jason kept his tone soft. "I appreciate what you've done. I know it wasn't how you would have liked it, but it means a lot to us both."

"I would have done it sooner," Nicholas said, while his fellow knight Phillip frowned at him. "It had to be done before tonight at least, before the gala."

"Nicholas," Phillip said sternly.

And Jason understood. Nicholas had used tonight to push for official recognition, but Emberline and Phillip had resisted until the very last minute. *Well. Maybe I'm not that welcome in the family after all.* Still, it was nice to know Nicholas had cared enough to advocate for Jason so hard. That was extra meaningful.

"Don't worry about that," Lisbeth said. "We all still agreed on this. Everyone voted on bringing you in early. I hope you can forgive us if we're still somewhat…" she gave a strained smile, "unfamiliar with doing things differently."

"Of course," Jason said.

"There's still one stipulation," Phillip said, and turned to Nicholas expectantly.

"Yes. Unfortunately, son, we still can't let you live here. You are family in truth, but without marriage, we can't condone you and Silvana living together. It would be improper."

Jason and Silvana exchanged a glance. "You know we're already…" Silvana started.

Nicholas held up his hand. "Please. There's no need to say it." Jason couldn't help smiling at his old-school attitudes.

"It's ok," Jason said. "I'll visit as often as I can." He put an arm around Silvana's shoulder and pulled her close. "So, you said we had to leave soon?"

"Any minute now," Phillip said. Yet, no one moved.

"So, uh, where are we going?"

Phillip shrugged. "Don't know yet."

Jason blinked. "When will we know?"

"When we get there."

Jason stared around the room. No one seemed bothered by this statement. He took another sip of champagne, wishing it was a simple beer instead.

A faint stirring of noise like the gentle rustle of clothes came from nearby. Jason looked up from his drink.

Two women now stood in the room before him, where no one had been a second earlier.

Jason stepped forward, shielding Silvana with his body. His free hand went straight to the handle of his sword.

"Now now," said a husky voice. "Is that how thou wouldst greet a guest?"

Jason recognised them now. He immediately let go of his sword and held up a hand to show he was not a threat. "My apologies. I was only startled. Please do not take offence."

That was the exact phrase Nicholas had schooled him on. He'd delivered it flawlessly. Yet the two women remained silently staring at him with faces hard as iron.

"It's telling, isn't it?" said the woman with bright red hair, blue eyes and fair skin. "You look upon the Vigiles of the Immortal Imperium, and what does your instinct have you do? Reach for a weapon and stand guard of your beloved. I cannot say if you are incredibly foolish," she paused to smile, like a beautiful predator, "or incredibly wise."

Vigiles. Immortal wizards of great power, and the enforcers for the Imperium. Jason barely knew what they were capable of. Had he just given them cause for offense?

The second Vigile took a single step forward, her heels clicking on the stone floor. "Neither. Thy action, however motivated, is entirely inconsequential." The older woman had black skin and long dark hair that was braided from head to waist. She wore golden necklaces, bracelets and dangling earrings. Both women wore tuxedos almost eerily similar to Jason's own.

"Welcome, Vigile Desdemona and Vigile Portia," said Nicholas with a modest bow. "We are delighted to have you with us."

Portia, the younger redhead Vigile, stared across the parlour room and shook her head. "Wish I could say the same. This place hasn't improved at all."

Jason inhaled, ready to launch out a counter insult but Silvana pulled at his arm. Somehow, she had sensed him tense up.

"We shall be thy escorts for the evening," Desdemona said. "We shall take thee to the location, and return thee home in precisely four hours. Any member not returned to the location will be abandoned henceforth, and the privilege of travel rescinded. Doth thou agree to these terms?"

Jason struggled to keep silent. It was only his respect for Nicholas that helped him stay still. "We do," Nicholas said.

"Then stand together," Portia instructed.

Everyone began to take the hand of the person next to them, forming a circle that included the Vigiles. Silvana took Jason's left hand. He reached out to the right, and saw Desdemona staring at him. Up close, her eyes were black.

"Come hither, mortal. I doth not bite," she purred, but her tone implied that was exactly what she did.

Jason swallowed and reached a steady hand towards her. She snatched it up with a jerking motion. Jason managed not to flinch, though his heart was racing.

"Portia," the older Vigile said.

"Ready, mistress."

"Wait, what's happening?" Jason said.

"Silence," Desdemona hissed. She shut her eyes and Portia followed.

And something began to…shift.

The air around them began to bend, as if viewed through a mirror with fractured glass. It looked like the room was folding around itself. The roof moved sideways, the walls moved up, and the floor seemed to race away from them in all directions while never getting any further away. And Jason could feel magic surrounding them. It was beyond anything Peter had ever demonstrated. It felt like an electric current burning his skin, but somehow chilling him with bitter cold as well.

"Hold your breath," Portia commanded.

"Wha—"

The floor dropped out from beneath Jason, and suddenly he was falling.

Chapter 4

The entire world was a black sea of nothingness. There was no light. No sound. Jason knew this, because he was waving his arms frantically, and he was screaming, yet saw or heard nothing.

Where am I? Where are the others?

He shouted into the silence. "Silvana!" Then, "Desdemona, you asshole!" No sound came out.

Then somehow, something moved within the void. Darkness filled his vision, but it was different now. It was no longer just emptiness. It was… night time. Stars shone in the black expanse of sky. Lights were flickering past. He realised the world was folding in around him, just as the mansion had folded away before. He could see the light from buildings. Concrete flooring. A city landscape. A towering structure of blue steel and golden light.

A hard force hit him in the chest. He let out an 'oof' sound, and he heard it clearly. Everything had stopped moving around him except the hustling of people.

There was a large crowd of one hundred people in front of him, all dressed in fine evening wear and sipping drinks. Only a few had noticed him. Jason realised he was on his belly, lying on the concrete floor. He did a push up and stepped to his feet.

"Silvana?" he called.

"Well," said a husky voice. Jason spun around and found his whole family right behind him. All of their hands were still locked in a circle except where he had fallen out and left a gap. Desdemona was shaking her head at him, her long braided hair swinging with every shake. "Dear knight, hast thou lost thy courage so quickly?"

"You dropped him on purpose," Silvana snapped. "He was ripped from my grasp."

"And yet, thy love hath arrived here, at the agreed upon location. Tell me, how wouldst thou have teleported him?"

Silvana glared back. She clenched her hands into fists, and the slightest hint of red entered her eyes. Jason stepped in. "Thank you, mighty Vigiles, for your…gracious…ness." He grimaced at his wording.

Emberline clicked her tongue.

"Oh, how charming," Portia said with a laugh.

"Well, here we are," Nicholas said. "Hey, welcome to the party, pal!" He grinned boyishly.

Jason frowned at him. "Die Hard? What happened to Dirty Harry?"

Nicholas shrugged. "I'm trying new things." He cleared his throat. "Ok listen up." He drew out a large, golden pocket watch. It had a long chain attaching it to his waist, and Jason had to supress the urge to smile. "It's six o'clock by British time. If we are where I think we are, that means it is ten o'clock here."

"Where do you think we are?" Jason asked and looked around. They were standing on a balcony, outside under the stars, while a hundred people were already gathered inside in a massive event hall. There was nothing to suggest where in the world they were. "I just assumed we were in London."

"Look down, darling," Silvana said. Jason ran to the balcony railing, and gasped.

They were hundreds of metres off the ground. Beneath them was a sea of skyscrapers, maybe thirty or forty giant buildings in total, yet all far below where Jason was standing. He was in the tallest building of them all. At the ground level was a huge eight lane highway that ran right through the heart of the city. There was even an intersection with another highway of equal size running in the opposite direction, with a dozen pathways leading off the highway overlapping each other. Yet beyond the city was…only the darkness of night. There were no lights that marked the city outskirts or suburbs. It was just skyscrapers, then nothing.

"Where…" he muttered.

"Want me to tell you?" Silvana asked. "Or can you guess, detective?"

Jason could only shake his head. He was still in shock. About everything.

"I'll give you a hint. This building we're in? It's the tallest in the world."

Jason swung around, looking at her with wide eyes. Silvana was grinning back. "Tallest in the world? That's in Dubai. How…what… we're in Dubai?"

"In the Burj Khalifa."

"Oh god." Jason looked out the window again. "Are we on the top floor?"

"We're on the one hundredth floor. It goes up to one hundred and sixty three."

Jason turned his head around to look up. Sure enough, the skyscraper stretched far above them towards a single blinking red light at the top of the spire.

"Whoa."

"Come on. Nicholas is still talking." She dragged him back to the family, but Jason couldn't stop staring over his shoulder at the view.

"As I was saying," Nicholas resumed. "We were invited for four hours. That means two a.m, local time. 10 o'clock London time. We must be back here at this exact spot for the Vigiles to return us home. Don't miss that cut off."

"Right," Jason said and reached for his phone to set an alarm. His pocket was empty. He slapped at his chest and found nothing. "Where's my phone? Shit, it must have fallen out during that… transit."

"Hey, mine's gone too," Silvana said, looking through her sequined décor clutch.

Portia scoffed. "You will not need your phones here," she said in a scolding voice. "We can't have you recording videos and posting them to the internet. Nor can we have you tracking the whereabouts of the Imperium elite."

"Where is my phone?" Jason said flatly.

"In your home. It probably fell to the floor. I hope you have a hard case." Her eyes glinted.

"Thou shouldst also know," Desdemona said, speaking to the group. "This event is under an enchantment. None may do violence upon another while here. Attempts to do so will incur the wrath of the Vigiles." She smirked at the word wrath.

Portia gave a polite laugh that made Jason shiver. "Your evening beckons. Remember, return to this point in precisely four hours, or you shall have to make the return trip on your own." The two Vigiles stepped out of the circle, came alongside each other, and walked into the crowd without a backward glance.

Jason watched them leave. *I wonder if they're a couple.* His mind automatically imagined them having sex. *They'd probably do it on an altar of human sacrifices.*

"Alright," Nicholas said and Jason drew back his attention. "Let's go over our plan. Lisbeth and I will be speaking with my cousins, the Glucksburgs." Jason tried to commit the name to memory. "Royal house of Denmark," Nicholas added.

"Oh. You're related?" He noticed Phillip shaking his head.

"Immortals are all distantly related," Nicholas said. "Normally we'd explain this when you became heir, but the Glucksburgs married into the Romanov House. You know my forbearer, Nicholas the Second? His mother was a Glucksburg."

"Oh! The grandmother from the animated movie."

Phillip shook his head again.

"I'll take your word for it," Nicholas said. "But that will be my focus tonight. Phillip and Emberline?"

"We have a list of possible contacts," Phillip said. "Starting with my cousins, the Windsors. It's a big list. We'll find someone."

"Good. And Silvana? Jason? You've got the harder job. Talk to anyone you can. Strangers, even. Maybe go for other young people? You don't have to make deals. Just make friends."

"Yes sir," Jason and Silvana echoed.

"Good. Now, let's get out there and represent House Romanov. Let's find new allies, and let's make some deals."

"And not embarrass ourselves," Phillip said as he looked at Jason.

"Yes, please don't," said Nicholas. "Cause if tonight does go badly, 'I promise I will never even *think* about going up in a tall building again.'" Nicholas grinned. No one reacted. "Really? That was also Die Hard."

"This isn't the time, my love," Lisbeth said with a gentle pat on his arm.

"We're in the tallest building in the world. If not now, then when?" Jason couldn't help laughing.

"Come on, my love," Emberline said and pulled Phillip forward. "I think I see my cousins." The couple disappeared into the crowd.

"Good luck, Jason," Lisbeth said. "I'm sure you'll do us proud."

"Thank you," he said, meaning it.

"And if you get nervous, son," Nicholas whispered, "just remember these wise words."

"Please don't…"

"Yippie Kay Yay, mofo!"

Jason rolled his eyes. "Well done, sir." Nicholas bumped his fist on Jason's shoulder and walked stiffly forward, leaning on his vampire wife.

Silvana clutched his hand tightly. "I won't leave your side."

"And I won't leave yours." They held hands as they walked forward.

It was a varied group of people. All shades of skin colour, and all ethnicities seemed to be represented in equal numbers and many dressed in a way to honour their country of origin. Jason noted the colourful gowns from east Africa, made from cotton fabric and decorated with bright headpieces. Several black women were wearing their hair tied up in bold shapes like a cone, a halo, and even a crown all formed out of their own hair. Other outfits were unmistakably Chinese. Silk skirts, tied off with a golden sash as high as the ribcage, and sleeves with long drooping wings underneath. Nearby, Geisha women were painted with white faces, red lips, and wearing traditional kimonos.

Several indigenous cultures were there from South America, Australia, Mongolia, and others Jason couldn't recognise.

Mixed among them were the Europeans. Men in military vests and women in ballroom gowns almost exactly like Silvana's aunts and uncles were wearing.

And there was Jason, in a standard tuxedo made of cheap synthetic polyester. It was the fanciest thing he'd ever worn, but here, he looked like the serving staff.

Well, at least I have a cool sword.

Yet what stood out most to Jason was the jewellery. Everyone was wearing necklaces of pearls, rings studded with precious gems of black opal and blue diamonds, and crowns of gold and silver. The combined wealth being worn in this room made Jason think of his struggling early life in Plymouth, and the nights when his parents couldn't afford dinner.

Unbelievable. Just one of those items would set me up for life.

He found himself squeezing Silvana's hand too hard, and softened.

"You ok?" she asked.

He nodded. "Everyone looks…"

"Human?" she offered.

"I was going to say rich."

It was the most opulent place Jason had ever seen, and it made him sick to his core. The room had a massive bar lit up with neon blue lights and was packed with serving staff. White lounges were set up all over the floor with Immortals gathering into groups and speaking in hushed voices. There were no walls around the outside of the room, only glass panels to give a better view of the city lights. In the centre stood the elevators, stairwells, and bathrooms, but aside from that, the whole room was as open as possible.

A man resting on a lounge flicked his hand, and a goblet flew off the nearby serving tray straight into his grip. Jason's breath sped up. *A wizard. I just saw a wizard do magic. Holy hell.* Jason had almost forgotten what he was looking at.

There were no Vulcan ears, or house elves, or cave trolls. This could have been a meeting of regular mortal kind among the super elite. Except for that glimpse of magic.

"You're right," he said. "They all look human. But they are not human."

"You have to remember, Jase," Silvana said coyly. "This event was invite only." She looked at him with her eyebrows raised. He looked at the crowd, then back to her.

"You mean… some Immortal races are excluded?"

She nodded. "This ball is for the mentally enhanced Immortals only. You won't see any physically enhanced here. Except, technically, vampires." She sniffed loudly. "Although…"

A waiter appeared, a young man with brown skin and a dark-haired fringe, holding a tray of drinks in bronze goblets that looked like antiques from a museum.

"Champagne, honoured ones?" the waiter asked.

Silvana took one, so Jason copied her to not seem rude. The waiter bowed and withdrew. Silvana stared at his back and whispered, "A Metamorph."

Jason gripped his bronze goblet a little tighter. "So the Skinwalkers are only allowed to be here as servants. Doesn't that seem wrong to anyone else?"

"Careful, Jason. You'll see more of that tonight. No matter what, you must remain polite." He nodded at her, and deliberately did not drink any alcohol.

A noise came from behind and Jason spun to see another group of people appearing out of nowhere onto the foyer floor. Two Vigiles held a group of people in a circle and finished their transport spell. The group relaxed, and Jason caught a glimpse of their faces.

"Oh my god," he said. "Is that…Prince William?"

The Duke and Duchess of Cambridge had arrived with their entourage, looking exactly like they always did on TV. Except their two Vigiles remained on either side of them as a menacing escort.

"Let's go," Silvana said and tugged Jason away, beginning to walk around the outskirts of the room.

"But…they're the Windsors. Aren't they your family?" He blinked. "*Our* family?"

"Different side of the family. There's a feud."

"What?!" Jason said, but Silvana forcibly lead him away.

"The Romanovs begged the Windsors for asylum, but they denied the request. That's why Nicholas the Second and his family were slaughtered."

"But…that was a hundred years ago."

"Jason, a hundred years is well within the lifetimes of most of these Immortals. We haven't forgotten."

Jason couldn't help swearing in awe. Now he understood exactly the type of people he was rubbing shoulders with tonight. These would be the royalty of the world. Or the power *behind* that royalty. It occurred to him how much knowledge he had access to. He could discover the secrets behind all modern civilisation, and uncover the mysteries of the world's ancient past.

Captain Kader's voice came to him. *"If you come across an opportunity to learn more information on this world, let it pass. There's too much risk tonight as it is."* She was right. He should be cautious.

Then Freddie's words came back to him, like the devil perched on the opposite shoulder. *"If I were you, I'd be trying to learn all I could about the Immortals."*

Jason shook his head. *Get behind me, Freddie. I'm playing it safe.*

"So, do you know anyone here?" Jason asked.

"Not many," Silvana said. "I do know one guy. An alchemist. But he's…unusual."

Jason watched as he moved around the crowd. A few people stared at him, and looked at his outfit with derisive sneers. He tried not to glare back. "Let's go talk to him."

Silvana led him through the crowd. More people glanced up at Jason as they passed, giving him brief glimpses of curious or scowling faces, some with Oriental face paint, others with dark skin and bright smiles, and one woman who's red vampire eyes were on full display. Someone bumped into Jason, whether by accident or intention was unclear, since he didn't see who it was. He kept one hand on Silvana, and another near his belt, and watched each passer-by with suspicion.

"Hello Edward," Silvana said, and Jason spun around.

The man before them was dressed like a high lord from the Middle Ages. No, Jason thought, he looks more like a modern person *trying* to dress that way. Like a cosplayer, or a guest at a medieval festival. This man wore a bright red puffy gown with white frills under the collar and neck. He had long matted hair that hung loose and covered half his face. He had a thin mouth and a slightly too long nose, but handsome blue eyes.

He glanced up at Silvana, before his eyes darted away again. "I can't help you, Ms Clarke. I don't have any elixirs on me."

Silvana pressed her lips together. "I'm not here to buy, Edward. I've come to say hello." Edward nodded, but said nothing in response. He stared past her into the middle distance, so Silvana sighed and said insistently, "Hello, Edward. How are you?"

"Fine," he said. The silence stretched.

"Aren't you going to ask me who this is?" Silvana gestured to where Jason stood beside her.

Edward shook his head. "You're about to tell me anyway."

Silvana gave a huff of annoyance, but Jason stepped in. "I'm Jason. Silvana's husband. I'm pleased to meet you, Edward."

"Jason," Edward said flatly, like he was committing the name to memory more than returning a greeting. He still didn't make eye contact, instead looking just beyond Jason's shoulder.

"How long have you been an alchemist?" Jason asked.

"One hundred and thirty-four years, and three months."

Jason blinked. *And three months?* A smile began to creep onto his face. "And you sell elixirs to Silvana?" Edward said nothing in response. "Well, in that case, I must thank you for saving my life." Edward didn't react, but Jason had suspected that would happen. "Six months ago, your healing elixir brought me back from the brink of death. I owe you, Edward."

The alchemist shook his head. "No. Clarke's healing elixir was already paid in full. Four hundred and seventy English pounds, by bank transfer, on February thirteenth."

Jason chuckled. "No, I just mean I owe you my thanks." He gave Edward a formal bow of respect to show what he meant. Again, Edward said nothing in response.

"Aren't you going to say 'you're welcome'?" Silvana asked.

"Why would I?" Edward asked.

"Oh forget it," Silvana snapped. "Let's go." She tugged at Jason's arm and tried to lead him away. He pulled out of her grip. "Jason? What are you doing?"

"What are *you* doing?" he blurted out.

She glanced at Edward, before pulling Jason a few steps away to whisper where he couldn't hear. "That man is being so rude. He's always like that. He can't follow the simplest social custom. I can't stand him."

"Silvana, of course he can't."

"What do you mean?"

Jason leaned down to whisper. "He has autism."

Silvana only stared back. "What?"

"Autism." He blinked. "He was avoiding eye contact, he missed social cues, and took things literally. Surely you noticed? Didn't you study medicine?"

"Yes, Jason," she said, sounding unimpressed at his question. "I learnt surgery and general practice. I never looked into all those mental disabilities."

Jason blinked at her. "All those disabilities? Silvana?"

Silvana softened slightly. "Oh," she said. "You must think I'm being very rude right now."

"Honestly, yeah. Kinda." He saw the regret on her face, so he tried to soften his tone and placed a gentle hand on her shoulder for reassurance. "Is this how all Immortals are? Do you ignore disabilities?"

"I don't," she insisted. "When I was young, they discovered Post-Traumatic Stress Disorder for the first time, after The Great War. I believe in that condition!"

Jason nearly rolled his eyes. She believed in PTSD, and thought she was being progressive for it. *I forget how old she is sometimes.* "Silvana, Edward's brain is fundamentally different. Not wrong, just different. It's very common for people with autism to have poor social skills. When you expect him to act with all your social graces, it's like asking me to cast a spell. It just cannot be done."

They looked back at Edward. He was still standing alone. In fact, he looked quite content to stand alone all night. His eyes were still downcast, but they flickered towards Jason and Silvana briefly. When he saw them watching, Edward looked away again. He kept poking his two index fingers together, unconsciously tapping at a consistent speed.

"Come on. I'll show you how to talk to him," Jason said. "All you have to do is find a subject he's interested in, ok?"

Silvana nodded in agreement and followed him back to Edward's side.

"Hi Edward," Jason said. "I had a question about your healing elixir."

Edward gave a 'hmm?' sound in response.

"After it healed me, I was *super* hungry. I was wondering…"

"It's supposed to do that. The potion was working perfectly. I won't be processing a refund." He'd spoken all in a rush, and Silvana twisted her lip upwards like she was ready to snap back.

Jason spoke calmly. "I know. So why does that happen?"

"It's complicated," Edward said.

"Can you tell me? I'd like to know."

The alchemist glanced at Jason's feet, then shrugged. "Healing elixirs accomplish both matter conversion, and cell growth acceleration. The acceleration requires large amounts of fuel from a nearby source, otherwise it's likely to latch onto vital organs and cause a complete shutdown of body functions. So matter conversion steps in, turning non-essential cells in the body into fuel for the growth. The least essential cells are always the newest, or those still foreign to the body. Conversion's first step will be to empty the stomach's contents, then into the digestive system, burning through food, water, faeces and urine."

Jason stared at him for a moment. "That is extremely cool!" he said with a laugh. "You used my own shit to save my life. You're brilliant!"

Edward's mouth hung open, like he was frozen mid-speech. He looked up and met Jason's eyes for a whole second before looking away again. "There's a magical component, of course. I can cast enhancement spells on my elixirs to help them reach potential. And I have an exclusive healing elixir that can revert death, if administered within minutes of passing. I always carry some on me."

Jason grinned broadly. He looked to Silvana with raised eyebrows, but she was still frowning.

"Well, that is fascinating. I'd love to learn more about alchemy."

"I can't teach you. A mortal can't do spells."

"I know. But I'm very new to the Immortal world. I only met Silvana seven months ago. That was the first time I learnt vampires existed. I'm not from any Immortal House."

Edward nodded. "I'm from Swansea."

Jason blinked at the sudden topic change. "Swansea. Is that in Wales?" Edward nodded. "How about that! I'm from Plymouth, England. That's only a few hours' drive away."

Edward looked up at him sharply. "Can you use the internet?"

Jason couldn't help laughing. "Well, yeah. I use it every day for work. I'm a police officer. But I'm no internet expert."

"Can you teach me to use the internet? I've heard of this thing. Google. It's how mortals do research, and I'd love to know how to use it."

"Oh…" Jason stared at him for a long moment. "Uh…sure. Yeah."

"Great. You can come by next weekend and stay the night. What alchemy would you like me to show you?" He pulled out a pen and paper from somewhere in his colourful robes, wrote his address down and handed Jason the slip of paper.

Jason's mind was scrambling to catch up. He did not want to drive to Swansea on his weekend and spend the night with someone he'd just met. Yet how often would Immortals give him such access to information? This could really help with the Immortal Investigations. Then he had a brilliant idea.

"Can I bring a friend?" he asked. "His name's Freddie and he's something of a genius with computers. A real expert! He's mortal too."

Edward nodded. "Fine, fine, bring Freddie too. I want to fully understand this internet."

"Ok. Sounds like a plan." Jason smiled, and turned to Silvana with a raised eyebrow.

Silvana's mouth was hanging open. "Edward," she said gently, "I'm sorry I've been so rude to you."

"Everyone's rude to me," Edward said flatly. "I'm rude to everyone. That's why I don't leave my lab. I'm only here because I was told it was rude to decline the invite. My plan is to stay in this corner and avoid people. That way I'm not rude to anyone."

Silvana let out a gasp. She reached out to touch Edward's arm, but he stepped back out of reach. Jason shook his head at her. Silvana looked between them, then said, "I like superheroes." There was an awkward pause. "Uh…do you like superheroes?"

"I like Captain America," Edward said.

"Me too!" Silvana cried. "He's my favourite. He's the most noble of them all. And he's like a vampire in strength."

"I like that he was made strong with alchemy."

"Alchemy?"

"The super soldier serum that turns him into Captain America. It's an elixir."

Jason and Silvana looked at each other. "Wow," Silvana said. "I'd never thought of it like that. But yes. I guess that's true. That's really cool."

Edward nodded. "Do you use the internet?"

Silvana smiled. "Yes, Edward."

He nodded to himself. "You can come next weekend too."

Silvana startled. Her mouth went up and down several times as if about to speak. Then she simply said, "Thank you, Edward." She looked at Jason, and he nodded.

"It's been really nice talking to you, Edward," he said.

"Yes, it's been really lovely," Silvana echoed. "Are you...ok here by yourself?"

Edward nodded. "Goodbye," he said simply. "I'll see you on Saturday."

Jason smiled. Edward had learnt enough social graces to know when someone was leaving, even if he was a bit too dismissive. He and Silvana said goodbye and moved away into the crowd again.

Silvana suddenly turned and hugged Jason tight around the middle.

"What's this?" he asked with a laugh.

"Thank you, Jason," she whispered. "You are just so wonderful." She leaned back and smiled up at him. "I can't believe how nice he was to talk to, when you just let him be himself. He's really smart. And I..." she made an angry face. "I can't believe how rude I've been to him all these years. I've been so horrible. I thought he was doing it on purpose."

Jason nodded. "But you learned how to be better. That's the important thing."

"It occurred to me. You were nice to me, back when everyone in my family was always pressuring me to marry quickly, and follow all the Imperium's rules. I remember what a relief it was to have someone who wasn't trying to force me to be a certain way all the time. Then," she sighed, "I realised that's what I've been doing to Edward all these years. Trying to force him to fit my worldview. It's unfair. And it makes people miserable."

Jason said nothing. He waited for her to collect her thoughts. She looked up at him and shook her head. "How did I get so lucky? You're a great man, Jason. You make me a better person. And I'm…sorry I don't appreciate you properly."

His mind started racing. *Don't appreciate me properly? What's this about?* He thought back to that afternoon, when she'd dragged him to her bedroom. He had felt pretty damn appreciated! But maybe she was feeling guilty about that? Especially if she only did it to get back at her aunt Emberline.

If that was the case, he honestly didn't mind. He wasn't Emberline's biggest fan anyway. And there were worse ways to be underappreciated.

Jason didn't answer out loud. He simply leaned down and kissed Silvana, and after a brief pause, she kissed him back.

A loud chime rang through the foyer like the clink of a bell and all conversation died down. Jason took Silvana's hand again and searched for the source of the commotion.

A single Vigile stood at the top of a grand elevated platform. He was a large man with dark skin and long dreadlocks, wearing a tuxedo similar to Desdemona and Portia. He stood with his hands clasped together.

"Ladies and Gentlemen," he said. "Distinguished guests, honoured persons, and members of the exalted Houses. It is my duty and privilege to announce, his illustrious majesty, ruler of the Immortal Imperium…"

A cold chill ran down Jason's neck and spine. *Ruler of the Immortal Imperium? THE ruler?*

People in the crowd were whispering all at once. "Surely it cannot be."

"He hasn't been seen in public in decades."

"We shouldn't have come."

The Vigile gestured behind him and a resplendent figure emerged from an archway, dressed head to toe in red robes with golden trims on the outside. Every inch of this man's clothes was woven with diamonds that sparkled in thousands of micro reflections of light. He wore a giant crown made in the style of the British crown jewels, with a golden circular base, a bright red cushion in the middle, seven half arches of silver folding together above the headpiece, and a holy cross on the top. The man was Caucasian, and he looked as old as Nicholas. *For an Immortal to look that old, this man must be ancient. Eight or nine hundreds years old.*

The announcer proclaimed, "All bow before the great High King, Reynold the First."

At his name, every person on the room fell onto their knees. Jason was slow to respond and was one of the last down. Everyone's face was pressed to the floor. He copied them and they all stayed like that for several seconds.

"Rise," came the old, raspy voice of King Reynold.

Everyone staggered to their feet again. The King moved forward off the platform and stepped into the crowd, becoming slightly obscured from sight. The murmur of the crowd resumed, and Jason breathed easily.

"High King?" Jason whispered to Silvana. "Is he, what…" he

struggled to find the words, "…the ruler of Earth?"

"One of them," Silvana whispered. "There are seven High Kings that rule the Imperium. All of them are wizards of the highest power possible. But Reynold…you might consider him the first among equals. He's the greatest of the High Kings, and everyone knows it."

Jason's heart was pounding in his chest. "How…" he trailed off again. "Where does he come from? Is he English?"

Several people nearby seemed to glance in his direction. Silvana leaned in close to whisper back so no one could overhear.

"He's the ruler of House English."

Jason frowned. "Wouldn't there be multiple English Houses?"

"Not an English House, Jason. Reynold is from *House English*. That's his last name. That's why his country is called England, and why his language is spoken around the world."

Jason's mouth dropped open. "How have I never heard of this guy?"

"You've heard of his younger brother. William the First, Duke of Normandy. Better known as William the Conqueror."

Jason stared at her with wide eyes. "From 1066? Battle of Hastings? That William?"

"Yes, that William." She stared towards the platform, where Reynold had stood. The cross on top of the royal crown could still be seen above the crowds. "There's a reason England has been a major world power for the last thousand years. Why the English Empire is a global superpower today. And why English is the most popular spoken language of the world and the official language of the Imperium. Because Reynold the First has made it so."

Jason watched carefully as the giant, golden crown weaving through the crowd. "But British Imperialism has done some horrible things over the last one thousand years," he said. "Strip mining. Slavery. Mass genocide."

"Yes," Silvana whispered. "And you've just seen the person most responsible for all of it."

Chapter 5

The crowd was subdued. Jason could hear the raspy old voice of the High King from across the room. He found himself backing away from the sound.

"I don't know about this," he whispered. "My training never covered High Kings. We had no idea someone so high up would be here."

"We couldn't have known," Silvana said. "High Kings never attend functions like this. For even one of them to appear, let alone Reynold himself, is a sign of something big." She looked at Jason. "We could be in very serious danger."

"They we should go."

"We can't. The Vigiles won't take us home before our four hours are up. Besides," she clutched her hands around Jason's palm and gripped him firmly. "This doesn't change anything. We still need to make allies. Let's just try to avoid the High King."

"Ok, ok," Jason muttered. "Um...do you know anyone else here we should speak to?"

"Not really. We have cousins, but my aunts were going to speak with them. Maybe we should...speak to someone new?"

Jason shuddered. Socialising was never his strength. He'd always had a grouchy face, and growing up in the foster system gave him a tendency to live in isolation. If that wasn't enough, he was also the biggest fish out of water in the whole room. And he was anxious about the High King.

"Don't worry, I'll find someone," Silvana said. "Maybe another vampire would be a good move." She scanned the crowd, inhaling sharply. "Oh look, there's another young couple. I think the guy might be a mortal."

She led him through a gap in the crowd, towards a young couple standing by themselves. The woman wore a bright pink kimono with white flowers. Her long black hair reached the small of her back and hung without any adornments. The man beside her had matching black hair worn shorter, with a fringe that partially covered one eye. He wore a black cloak over a folded white vest and loose fitting grey pants. He almost looked like a stereotypical kung fu master in American films. They both appeared like regular humans, so Silvana must have smelt a difference between them with her vampire senses. If the guy was mortal, then what was this woman in the kimono?

The couple looked up as Silvana approached, Jason at her side. Their eyes were cold and wary. Silvana stopped short and bowed with her hands clasped together. "Greetings, friends. I am Silvana, of the House Romanov. This is my husband and Knight, Jason. We would like to make your acquaintance."

Silvana remained in her bow. The couple stared back with guarded expressions. The man looked towards the woman in question. She nodded and spoke.

"Greetings, Silvana and Jason. I am Hana. This is my Knight, Mikeru."

Jason recognised what this meant. Hana had given the simplest greeting possible while remaining polite. She'd also avoided mentioning her House. This meant she was open to talking, but would not volunteer information about herself. *That's ok. We can work with that.*

"I like your outfits," Jason said. It felt blunt, but he meant it. "You're a beautiful couple."

Mikeru eyed him up and down. "Your outfit is…elegant in its simplicity." He grinned. Jason gave his best polite grin back, choosing to assume it was a compliment. "That is an impressive sword. Are you familiar with its forms?"

Jason forced his smile wider. "I don't like to brag."

Mikeru pulled back his jacket, revealing the black handle of a katana at his hip. "If not for the enchantment, I would love to duel an Englishman. We could both learn so much."

Oh, he means the anti-violence enchantment. Well. At least we're talking. "Another time," Jason said, and Mikeru smirked in amusement.

"I think I've heard of you," said Hana. "Jason Turner, the mortal knight who slew the rogue wizard, Peter Erikson. I was astounded to hear that the Vigiles pardoned you."

Jason blinked. He hadn't realised news of his actions had spread. Silvana was quicker to respond. "One does great deeds in defence of one's home and family," she said.

"Indeed," Hana replied. "Tell me, is there a business venture you were hoping to propose?" Silvana paused, but she was quiet for too long, revealing she had nothing planned. Hana smirked. "I didn't think so. I intend no offence, but we were hoping to negotiate certain deals tonight."

"This was more about offering friendship," Silvana said warmly.

"Then you can consider the friendship established and our need for communing ended." Hana's tone was decidedly not friendly as she turned to go.

"We're looking to purchase property!" Silvana blurted, startling Jason with the rise in her volume.

"Property?" Hana asked with a faint hint of derision.

"Yes. I have a portfolio outlined with suggestions. However, if I could bring in other investors, there are greater options available to us."

"Interesting. What options?"

Silvana smiled brightly, yet Jason could see her uncertainty. "I had several houses outside London lined up. The value increase in the area is set to explode over the next five to ten years. And with other investors, we could purchase whole streets. Whole suburbs."

"And corner the market?" Hana giggled like a schoolgirl in an anime. "Has House Romanov fallen so far?"

"What?" Silvana said as her face fell.

"You want to buy houses. *Dasai Baka,* that's how you *start* a portfolio of investments. Are you telling me that you haven't even purchased your first property yet?" She smiled sweetly. "And you expect me to invest in your schemes? You probably want me to buy it for you because you can't afford it yourself." Silvana flinched. "Oh, did I guess right? Too bad. Your House has a strong name and a good reputation. But without any real power…"

"We have cash," Silvana cut in. "I can invest in your property instead. What is your counter proposal?"

Jason tried not to let his surprise show. He had no idea they had cash anywhere. Was this why Silvana was tense all evening? She was preparing to make deals of this magnitude? He remembered the torn up papers on her bedroom floor. Investment plans? Maybe he shouldn't have taken her nervousness so personally. She seemed to have bigger plans.

Hana studied her through narrow eyes. "I have a construction company. We're building skyscrapers in the business districts of several major cities. One in London, in fact. The London building is only months away from completion. You can buy shares now, and make your money back when we sell. The turn-around is short, which I suspect would meet your needs most adequately."

Silvana gave a relieved smile. "I would be most interested." She held out a business card, and Hana only paused a half second before she extended her own for the swap.

"I'll await your contact," Hana said and bowed low. Jason understood the bow was a dismissal. He and Silvana returned the gesture, then backed away from the couple.

"That was brilliant," Jason said. "I had no idea you'd done so much preparation for tonight."

"Well, some of that was improvised."

"I've got to ask. How sure are you that we can trust them?"

"They're Immortals doing business. Of course we cannot trust them." Silvana said with a smile. "But I'll be ready for—"

A woman's shriek ripped through the noise of the crowd. Jason spun. The cry was cut off suddenly after only half a second. Everyone kept talking as if nothing had happened.

"What was that?" Jason whispered. Silvana could only shrug. "I've got to see." He forced his way through the crowd. People were moving towards him at an unhurried pace, like they were fleeing in a calm state so as to not look like they were fleeing. Jason caught sight of a golden crown with a cross on top. He froze in place and the crowd parted around him.

Reynold the First stood before him, dressed in his golden robes and covered in gemstones. He stood in front of a woman in a dazzling red ball gown. And he was openly groping her.

He had his leathery old hands on the front of her dress. The fabric had torn and part of one breast had come out. The King was squeezing the exposed flesh with a sneering grin on his lined face. At once, Jason understood. Reynold had seen this woman's large chest and thought nothing of seizing her then and there. She had screamed, then cut off when she realised who it was. Now the woman was doing everything she could to keep still and leave her face expressionless, but Jason could see the fear and revulsion in her eyes.

"Jason," Silvana hissed and tugged at his arm.

"We have to stop this."

"Jason, there's nothing we can do."

He turned to her sharply. "That's a sexual assault happening right before my eyes. I have a duty to protect people."

"He will kill you with a word and think nothing of it," she said. "Why do you think no one else is challenging him? Cause he can do whatever he wants. Now come on." Jason felt himself being ripped back by Silvana's greater strength. He glanced once more at that poor woman, just as the King slapped her on the face. It was a feeble slap with no power, clearly done just to humiliate.

Then Jason's hand was on his sword.

Silvana's hand came down on top of his, preventing him from drawing it. "Wait."

"He has no right. No amount of power makes that ok."

"Jason, you are my knight, and I'm ordering you to stand down."

He blinked. A moment of calm burst through his rage, and he looked at Silvana. "I'm sorry. Did you just say you're ordering me?"

She blushed. "Yes. Technically I have that right."

"Huh."

"Are you mad?"

"I… don't know. But we should discuss this later." He turned back, and saw the High King had moved away from the woman. Everyone was pretending nothing had happened. The woman was scrambling to pull her top back up, though it seemed like too much fabric had been torn.

"Let's help her."

"Jason, no. We should act like everyone else. Besides, she's probably feeling humiliated."

"Hey, you wanted to make allies, right?" he said. "I've chosen who I want to speak with next." Silvana hesitated a moment, then nodded, and together they rushed to the woman's side.

"Excuse me," Jason said. She looked up, and Jason was instantly struck by her obvious beauty.

She had flowing blonde hair, eyes of the brightest blue, and a face like a movie star. Yet her eyes were red with unshed tears. She held her jaw in a steel clench, and her youthful face was tightly controlled. Jason now saw, her gown had been ripped down to the waist in a single tear. It was unsalvageable.

"I have no wish to talk," the woman said in a flat tone. Her accent placed her as an American, though Jason couldn't recognise where specifically.

Jason had his jacket off in a moment. "Please, take this."

"And what will it cost me?"

"Nothing. You can have it."

She glared at him. "What game are you playing?"

"He means it," Silvana said. "He's trying to help."

The woman frowned at Jason, and he shrugged. "I'm new to all this," he said, nodding his head to the wider room.

"You must be," she said and took the jacket. Jason averted his gaze when her gown started falling open while transitioning into the new clothing. She did up the suit buttons. It was low cut and revealed a lot of cleavage but she was large enough to fill it out. "I must say, this is actually a rather good look." She was right. Her red gown with the black jacket combined a formal and informal style. She looked directly at Jason and bowed her head. "Thank you, sir knight."

"I am Lady Silvana, of House Romanov," Silvana said proudly. "This is my knight and husband, Jason." She clung to Jason's arm and kissed his cheek.

And now she's jealous of me. Oh Silvana...

The woman gave Silvana the same bow, with her head only. "Samantha, of House Kennedy."

Jason raised an eyebrow. *House Kennedy? Could she be related to John F Kennedy? She's American, after all, and they're a political family.* "Well, it's an honour…" But Samantha wasn't listening. She was glancing over Jason's shoulder with a blank expression that couldn't hide the tension around her eyes. She was afraid, but trying not to look afraid. Silvana had the exact same appearance as she looked past Jason, though she didn't hide it as well. Jason turned.

The High King was standing right behind him. Watching.

Reynold the First stood only slightly shorter than Jason, except his crown made him loom taller. He would have been a handsome man in his youth with a strong jawline and blue eyes, though now his eyes had puffs of red and his jaw had sagging skin folds. Yet there was something in the way that he stood, watched, and simply existed. He was powerful, and he knew it. This was a man who had never known fear.

Jason forced himself to take a bow, despite his revulsion at what this man had just done. "Your Majesty," he said, bending at the hips. It was possible he should take a knee before the High King, but Jason drew the line there.

"Why help her?" Reynold asked. His voice was still strong despite a slight rasp, though his tone gave away nothing of his feelings.

Jason had no idea how to answer that. Should he tell the High King that he was disgusting for assaulting a woman? It'd probably get Jason set on fire. He glanced back at Silvana and Samantha, hoping one of them would give a clue. Both only looked back with thinly veiled fear. Jason knew what was expected of him. He should give some polite lie that would avoid offending the king. But it just felt wrong.

"Because she needed help," Jason said flatly, looking the King dead in the eyes.

Reynold raised his head slightly and Jason braced himself for pain. "You are brave," Reynold said. "Perhaps the slaying of a wizard has taught you pride." Jason's eyes widened at the reference, and the High King gave the slightest satisfied sneer. "Yes, I know who you are. The Mortal Knight, Jason Turner."

Fear surged through Jason's body like hot fire, begging him to run and hide from this man. His skin crawled to hear his name spoken from Reynolds lips. It took all his training to make himself bow again and speak calmly. "I am honoured to be known by you," he said.

"This one," Reynold said, gesturing to Samantha Kennedy. "You could benefit from a friendship and improve your prospects. But do not forget, you are greater than she."

Jason had to keep a frown from lining his face. "I am, sire?"

"You are a man," Reynold said simply. "While a mortal must obey an Immortal at all times, always remember the place set for us by the Lord God Most High. The right to rule is given to men, as He decreed. Remember your birthright, even as you must give praise in public."

Jason couldn't believe what he was hearing. Reynold was advising him that all women were lesser, even Immortals. An image flashed into his mind, and he remembered his father, standing over his weeping mother, screaming at her to submit to him because he was the husband. Here was the exact same belief, ten thousand kilometres away and spoken by arguably the most powerful man in the world. Jason couldn't speak. He was too angry, like the small child he had once been, too helpless to fight back against his father. He didn't trust himself to act with control.

So he simply bowed again and said, "Thank you, sire."

Reynold seemed to accept this. Without another word, he turned and walked back towards the crowd, many of whom had been watching while pretending not to. Jason stared at the High King's back and the train of robes and gems that decorated him, and pictured hitting the back of his head with something heavy. *Calm down, Jason. Get control of yourself again.* He took a long breath and focused on letting his nerves settle.

Silvana appeared at his side and placed an arm around him. "You did really well," she said. "I know how hard that was for you. I'm so impressed." She kissed his cheek, and Jason's heartrate began to slow.

"Thanks, darling," he said.

"Sam!" a voice cried. A dark-skinned woman appeared beside Samantha and wrapped an arm around her shoulders, squeezing her tightly. Her lean face showed concern, which hardened into a dark fury when she saw Sam's ripped clothes. This woman had her hair done up in an elaborate style of curls, and her Arabic gown of emerald green embroidery only accentuated her beauty.

"By Allah, Sam. I just heard what happened. Are you ok?" Jason was surprised to note her distinctly British accent.

"I'm fine," Samantha replied. "My new friends have come to my defence."

"Not exactly," Jason grumbled. "I wish I could have intervened directly."

Both women turned sharply to stare at him.

"What?" he cried. But Silvana was shaking her head at him.

"It is unwise to suggest challenging a High King," the Arabic woman said.

"His will is the law of the world," Samantha said, bitterness in her tone. "There is none who can defy it. I would hope you would never be so foolish as to try."

"No, I guess not," Jason murmured.

The Arabic woman in green offered a tiny bow. "Greetings. The helpers of my friends are my friends as well. I am Khadija, from the House of Al Khalifa."

God, I hope I don't have to repeat that name.

"Al Khalifa?" Silvana said in a tone of reverence. "So that means… you're our host."

Khadija smiled warmly. "That is correct. My family own this building. And you are all very welcome here." Jason looked at Khadija with new appreciation as she clapped her hands together. "I think tonight has been tougher than we expected. How about you all join me for drinks in a private booth?"

Before Jason could even process this, Sam answered, "That would be lovely. I could use some peace and quiet. And a strong drink."

"Excellent. Besides, we'd both love the chance to get to know our new friends." Khadija linked arms with Jason, and Sam linked arms with Silvana, and he felt himself being pulled away.

What just happened?

Chapter 6

The 'private booth' was the entire hundred and first floor, with about ten wait staff dedicated to Khadija's needs, and not a single other guest in sight. The layout was similar to the lower level. A large bar lined one wall with several staff stacking glasses and bottles in preparation. Electronic dance music was blasting slightly louder than Jason would have liked. The dance floor was empty, and the whole lounge area had dozens of leather couches with velvet cushions left completely unused. The floor had dimmed lights from above, and blue fluro lights on the ground.

Khadija gave a whoop as she downed her second shot. Sam copied her as she adjusted herself inside Jason's jacket and shuffled her hair. Jason and Silvana sat on a couch opposite like nervous atheists at a Pentecostal church.

"Aren't you drinking?" Sam asked.

"I had a few beers before arriving. I'm trying to slow down."

"And you?" Khadija asked, looking expectantly at Silvana.

Silvana gave her a warm smile. "I've had several wines already," she lied.

Jason didn't so much as glance at her, lest he give her away.

Khadija gave a polite smile. "You know, I can get you whatever you need. You are…vampiric, right? House Romanov and all? Cause I can get you something stronger than wine."

Silvana gave an honest-to-God gasp. "Are you suggesting I drink someone else's *blood?* Someone other than my husbands?"

"What? No," Khadija said with a polite laugh. "I never meant to cause offense."

"Hang on," Jason said, "you sounded unsure if Silvana was a vampire. Can't you smell her?" Everyone stared at him. "Oh. You two are not vampires? My mistake." He shifted awkwardly on the couch and cleared his throat. "So what are you, then? Witches? Telepaths?"

"Wizards," all three said at once.

Cold rushed through Jason's body. They were both wizards. And unlike Peter who had only appeared like a nineteen-year-old, these women appeared in their early thirties. That meant they were nearly two centuries old.

Nicholas had explained the maths to him. Immortals aged like normal humans until they turned sixteen. Then the aging process slowed dramatically. For every one hundred years of life, they aged about eight mortal years. It took a bit of effort to calculate, but Jason was getting the hang of it. *If these two Immortals appear about thirty years old, then take away their first sixteen years when they aged normally, that leaves fourteen years aging at the Immortal rate. At eight years per century, that's one hundred and seventy five years. Plus the original sixteen, it's about one hundred and ninety. Assuming I guessed their age correctly.*

That meant these were not young, inexperienced wizards like Peter Erikson had been. They would have fully come into their magic and be several magnitudes of power greater.

And the four of them were alone.

"It's alright," Khadija said with a laugh. "You can relax, sir knight."

"There's an enchantment," Sam droned like it was obvious.

"And even without it. You're our guest and our new friend. You have nothing to fear."

Jason gave her a wary look. Yet Silvana seemed to relax. Perhaps these words constituted some sort of promise.

Khadija smirked. "Though I have to admit, you probably have more cause to fear than most. Didn't you kill a wizard?"

"Yes. But we fought him together." Jason gripped Silvana's hand. "We're a strong team."

Sam gave a dark laugh, and her chest shifted with the motion. "Please. You fought a baby wizard. And he'd already fallen victim to the first sin of wizardry."

"First sin?" Jason asked.

The wizards went quiet and glanced at each other. "Should we?" Sam asked. Khadija spoke, but no sound came out of her mouth. Jason thought maybe the music was just too loud, until he saw Sam gesturing wildly and speaking in what was clearly a half-shout, still making no noise. *Some sort of magic mute button?*

"Alright, we'll tell them," Sam's voice cut back in.

Khadija offered another charming smile. "Sorry for being so rude with the sound bubble. It's just easier than getting up and moving. That shit is exhausting!" She laughed at herself, and Jason couldn't help smiling. For a powerful wizard and insanely wealthy person, Khadija was refreshingly direct. "So, we'd love to tell you a little about wizardry. Free of charge."

"What?" Jason asked, glancing at Silvana in confusion.

"You won't owe us anything. You've been kind to my friend tonight, so I want to gift you with something precious. These are rare secrets, after all."

"Thank you," Silvana said simply.

Jason nodded along, but his thoughts were going wild. *This seems too easy. There's something else going on here. Why are they being so friendly with us? We're a low House.*

Khadija leaned forward. "Have you ever seen a wizard cast a spell?" They nodded. "Have you tried speaking the spell yourself?"

Jason blushed. "Yeah. I heard Peter say a spell, think it was *Khàd Nga.*" The wizards both nodded in recognition. "I tried saying it a few times. Nothing happened."

"That's right. So logically, that means the word itself is not the source of power."

"Then what is?"

"Thoughts."

Khadija smiled brightly again, but Sam rolled her eyes as if in disagreement.

"When we cast a spell, we must have utter assurance that the spell will work. Our entire will must be solely focused on that fact. If we doubt even a little bit, the spell won't work. We need the purest of faith and the surest of thoughts."

Jason frowned. "So you're saying magic works because you *believe* it works?"

Khadija pouted her lips. "It's an oversimplification of things, but yes."

Sam gave an exasperated sigh and shifted forward on the couch, seeming unwilling to trust Khadija to explain anymore. "If you said a spell now, it wouldn't work, because on some fundamental level your brain will tell you it was impossible. You're too old to learn. As an adult, you've already decided how the world works. You don't believe that you can break the laws of physics. That's why we start our training as children."

"What? Children?" Silvana cried, a hand to her chest.

"Oh relax. It's nothing inhumane," Sam drawled. Jason noted Sam being dry and sarcastic again. He had thought she was acting that way after the incident with Reynold, but it appeared that was just her whole mood. "We teach the firstborn in a wizard family that spells are natural. We perform magic in front of them all the time. And we tell them that one day, magic will work for them. When that day comes, we perform a ceremony, or lay hands on them, or 'speak the magic words'. Then voila, you can now do magic. And the child *believes* it. You might call it psychological conditioning."

"That's right," Khadija interrupted. "That's why no one can discover magic on their own. You'd never have enough faith for it."

"Indeed," Sam said. "If you look at the High Kings, most of them are religious. They've convinced themselves that their power comes from God. That's why religion is so widespread around the world. Wizards need the faith to fuel their power. Whether that faith is real or not is irrelevant. It's real for them, so it works for them. "

Jason became aware of his jaw hanging open, and he quickly closed it to try to look more distinguished.

"So let me get this straight," Silvana said. "You teach these children that the entire world, the very laws of nature, will bend to their will?" She turned to Jason. "My God, no wonder wizards are known for their arrogance. They've been brainwashed to think they're a superior race. No offence intended."

"None taken," Sam drawled.

"But more than that," Jason said. "If wizards teach that their power comes from God, they have to constantly reinforce their religious beliefs to support their power. Religion is a foundation to support their magic." He looked at the two wizards. "Is that right?"

"It is exactly right," Sam said.

Jason shook his head. "And these power-hungry psychopaths rule the world."

Sam coughed politely "Psychopaths?" she whispered.

Oh crap. "I'm so sorry," Jason began

"We meant no offense," Silvana said quickly.

"Now now," Khadija cut in with a wave of her hand. "Our

guest makes a good point. You have to admit, Sam, wizards are often too proud, too sure of themselves, and rule without any regard for their subjects. That's why pride is the wizard's first sin I mentioned. Too much power and overconfidence can lead to stupidity and recklessness, like your former enemy Peter Erikson. But the alternative is the sin of doubt, where we lose our powers through weakness and insecurity."

Jason asked, "You can lose your powers?"

Khadija nodded. "Mmhmm. If a wizard speaks a spell with doubt just one time, the spell won't work for them ever again."

"Never?"

"That's right. Because doubt has started. The wizard will forever wonder if the spell will work next time, and the act of wondering causes it to fail. Do you see? Our faith has to be *absolute.*"

"If you don't mind my asking, Khadija, have you ever lost spells?"

Khadija eyebrows flattened into a straight line. "*'Ana? La samah allah!* I don't use spells."

Sam huffed loudly and rolled her eyes.

"But you're a wizard?" Silvana asked.

"Technically, we're different types of wizards," Sam said, "who follow different schools of thought. There are multiple ways to achieve the focus of will required for magic."

"Yes, you must forgive us!" Khadija said with a warm laugh. "If Sam seems impatient, it's because we've been having this same argument for literally a century."

"You have no idea how tiring it gets," Sam said dryly, to a polite round of laughter.

"So Samantha here is a modern wizard. She uses the power of words." Khadija patted Sam on the shoulder. "She believes the words themselves will always work. Whereas older wizards have the power of God. They believe they are like Zapherahleous himself, speaking creation into being. But I am a new type of wizard."

It took Jason a moment to remember the name. Zapherahleous, the first wizard who created all Immortal kind. He was often mistaken for God in historical retellings. He was exactly how most wizards would imagine themselves.

"So if you're not like Zapherahleous," Jason said, "how do you use magic?"

Khadija gave a coy smile. "Through my thoughts."

She reached her hand towards the table, and her glass suddenly flew up on its own and floated into her hand. She hadn't uttered a word.

"You're a Jedi!" Jason shouted.

"Yes! You get it!" Khadija laughed and gave a loud whoop. "Technically, I did it first. But ol' George must have seen it somewhere. It was too perfect for it to be chance."

"Wait, I don't understand," Silvana said. "You move things? Is that it?"

Khadija laughed. "No, silly. The benefit of using thoughts is that I don't need words. This means I can never lose a spell." She grinned broadly and bowed as if to a crowd. "Cause thoughts are already flexible. They're much more fluid than words. So if they don't work once, it's only natural to blame it on the thoughts of that particular moment. I've had mental spells fail, then work again later."

"But you're slower," Sam said, with an edge in her voice. "Everything takes you more time. And you still can't do really big magic."

"Alright, judgey much?" Khadija said playfully. She gave Jason a sweet smile. "It's the same for many Immortals with mental enhancements. Alchemists, witches, telepaths, they can achieve their power through focus of will and belief in their power. Just to lesser degrees than wizards. It's basically the same thing."

Jason sat back in the lounge and let it all sink in. So modern wizards used the words of magic, the older wizards used religion and the power of faith, and Khadija used thoughts. But it all came down to believing it would work. He wanted to shudder. If magic only required belief, then theoretically, there was no limit to how much power a wizard could have.

He took a long sip of the drink that had been sitting beside him the whole time. *Shit, that's good.* He stared at the liquid. It was bright pink. *Ok sure. Why not?* He sipped it again.

"I can't believe I've never heard any of this before," Silvana said. "I'm ninety years old, and in all that time I've never heard even a hint of this."

"Oh, yes you have," Sam said. "You ever read the Good Book?"

"What, Lord of the Rings?" Silvana asked. Jason laughed and they high-fived each other with a satisfying clap.

"The Bible," Sam said, unimpressed. "You ever heard that verse, where Christ said if you have even a little faith, you can tell a mountain to get up and move, and it will. Magic is just like that."

"Wait, what?" Jason said, sitting forward sharply. "Are you trying to tell me that Jesus, *the* Jesus, was a wizard?"

Everyone was staring at him, blinking in confusion. "Oh," he said. *They all thought it was obvious.* "Right. I guess that makes sense." He turned to Silvana. "You once told me that God was probably a wizard called Zapherahleous. Makes sense that His son was a wizard too."

"Funny you should mention it," Khadija said. "The Christ was determined to undermine the Imperium of the time. You ever read what he preached? He taught the value of all life, and the equal value of all beings. He fought against racism, sexism, and classism, all the things that the Imperium uses as tools to make themselves more powerful."

"Khad," Sam hissed in a warning tone. Their host cut off suddenly.

"I misspoke," Khadija said with a laugh. "But I'll show you what

I mean. Hey!" She called to a nearby waitress and pointed at her directly. She said something in another language, perhaps Arabic. The waitress came forward and bowed low. She looked barely sixteen years old.

Khadija spoke in English. "Can you please show our guests what you are?"

The young waitress hesitated, but only for a moment. "As you wish, mistress," she said in a strange, exotic accent, then held out her hand. She unbuttoned her sleeve at the wrist and rolled it up above her elbow.

Her white skin became a dark brown and began to change shape. Jason stared in disbelief for several moments, until he recognised the form. It was bark. Tree bark. The arm kept growing outwards and spread into several branches. Bursts of green leaves fell outwards, and white flowers bloomed.

"Whoa," Jason said.

"A Fae!" Silvana gasped. "A real life Fae. I've never seen one before." She blushed. "I mean, never seen one so lovely, I mean."

The waitress blushed, but from embarrassment. She was clearly waiting to be dismissed. At last Khadija waved a hand. "Thank you. You may go." The waitress bowed and Khadija was already speaking before the tree arm shrunk back and reverted to a human.

"The physically enhanced will always be seen as lesser by the Imperium," Khadija said. "And mortals even less so. Even the Fae, who were here before even Zapherahleous himself, now serve our kind. Does this seem fair to you?"

Jason stared after the waitress. "Wait. The Fae were here first? Before any other Immortal?"

"Mmhmm," Silvana said. "They are part fauna and part spirit. They have deep ties with the earth and nature. Some believe it were they who kicked Adam and Eve out of the Garden of Eden for crimes against the earth. But the Immortals fought back, and eventually won."

"My God," Jason said, rubbing his temples with his forefinger and thumb. *I feel so lost. I've been learning and unlearning for six months now, and I still have no idea what's going on.*

"You see what I mean?" Khadija said. "This is what the Christ was warning everyone about. If we see one life as being worth more than another, then we will always commit great evils."

"So that's why they killed him?" Jason asked.

"Yes," said Khadija, her face shining with another smile. "Removed the man who challenged them. Dumbest thing they ever did because it made him a martyr. The Imperium had to change their policy about dissidents after that. Now they vilify them first. Or use propaganda to twist the original meaning…"

"Khad!" Sam hissed again, and Khadija cut off.

"Right. I'm sorry. I've been drinking. I didn't mean to… say…"

Jason stared at the two wizards, squinting, his mind processing their strange behaviour. He glimpsed at Silvana, and saw her thinking too.

Then in a flash, he understood.

"I know what this is," he said. He saw the wizards tense up. "This isn't just friendship. You're auditioning us!" The shocked look on their faces confirmed his suspicions. "So what is this then, some sort of *resistance* movement? An underground rebellion against the Imperiu—"

"Quiet!" Sam hissed. Khadija pressed her hands together, and the whump of the music cut off. Suddenly everything was silent. Jason could see the shimmer of air around them. They were in a sound bubble. In the stillness, Jason's pounding heart sounded like thunder.

"You could get us all killed with that loose tongue," Sam hissed. Her hands were clenched into fists at her side

Jason pointed a finger. "Then it's true. You chose us because we helped you, after the High King's attack. We were the only ones who even *implied* that he was in the wrong. Then you offered Silvana blood as a test, to see if she was willing to defy Imperium law. And this…" he gestured at the two wizards, "…sharing of secrets 'free of charge'. It's all to get us to trust you. You even implied you're like Jesus, cause He spoke up for human rights!" He laughed. "I mean, come on! You think you're the first to use that name to get something?"

"Alright," Sam snapped. "Then what do you want?"

"I want to know why." Jason gestured around him. "Everyone is here tonight to make deals. To network and make allies. So what's your angle in all this? An alliance?"

The wizards were still and silent, casting furtive glances at each other and the serving staff beyond.

"The wizard we slew," Silvana said, her voice quiet with confidence. "He wanted to destroy the Imperium so he could reinstate the monarchies. He and his allies wanted to come out of hiding and rule the mortals in the open. Is that your plan?"

"Of course not," Sam barked. "That's just the goals of radical extremist youth. The Royalists are fools. We're nothing like them."

Royalists. Jason noted. *So that's what they called themselves. Extremist who want to bring back the monarchies and rule the mortals openly.*

"Then what is your goal?" Silvana asked.

"To remove the old systems of power," Khadija said, suddenly snarling in a zealous rage. "To bring down the ancient fools that hold back humanity and keep us divided. To break down the walls of ignorance and free the oppressed." She hissed. "I want to end the rule of the High Kings!"

Noise rushed back to Jason's ears, and just as suddenly, Khadija was laughing pleasantly. "You are so funny!" she cried and patted

Sam on the arm. Khadija must have ended the sound bubble before it got suspicious. He could feel the wait staff watching them.

He also noticed the way Khadija's fingers stroked Sam from shoulder to cuff.

I think I know exactly what you want to achieve. Jason nodded thoughtfully. *You want to be with the woman you love, but the Imperium won't let you. So you'll destroy anyone who stands in your way. Even High Kings.*

"Will you think about our business proposal?" Sam said.

Jason looked at Silvana, and bowed his head to her respectfully, signalling his support of whatever she decided.

"We will consider it," Silvana said at last. "And we will use our… discretion." She held out a business card for House Romanov.

Khadija handed back a card for House Al Khalifa.

"I look forward to working together," Khadija said in a sweet voice.

Chapter 7

The elevator doors pinged and opened, and Silvana found herself back on the one hundredth floor. She and Jason stepped into the original room filled with strange people. An hour had past, yet the crowds were still arranged in the same way with some grouped together on the lounges and others standing by the bar. Though a few were showing signs of intoxication, laughing louder and longer than necessary.

"Well that was weird," Jason said. "Do you want a drink break?"

"Maybe just some fresh air," she answered. She knew she should be concerned that some free thinkers had tried to recruit them, but all she could think was that she now had *two* business cards in her possession. This was a massive victory for her family, and an even bigger win for her and Jason. Her family were sure to be jealous.

No sooner had she thought about family when she caught a familiar scent nearby. "Uncle Nicholas?"

Nicholas the Third appeared from between a gap in the crowd. His old weathered face lit up when he saw them. "Ah, Silvana. And Jason, my boy. How goes your evening?"

"Pretty good. Where's Auntie Lisbeth?"

"She stayed at the side of the Glucksbergs. Unfortunately, I needed my second bathroom break for the night. Worst part of my eighties."

He gave Jason a long-suffering eye-roll, much to his amusement.

"How are things going on your end?" Jason asked.

Nicholas grimaced. "Truth be told, not well. The power behind the Glucksberg throne is the wizard Ingolf. He's nearly five hundred years old and about as powerful as a wizard gets." He shook his head. "We are so far beneath his notice. I confess, your aunt and I have been mostly lingering nearby him, waiting for a gap in his conversations to insert ourselves. It is quite humiliating."

Silvana scowled in annoyance. *So Lisbeth doesn't want my investment plan, but will loiter around a rich guy like a sycophant. Oh yeah, that's much more honourable.*

Jason gave a shrug. "Is there anything we can do to help?"

Nicholas smiled back. "No offense, son, but an hour ago you didn't even know who the Glucksbergs were."

"Oh. Right."

"The offer was most noble, regardless. So, have you two made any friends?"

"A few, actually," Jason said proudly and puffed out his chest.

Silvana cut in, "We met the Al Khalifa princess, the host of this event. I even have her business card."

Nicholas's eyes widened. "My god!" he laughed. "That's incredible. Well done, both of you." He gave Jason a firm clap on the arm. "I best be returning…"

"Sir," Jason asked. "I have a question." He leaned in close and whispered in Nicholas' ear, where Silvana had to use her vampiric senses to hear. "Does everyone in the Immortal community…*like* the High Kings?"

Nicholas gave a polite laugh. "What an odd question."

"Well I know us Brits love to bash on our mortal leaders. I was wondering…"

"Ah! But even your mortal king and queen are still leaders of a democracy. You're expected to mock them. Our world is a true monarchy. Disliking our leaders is considered treasonous, and that's a capital crime."

Jason's mouth fell open. "That serious?"

"Son, we're talking about the divine right to rule. I know it is an old concept for us mortals, but Imperium laws haven't changed much in the two thousand years since its formation. The High Kings are considered God's personal representatives to earth, the highest authority."

"But did you see what the High King did to that woman?"

"Ah." Nicholas gave a knowing nod, as if he finally understood Jason's true question. "Son, it's not a perfect system. But there's not much we can do. Our family barely has any power here anymore. I know it's hard to accept. Still, please don't try to change the whole system tonight. Work within it to do good, ok?" Jason clearly had more to say, but Nicholas patted his arm again. "We can talk about this again some other time, ok son? But I really have to get back."

"Of course."

They parted ways. Silvana took Jason by the hand. He was staring at the ground with empty eyes and a deep frown, but he didn't say anything. So Silvana took him back through the room to the outside balcony.

The dry night air was quite warm, despite the balcony winds at this height. Silvana leaned against the railing and looked down to the city below. The world was silent except for the occasional honking of car horns in the faint distance. Twin red lights in the sky were descending towards the airport runway.

"You ok?" Jason asked.

She felt herself relax at the sound of his voice. His presence was so comforting, his scent, his quiet confidence, seemed to hit a button that calmed her nervous system.

"I'm fine," she said. "How about you?"

Jason only shrugged. "It's a lot to take in. But right now, I'm worried about you. You've been awfully quiet. What's on your mind?"

She smiled. He was trying to connect with her, even now. She should open up. "Honestly? I was so happy that we have two business cards. Yet I know…my aunts are just going to ignore this too."

Jason was quiet a long time. Then he said, "Those papers on your bedroom floor. They were financial reports."

She nodded. He was using his 'detective' voice.

"I take it things are not going well."

"I shouldn't talk about this," she said. The balcony was mostly empty of people. Silvana could not smell a vampire among the others, so they must have only natural hearing. Still, she leaned close. "Our family is nearly completely broke. I haven't explained just how bad things have become."

"I guessed. That hole in the wall was a bigger clue than most."

She smiled even as she rolled her eyes. "The problem is my aunts don't understand modern investment. They're terrified of moving money around to create profit. They don't understand that we don't have any other choice left to us. The only money remaining is in assets. If we keep trying to preserve our assets instead of using them, we'll lose everything."

"I see," Jason said, looking surprised.

"I'm sorry I didn't tell you sooner. Are you angry?"

"No, no. I'm just…" he blinked. "So you're not bothered at all by what just happened?"

Oh. Of course he's more worried about those wizards. I should have realised. "Sorry, Jase. I've got bigger problems to worry about."

Jason frowned. "If you need financial help, you could ask Sam and Khadija. It might be a good test of their character."

"Maybe. But if they disagree with the Imperium, it could be too risky to join them. The Imperium could discover them and wipe them out easily. We could sink with their ship."

"They're over a century old, sweetheart. I suspect they've been surviving pretty well." Silvana only shook her head. Thankfully Jason moved on. "Well there is that other couple we met. The…I want to say Korean couple?"

"I don't know," she admitted. "Yes, there's them. But it wouldn't be a joint venture. I wouldn't even be a junior partner. They asked me to invest like any mortal."

"Well. I hate to say it. But aren't we that desperate?"

"Maybe." She looked up at Jason, and noticed he was still missing his jacket. His white shirt was tight across his chest. She smiled. "I'm sorry you've come into my family just to inherit its problems."

"Hey, I already had financial problems. Nothing's changed." He smiled. "Besides, I'm grateful for your financial problems. Meant you had to marry 'beneath your station'" He held up quoting fingers and made a mocking voice. "It meant we found each other."

His words swept aside all the anger and frustration inside her. She was calm again. A single thought occurred to her. *Arthur never said anything like that. He never said he was grateful to know me, or share in my problems. He always blamed me for the whole situation.* She looked at Jason, and saw the utter sincerity in his eyes. *He means it. Somehow. He really is happy to be with me.*

"Why are you so nice to me?" Silvana said.

"Honestly, I'm just grateful you're not breaking up with me."
She blinked. "What?"

Jason gave a nervous laugh and scratched his head. "I mean, we had sex pretty suddenly, and I assumed it was out of pity."

"Jason?!"

"I'm a foster kid, remember?" he said as if it were a joke, but there was real anxiety behind his eyes. "I'm used to changing homes and families every six months."

"Do you really think I'm going to leave you now it's been six months?"

"No! Silvana…" he clearly didn't hear the levity in her voice. "Look, I'm sorry, but I'm very insecure about this sort of thing. I'm uncomfortable with long term relationships cause everyone always leaves, so I don't know how to handle someone who wants to stay. My stupid brain keeps telling me that you'll leave one day and there's nothing I can do. I don't actually believe it, but the thought is there. It's just really hard and I'm scared all the time." He held his hands up in surrender.

She stared back at him and had to force the truth through her lips. "My stupid brain keeps telling me that you're going to slap me," she whispered.

"What?" Jason cried. "How could you say…" then he went silent. "Oh."

"See? I know you never, ever would do that. But I'm still scared of it all the time." She gave a bleak laugh. "I'm trying to say I understand, though I don't know if that's coming across."

Jason clutched her hand. "I'm never going to hurt you," he said.

"And I'm never going to leave you." She cupped his cheek and pulled his face lower, before she pressed her lips against his.

"Excuse me, miss?" someone called out in a tone to get attention. Silvana looked up.

A young man was approaching them, making direct eye contact with her. She could smell his vampirism straight away, like the scent of the iron in blood, but stronger than it appeared in any other type of person. Behind the man was Aunt Emberline and Phillip, giving chase. Phillip reached for this man's shoulder to restrain him, but the young vampire shrugged it off.

A strange scent was coming from her aunt, like bitter wine. Her heart was thumping loud enough for Silvana to hear. *She's terrified.*

"Young lady," the man said. "What is your name?"

The man was dressed all in white, though his jacket was stitched with bright squiggly lines in random arrangements. The sleeves were white too, except for a thin strip of patterns by the wrist. He looked far too poor to have fit in here. Silvana instantly didn't like his tone. She squared her shoulders. Jason obviously had the same thought and moved alongside her, his hands at his hip. "First give me your name, stranger," she said curtly. "Then I shall give you mine."

"Dorin," he said impatiently. "Now yours!"

"Excuse me, sir!" Silvana snapped. "You have no right to demand anything."

"All right," Dorin said, holding up his hands and stepping closer. "I'm sorry for pushing. Please, just tell me your name! It's important." Dorin's voice was nearly shouting. He reached for her.

Jason had his sword out and extended in a flash of movement. Dorin stopped short, his throat an inch from the blade, his short curly hair flicked as he jerked to a halt. "Your behaviour is threatening, sir," Jason said in hard command, his voice like steel. "Stand down."

Dorin sneered, "You cannot hurt me. There's an enchantment."

Jason's voice was a low, husky growl. "And it will not save you, if you threaten her again."

Oh God, I'm going to swoon.

Phillip and Emberline appeared on either side of him now, ready to step between Dorin and Silvana at a moment's notice. Dorin stood up straight. He looked to be in his early twenties. His baby blue eyes were wild with panic as he kept staring at her.

"I'm not going to hurt her," he said. Silvana could hear the promise in his voice now, and the accent of Eastern Europe. "I would never hurt her. Especially if she is who I think she is. Please, miss." He lowered his voice to a soft whisper, but it still couldn't hide his desperation. "Can you please just tell me your name?"

"She will tell you nothing!" Emberline snapped. And it wasn't just a declaration. It was a command, directed at Silvana.

Is that so, dear aunty?

"My name is Silvana."

Everyone stared at her. Jason lowered his sword in surprise, and Emberline's eyes widened to their maximum. It was worth it just for that look on her face.

Silvana stepped past the others and reached out to shake hands with Dorin. He gave her hand a gentle squeeze. A second later, his eyes widened even more than Emberline's.

"You," he whispered. "It's the wrong name, but it is you. I'm sure of it. It should be impossible. I've searched for years. Yet here you are. I don't understand."

Emberline snatched the man by the scruff of his lapel and pulled him back out of Silvana's reach. "You stay away from my daughter," she hissed. "Or I'll tear you to shreds."

"She is not your daughter," Dorin said in a flat tone, barely giving Emberline a glance.

Everyone went quiet, and Silvana's heart began to surge with sudden terror and excitement. She pushed through the people surrounding her and laid a hand on the square of Dorin's chest. She could smell him now. Beer, tobacco smoke, and something else. Honey?

"Who are you?" she asked.

Dorin stared at her with those bright blue eyes.

Blue eyes.

A sudden explosion roared all around her, powerfully loud like a crack of thunder in close quarters. Metal shrieked, glass shattered, and within the same instant, Silvana dropped. The balcony was ripped away, and at once she was falling.

Falling.

The world was spinning. Lights flashed past her in a blur of red, yellow and purple. The wind howled in her ears, louder than a jet engine. Yet she could still hear herself screaming at the top of her lungs.

What the hell just happened!

She had started falling so suddenly she had no idea how long it had been happening for. A second? Five seconds? What had caused it? Was this Dorin's doing? She was spinning wildly as she dropped down the outside of the skyscraper. Concrete blocks and metal debris were falling all around her amidst the shattered remnants of the balcony, mixed with the screams of other people.

Jason! Auntie!

She flung out her hands to try to stabilize her spinning. The ground was rushing towards her. Jason was floating to her left, tumbling, his sword spinning nearby. A gush of blood was smeared across his forehead. His eyes were closed.

"Jason?!" she screamed over the roaring wind. He didn't move.

I must save him!

She angled her body towards him, and the wind helped blow her closer. She caught his arm. She reached out and snatched his sword, then she turned towards the side of the building. The ground was only seconds away.

This has to work, or we're both dead!

She put all the power of blood she had available into her hand, and rammed the sword into the side of the building to try to slow their descent.

The sword clanged and bounced off.

NO!

Someone appeared in front of her. A woman in a black suit with red hair that flapped violently in the wind. She grabbed hold of

Silvana and Jason. The world folded around them.

Then something hit Silvana in the chest. She gasped in pain and pressed down with her hands, and felt solid concrete beneath her. She was lying motionless on the ground. She had landed. *I'm alive!*

Portia was standing over her, panting, her long red hair half covering her face. "Damn, I'm good!" she growled through a gritted smile.

Silvana was panting as she sat up. Jason was beside her, still unconscious but clearly breathing. His sword was still in Silvana's hand. She looked up. The Vigile Desdemona was standing over Emberline and Phillip. Neither looked harmed.

"What happened?" Silvana asked.

"I was about to ask you the same thing," Portia said, still panting. "You're lucky we warded you for danger, or we would have been too slow. As it was, you were a second away from being a smear."

Silvana looked up. Far above her, the flickering red light of flames were burning halfway up the sides of the Burj Al Khalifa.

"You're lucky you didn't fall straight down," Portia went on. "You would have hit one of the lower tiers of the building. The explosion must have thrown you far off the side."

"Explosion?" Silvana cried. "But there was an enchantment. No violence allowed. How did this happen?"

Portia scowled. "I don't know." It seemed hard for her to admit this.

"Where's Auntie Lisbeth? Where's Nicholas? Did you have them warded too?"

Portia shrugged. "My wards don't show me where they are, exactly. But I know they're not in any danger."

Silvana froze. *Does that mean they're dead?* She couldn't think about it. "Wait, what about that man I was talking with? Dorin? Where is he?"

"He wasn't my charge."

Silvana was on her feet, scanning the area. They had landed in an outdoor courtyard that had probably looked beautiful before the debris of the destroyed balcony had smashed it all to bits. Silvana couldn't see any bodies, no blood stains, and no gore. Another Vigile was standing over a pair of strangers nearby. They must have caught everyone.

Dorin was gone.

Had he fallen onto the side of the building? Was he stuck halfway up there somewhere? Silvana stopped herself. Why did she care? She had family to worry about.

"Take me back up there," Silvana said.

Portia raised an eyebrow at her. "You dare make demands of me?"

"They're my family!" Silvana shrieked.

"You care not for your lover?"

She glanced down at Jason. He was motionless. The cut on his forehead hadn't gotten any worse and she couldn't smell his blood anywhere else on his body. It was extremely likely he was not injured further. *But not certain.* She still turned back to Portia. "Take me back there."

Portia sneered. "I have no desire to. And you can't change that."

Silvana thought carefully. She couldn't plead or threaten the Vigile, no matter how desperate she felt. Then it occurred to her. "My family are your charge. If harm has befallen my aunt and uncle, the Imperium will be liable for recompense. Your failure to protect them will go on your record and damage your standings in the Imperium's eyes."

Portia merely blinked in surprise. "You bloodsucking bitch," she said calmly. "I ought to take you back up there in the hope you do come to harm."

"I'll take that chance," Silvana said and held out her arm.

Portia stared back at her, her eyes flat and unimpressed, then snatched her hand. The world bent around them and Silvana glimpsed Jason lying on the pavement, bleeding.

I'm never going to leave you, she had said.

Chapter 8

Silvana's heels touched down on the floor, and immediately her senses were assaulted by a thick cloud of black smoke.

A shallow cough racked her entire body, but it didn't help to clear her airways. There was no clean air to be found. Then the smoke was ripped back, and a bubble of air surrounded Silvana. She found Portia standing beside her, her eyes hard and hands outstretched as if holding back the smoke.

"Thanks," Silvana said. "Now can you do that for the whole room?"

Portia's face seemed to harden. "I will not."

"Can you try?"

"My charge is to protect you, and you're protected."

Silvana stared at her a moment. *Maybe she's not sure the spell will work, so won't risk failing in her attempt and losing the spell forever.* If that was the case, Portia would never tell Silvana that. "Alright, which way?"

"I can't sense the wards on your aunt and uncle," Portia said. "They only appear when they're in danger."

"Fine. Let's move. I should be able to smell them."

Portia barked a laugh. "A sniffer dog? Just when I thought you couldn't be any more of a bitch." Silvana clenched her jaw and fists, but said nothing.

They made their way through the rising plumes of black smoke, with their air bubble carving a way forward. Silvana recognised the pattern of tiles on the ground. They were back on the hundredth floor. It was completely vacant now. Silvana could barely hear the sounds of distant voices, even with her supernatural hearing, which meant everyone was either dead or had fled the premises.

"How did the enchantment fail?" Silvana asked. Portia did not answer her. She just looked pissed off. "That explosion must have happened on the floor beneath ours, or several floors down. Notice how there's no flames or heat here, only lots of smoke?"

"No shit, Sherlock," Portia growled. "Do you smell them yet?"

"Not yet. The smoke's making it hard."

She led Portia towards the sound of voices. The smoke began to clear slightly and Silvana caught glimpses of lights and shadows flickering across her vision. Then she smelt it. The unique acidic scent of blood.

"Someone's been injured," she said.

Silvana crouched low, creeping forward and sniffing deeply. The bubble of air pushed back the smoke and revealed a figure on the ground, wearing a man's jacket. The person wasn't moving. They lay crumpled on their side, their long blonde hair sprawled out behind them. Their red dress did not disguise the thick sploshes of blood all down the length of the garb. The smell of blood was overpowering, and yet, she could also smell Jason, somehow.

It can't be. Silvana dropped to the figure's side and rolled them over.

Samantha Kennedy was dead. The wound across her throat was jagged and brutal. Her neck had been half severed from her body. Her eyes were wide open as if merely in shock. She still wore Jason's jacket.

"Shame," Portia said. "Must have been killed by shrapnel. That's a vicious wound."

"She was alive…just minutes ago…" Silvana murmured. She had felt jealousy towards Sam, for her obvious beauty and the way Jason had rushed to help her. Yet she also felt respect for the woman's strength and confidence, and had wished she could feel that way about herself. Sam didn't deserve this. *I am one of the few who know the truth. Sam was resisting the Imperium. This may not have been an accident. Good Lord, am I at risk too for being near her?*

"Are you done?" Portia asked.

"Sorry." Silvana leapt to her feet. "I'm just in shock. I haven't seen anyone dead…"

"Since the last wizard you killed?" Portia sniffed sharply. "Come on." She stepped over Sam's body, being careful to avoid the pools of blood. Silvana stepped around her.

The sound of the voices had grown louder. Someone was shouting now. Silvana heard something else. Heavy breathing and something scratching against steel. A sharp hissing sound. *What the hell am I hearing?* Silvana sniffed deeply, and caught the hint of something foreign. It smelt of leather and tender meat, like the time she'd visited her cousins and they insisted on serving an exotic dish with crocodile as the main meal. *Am I smelling something…reptilian?*

Then she understood.

"Skinwalkers," Silvana hissed in warning.

Portia crouched low, alert. Her hands raised up to her chest, palms facing outwards.

Something burst out of the blackness of the smoke. A large reptilian head appeared with a wide jaw and rows of teeth, rushing at them with full speed and barking with deafening sudden noise. Silvana screamed.

"*Haš Edün!*"

Portia had thrust out a hand as she spoke and the creature was thrust back into the smoke, yelping loudly as it flew backwards. Portia panted heavily. "Well," she quipped, "the no violence enchantment seems to have completely failed."

"What was that thing?" Silvana asked.

"Some sort of dinosaur."

"Dinosaur?" Silvana cried in disbelief. But she remembered the brutal gash on Samantha's throat that had nearly severed her head. *So this thing killed Samantha, God rest her soul.*

Something started creaking nearby, like the sound of someone trying to gargle pebbles in their throat. "Watch my back," Portia said, and the pair stood back to back to watch the smoke.

"This was a coordinated attack," Silvana said. "The explosion. Now Metamorphs. This has to be an attack on the High King."

"Or meant to look like one," Portia said. "You still want to find your family?"

Silvana hesitated only a second. "Yes."

"Then we fight."

The creaking and gargling sounds grew louder. Silvana watched over her shoulder. The noise was coming from Portia's side. She kept her vampire teeth at the ready, and the blood in her core, legs, and forearms, ready to strike at a moment's notice. The creature gave a sharp bark from somewhere near Portia. "He's coming!" Portia shouted and braced for attack. Silvana turned to face the Vigile.

Then stopped. *Didn't I see this in a movie once?* She turned back to her own side.

A scaly head leapt out from the thick smoke, its wide snapping jaws coming right at Silvana.

Clever girl.

Silvana crouched and leapt at the velociraptor, catching it in the middle and tackling it backwards. She heard Portia shouting more spells and felt searing heat wash over her. The creature underneath her began squirming frantically, its jaws snapping at her face. She buried herself down against its chest and pressed her elbow under its jaw, forcing its head away from her.

Something sharp sliced through her gown and cut her leg. She glanced down only for a second. The raptor's long, hooked claws slashed at her dress, its talons trying desperately to reach the flesh beneath. Silvana pulled her legs up onto its chest to pin it down and grabbed its jaw with both hands. The talons scratched at her forearms but she ignored them, instead pouring her strength into her arms and twisting the dinosaur's neck.

The raptor changed shape and shifted out of her grasp. It was now some sort of small house cat. Yet only a second later, it shifted into a full sized kangaroo. Its giant legs caught Silvana in the stomach and sent her careening backwards.

She flew past Portia and into the black smoke. As she passed, she caught a glimpse of the Vigile holding back two more great lizards with streams of blue fire from her hands. Silvana tucked in her feet and twisted in the air. She hit the ground on her feet and fists, then launched at the nearest raptor.

There was too much smoke to see, so she aimed at where the raptor had been a moment ago. Her hands touched upon scales. She snatched the back of its head, then used the momentum to throw a kick at the second raptor. Both collapsed, and Silvana landed between them. Portia was watching, her back unguarded as a shadow rose up from the smoke.

"Behind you!" Silvana screamed.

Portia roared, *"Tàb Izī!"* and the raptor that had been the kangaroo was suddenly wreathed in blue flame that poured from Portia's hand with a loud whoosh. The creature shrieked hideously for a mere second, then went still.

Holy shit. That...that was a person.

The two remaining creatures made barking sounds and fled into the smoke. Silvana stared after them, panting, and clutching her chest as the pain settled in. Portia stood beside her and surrounded them both in the bubble of air again.

"Not bad," Portia said. "For a glorified mosquito."

Silvana turned sharply to look at her. "What the fuck is your problem?" Portia only snorted, but she was smiling in amusement. Silvana checked her wounds. She had scratches across her belly and along her forearms. None were dangerous, yet she still used up some of her blood supply to begin healing quicker than normal.

Portia kept moving, and Silvana followed before her healing had made much progress. Just seconds later, the smoke grew less thick, and Silvana finally emerged onto the open floor. A few people were crowding around the doors to the stairs, shouting and gesturing with fists, though they looked more annoyed than scared. Vigiles were spread among them, watching the smoke with alert eyes.

"Aunty Lisbeth?" Silvana called. Several heads glanced up, but no one answered.

"Are we evacuating?" Portia asked.

One of the Vigiles faced her, an older man with a gravelly voice and a white fuzzy beard. "We're holding them here. There will be an investigation, and we'll need to know who was in this room."

"We're searching for my family," Silvana said. "Do you know what other rooms had guests in them?"

The older Vigile glanced at Portia with eyebrows raised. Portia groaned, "I vouch for her."

He growled in response, "The two floors above this one."

"What about below? Where the explosion came from?"

The man shrugged casually. "Staff area. Don't worry. No guests were allowed."

Silvana stared at him. This man saw no problem whatsoever with serving staff being attacked. *God, Khadija had a point.* "Is anyone checking on them?" Silvana asked.

"Absolutely. Vigiles are doing what they can to contain the flames."

"But the staff? What about the people?"

"They're doing their jobs, madam." Silvana's mouth fell open. She prepared to shout back.

"Hey," Portia said, interrupting Silvana's upcoming outburst. "You want to find your family? Then we need to check upstairs." She grabbed Silvana's arm and started pulling.

"We're going downstairs."

Both Vigiles looked at her sharply. "Are you giving orders?" the old man said with a bemused smile.

"Yes. We're going to find any injured down there and help them. Portia, you can offer any healing spells you know. I have mortal medicine training."

"I came here to help you find your family."

"And now I'm going into danger again. You best protect me."

"I won't let you get anywhere near danger." Portia's voice had become a threat.

"Well that's too bad. Because I can smell my aunt. She's already downstairs and helping."

Portia's eyes squinted. "You're lying."

"How would you know? Now let's go help the injured."

Portia's lip twisted, like she wanted to curse. Instead she said calmly, "I don't know any healing spells. I'm a warlock. My magic is for battle, not for helping those defeated."

Silvana scanned the crowd nearby, searching for any sign of help. She spotted someone in a bright red puffy vest, and a white flowery hat. "Edward!" she shouted, and the alchemist looked in her direction without making eye contact. "You always carry healing elixirs on you, right? I need to buy them."

"There's a premium right now," he said, his hands fidgeting nervously and his fringe covering one of his eyes.

"Fine. Bring them. You're coming downstairs with us."

"I don't go into the field," he cried. His hand movement sped up.

"There can be a premium for that too," she answered, and he went quiet. She took that as agreement. "Fine. Both of you, come with me."

The vampire, wizard, and alchemist forced their way through the crowd and past the Vigiles guarding the stairs. Silvana led the way down. The stairwell lights were flicking rapidly like they were stepping into a horror film. Voices shouted from somewhere above them, echoing down the corridor. They reached the next floor down. The door was shut. Silvana tested the handle and found it to be slightly warm.

"Stand back," she warned, and forced the door open.

A burst of heat rushed through the entryway. But it was only hot air. Silvana opened the door all the way, and saw a scene of devastation. Everything had been shredded apart by an incredible force. The walls and roof were on fire, and the hallway was glowing red.

"This is crazy," Edward said. "I don't have my fire-proof elixir."

"We'll protect you. Just have your healing elixirs ready," Silvana said.

"Why bother?" Portia replied. "Look at this place. It's unlikely there are survivors. We should return to the higher floors."

"We'll conduct a search first," Silvana said flatly and stepped into the corridor. "We'll need to go further in before I can smell anything reliably."

The flames looked like they had already died down a lot from the initial explosion. Small patches of shredded materials were still lit up and smouldering. The roof panels had fallen and pieces of white foam had sprayed everywhere. The foam burnt with a brief flash whenever the flames touched it. Silvana stepped on scattered ash, her heels clopping softly across the once white-marbled floor. She listened to sounds of cracking heat, vigilantly listening for creaking beam sounds that might warn of a collapse.

She opened the closest door to find a storage room of medical supplies. No one was in here. Still, she grabbed a first aid kit and moved on.

She smelt blood. She held up a hand for silence and led the way down the corridor towards the corner. There, she found a body lying face down and motionless. A trail of blood was smeared behind them for several metres. This man had dragged himself from where he fell.

"The Skinwalkers probably came from here," Portia said. "They would have been on the staff or disguised as staff members, since there were no Skinwalkers as guests. They would have killed any witnesses."

"They might still be nearby," Edward whispered. He was holding two vials in his hands, as if ready to throw them. His head was jerking around in all directions, searching for the first sign of danger.

"It's still quiet here," Silvana said. "The Skinwalkers have probably moved on." Silvana leaned down to check the body's wrist. No pulse. She sighed and kept moving.

More red light flickered at the end of the corridor. She moved down there with vampiric silence. Here she found the kitchen area and the greatest presence of flames. They crackled and roared up the sides of the building. Black char smeared all the walls and surfaces. Several bodies lay strewn across the floor. Some had limbs blown off. Silvana studied the angle they'd fallen at, and noticed their feet faced the left wall. They explosion had come from there, where the flames were hottest. She could just glimpse the open night through the broken walls.

Portia arrived beside her. "That's where the blast came from," Silvana told her. "It must be directly under the balcony where I was standing. It took out the walls with its blast."

"You're surely mistaken. I don't detect any magic here."

"Then it wasn't magic," Edward said. They stared at him, and he spoke while staring at the ground. "Industrial kitchens have gas canisters. Can't you smell it? It must have ignited and sucked all the air out of the room. That's why the force of the explosion went up."

"Thank you Edward." Silvana looked at Portia. "So gas canisters went off. Maybe that's how it got past the enchantment. It was not an Immortal device, or intended for violence. This could all be an accident."

"Or meant to look like one. I would bet the Skinwalkers rigged the canisters to blow then got to a safe distance. The enchantment might have fallen because the explosion injured people. That's when the Skinwalkers rushed back in to kill witnesses before they began their main assault in the confusion."

"Main assault?" Silvana said. "The High King?"

Portia nodded. "Who else?"

"But why?"

"There's always a reason. At any rate, there's no use hanging around any longer. These poor fools are dead, and that fire is too strong right now..."

Edward pushed her aside. Portia gasped. "How dare you!" she hissed and raised a hand. But Silvana stepped in and blocked the Vigiles from reacting. Edward was staring straight ahead with wide eyes. *Has he forgotten we're here?*

He nodded. Then threw a glass vial into the heart of the flame.

"Alchemist!" Portia snapped.

The vial cracked open, and the liquid inside turned into a swirling white ball of air. A loud hissing sound reverberated off the walls before an intense rush of air filled the kitchen. The white ball was spinning faster, forming a vortex. Waves of shimmering hot air from the flames was rushing into the ball, and disappearing. The flames were going down. Already it was half the size. Just a few seconds later, the flames winked out, and the white ball of air simply ceased to exist.

"I thought so," Edward said, then turned back to Silvana and Portia. He had a satisfied glint in his blue eyes. There wasn't even a hint of smugness. "Two thousand four hundred pounds," he said.

It took Silvana a moment. "Right! Pounds. I'll send you the funds." She shook her head, not wanting to think about how she'd explain this expense to her aunts. "Well, guess the fire is not too strong anymore. Let me check these bodies, then we can head upstairs." Silvana began to check the pulse of each one.

The second one was still alive. "Edward! Healing!" Silvana cried. The alchemist was at her side.

"Five hundred pounds," he said. Silvana rolled her eyes and nodded. Edward cracked the vial open and poured a few drops over the unconscious person's open mouth. Silvana could smell the wounded man. He smelt just like the Fae in Khadija's private booth: like oak and ash and flower buds.

"Looks like a head injury," Silvana said. "Blunt force trauma, but no visible wounds. Probably internal bleeding from concussive force to the chest."

"He'll be fine. The elixir will fix him soon," Edward advised.

Silvana rushed to the next body. She found another Fae male alive. He had a severe gash on his chest, and shrapnel was buried in several places on his body.

"The elixir won't work with him," Edward said.

"What?" Silvana asked. "Why not?"

"Healing elixir won't remove foreign objects. You'll have to do that yourself if you want to stop the bleeding. Then we can heal it."

"Understood."

Silvana opened the first aid kit, found a scalpel and some tweezers and started pulling the metal out of the wound. Silvana lost herself in the work. Her hands moved with her vampiric speed. Yet she felt her first wave of fatigue and thirst. She'd used up a lot of her stored strength tonight. She'd need more blood from Jason in the next day or two to remain in good health. And if she had to fight anyone else tonight, she'd be in real trouble. Still, she used her power to patch the wounded Fae faster. After a few minutes, she was confident she'd removed it all.

"How are there any survivors?" Edward asked as he administered another elixir. "I don't understand. The Skinwalkers killed the others on this floor."

"They probably thought these were already dead," Portia said coldly from where she loomed over the working pair.

"This one will do for now," Silvana said. "I need to double check the others."

She moved around the remaining bodies. They were already dead and growing cold. No wonder the Skinwalkers has assumed them all dead. The ones standing closest to the explosion were in multiple pieces. They were…grisly sights that made Silvana woozy. She pushed through and checked every last one.

She found a third survivor. A young woman who appeared in her late teens, with a weak pulse beating away in her wrist. But her scent was different. Not Fae at all.

Another Skinwalker.

Silvana hesitated. Was this woman one of the conspirators? Was she lying in wait? But that was impossible. She was at deaths door. There was no way…unless she was a conspirator and had just been in the wrong position when the attack began. *Maybe I shouldn't take the risk.*

Or maybe you're being prejudiced. You have no way to know what this person has done. She needs care. Silvana took a deep breath. Jason would have insisted on helping her. She should help.

But Portia...

The image of that shrieking dinosaur burning under Portia's blue flame came back to mind. Silvana shivered. If Portia found out this was a Skinwalker, she would assume the worst and this woman would be as good as dead. *And Edward might give her away too. I have no idea how he thinks.*

"Edward," she said calmly. "Let me administer the elixir."

"It won't lower the price."

"That's fine."

Edward handed the vial over and there was only a few drops left. Silvana poured them all into the Skinwalker's mouth then began checking over for wounds. There was a severe gash across her thigh that had bled heavily, but the elixir was already closing it off. Silvana touched the girl's face, lifting an eyelid with her thumb to check for responsiveness.

A hand shot out and grabbed her wrist.

Silvana froze as the Skinwalker's eyes settled on her. She nearly punched that face. Until she saw her own fear reflected there. The young girl was glancing past her, towards Portia.

"We're helping you," Silvana said. "You've been wounded. I gave you a healing elixir."

The girl was panting, her breaths shallow. She clung to Silvana and started speaking faintly in another language. Silvana didn't recognise it, so she just offered a big smile and said in a calming tone, "Everything's going to be ok." Yet the girl looked around the room with frantic eyes, as if searching for someone.

"Are we done here?" Portia asked.

Silvana scooped the girl off the ground and held her gently, so that she relaxed into Silvana's grip. The two wounded Fae were awake now. One was standing. The one with the chest wounds was wincing in pain.

"Can you transport us out of here?" Silvana asked.

"Not this many," Portia said. "Come on. The stairs aren't far." She saw everyone staring at her, then she sighed. "Fine. I'll carry this guy."

Chapter 9

Silvana and her entourage returned to the main floor. The fires and smoke had mostly faded, leaving only scorch marks and the thick lingering scent of ash. People were starting to wander out of the side booths and stairwell as Vigiles watched over the bustling crowd. Silvana anxiously scanned their faces. Still no sign of Aunty Lisbeth and Nicholas.

She did see Khadija sitting on the steps near the bar and panting. She was nursing a bruise on her face and a cut on her forearm, and she was surrounded by security guards.

A half dozen witches were roaming through the crowd wearing black pointy hats. They were obviously on staff for the event tonight in case of just such an emergency, since they were seeking out any wounded and speaking enchantments.

"Hey," Silvana shouted to get a witch's attention. She pointed out the injured wait staff with her and let the witch get to work. Then she moved toward Khadija.

"I told you, I'm fine," the wizard host shouted again. "You need to be looking for Sam. She had just stepped outside when the explosion happened, and I haven't seen her since."

Silvana stomach clenched tightly. *She doesn't know about Sam. How will she react?*

Khadija saw her nearby. "Silvana! Hey, did you see Sam anywhere? She was out on this floor when—" she cut off with a groan of pain and clutched her head.

"Has a witch seen to you?" Silvana asked gently.

"Yeah. But they've got limited power to spare tonight, and apparently my situation isn't life threatening." She rolled her eyes. "A fucking dinosaur hit me with the club on its tail, and she tells me I'll live. The fucking nerve of some people. Now, did you see Sam?"

Silvana's breath caught in her throat. She couldn't speak. Khadija noticed the silence and finally looked up at her as a shadow spread across her face.

"There were more dinosaurs on this floor," Silvana said. "I fought them. But…they'd already gotten to Sam."

Khadija laughed. She actually laughed. "I bet she fucked them up good. She's a hell of a wizard." Silvana didn't know what to say in response. Khadija looked up at her again, and the smile bled from her face. "Silvana…she isn't…"

"I'm so sorry," Silvana replied. She reached out to comfort Khadija, but stopped when a dark scowl crossed Khadija's face.

"Take me to her. *Now.*" Each word laced with poison. Silvana didn't dare refuse. She tucked an arm under Khadija and helped her cross the room through the dying column of smoke.

Please don't be there. Please don't be there. Let me have imagined it.

There was a body, exactly where Silvana feared it would be. Blood still pooled around the torn throat. Jason's jacket still covered her.

Khadija let out a piercing shriek, and Silvana nearly dropped her in terror. The wizard collapsed by Sam's side and howled, *"NO! SAM NO!"* Her voice echoed around the chamber, ringing with desperation and agony. She screamed wordlessly now, her voice was more animalistic than human.

Silvana watched helplessly. *She must have really loved her. God, how would I react if I lost Jason?* She thought of her partner, probably still unconscious a hundred stories down, and felt a twisted pang of guilt.

"Did you kill them!?" Khadija shrieked.

Silvana stammered. "Uh...what?"

"The fucking changelings! The bastards who did this?"

"Wha..." Silvana struggled to answer. *She just called them changelings. That's the mortal word for them, and highly insulting.* "We killed one of them," she said. "Portia...burnt it to death."

"Still too good for it," Khadija cried. "After I fought my family for years, begging them to employ those bastards. After Sam and I fought for their rights. By Allah, look what they've done to her! This is the thanks they give!"

The mortal security guards swarmed forward now, cutting Silvana off from Khadija. "Mistress, we have to get you to safety. There are still insurgents unaccounted for."

"Then let's go hunt the fuckers!" Khadija said as she stood up, but immediately staggered and fell. Her guards caught her. She went limp as she nearly lost consciousness. Yet she kept muttering to herself. "Those fuckers...changelings...kill them..."

Silvana turned away from the sight. It was too hard to watch. She scanned the crowd once more from a different angle, and finally, she saw the faces she'd been looking for.

She rushed forward. "Aunty!" she cried.

Lisbeth and Nicholas had just emerged from the stairwell in the centre of the room. Silvana pushed her way through the crowd. Several people turned their noses at her in disgust, probably from the smell of smoke and blood, and the deep tears in her dress. *It's a fucking emergency, and still they look down on vampires.* She didn't care. A moment later, she wrapped her arms around her aunt and squeezed her tightly.

"Oh my darling," Lisbeth cried. "We've been so worried."

"Are you ok? Are you injured?" Nicholas asked, his hands touching her arms and cheeks, searching for wounds.

"Fine," Silvana said. "Everyone else is fine."

"We checked everywhere for you. Where were you?"

"Uh…" Silvana grimaced. "Don't freak out, aunty, but the balcony collapsed while we were on it."

Lisbeth gasped. "Good Lord! Are you serious? How could that happen?"

"The blast…"

Lisbeth talked over the top of her. "I can't believe the Al Khalifa thought they could do this. Faulty workmanship, as if we don't have enough to worry about."

"The Vigiles caught us…"

"They better have! It's bad enough the Imperium has let this happen at a sanctioned event. There was security everywhere. And how did they get past the enchantment?"

"I said don't freak out!" Silvana cried, her voice rising.

"Well, how do you expect me to react, Silvana?" she shouted back at her with matched volume. "We searched multiple floors for you! I kept expecting to find you dead. Do you know what that's like for a mother to go through?" She stopped. "Sorry. An aunt."

Nicholas stepped forward, placing his shoulders between them. "We're just glad you're ok. You must forgive us, if our fear for you has left us upset." He patted Silvana on the arm. "So where are the others now?"

"On the ground, outside the building."

"Well, perhaps that's where we should go next. Reunite, and make our way back home." He paused and frowned at her. "How did you get back up here?"

"Portia transported me."

"Oh." He looked thoughtful. "How long ago?"

"I don't know. Half an hour?"

His eyes shifted to the side. "But we've been looking for you all this time. You never saw us?"

"We were fighting Skinwalkers."

"My God!" Lisbeth cried. "You saw the Skinwalkers who orchestrated the attack? And you fought them?"

"Portia was with me."

"They've killed people, Silvana! You shouldn't have come back up here. How could you be so careless?"

"I was here looking for you!" Silvana shouted. People were staring now, but she didn't care. "I didn't know there'd be Skinwalkers. But the two of us *beat* them, aunty. So stop treating me like a little girl."

"That's enough," Nicholas said, cutting in again. He spoke in a softer voice. "So you were fighting them the whole time?"

"No. We went downstairs to investigate. We found three wounded people and helped them. They're over there now." She pointed out the three wait-staff, sitting together with a witch working on their wounds.

"Oh Silvana!" Nicholas smiled brightly, relaxing. "Of course you went to help people. I am so proud of you." He patted her on the shoulder. "I was just worried that you had been in danger, and seen something horrifying."

Nicholas, you can be so patronising sometimes.

"I did." She swallowed, but spoke with a calm detachment. "There were dead on the floor below. People blown to pieces." She looked between them and saw the shock on their faces. "How come no one went downstairs to help them? Those people would have died without me. There are so many powerful wizards and witches up here who could have saved them."

Nicholas offered a sad smile. "The people here tonight are VIPs. In fact, they're the most important of all VIPs in the world. The staff would have cared for them as a priority."

"But that shouldn't matter. Most of these guests had the power to protect themselves. The wounded…"

"Honey, please stop," Lisbeth said, her eyes suddenly wide with terror.

"They had been helping us all night. Why couldn't anyone help them when they were literally dying? They didn't do anything to deserve this."

"Silvana…" Nicholas warned, gesturing behind her, but Silvana was too frustrated to stop.

"And if we don't help them, what right do we have to rule…" she trailed off when she saw her aunt and uncle bowing their heads. She turned around.

The High King, Reynold the First, was right behind her. His weathered face was scowling and his eyes were focused right on Silvana.

"Please, young lady," he said in a gravelly voice that had deepened with age. "Don't let me interrupt. Pray tell. By what right do we rule?"

Oh my god. He heard everything. Will he be offended?

"Your…excellency," she said and bowed low. "Forgive my words, they were hastily spoken. I am merely in shock after the events of the night."

The King was silent. She rose from her bow so she could see his face. He was still staring at her. "I detest waiting," he said. "I've done plenty of it, over nine hundred years." He spoke the number with a clear tone of emphasis.

Waiting? Oh, he wants an answer. "Yes, your majesty. I…" Silvana swallowed. "I was expressing my regret that so many serving staff were killed tonight, and no one could help them. I…I wondered how such power as was here tonight could still be… limited."

Silvana could hear Lisbeth's sharp intake of breath behind her. Silvana braced herself, maybe for a decree of punishment, or maybe he'd do it himself with magic.

Yet Reynold only offered her a smile. "The greatest sin has always been pride," he said. "No wizard is omnipotent, and it is a sin to think so. Only God has the power over all. We are but His vessels. It is for Him to choose who lives and dies, and for us to marvel at His wisdom. However," he paused, and reached a slow-moving hand towards Silvana's cheek. "It is only natural, for one of such beauty, to hate the ugliness of violence. I wish every soul was as pure as yours."

His hand touched her cheek with gentleness as his fingers ran along her chin. He paused in his speech, as if waiting for something. "Thank you, your Highness," Silvana said politely.

Reynold nodded, as if seeing what he expected. "You are vampiric, are you not?" She nodded, and he smiled enough to spread wrinkles across his face. "Truly, the great beauty of Eve, mother of your kind, shines bright still." He lowered his hand to cup her chin. Yet...

The back of his wrist was resting against her décolletage, and his forearm was just brushing against the fabric covering her breast. And his hand stayed there. Silvana went rigid and her teeth clenched. *What is he doing? Is he about to grope me, like he groped that poor woman? Even with my family watching?* Reynold kept staring, smiling at her with a glimmer in his eyes, then at last she understood.

He's trying to seduce me! He honestly believes that calling me beautiful and touching me like this is all it takes to attract me to him. The idea was absurd. She was too afraid to feel any sort of endearment. And yet, he was High King Reynold the First. If his title alone wasn't enough, he was one of the most powerful wizards in the world. This man could singlehandedly cause earthquakes, tsunamis, hurricanes. He could wipe an entire city from the earth if he wanted to. Maybe he was so powerful that this is all it usually took for him to have his way.

So playing along, she smiled back and pressed her chest forward slightly into the back of his arm.

He pressed down slightly harder in response. *I was right. He is coming on to me.* She stepped back out of his reach. Surprise flickered on Reynold's face, but before he said anything, Nicholas stepped forward.

"Thank you for your kindness, your excellency," Nicholas said, coming forward and bowing.

The High King lowered his arm. He studied Nicholas for a long moment. "You look familiar," he said. "That sword…House Romanov?"

"Your majesty is most wise."

"Then that would make you…Nicholas the Third?"

Nicholas's eyes widened. "My lord, I am honoured to hear my name spoken by you."

"Nonsense. I knew your namesake quite well. And I was thrilled to hear your parents had named you after him. Most fitting."

"It's an honour I've known all my life, and yet have never tired of."

Reynold smiled again. "Tell me. How is House Romanov?"

Nicholas didn't falter. "We hold land, and many priceless heirlooms and artefacts. We are the proud caretakers of the past, and stewards for the future."

"Ah. It is good to hear someone around here still remembers the past. With every day, I feel the old ways slipping. I take comfort in knowing God does not *slip*." He looked up at the ceiling, and artificial lights cast shadows over the lines on his face. "Yet, change is a constant. You would not believe how much the English language has changed in my lifetime alone. I have to relearn my own language every hundred years, lest I forget how they speak it now." He gave the slightest laugh, and suddenly Nicholas and Lisbeth were laughing with him, much louder than necessary. Silvana could barely crack a smile.

"It pleases us all to see you in good health," Lisbeth said. "After the danger of tonight, we thought surely some fools would attempt to challenge you."

"I thank you for your concern, but you need not worry. God is alive within me, and His power permeates the blood in my veins. None may touch me."

Silvana remembered what Khadija and Sam had told her, about a wizard's source of power. She understood now. Reynold was constantly talking about God, because it was linked with his faith. He was constantly self-assuring to keep his faith and his will at maximum. *He must be near limitless in power, after nearly a millennium of faith.*

"My lord!"

A voice shouted, and all background murmuring of the crowd cut off. Reynold turned, and everyone followed his gaze.

A young man marched across the floor from the opposite stairwell, dressed in an Asian styled male jacket and loose pants. A beautiful woman in a pink kimono marched alongside him. *I know them. Hana and Mikeru, the couple who gave me their business card.*

Mikeru lifted something above his head. "I have slain one of the aggressors!"

He was holding the severed head of a velociraptor in one outstretched hand, and his katana rested at his side in his other hand, the blade dripping with blood.

A hush fell over the crowd. Then the High King gave a barking laugh and clapped his hands. "A mortal knight has slain a dragon! Here is a deed worthy of legend!" The crowd broke into applause, and Mikeru stood before them with a straight face as he soaked up the praise.

The sound of applause died down as another Vigile stepped forward. Silvana recognised the older bearded man who had spoken with her and Portia earlier. "My lord, we've reported three insurgents so far who attacked in the chaos. All Metamorphs. Thanks to this knight, two have now been slain. The third is still at large. We believe they became a bird and flew off the building."

Reynold ordered, "Then find them. Half of the Vigiles must start searching. The other half, take our guests home and out of danger." He turned to face Silvana once again, his eyes boring into hers. "We must protect those we rule over, or else, what right do we have to rule?"

Silvana had to supress a cold shiver. This powerful man had noticed her. She began to fear she would never escape his notice again.

Chapter 10

Jason was sitting on the edge of a garden wall, his face in his hands, his legs shaking with anxiety. There was nothing he could do. And he hated it.

Desdemona stood watch over him, and Emberline and Phillip hovered nearby. It had been an hour since Jason woke up. He only had a slight headache, which was a positive sign, leading him to suspect he had just passed out from the shock of the fall, rather than any serious head wound. Either way, he'd been left behind when Silvana went searching for the others and Desdemona was unwilling to take him back. So there was nothing to do but wait.

I will never leave you.

Silvana's words echoed through his mind again. *Stop that. You're being unfair. She had to go help her family in an emergency. Grow up and stop taking it so personally.* Still. If he was being honest with himself, her leaving him like this really hurt his feelings, plain and simple. Even though he knew it shouldn't.

Something moved in front of Jason and he stood ready and alert. The air in front of him bent around itself as light reflected in paradoxical ways. Four figures emerged between the folding of space. In a second, Jason had covered the space between them.

"Silvana!"

She was there, her dark hair and blue eyes singing to him. He glimpsed the torn up dress and blood smears on her hands but judging by the way she leapt into his arms and squeezed him tight, she was uninjured.

"Jason! I'm so glad you're ok."

Liar.

He was shocked by his own thought. Yes he had felt a little hurt by her leaving, but he understood her actions completely. He might have done the same if there were people in danger. He had to get over that.

She cupped his face and scanned his forehead. "How's your head? Are you woozy?"

"I'm fine. Just a little tender."

She sighed in relief. "I'm so sorry I left you here. I feel terrible. But I had to go back for Aunty Lisbeth and Nicholas. I hope I didn't worry you."

"We've been worried sick," Emberline said, and Jason couldn't hold back the loud groan of annoyance that escaped his lips.

"I'm sorry, but can you two not start up again?" Jason snapped. He knew he was losing his temper, but he didn't care. "It's been a hell of a night, and we don't need to start pointing fingers and blaming each other. We should be grateful we're all alive!"

Emberline glared at him.

Phillip stepped before his wife. "Listen here, you filthy beardsplitter..."

"Jason's right," Nicholas cut in with a louder voice. "If tonight has taught us anything, it's that it can all be taken away so easily. Let's not fight. Right now, we should return home." Emberline was making hard eye contact with Jason, but Phillip's expression softened and he gave Jason a nod of truce.

"Thou art most generous, Nicholas," Desdemona said as she

approached, 'in granting thy permission. Hast thou any more demands to place on thy servant?" she gave a mock bow. Portia was smiling behind her. The two had been standing close together a moment ago.

Were they...embracing while we were distracted?

"My apologies," Nicholas said. "It's been a long night, and I misspoke. Mighty Vigiles, would you be willing to return me and my family home ahead of time?"

Desdemona snorted. "Well, far be it from me to disappoint."

The group came together and linked hands as they had done mere hours ago. Jason was sure to grab Silvana's and Lisbeth's hands before either of the Vigiles could step beside him. The wizards muttered *"Silaurudu!"* and the world bent around them again.

This time, Jason didn't fall. Though he did shut his eyes.

A few moments later he found himself in the front parlour at the family mansion, north side of Plymouth, England. The air was immediately colder and more humid.

"Ah!" Phillip said. "Bloody good to be back. You know, I don't think I ate anything at that party. Damn Skinwalker zounderkites. Anyone else hungry?" Phillip made his way to the kitchen, but Jason wasn't listening. He searched the floor for his phone and found it face down on the carpet. He snatched it up and breathed a sigh of relief. The screen wasn't cracked. He didn't have the cash for a new phone.

I just saw a room full of people with blue diamonds, and I can't afford a new phone. He shook his head.

"Any messages?" Portia asked with a bemused smile.

"Well no, but that's not the point."

"I was with him all night," Silvana said. "Who else would be texting him?"

Jason groaned inwardly. It was a hundred percent true, but

admitting it seemed pathetic.

"We declare," Desdemona said in a loud voice, "that thou art returned to thy home as thy left it. Our contract with thee hast been fulfilled."

"Hold on," Lisbeth said. "Look at my daughter's dress? It's been torn to shreds. Surely that's not the same condition we left in."

"That was caused by her decision to return to danger," Portia said. "We take no responsibility for her decisions."

"What about our near-death experiences?" Emberline sneered. "You can't say that falling off the side of the building was our decision. What about my mortal husband's health?"

"Thou were caught in time."

Emberline and Lisbeth looked ready to yell some more, but Jason cut in. "Can we expect news?" he asked. Everyone turned to him. "Updates into the investigation. Will the Imperium tell us what happened tonight, and why?"

The Vigiles both sneered in unison. Desdemona purred menacingly, "Thou can count upon it."

"Now if no one else has any complaints," Portia said, "then we wish you all a good night." She clung hands with the older woman beside her and the air folded around them once more. Between one movement and the next, they were gone.

Suddenly, everything felt normal again. The Imperium were gone, all Immortal culture was left behind them, and it was like the night and the attack had never happened. Yet Jason could still feel the tension in the room. Emberline and Silvana were avoiding each other's gaze. His own mind was filled with questions. Actually, it was just the same question over and over in variations of 'what the hell was that?'

"Well that was a disaster," Lisbeth said with a sigh. She moved to one of the ornate armchairs and collapsed onto the cushions with a rather undignified 'oomph'. "It's not even eleven. We were supposed to have until two tomorrow morning to network. I barely made any headway with the Glucksbergs. Did anyone else at least have more luck?" She scanned the room, but no one looked up at her. "Emberline, surely you had some success? I saw you talking with so many different people?"

Emberline had just draped herself over the fainting lounge, laying on her side and raising the back of her hand to her face in a dramatic sigh. "No one wanted to make a deal," she said, her voice flat and lifeless. Then she pulled the diadem out of her hair and let her hairstyle fall back to normal.

"We had some success," Jason cut in. "Didn't we?"

He looked towards Silvana whose cheeks blushed soft crimson. "Yes. I have two business cards. A vampire and her knight from Japan, Hana and Mikeru. Though, they didn't tell me their House name."

Emberline gave a loud huff of annoyance. Jason had half a mind to draw his sword on her then and there, until he remembered seeing her in battle where she had wielded a sword with far more strength than he was capable of. *She'd kick my ass easily.*

"You cannot trust people who hide their House," Emberline said. "That's what cheaters and con-artists do. You can save us all time and throw both those business cards out right now, if that's all you…"

"The other card is from the House of Al Khalifa."

The room went quiet. Jason couldn't help beaming at Silvana, especially at the look of confidence in her eyes.

"Maybe you've heard of them?" Silvana said coyly, and Jason had to hide his smirk. "Royal family of the United Arab Emirates, one of the wealthiest modern families in the world, and quite possibly the royal house that has retained the most power in this century. But hmm…maybe I should throw that card out. Don't you think, Aunty?" Silvana glared at Emberline with a fierce defiance.

Emberline's nostrils flared. "I don't appreciate your tone, daughter."

"And I don't appreciate yours. After all, I'm the only one here who made any contacts tonight. I would expect a little more gratitude."

"As the one who raised you, I should say the same!"

"Ladies," Nicholas tried but his voice was barely noticed.

"I've taken you in," Emberline growled. "Cared for you for nearly one hundred years. I shouldn't have to *ask* for your respect."

"You've spent one hundred years treating me like a child."

"Because you *act* like a child."

"Alright," Nicholas snapped, and the slightest rise in voice was enough to calm the room. "That's enough."

A terrible chill rang through Jason at the sound of that commanding voice. He caught a glimpse of Nicholas as knight, warrior, and king, and it impressed him as much as it scared him.

"There's been far too much disunity in this house," Nicholas said in his calm, commanding voice. "We've all been through hell tonight. If everyone accepts, I propose an emergency family meeting in thirty minutes, once everyone has had the chance to calm down, eat some food, and slip into something more comfortable. All agreed?" There was a nod from Phillip and Jason, and no one else. "Great," Nicholas said, then sighed. "And I thought only John McClane could drive somebody that crazy."

Jason tried to hold back his laugh, and instead let out a loud snort. Nicholas winked at him.

Silvana was the first to leave the room, moving fast enough for her dress to audibly swish. Jason followed her at a brisk pace. He expected her to turn towards her bedroom, instead, she moved down the east wing. "Where are you going?"

"Kitchen," she said. "The family is hungry. They're expecting me to fix them up something."

Jason frowned. "You were just in there demanding respect. And now you're going back to being a servant?"

"Get off my back!" she snapped, whirling around. Yet her face softened immediately and her mouth fell open. "Oh…I'm sorry Jason. So sorry. It's been a long night."

"No it's ok." He came forward and held her shoulders in a soft grip. "Tell you what. I've got an idea that will help with food. And it'll give you the chance to fill me in on everything. Sound good?"

* * *

Half an hour later, Jason and Silvana walked into the family dining room. Everyone was seated around the table in their usual positions, though now with slightly less formal clothes, with the men in jackets and the ladies in long silk gowns.

"Was that a knock on the door?" Emberline asked

"Did you get food, sweetie?" Lisbeth asked at the same time.

Jason grinned. "Yep! Uber driver just dropped it off. Bon appetite!" And he set down four bags of McDonalds as Silvana set down the drinks. Jason grinned broadly and said, "Oh how good does that *smell?* I can't believe how quickly it got here." Jason sat down with an entire bag for himself.

"What is this greasy shit?" Phillip growled, picking up a cheeseburger and eyeing it sceptically.

"Hear hear," Emberline echoed. "I can't believe you thought this would be acceptable. This unhealthy slop is inappropriate for men of Nicholas's age. Do you know how bad it would be for his heart?"

A bag ruffled and everyone turned to see Nicholas already biting into a cheeseburger. He paused with the burger in his mouth and made a 'mmm?' sound.

"So let me get this straight," Jason said. "You expected Silvana to get dressed and settled in the same amount of time as you had, but to also cook an elaborate meal? Does that seem fair to you?"

"She is the youngest," Emberline said. "It is her duty to this family…"

"Then it's also *my* duty, as her knight," Jason said. "That's why I paid for this meal. You're welcome, by the way. And if you're not prepared to lift a finger, then you'll eat what you're given."

"You treat us like children," Phillip snapped.

"Interesting. I wonder why that is."

Jason stuffed a handful of chips between the buns of his burger, and bit down with a satisfied moan. Sauce and mayonnaise dripped down his hands and smudged on his cheeks. He looked up and offered the table a closed-lip smile.

"Jason," Nicholas said, "My son. You know I called this meeting to deal with the tension in the family. Why would you start by antagonising your aunt and uncle?"

It hurt to hear Nicholas call him son but with disappointment lacing his words. Jason nearly backed down then and there. But he swallowed and spoke in a more formal tone. "I'm sorry, sir. But I believe the tension comes from this family still treating Silvana like a child. She is smart, strong, and extremely capable. It is time for us all to see her as an equal."

"Oh really?" Phillip said and pointed at Jason. "Then why are you acting as her lawyer, instead of letting her speak for herself?"

"Don't deflect from my point. Silvana secured a powerful ally for this family, and she had to shout over you all to get the appreciation she deserved."

"Begging your pardon," Lisbeth cut in. Her volume was half what Jason's had been but still held an air of authority. "I think we can all agree that Jason has a good point. Silvana, I would like to take a moment to commend you on befriending the Al Khalifa family. Well done."

A muttered chorus of 'well done Silvana' went around the table. Silvana had a quiet, proud look on her face.

"There is another issue," Nicholas said gravely. "Miss Al Khalifa was attacked directly tonight. In fact, I think it's safe to assume that she was the sole target."

Jason hummed at that. It made sense. Silvana had told him about the three Skinwalkers in velociraptor form who had likely rigged the gas in the kitchen, then swarmed towards Khadija. She had barely survived. Silvana had thought the High King was their real target, but Jason wasn't so sure. If anything, the real target was probably Samantha Kennedy. What were the odds that the two people attacked directly where the two who had approached him with an offer to resist the Imperium?

"Which raises the question," Nicholas went on. "Is it safe to ally ourselves with them right now?"

A thought hit Jason and he couldn't help wondering, what if there were already a target on his family's back? He and Silvana had spent an hour talking with the wizards. Sam had died wearing his jacket. *Shit. Those Skinwalkers could be working for the Imperium. They could be some sort of black ops military.* But then, why had they attacked Silvana and Portia? Were the two of them just in the way? But why would they attack a Vigile if they were working for the Imperium?

"I think it's perfect timing for us," Silvana said. "I'm sorry to sound callous, but if the Skinwalkers did attempt to kill Khadija, then House Al Khalifa will be looking for allies. Maybe we'll have the chance to prove ourselves in the coming days."

"What if this wasn't the only attack?" Emberline said. "If we ally ourselves with them right away, we could get caught in the crossfire.

The best thing to do would be to wait and see if they endure."

"How long can we afford to wait?" Silvana asked.

Emberline drawled, "As long as is necessary to survive."

"Ok, but keep in mind," Jason said, "Khadija is a wizard. She was attacked by Skinwalkers. I'm no expert, but even I know wizards are *far* stronger than Skinwalkers. She's in a different weight class."

"Yes, but so was Samantha Kennedy," Nicholas said. "You can't kill a wizard by matching them with power. It has to be through surprise, ambush or just plain treachery." He shuddered, like the very thought of betrayal left a sour taste on his lips. "That's not the least of it, my son. The Skinwalkers were just the tip of the sword. The most *expendable* tip. We have no idea what might be thrown at Al Khalifa next."

"Alright," Jason conceded. "So let's investigate the situation. Crack the case, figure out who's behind the attacks. Then we can rescue a powerful new ally and save our family fortunes in one strike." Jason's voice had raised an octave in his excitement. He had goosebumps. *A detective case. And for Immortals! Another chance to expand the Immortal Investigations, and save the family. God this is too perfect!*

"It's too risky," Emberline said, and Jason began to sigh. "Getting involved will put a target on our heads."

"I don't think so," said Silvana, her voice also growing with excitement. "Jason's great at investigations. He caught Peter Erickson. He put all the clues together. I think we should let him work on this."

Phillip shook his head. "Jason did well in defeating that zounderkite Erikson, I'll admit. But he also led the wizard into our house and forced a fight we barely survived. Our front parlour room still hasn't recovered." He waved a hand towards the hallway and the discarded stones still piled there.

"I've learnt a lot since then,' Jason said.

"The alternative is to do nothing," Silvana went on. "I am all for making contact with Khadija right now, but if you're all too nervous about attacks, then let us hire Jason as our PI. He can gather the information and prove who's behind the attack."

Jason and Silvana looked at each other. They smiled, and held hands under the table.

"Let's put it to a vote," Nicholas said. "All those in favour of tasking Jason with finding the culprit behind tonight's attack to help us win a powerful ally, please raise your hand."

Jason and Silvana's hands shot up. They were the sole votes.

"All those in favour of waiting for events to proceed on their own, and afterwards consider an alliance with Al Khalifa, please raise your hand."

All four of the others raised their hands.

Jason couldn't help staring at Nicholas in shock. The old knight had sad eyes, but his face was flat and hard. "Motion carries," he said. "We will wait."

Silvana silently pushed her chair back and left the room without a single word.

"Well, I dare say that concludes the meeting," Emberline said. "We shall retire. We bid you all a good night." She and Phillip left together through the same door as Silvana.

Jason remained where he was.

"My son?" Nicholas asked. "What troubles you?"

"I just don't understand."

"What's that, deary?" Lisbeth said.

"Silvana's trying to help this family. Yet all of her ideas get shut down. I just don't understand why no one listens to her. She's the third oldest in this family, and she's probably the bravest, when you consider her actions tonight. What has she ever done to earn your distrust?"

There was a moment of silence. Jason stared at the table without looking up.

"Son," Nicholas said. "You have a good heart. You care about Silvana and this family, and we are proud of you for it." Despite all the anger Jason felt, he still experienced a wave of pride at Nicholas's praise. "We appreciate the ideas Silvana is putting forward. We just know more than she does about this world."

"It's not an insult," Lisbeth said, her husband nodding in agreement. "I'm much older than she is. And while Nicholas is ten years younger, he has had more dealings with the supernatural community as leader of his house. The event tonight is far more complicated than Silvana realises."

"But she was there. She fought for her life."

Nicholas took a long breath. "Let me ask you something. Why was Reynold there tonight?"

Jason frowned. "Wait. You think he was some kind of distraction?"

"Or bait? I don't know, son. But I know the High King hasn't made a social appearance like that in decades. I also know our family hasn't been invited to an event like that in years. Do you see? There's already plenty of unusual things about this situation."

Jason sat up a little straighter. "Do you think…we might have been targets? I guess we killed a wizard. That might have pissed people off."

"We can't rule that possibility out," Lisbeth said. "Even if my feelings tell me that is unlikely. But the main question here is why did the Skinwalkers attack Al Khalifa, when the High King was in the room? Surely he's the bigger target?"

Jason shrugged. "He's too strong. Doesn't he basically have the powers of a god?"

"Even High Kings can be killed." Lisbeth gave a grim laugh. "It's never happened before, but it's theoretically possible. That's why they usually have an armed guard."

"But Reynold didn't have any guards."

"Yet another unusual thing."

Jason frowned. "So Reynold was exposed and more vulnerable than anyone's seen in years, and they still didn't attack him."

"Can you think of no reason why?"

Jason understood immediately. "Are you suggesting…they were working for him?"

"Ah!" Nicholas pointed a finger. "And we come to the heart of the matter. The simple answer is we don't know. But it's possible. The very fact that there's even the slightest possibility that Reynold *might* be behind the attack, means that there's no way we can risk investigating it."

"Standing against one of the Imperium and the Seven High Kings is a sure way to have your House utterly obliterated," Lisbeth said. "It's happened many times before."

Jason sighed. "I should have considered that. My mind hadn't gotten around to it yet."

But even as he acknowledged their point, he knew he couldn't let this go. It wasn't in his nature. He was a detective, even if it wasn't official, so he had to uncover the truth. The thought that someone might commit injustice and walk away made his skin crawl. Still, he couldn't say that out loud. Instead he smiled politely. "You two would make good detectives."

Lisbeth gave a polite laugh. "We've just been around longer. You'd be surprised at the skills you can learn with more than one lifetime."

Nicholas held his wife's hand. "Don't worry, my son. This house has stood strong for hundreds of years. We'll find a way to endure. We always do. But we must avoid being overcome by fear and taking dangerous risks." He stood up, and his chair squeaked against the floor. "I confess I am exhausted. I'm usually asleep three hours earlier."

"Good night, Jason," Lisbeth said and she put an arm under her husband and helped him away.

"Nicholas," Jason called, "why do you keep calling me son?"

The old knight glanced over his shoulder so only the profile of his face was visible. "Does it bother you?"

"No. No, I just…don't understand."

Nicholas smiled. "Because I always wanted a son. You are the answer to a prayer I made seventy years ago."

Then he walked from the room, leaning heavily on his wife for support, leaving Jason alone as his eyes began to well up.

Chapter 11

Jason spent the night at the Romanov home and slept with an arm over Silvana's stomach. She woke before him and he flopped over in the morning to find the bed empty. He let out a groan from the effort of waking.

"I'm here," her voice replied from nearby. He blinked open blurry eyes.

Silvana was sitting at her desk. A wooden pedestal with a notebook was propped open before her and she was quietly drawing. Jason stared at her back for a long time in quiet appreciation. She wore only a silken nightshirt with thin singlet straps that barely covered her shoulders. Her hair was tangled, hanging partially over her face. On the notepad were black pencil scratches. No colour. She was drawing a woman in a dark mask and black cape.

"You ok?" he asked.

"Mmm," she murmured.

Jason recognised this mood. After six months together, he knew when she was frustrated with her family, but Silvana would never speak a bad word about any of them, and so would draw for hours on end. He knew there was little chance getting through to her while in this state. Jason crawled out of bed, dressed in slacks and a t-shirt, and used the bathroom. Then he stood near her and watched her draw over her shoulder.

"Do you want any breakfast?"

"I'm not hungry." She didn't look up, only continued to carefully lay down each pencil stroke.

"Do you…need any blood?"

"No, sweetheart. Thank you for offering."

Jason stepped closer, holding his wrist at a distance but within her line of sight. "Are you sure? Cause I know you had to fight last night, and that would have used up some of your strength. So it's ok if you need more a bit early."

"It's fine. Really."

Jason nodded. "Ok. Well, I have training with Phil and Nic this morning, so I better get some food."

"Mmm."

She's not ignoring you. Don't take it personally, he told himself. He held back a sigh, and instead made his voice soft to whisper, "I love you, Silvana."

She spun around. The sight of her eyes staring at him, focused on him with warm recognition, put him at ease with the world. "I love you too, Jason," she said. "I'm sorry if I'm being weird. But I'm fine. I just want to draw for a bit longer."

"Ok. Thank you." He bent over, and they exchanged a quick kiss. Then he left.

Jason walked towards the kitchen and made himself some butter and toast. He sat down by himself to eat in silence and briefly considered opening his laptop and working on his report about last night. But the thought was overwhelming. The Immortal Investigations would require a huge write up to cover everything that had happened. It would take three to four hours, and he only had one hour to spare before training. So he finished his meal and wandered through the mansion. On a whim, he went upstairs to kill some time.

He rarely went onto the second floor and didn't know the area well. He stepped lightly as he moved down the corridors. Dust clouds sprung up from the carpet with every step. Rows of doors lined the hallways, in various colours and different levels of deterioration to the wood and paint. He checked the closest one. Inside was a small room stacked with old furniture. The air smelled of dust.

He moved to another door. An old bedroom with green wallpaper. *That's hideous.* He started to leave, but something caught his eye. Several stacked billboards leaned against the wall. He walked over and pulled one back.

It was a picture of Nicholas, though it took a moment to realise it. This was Nicholas in his late thirties. Underneath was the graphic, '*Nicholas Clarke. Vote Conservative.*'

Jason barked a short laugh. *Nicholas ran for office?* He whipped out his phone and googled it. A second later he found it. *Nicholas Clarke, conservative independent for Mayor of Plymouth in 1977. Received 2.8% of the vote.*

"Ouch," Jason groaned. There was no further information. Apparently this was the Romanov family's one and only attempt to adapt to the politics of the time. *Only 2.8% of the vote. No wonder they're so scared of change.* He closed the door and left.

As he came back into the hallway, he heard the slight murmuring of voices. He crossed to the end of the hallway and listened. Two women were conversing. He reached for the handle, then stopped and knocked instead.

"Yes, darling?" Lisbeth called out.

Jason went in. "Hi. I just wanted to…"

He cut off.

Emberline and Lisbeth were in a studio. They were dressed in painter's overalls with their hair pinned back. And before them was a canvas large enough to cover the entire room.

"Oh my god," he whispered.

"What are you doing in here?" Emberline snapped.

Jason couldn't stop staring. The painting was gorgeous. He hadn't been able to take his eyes off it since he walked into the room. It depicted a vast ocean of blue and black. A storm front was rolling across the shoreline. On Lisbeth's side was a setting sun reflecting golden light over a peaceful sea. Near Emberline, the painting was a swirling black vortex of storm that lashed the sea with tumultuous waves. And in the middle, where they met, was a perfect blend of darkness and light, sea and storm, flowing together and interweaving.

"We did not invite you in."

"Actually, Lisbeth did," Jason replied without looking away from the painting.

"I thought you were Nicholas," Lisbeth said. "Didn't you hear me say darling?"

"In fairness, you call me darling all the time."

"Yes, but the tone is different."

Jason just shook his head. "This is amazing."

"It's not finished," Lisbeth said, waving her hand dismissively. "No one's allowed to see it until then. I haven't got the colour right on the reflections. Sunlight on water is tricky. It needs to reflect off the surface, but not look like it's coming from the surface. I need months more…" she trailed off. "Jason? Are you ok?"

Jason couldn't explain it. But for some reason, he found himself wiping a tear from his eye. "It's beautiful," he said in a choked voice. He had to swallow back a sob, and coughed to clear his throat. Jason was not very artistic himself, but art always moved him in strange ways, and this piece was even more effective than normal.

"I've never seen a man cry so much," Emberline said, shaking her head.

"I think it's sweet," Lisbeth said. "And flattering. I consider it high praise."

Jason couldn't help a laugh. "What do you mean I cry too much? You've seen me cry only twice in six months."

"I've been married to Phillip for forty years, and I've only seen him cry once."

Jason shook his head. "Yeah that's healthy," he mumbled to himself.

"Healthy is exactly what it is," Emberline snipped.

Damn. Forgot about her vampiric hearing.

"Look, I'm sorry to intrude. But I'm not sorry to have seen this. It's is such a beautiful painting!"

"Thank you," Lisbeth said with a smile.

"And you know, Silvana is in her room drawing as we speak. I like that you have so much in common." He took a step towards the door. "Well sorry I interrupted. I'll be going—"

Emberline cut him off with a sigh. "Well since you've already seen it, you might as well come have a closer look." She turned away as if uncaring, and Jason couldn't help smiling. *She's showing off.* "We have spent over eight months working on this. And it probably still has four months left to go."

"Give or take six months," Lisbeth sighed. "This damn reflecting sunlight is driving me crazy."

"It looks finished to me," Jason said. He stepped so close to the painting that he could see the fine, delicate brush strokes on the canvas. The colours were even more vivid up close. He wished he could step into it.

"Well clearly you don't have two hundred years' experience," Emberline said.

"So wait. All those other paintings in the house. Are they all yours?"

"Mostly," Lisbeth said. "Some we keep around because we love them too much to bear parting with them. Others, well…we've never found buyers."

"That's too bad. What about this one? Is it for something special?"

"It's to fix our hallway." Lisbeth said with a dark laugh. "A big masterpiece like this could sell for a million pounds at auction."

Jason nodded in understanding. This explained what the women did with most of their time. He always assumed they just kind of free loaded around the place, doing vampire things and thinking Immortal thoughts. This almost humanised them. They worked a job.

"This looks like the stuff you see in museums."

"Well, I should expect so," Lisbeth said. "Many of those artists were also our teachers."

"Or students," Emberline said.

"Anyone I would know?"

"Oh yes. Pierre Renoir taught us for some time." Lisbeth smiled fondly. "Wonderful man. A little strange, but brilliant."

"Oh him!" Jason said, having no idea who they meant. "Have you ever taught Silvana?"

Emberline snorted. "Tried to. She has no interest in working with *oils*." She sneered the last word. "Prefers her sketchbooks and pencils, and those damn superhero comics. At least with this she could make some real money."

Jason blinked. "Uh…pretty sure there are comic books worth millions of pounds."

"Ridiculous."

Jason found himself laughing rather than being annoyed. "Well this has been very nice, but I have to start the day's training soon."

"Don't let us keep you," Lisbeth said.

"And don't tell the others what you saw!" Emberline growled. "No one was supposed to see this until the unveiling!"

"Ok, I promise I won't tell." Jason offered a low bow to show respect and left the studio behind. He couldn't help smiling. *That was probably one of my better interactions with the two of them.*

He hurried back down the hallway and ignored the remaining doors. *Another time.* Instead he headed downstairs and along the west wing hallway. Soon he reached the gym, where he often worked out with Silvana. He looked longingly at the weight racks, benches and cardio machines, planning what he might do this afternoon if he had any energy left. But for now, he only walked through the gym to reach a side door that led onwards, into the training grounds.

The floor was made of hardwood sleepers that had a pleasant varnish scent. Four pillars marked the boundaries of the practice ground. On the far wall was a series of weapon racks lined with swords short and long, claymores, halberds and fighting staffs. And by the entrance were two suits of armour for medieval knights.

Jason began his stretches immediately. He was halfway through them when Nicholas and Phillip arrived.

"Well well," Phillip said. "'Blessed is that servant, whom his lord when he cometh, is found so doing the master's will.'"

Jason smiled. Phillip was always in his best mood while training. Perhaps bossing Jason around and swinging weapons at him may have something to do with it. "I'm keen to begin today, sir," Jason said. "After I spent last night's fight sitting on my ass."

"You got dropped off the side of the world's tallest building," Nicholas said. "I think you were hardly sitting on your ass." He frowned at Jason. "Where's your sword?"

"Oh. Sorry sir, it's in Silvana's room."

"Won't do much training with it there, will you?"

Jason was on his feet. "I'll fetch it right away."

Nicholas merely held up a hand. "You can use a staff today."

"But I haven't used a staff before."

"That's to be expected when you forget your primary weapon."

Phillip was grinning broadly. Jason didn't give him the satisfaction of showing his disappointment. He took a long staff off the rack without complaint. It was 1.5 metres long and made of thin bending wood. He gripped it firmly and gave it a test swing, whipping it through the air with a whoosh.

"I'll be quicker with this," Jason said in warning.

"Will you now?" Phillip said. "Well perhaps I should surrender." He chuckled, and Jason did not like the sound of it.

Nicholas sat down on a nearby bench, threading the sword at his hip through the gap in the chair. "We won't be learning any new forms today," he said. "Instead, I want to teach you how to spot an opportunity. Winning a fight is often more about seeing a chance to strike and taking it."

"So it's training my mind to act?" Jason asked.

"Partially. But your body has a mind of its own, so to speak. Sometimes your body will do things you didn't tell it to do because of its own system. You've heard the terms flight, fright, or fight?" Jason nodded. "People think that's about the choice you make in the face of danger. But it's not a choice. It's your body's automatic reaction, and it's largely involuntary."

"Until you've trained for it," Phillip said. "You have to practice a fight response over and over, otherwise your body will react on its own and make its own choice. For example..."

Phillip launched forward. His sword swooped high overhead.

An eagle strike. Jason swung his staff. Rather than catching the sword head-on with an unfamiliar weapon, he swept the staff sideways, catching the sword and deflected it away. He raised the staff up to cover his chest.

Phillip didn't move again. "Very good," he said. "You saw a sword coming. Did you have to think about it?"

Jason frowned. "No. I didn't think. Though, I did decide not to block directly in case you cut through the staff."

"Smart. That was a possibility."

"Good," Nicholas said. "That's an example of what we mean. Your body reacted with a fight response. This freed up your mind to consider the action, instead of forcing your mind to spend those precious seconds trying to get your body to act."

Jason nodded. "Cool."

"But you can't always control when your body freezes. Hey Jason?" He looked at the old master.

Nicholas had a gun – his silver magnum – pointed directly at Jason. *What the hell? Is he going to shoot me? Why? How would that help? Unless it's a betrayal! Nicholas never would. God, there's too much distance. Wait I could throw...* Jason raised his staff overhead.

"That's enough," Phillip said and stepped between them. He smirked. "You're dead, my apprentice. You stayed still too long."

"What are you experiencing?" Nicholas said. He saw Jason wasn't listening and spoke louder. "Jason. My son. Tell me, what are you feeling right now? What is your body doing?"

"I..." he struggled to catch his breath. "I can't...speak. I'm...panting. I'm trying not to start hyperventilating?" He put a hand to his chest. "God, Nicholas! What the hell was that?!"

"Sorry, my son. I would never hurt you. But we had to trigger a fear response."

"Oh. That makes sense."

"What else are you feeling? Notice the little details."

"Um...nausea, high heartrate. Uh...it's like a fog on my brain."

"Good, Jason. Well done. Now that you know what a fear overload is like, we can practice dealing with it. Now my son, I'm going to point the gun at you again. But I won't fire. It's not even loaded. And you're going to practice controlling your thoughts and your body."

Jason nodded, and Phillip stepped aside again. *This won't be hard.*

Nicholas just told me there's no threat. Then the gun was raised, and Jason immediately felt the exact same fear with all its horrible intensity. He froze. He stared at the nozzle and just kept imagining it going off. He could feel the phantom pain in his chest from a fictional bullet. He thought of Silvana, his police captain and workmates and Freddie all grieving for him. *I still haven't moved!* And he fell backwards onto the floor.

"Ok that's enough," Nicholas said and put the gun out of sight. "It's still confronting to see a weapon pointed at you, even when you know it's safe."

"Shit yeah," Jason groaned and lifted himself. He'd landed on his back, and his staff had dropped out of his hand and clattered away. "God, I really fell apart there."

"That's alright. Better you fall apart in training," Phillip said. Then he patted Jason on the shoulder with two firm claps. Just when it seemed like an affectionate moment, Phillip roared with laughter. "But I'm going to remember you falling over backwards for a long time. Seriously, how was that going to help?"

"Alright, sir," Jason drawled. "But what can I do in that situation? Nicholas is seven, eight metres away. There's no way to cover that distance before he can fire. And there's nowhere to run in this room. No cover."

"You're missing the point, zounderkite," Phillip drawled back. "The goal is not to stop bullets. The goal is to train yourself to *act*. Once you can control your reactions better, we'll start talking about what to do next. For now, the goal is to control your fear."

Jason picked up the staff and took position, knees bent, one foot pointed forward and the other turned side on. "Any tips on staff fighting?" he asked.

"None!" Phillip shouted and started swinging.

The master knight and the apprentice traded four quick blows.

Phillip was all on the attack today. Jason found himself naturally holding the staff at one side like a longsword and using its full reach to keep Phillip at a distance. Its extra length made it quicker. But Phillip's sword was stronger. His footwork was neater, more controlled, less wasted energy. He stepped forward with each strike, and Jason was hard pressed to keep the blade away with sweeping strokes, even as he backed away. He could only deflect or risk snapping his weaker weapon.

Nicholas was behind him, sitting calmly as Jason was forced towards him. Then he raised his weapon. "Look out for the gun!" Nicholas roared, and Jason dropped to the ground to duck. Phillip was on him a second later. Two quick strokes knocked his staff aside before the blade rested at his throat.

"Fuck!" Jason growled.

"Alright, stop and focus, son," Nicholas ordered. "Examine your mindset, your body, your feelings. What are you experiencing?"

Jason huffed for breath. "Anger at being caught off guard and not reacting better. Adrenaline from the fight."

"What about blinding fear?"

"Not as much as before."

"See?" Nicholas smiled. "When you saw the gun, you immediately *moved*. You took action, even if it wasn't an effective action. You didn't freeze because the adrenaline from the fight was keeping you alert."

Phillip moved his sword and let Jason stand up. "Let's try it again." They moved back to the centre of the floor and took positions. Jason placed his feet wider, lowered his body mass even closer to the ground for greater balance, and moved his right hand further up the staff. Phillip had a two-handed grip on his sword, held directly in front of him.

Jason launched first, lunging in a jab straight for Phillip's chest. Yet

Phillip seemed to anticipate him. With a simple sidestep and thrust, his own blade caught Jason over the heart.

"Fast, but clumsy," Phillip said. "I hope I'm not also describing your lovemaking."

"Stop flirting, old man," Jason said, "or I'm gonna fall for you."

Phillip blinked. "What the…"

Jason jabbed his staff and caught Phillip's wrist. The old knight growled as he drew his injured hand back in pain. Yet he immediately moved the sword with his one good hand and resumed his assault. He came on with bold steps forward, controlling the field with precise shifts forward. Again Jason was back-peddling on the defensive. But this time Phillip's blows were faster in the one-handed grip. Less strong, but sudden and random with combinations of jabs, slices and thrusts. Jason kept trying use his long staff to keep him at a distance. But Phillip was unstoppable. It's like he knew where Jason would step and was already ahead.

Movement in the right corner of Jason's eye. *Gun!*

Jason stepped sideways to the left. Phillip was caught off-guard and spun to protect his flank. And he perfectly shielded Jason from Nicholas's gun.

"Good move," Nicholas shouted. "Using your opponent as a shield can be effective. But Phillip need only step aside…"

Jason swung wide at Phillip, coming in hard from the side then spinning to strike on the opposite in quick succession. It forced Phillip to defend and kept him in place. The old knight tried to step sideways to let Nicholas take a shot. Jason used the length of the staff in long sweeps to keep him in the centre.

Phillip suddenly thrust his sword forward. Jason was caught unprepared. The staff wasn't in the right position to block…

So Jason grabbed the staff by both ends and caught the blade in the middle. The blade struck into the wood and wedged there. Then

Jason charged forward and forced the sword up over both of their heads. He overpowered Phillip's straining arms, forcing him to let go of the sword with one hand. Then Jason pushed the staff and sword all the way down behind Phillip's back, grabbing him in a bear hug. He pinned the sword arm down and squeezed.

Jason growled, "I have you now—"

Phillip's free hand gripped him around the throat. He started choking Jason. *Son of a bitch!* Yet Jason could handle it and refused to give up. Phillip tried to sidestep again to break his grip, so Jason seized him tighter and yanked him back into the path of Nicholas. Phillip had dropped hold of the sword and started jabbing Jason in the ribs, stomach, chin…

Jason moved the staff behind Phillips head. Phillip tried once more to side step, and Jason was ready for him this time. He spun in the opposite direction as Phillip and successfully locked the staff around his throat in a headlock.

"Yield!" Jason roared.

"I yield!" Phillip roared back, and Jason released him.

"Unbelievable!" Nicholas gave a cheer and waved his hands above his head. "I can't—"

The gun went off.

Chapter 12

The boom was deafening. Jason and Phillip dropped to the ground and covered their heads.

"Shit! Sorry! Sorry!" Nicholas cried and lowered the weapon. "My fault. Accidental. Here, I'll take the other bullets out."

"You said it wasn't loaded!" Jason shouted. Then added, "Sir!"

"I just told you that so you'd relax."

"Are you kidding me?"

"My finger wasn't near the trigger during practice."

"Oh my god!" Jason cried.

"Put the damn thing down, zounderkite!" Phillip growled. "And you can sub in next, since I'm busy having a heart attack over here." Phillip staggered to the bench and sat down. Nicholas sighed as he put down the gun, stood up, and reached for his sword. The silver of his blade was just visible above the scabbard when Nicholas seemed to freeze in place, the sword still mostly sheathed.

"Sir? You ok?"

"My apologies," Nicholas said as his sword hand started to tremble. "My wrist is hurting. It must be from the recoil of the gun. I can't seem to grip the sword properly."

Phillip muttered to himself and Jason swore he caught the word 'justice'.

"Can I help you, sir?" Jason asked.

Nicholas shook his head. "I just hate getting old. If I could put my brain into a young body, oooh I could show you some sword skills!" He slid his sword back into its sheath and sighed. "We'll have to run through the sword forms after all. At least until Phillip is recovered."

Jason nodded and took starting position with the staff, feet together and weapon held in two hands on the side. He took a deep breath and started to move. He followed a pattern of thrusts and slices, followed by long sweeps and powerful steps as the two old knights started calling out instructions from the sidelines.

"Bring your left foot further in, you don't need to jut it out so far."

"Lower your elbow. You're not trying to flap yours wings."

"Thrust from the shoulder and hip together, not just with your arms."

Jason focused on the movements until he had worked up a sweat. In a distant part of his mind, he noticed that none of the women had come to investigate the sounds of the gunshot. *Says something about us men, if they didn't even react.*

"Can I ask you both a question?" he said as he panted for breath.

"Of course, my son." Phillip also gave a grunt of agreement.

"I've been wondering for months. Why does Silvana call Emberline and Lisbeth her aunts, instead of mothers? And why does she call you by your names, instead of uncles?"

"Ah. Well, It's very common in vampire families," Nicholas answered. "Vampires choose their heirs and adopt them, since they can't have their own biological children. For them, it's the vampire venom that marks their offspring, not their DNA."

"So all vampire children call their parents aunt and uncle?"

Phillip glanced at Nicholas, and slightly shook his head. But Nicholas shook his head back. They began muttering in hushed voices. Jason kept moving in his forms and pretended not to notice.

He kept his breathing to a minimum so he could listen well. He caught the words, 'already family', and 'not yet'.

He stood still. "Sirs, I don't want to cause a problem. I can just ask Silvana."

"That wouldn't help," Phillip said, before wincing and turning away.

"Oh we have to tell him now," Nicholas said. Philip growled as he nodded agreement. "Jason, some vampires will call their birth parents mum and dad. Others consider their parents to be whoever *bit* them."

Jason thought about it. Whoever bit them. "Wait," he cried and fell out of his fighting form. "Are you saying Silvana is not their biological child, and wasn't turned into a vampire by them either?"

"Correct."

"So she's adopted? In both the mortal sense and the Immortal?"

"Yes. And she knows this."

"Then…who turned her into a vampire?"

Nicholas shrugged. "We don't know."

"Our wives found her eighty years ago," said Phillip.

Jason did the maths. "Do you mean, during the second World War?"

"That's correct," Phillip said. "It was chaos. There were millions of refugees from all over Europe."

"And the British were terrified of them," Nicholas said. "The world doesn't like to talk about it, but I remember. We were all convinced the refugees were Nazis in disguise who would infiltrate and sabotage our defences and assassinate our leaders. So the refugees were outcasts from society. No one would take them in."

"Did Emberline and Lisbeth take them in?" Jason asked.

Phillip chuckled. "They *were* the refugees."

"Wait, what?"

Nicholas smiled. "Alright, full story. Emberline and Lisbeth are biologically cousins. But they were both turned by the same family member in the late 17th century, so they're sisters on the Immortal side. By 1939 they were living in France with their then-husbands. When the war came and France was overrun, their vampire parent was killed. That's when they tried to flee to England. They found a refugee camp in northern France that had a high population of Immortals displaced by the war. The unwanted of our society. People who were completely valueless to the Imperium, the physically enhanced and such, and were therefore abandoned. That's where our wives were hiding. And that's where they found Silvana."

"She was a war orphan," Phillip said.

"At just twelve years old."

"My God," Jason whispered. "She never mentioned it. What happened to the rest of her family?"

"Impossible to know," Nicholas said.

"But doesn't she remember?"

"Not exactly."

"Ah," Jason said. "Was it so traumatic she blocked it out?"

"That might have had something to do with it. But the more likely reason is…the frenzy." Jason raised an eyebrow and Nicholas let out a long sigh. "We're trusting you with this information, Jason. Please don't blame Silvana for this."

"I won't. I promise."

Nicholas nodded. "Silvana was not exactly a part of the camp. She was an outsider. She only came to the camp to…get what she needed…"

"She was feeding," Phillip cut in bluntly, and shook his head at Nicholas. "She was a predator praying on the refugees."

Jason blinked. "That seems unlikely. Surely Silvana…"

"She was in a frenzy," Nicholas said. "Silvana had been turned only a few weeks earlier. It's highly unusual timing. Most mortal children are turned before the age of seven. The body is young and underdeveloped, so it only undergoes minor physical changes to turn vampiric. But by your teens, morphing into a vampire requires a much more extensive change. I'm told it's excruciating. Some go mad with the pain or the sudden hunger. That's what happened to Silvana. When our wives found her, she was feral. Like an animal."

"Jesus…" Jason walked over to the bench where the two men were sitting, and he leaned on his staff, catching his breath. "But why? What could have changed her as a twelve year old? Was it…a war strategy? Create more vampires? Like recruitment?"

"It's possible," Nicholas said waving his hands. "You remember the Imperium law that no Immortal can kill another? That law was only created *after* the World Wars. It's sort of like our version of the Geneva convention. We made that law because our conflict spiralled out of control."

"But we're getting off topic," Phillip said.

Nicholas nodded in agreement. "It's possible that a vampire attacked Silvana at random. But it's far more likely that Silvana was the second child in a vampire family, and her elder vampire sibling was killed in the war. Meaning Silvana became the Immortal heir at an older age. But the change made her wild and separated her from her family."

"Or they abandoned her when she lost her mind," Phillip said.

Jason growled in frustration. "So what did Emberline and Lisbeth do?"

"They captured her to stop her attacks," Nicholas said. "Then they made their way to England with her in tow. For a time they stayed with their cousins."

"My side of the family," Phillip said. "It didn't go well. Silvana was still feral, and there was an incident with a…unexpected feeding."

"Shit. She attacked someone?"

"Yes. But shortly after Emberline was able to marry a wealthy man, and the family lived with him."

"So this was the husband before you, Phillip?"

Phillip nodded. "This was a while before we met them."

Nicholas pointed at himself. "I didn't meet Lisbeth for another ten years. She was still with...*Alphonse*," he drawled the name with derision, and Jason smirked.

"Well, it's lucky Emberline was available for marriage at that point."

The room went still, and the two knights failed to hide the slight frowns and pressed lips. Jason studied them. "What am I missing?"

"Zounderkite," Phillip muttered. "Emberline was single because Silvana *consumed* her husband."

Jason's eyes shot wide open. He stared at the floor in shock, unable to imagine the scene. Silvana had murdered someone. There were probably other murders in her attack on the refugee camp. Yet to know she killed Emberline's husband... *Well that explains the tension between them.* He thought of the way the two aunts still treated Silvana as a child at ninety two years old, and Emberline was always especially distrustful. It made sense if Silvana had been feral for a long time and was responsible for the death of her husband. But it seemed so unfair! Silvana was being punished nearly eighty years later for something she didn't even remember doing. *No wonder nothing she does is ever good enough for them.*

"Then I met Lisbeth," Nicholas said. "It was the late 50s, and even then, Silvana was still a difficult young vampire. There were times when she truly scared me. I can hardly imagine what she was like *before*." He shuddered.

"Wait," Jason said. "You said most vampires were turned before seven. But vampires are only allowed to get blood from their spouse? So how do they get blood as children? You don't make seven-year-olds marry, do you?"

"Children get it from their mortal family members. Parents, siblings, or cousins," Phillip said. "Silvana had cousins for that time. She didn't marry her first husband until her mid-twenties."

"That was Henry, right?"

"That's right," Nicholas said. "Normally vampires marry earlier, but it took Silvana some time before she calmed down completely. She became quiet. Very submissive. Never really spoke up. It's like her aunts trained her too well."

Jason came and sat down on the bench next to the old knights. He had one last question. And yet, it was the only question he'd actually wanted answered. It was the whole reason he'd steered the conversation in this direction.

"So that man at the party last night. Dorin." He sensed the old knights tensing beside him. "He might legitimately be a relative."

He waited in silence, staring at the room ahead.

"Yes," Nicholas whispered.

Jason nodded. "Then why don't we find Dorin again? Silvana can find out where she came from."

"No," Phillip said. "She can never find out."

Jason clenched his fists on impulse. He forced himself to relax and breathe deeply, speaking in a calm voice. "Why not?"

"Because then she would become someone else's heir," Nicholas said. "Silvana is currently heir to the Romanov line, and all the possessions of this family. If it was discovered she belonged to another House, especially a powerful one, then that House would have a claim to everything we own."

"It's possible that Dorin was a liar," Phillip said. "A scammer, as you might say. They're very common. He could have been intending to claim relation and con us out of our property. He might have heard of the circumstances of Silvana's adoption and thought it was worth a try."

"But isn't it worth the risk?" Jason asked. "She could find a family she's never known. And her family might become a powerful ally that could help us."

"*We* are her family," Phillip insisted.

"That's right," Nicholas echoed. "Here she is loved and appreciated. And I have no interest in finding an ally in someone who let their daughter run wild and unsheltered during a war." His voice changed into a hard growl. "We were fortunate that the explosion happened when it did. Let's hope we never hear of Dorin again."

Jason gave a nod. Yet inside, he was still not so sure. After all, why hadn't they discussed this with Silvana?

"So now that you know the truth," Nicholas said, "we must swear you to secrecy as well."

Jason blinked. "Are you telling me that Silvana doesn't know her own history?"

"That is correct, son. Silvana doesn't remember her time as a feral vampire. She doesn't recall her attacks on the camp, or her murder of Emberline's husband. We chose not to tell her because it would only make her feel guilty. She was not really responsible for her actions. All she knows is that she has memory loss from a traumatic transformation."

"So now that you know the truth," Phillip said, "you understand why we treat Silvana the way that we do."

"Oh I see," Jason said with false cheer. "You treat her like a second-class citizen in this family cause you think she might go crazy." The older men began to protest, but Jason talked over them. "It's been seventy years, and you're still holding this over Silvana. You need to talk about this and tell her the truth. Then move on and treat her like an equal."

"Jason, trust us," Nicholas said. "We understand this situation better than you do. If we told her the truth, Silvana might become so upset that she relapses back into that feral state. It could undo her last seventy years of progress."

"Jesus," he groaned. "You're asking me to lie to her. I can't do that."

"No, don't lie," Phillip said. "Just avoid the topic. Use your Imperium politeness training to steer the conversation."

"We're telling you this because you deserve to know."

"Oh, and Silvana doesn't?"

"Trust us. If you still feel strongly about this, we can discuss it further another time. The family can put it to a vote if we should tell her the full story. But for now, Jason, just understand why we treat Silvana this way. And why we don't want her to find her old family, who failed to care for her appropriately the first time. Understood?"

Jason let out a long sigh. He gripped his staff and stood up. "Fine. I'll keep your secrets. But if Silvana starts noticing something, I'll be back here asking for your blessing to tell her."

Nicholas gave him a smile. "It warms my heart to see you love her so much. Thank you, son. Now, shall we continue training?"

Jason nodded. Yet even as he continued through his forms, he couldn't let go of the unsettled feeling in his stomach that he would have to lie to Silvana.

Chapter 13

J ason knocked on the bedroom door. When there was no response, he waited several seconds and knocked again louder.

"Yes, come in," came Silvana's impatient voice

The room was exactly the same as he'd left it. Silvana was still in her desk chair, sketching pencil on her notepad. She was even in the same posture.

She's eccentric. Is that the result of being feral after her vampire bite?

Then he shook his head. That was unfair. There was no reason to treat her any differently because of something eighty years in her past. *I will not judge her for something out of her control. Damn you, Phillip and Nicholas, for telling me.* He crossed the room to her side, bent down, and softly kissed her cheek just the once. She gave no sign of acknowledging him.

"Babe?" he said. "You ok?"

"Yeah. I'm just really enjoying this."

He looked at the page. It was almost completely black. The scene was a vast cloud of smoke, with the snarling jaws of a draconic beast bursting out.

"Is that…what you saw last night?"

She stopped drawing and sighed, then pushed the pencil and paper away. "I don't really want to talk about it," she said and turned to face him. "Is there something you want?"

He immediately bit his tongue to stop his first response. He took a long breath. "I wanted to…" he trailed off, unsure where to begin. "I just needed to…" she was staring at him with cold eyes, and he suddenly felt on the defensive. "Bathroom. Training was hard."

"Ok," she drawled. Jason sighed, but went to the ensuite. He looked back at her. She was already drawing again. He shut the bathroom door all the way.

He stripped down to nothing and stepped into the white marble bathtub. Silvana's bathroom was designed in the 18th century. White tiles with decorative grey patterns lined the walls, and her hand basin was wooden and green, except for the white sink bowl. The shower head had clearly been installed more recently and held modern pressure options if you twisted the nozzle. Jason turned it on and let the warm water sluice over him.

Something was bothering Silvana, and he had no idea how to get through to her. Should he try confronting her directly and insisting on a response? Or maybe just sitting near her and waiting in silence?

Or perhaps he should do nothing. Let her come to him when she was ready.

God I have no idea how to do relationships.

It was late morning on Saturday and he had nothing else to do this weekend except write his report. He had plenty of time. Jason picked up the plug and slipped it into the bath's drain, then sat down and let the tub fill.

As the water rose and covered him, he thought about the details of the night before. Three Skinwalkers had attacked one of the most well-defended locations in the world. Not to mention, every single guest there was capable of significant self-defence. It amounted to a suicide mission. What threats or rewards had convinced those Skinwalkers to sign up?

The more Jason thought about it, the more certain he was that the target had been Sam and Khadija. There was a great chance that the servants in their private booth had been listening in and identified them as dissenters against the Imperium. It must be Reynold himself who ordered their deaths.

Unless it was another faction of rebels? Someone who knew Sam and Khadija were compromised and silenced them to protect the organisation.

If that was the case, would they come for Jason and Silvana?

Or had they already tried? The explosion had gone off directly underneath them. Surely that couldn't be a coincidence. *Shit. Is someone coming for us?* He pushed the thought away as just paranoia. Their family simply wasn't important enough for that. Besides, even if someone from the Imperium came for them, they'd be better off talking their way out rather than trying to fight. He'd have to…

The door opened, and Silvana walked in. She looked so…normal. Her hair down and slightly tangled, her faint pink nightgown hanging from her shoulders by two thin straps. This was how she always looked. Like herself. There was no reason for Jason to feel like his heart would burst. Yet that's exactly how he felt. Her simple presence was reassuring.

"Hey," she said. "Can we talk?"

He smiled. "Sure. I wasn't trying to relax or anything."

"Oh, of course you were. I'm sorry." She turned to leave.

"Oh God, no! I was joking! Silvana, please come back." She turned to look at him. "Sorry. I shouldn't have made that joke. Please come talk to me."

She pulled up a stool and sat down. Jason shifted up in the tub and leaned his shoulders against the rim. He almost grinned at having her so near while he was nude. But she didn't so much as glance at his penis.

Well that's rude.

"Can I ask you something?" Silvana said.

"Sure." He replied instantly. She still took several seconds to ask, and the sound of the flowing tap water filled the silence.

"Do you respect me?"

Jason blinked. "Uh…yeah! Of course I do. What do you mean by that question?"

She kept staring at the wall. Jason felt his insides squirming, but he forced himself to be still and wait. He had to show that he was listening.

"I'm ninety-three years old," Silvana said. "Yet I will always be a child in the eyes of my aunts. It just kills me that I'll never – *never* – be good enough for them. But somehow, I'm good enough for you. You've known me barely six months, and you show me more respect than they ever have."

"Cause you deserve it."

She gave a small smile. "I don't think they'll ever believe that."

His insides gave a painful twist. *Cause they think you're one step away from feral. Damn it, they should tell you the truth.* But he remembered what Nicholas asked him to do. Steer the conversation away from the topic. He would do it today. Tomorrow, he'd have to talk about it again. Silvana deserved to know.

"Silvana, it doesn't matter what they think. It doesn't even matter what I think. It's only important what you think. Do you respect yourself?"

She whispered. "I don't know. I thought if I avoided marrying you, it would prove that I can be my own person. Yet I don't feel like I'm any closer to that. If I can't get my family to respect me, how can I respect myself?" She sighed. "Maybe this is stupid, and you and I should just get married."

"You sure know how to make a proposal," Jason chuckled. She was silent. "Sorry." He cleared his throat. "Look, I'm happy to wait as long as it takes. For what it's worth, I think you've come a long way. Just yesterday, you were being very assertive and telling your family what you wanted. The old you would never have done that."

"But it wasn't good enough for them."

"It doesn't have to be. You don't have to change their minds."

Silvana groaned. "I know. But I still want to. I wish I could just flick the switch and turn off my need for their validation. But I don't think I can."

"Ah…" Jason nodded. "Well I understand that. Silvana…" the words were suddenly heavy in his mouth. He took a deep breath – *don't freeze. Act* – and forced out the words.

"You know what happened to my mother. How my father drove her to suicide after years of abuse." Silvana nodded. "And you know that I hate that man, and will always hate that man." She nodded again. "Well, it might sound crazy, but do you know that there's still a part of me that wants to call him? To see him for the first time in twelve years, after he nearly beat me to death? That same part of me wants to say 'I love you' to him, and hopes that he'll say it back."

"I didn't realise," Silvana whispered. "Well, I'm sure you could look him up. Any time you want to visit him, I'll come support you."

Jason laughed darkly. "But that's my point. My father is *evil.* He's toxic and cruel and dangerous to be around. Even if I wanted to see him, I *shouldn't.* Does that make sense?"

She frowned at him. "Surely you're not telling me to do that with my family?" There was a hint of ice in her voice.

"No, of course not. I'm just saying that you can want something even when you know it'll hurt you. My father requires very strict boundaries. In your case, very small boundaries. Just enough to help you to stop chasing their respect when they probably won't give it." *Yeah. Seems unlikely they'll respect her anytime soon, if she killed*

Emberline's late husband.

"Yeah. I think you're right." She looked at him, and abruptly her eyes lowered. "Oh my god…Jason I'm sorry. I've been so distracted. I've been ignoring you all day. I'm sorry."

He laughed and took hold of her hand. "You know you say sorry a lot for things you don't need to be sorry for."

"I know. I'm sorr— damn it!"

He laughed. "It's ok. You've been working through something this morning, I understand." He hesitated. "Was I…ok? I wasn't sure how to help. I just gave you space, but I wasn't sure if I should have tried to talk to you."

"No, you definitely should not have tried to talk to me. I would have snapped at you." She winced. "More than I already did. I'm sorry. And yes, I need to say sorry for that."

"It's fine, really."

She looked at him again, and this time her eyes were lingering over his body. "Well. I should let you enjoy your bath in peace. I'm sorry for interrupting."

She turned to go, but he squeezed her hand even tighter to hold her in place.

"Please! Interrupt!" he cried.

She blushed and looked away. "Do you want me to join you? Cause I'm not sure there's space."

Jason kicked the tap with his foot and shut off the water flow. The tub was only half full. "You're right. There's very little space. We'll have to squeeze very close together."

"Oh, very subtle."

"It wasn't meant to be." He smiled. She still seemed hesitant, so he lowered his voice and spoke gently. "Please. Join me." Then he reached down towards her pink silk nightgown, and gave the slightest, suggestive tug down.

"Alright, my love," she said. "But don't think you're getting lucky. Bathtubs are not a good place for sex."

"Uh-huh."

She slipped her singlet straps over her shoulder. She wiggled an elbow through the gap, then the other. For a moment, the nightgown hung from her breasts alone. She let it pause there, a glimmer shining in her eye. Then she shifted it a mere centimetre and showed just a fraction more skin and cleavage.

He reached for her gown, but she stepped out of reach quicker than humanly possible. "Oh my god, *please!*" he begged.

"Oh I like to hear that," she said. "Ask me again."

"*Please,*" he hissed. "Please take it off. I swear I'll…"

The gown dropped down to the floor. She wore nothing underneath.

"…Fuuuuck!"

She stepped back into reach, letting her hips sway with the motion. "You like?" He could only nod emphatically. "Would you like me to turn?" She spun around slowly, bending and swaying with subtle movements. He reached out and traced her hips with his fingertips, then cupped the curve of her cheek and pressed his thumb down.

"I thought you said I wasn't getting lucky," Jason said as he squeezed tighter. "I feel pretty lucky right now."

"God, you're cute."

She turned back to face him and went to step into the bath. "Wait," he said. "Can I touch you… here?" She gave a short hum of consent. Then he reached up between her legs and began to stroke, up and down the outer skin. His fingers moved higher, and deeper. Soft, slow movements. Letting her warm to his touch. Feeling her dampen.

"Ok," she said with finality.

She stepped into the bath, and the motion of her legs opening made Jason burn with desire. She faced him, crouched down and placed her knees on either side of his hips.

Water sloshed up the sides of the tub.

"Shit, I should let some water out," he said and tried to flick the plug with his foot. Until he was distracted by her hand clutching him.

"You seem ready," she said.

"Mmm. It was all that…spinning you did."

She lowered herself directly onto his lap. Jason was burning with desire from her being so close. His arms wrapped around her waist, his forearms braced against her thighs. She gripped the back of his neck to adjust her angle, then gracefully slid him inside. They both gasped in unison as she began to rock.

Yet the first motion set the water rolling in waves and splashing over the sides.

"Crap. Hang on," she whispered. She tried raising her body slightly and only moving her hips. It wasn't enough. Everything moved too much. Water splashed against Jason's chest and face.

"Damn it," she hissed. "Let's move to the bed. I don't care if it gets wet."

"Wait a minute. Just sit back." He gripped her hips and guided her off him, sitting her against his thighs. He kept her legs around him. "Let me do this." He slid his fingers back to where they had been a moment earlier. He started to work with his hand, and the water stayed still.

"God, that's…" she cut off with a gasp. "That's a good idea. Let me…" She reached for him and clutched down firmly. Jason felt his hips twitch forward. He focused and kept moving his hand. His fore and middle fingers curled upwards, and his thumb pressed down gently, moving at the same rhythm. Silvana gasped again.

"Wait, stop," she cried.

He immediately froze. "What is it?"

"I can't…concentrate," she said. "I'm trying to do you."

He smiled. "I can wait. Let me take care of you first."

"You don't have to…oooh…" she cut off as he resumed the motion.

She gripped the tub edges with both hands and tilted her head back. She had never looked so beautiful. Jason studied every single detail. The water came up to her middle, her breasts sitting on the surface as hundreds of water droplets lit up her skin. Her hair was mostly dry and hanging over her shoulders. Her mouth was wide open, and her eyes shut. She clutched at his arms, her fingers digging in slightly too hard. Jason didn't stop. She had come so far since he met her. She deserved this.

Her panting grew more rapid. She gripped him tighter. Then in one motion, she convulsed from head to toe. Her thighs quivered against him and squeezed hard against his hand. And the bathroom echoed with her rapid breathing.

She slunk forward and fell against him, gasping to get her breath back. She opened her eyes and stared at him. Water droplets rolled down her face. Or was that sweat?

"Ok," she muttered. "Your turn." She seized him and began to move.

"OH MY!" someone exclaimed from *right next* to them.

Silvana cried out, "Holy fuck!" Jason looked up.

A hooded figure was standing next to the bath.

Jason didn't pause to think. He launched out of the tub, spraying water everywhere. He stepped on the rim of the bath, jumped off, and crash tackled the figure to the tiled floor. He drove them down with a heavy thud. The voice that cried out was distinctly female. Jason pressed his hands down and slammed them to the ground. The woman had dark skin, brown eyes, and a lean feminine face.

"Jason!" she cried. He finally recognised her.

"Khadija?"

She glanced down towards his chest and beyond, then her eyes snapped up to make hard eye contact. "Uh…hey. Is that a fully erect penis digging into my hip, or are you just happy to see me?"

He became aware of the placement of his hips. *Yep. She's right.* Then he noticed the placement of his hands, half touching a boob. *Ah shit.*

"What are you doing here?!" he growled. She opened her mouth, and his eyes went wide. "Oh no!" He slapped his hand over her mouth. "You will not be casting any spells…"

Khadija just laid still, and raised an eyebrow. *Oh that's right. She can cast spells with her thoughts, remember?*

Silvana was beside him. The tendons in her arms were strained as she raised a fist over Khadija's face. "You try anything," she hissed, "and I'll smash your skull."

Khadija's eyes widened and she lay still. She held her hands up. She even held up one finger as if requesting permission to speak. Then her eyes drifted down Silvana's dripping wet form, her body heaving with ragged breaths, and Khadija's eyes widened further.

"Hey!" Jason snapped and covered her eyes with his other hand. "Bloody pervert, spying on people. You have no right to enter our home without permission. We should…"

Khadija's finger jerked up and pressed into Jason's head.

Words blared into his mind, as if someone was screaming into his ear. "I AM NO THREAT! I CAME TO ASK FOR HELP! I'M SORRY FOR INTERUPTING! PLEASE LISTEN!"

"Ah God!" Jason cried and shook his head against the intrusion into his mind.

Silvana slapped her hand away, yet Jason lost his grip on the wizard and staggered back. "Jason?" Silvana cried, then turned to Khadija, "What did you do to him?!"

"Nothing!" she cried. "I'm a friend! I'm a friend!"

Silvana's arm tensed, and Jason recognised her preparation to strike. He caught her fist to restrain her. She looked at him with wild eyes.

Feral eyes. My God, she was ready to kill her.

"She hasn't cast a spell yet. She had the chance if she wanted to."

"Yes," Khadija said with a hand covering her eyes and looking away. "Forgive me, I did not mean to trespass, especially on such a private time. Please take a moment to dress. But I must talk with you, as a matter of life and death. Please."

"Why should we?" Silvana growled. "You're the reason we were attacked last night. Just being around you puts us in danger from the Imperium."

"With all due respect, that's bullshit," Khadija snapped. "You are already in danger from the Imperium."

Jason and Silvana exchanged a glance. "Why should we trust you?"

The wizard's mouth twisted into a snarl and her voice burned with rage. "Because the Imperium killed my friend, and I will burn anyone who stands with them."

Chapter 14

"First of all," Khadija said while sitting in Silvana's desk chair. Jason and Silvana were standing over her, glaring. "I'd like to say how sorry I am to have interrupted…you know. I only meant to teleport to where you were. I had no idea you would be in such a state. For any offence or discomfort I caused, I apologize."

She looked at them with a strained, friendly smile. Jason tucked the bathrobe a little tighter around him, suddenly feeling keenly aware of the cold air wafting up his leg.

Khadija appeared to notice the icy stare on his face, and tried to give a polite laugh to ease the tension.

"Though, I have to say, I hope you'll think of me if you ever want to go non-traditional. Cause *damn!* I can't decide which of you is more attractive."

"What?" Silvana said, sounding genuinely confused.

Jason couldn't help letting out a sigh. "She's bisexual, Silvana. She likes men and women." He gave a knowing nod to Khadija. "Just like me." Khadija raised an eyebrow and gave a nod of recognition back.

Silvana gave a little 'oh' sound before she gave a scandalised gasp and crossed her arms over her chest as if Khadija could stare through the bathrobe. "You lecherous little whore!"

"Whoa!" Jason and Khadija cried in unison.

"You were staring at me! You claim you were sorry, but you made no effort to look away."

"Ok yes, I admit that's true," Khadija said. "But in my defence, I tried my best to look away. You can appreciate why I had some difficulty. Jason, back me up on this. Silvana is gorgeous and it's literally impossible to look away from her naked form, right?"

Damn straight. Out loud he said, "Just tell me how you got here. Can wizards teleport anywhere in the world like that? Or have you been spying on us for a while now?"

"No! Look, you know I'm smarter than your average wizard." She grinned. No one grinned back. "I cast spells with my thoughts. It means I don't have as much speed or firepower as other wizards, but they have several limitations that I don't."

"What limitations?" Jason demanded. "And no clever language. Be specific."

"Alright. You know wizards can lose spells, but I don't. Also most wizards can only teleport somewhere they've been before. But I can teleport to new places. Although, I need an 'anchor' to guide me. Such as people I know." She gestured towards the couple and held her hands out. "Happy?"

"What about that thing you did to me?" Jason said. "You touched my head, and I heard your thoughts. It was like…a telepath."

"A lot of wizards have partial telepathic abilities. I can't read your thoughts like a telepath, but I can put thoughts there if I have physical contact." Khadija grinned. "It's very helpful when you're in a business meeting and your partner is sitting beside you."

"That's irrelevant right now. Why have you come to us?" Silvana said. "You're rich and powerful. Surely you must have other contacts."

Khadija lowered her head. "Not right now." When she looked up, her eyes were wide and alight with rage. "Those bastards killed my Sam. They tried to kill me, and everyone thinks they're going to try again. It's too dangerous to be around me. No one wants to help." She clenched her jaw in a sneer. "Not even my family."

"I know how that feels," Silvana whispered.

"So you're on the run," Jason said in a voice far more calloused than Silvana's. "People are coming to kill you and no one wants to be too close by when it happens." He gave her a false smile. "Well, thanks for coming *here*."

"Believe me, I have no desire to hurt any of you. But I need your help."

Jason laughed in mockery. "What can we do to help you? The Imperium wants you dead. In case you haven't noticed, we're not that powerful a House anymore."

"It's not the Imperium."

Jason blinked. "What?"

"At least, I'm pretty sure it wasn't the Imperium."

"Why?" Silvana asked.

"Because the Imperium would never attack me at an event they were attending. It could damage their reputation, make them seem too weak to enforce their peace. Whoever did this was hoping to make Reynold look like a fool at the same time."

Jason looked at Silvana in question, and she gave a shrug as she said, "That does make sense. There were so many Vigiles on watch and a powerful enchantment against violence, yet this attack still occurred. This makes the Imperium look weak."

Jason rubbed his chin as he started to pace the room. Khadija remained in her chair, and Silvana stayed at her side, watching closely. "Alright," Jason said. "I'm not ruling out the Imperium entirely. But let's say for arguments sake it's not them. Who else could it be?"

Khadija lowered her voice. "You know what Sam and I did with you last night? Testing you? Trying to see if you might be swayed towards our belief?"

"Get us to join the rebellion, yes?" Jason said in a flat voice.

Khadija squinted at him. "It's nothing so serious as a rebellion. We're just people with ideas at this point. There are others like us…" she grimaced. "Like me. Sam and I were recruiting. And unfortunately, that means a certain level of exposure. There are several people who heard our ideas but didn't agree." She winced. "And there's one in particular who I think were angered by the mere suggestion."

"Oh?"

"Glucksburg."

Jason jolted. He made eye contact with Silvana as she made a short sound.

"Ah!" Khadija said. "You know them?"

"Yes. The Royal House of Denmark," Jason said.

"That's the one. There were two older men in the family, the wizard Ingolf and his knight, Wilhelm. We tried talking to them several months ago." Khadija gave a bitter laugh. "They were always close together. We thought they might have been a couple. I thought they would be willing to challenge the Imperium laws if it meant they could be together openly. But when we tactfully made the slightest suggestion about the two of them, well, let's just say it was considered especially offensive."

"Oh," Jason said.

"They might have cause to hate the two of us."

"Seriously? You think they'd murder you for just insinuating they might be gay?"

Khadija twisted her mouth. "I don't expect you to understand."

"Ok, can someone explain this to me?" Jason said. "What is the Imperium's problem with gay people?"

"They don't have a problem," Silvana said, though Khadija was definitely glaring at her in disagreement. "The issue is that every

Immortal has to pass on their immortality to someone. So every mortal family member has to marry and have offspring. You're allowed to be gay, but you still need to procreate."

"How generous," Khadija sneered. "Does that sound fair? 'Oh you're repulsed by the sight of men? Too bad! You must marry one and let him fuck you for most of your life.' Yes, how could anyone complain?"

"I didn't mean it like that," Silvana said, holding up her hands. "Besides, wizards are the exception. They don't have to get married. Even Reynold isn't married! Meanwhile, vampires die if they stay single."

"Wizards still face pressure," Khadija grumbled. "It's considered bad form to be unwed. Just ask my entire family."

Silvana gave a nod of acknowledgment. She finally backed away from Khadija and took a seat on the corner of her bed.

Khadija's face softened. "Listen. If you help me, I'll help you." She held up her hands. "A favour for a favour. If you find who's really trying to kill me and stop them, then my family will welcome me back and I'll have access to their fortunes. How's a payment of five million sound?"

Jason tried to keep a poker face. But Silvana gasped, ruining it.

"Then we're agreed," Khadija said. "Investigate the Glucksburgs for me. And I'll pay you back with money and friendship. We can do much more than just give you money, too. My family…" she cut off, and suddenly her eyes went wide.

Jason asked, "What is—"

"Magic!" she cried.

She held up her hands towards the walls, as if trying to push away from herself. The air moved. Light refracted, and the shape of the room began to bend around itself. "Step back!" Khadija ordered. Jason and Silvana leapt into the centre of the room as the roof seemed to fold down and swallow Khadija. When it folded back, she was gone and the room had returned to normal.

The bedroom door broke open a second later as a powerful force blasted through the lock and swung it open on the hinges. The sudden loud noise made them both jump.

Desdemona and Portia burst through the doorway, their hair swaying with their movement and their black suits darkening the room.

"Where are they?!" Desdemona roared, her eyes wide as she searched the room.

Jason took a step towards Silvana and covered her with his body.

"We sensed a wizard! Where is the spellcaster?"

Jason's mind flew into a panic. *Oh God, they know Khadija was here! Should we tell them? It could lead to her capture, and we'd lose the chance to ally with her. But they might know if we lie!*

"Answer her!" Portia screamed. "Who was here just now?"

"No one!"

Jason was surprised to hear himself say it. Silvana stared at him in shock. The Vigiles glared at him with eyes full of burning hellfire.

"I dislike thy tone, mortal knight," Desdemona growled. "Thou dare lie to us? We sensed a spell cast in this mansion, in this very room. Wouldst thou defy the Imperium?"

Silvana was looking at him. She shook her head slightly. Yet Jason couldn't help himself.

"We were having sex, alright?" he cried. "We just did it in the bath, and now we're moving to the bed to do it again. You can see for yourself." He gestured to the bathrobes he and Silvana were wearing. "No one was here doing spells."

Desdemona rushed forward, making Jason flinch.

She walked past him to the ensuite door and stared at the puddles of water on the floor. Slowly, she turned to study the two of them.

"Thou put on bathrobes? Between relations? Sounds like thy modesty was for someone else's benefit."

"It was for drying off," Jason said. "Don't want to get the bed wet. Then we'd have to change the sheets."

Desdemona took a step towards him, squinting her eyes in his direction.

"It's entirely possible," Portia said, "that this handsome young couple was being spied upon without their knowledge by means of magic." The room went still. Everyone looked at Portia, who simply shrugged. "I could see the appeal," she said.

"That's repulsive!" Silvana cried in outrage, and Jason relaxed to see her finally playing along. "Utterly deplorable. What sick delinquent was doing that? I demand an investigation!"

Portia looked to her mistress in question. "That seems fair. We can look around, as a courtesy."

"Hang on," Jason cried. "What are you two even doing here? What gives you the right to barge in here and violate our privacy? We didn't ask for—"

Desdemona muttered.

Something seized Jason around the stomach and squeezed his insides as he was hoisted off the ground.

"Jason!" Silvana cried.

He thrashed against his invisible bonds, but it only made the pain worse. Something was gripping his core so tightly he wanted to throw up. He kicked his legs wildly. He slapped at his core, but found nothing to push away. He let out a cry of pain.

"I've had enough of thy arrogance!" Desdemona growled. She stared at him with her arms flat by her sides.

Silvana leapt at the older Vigile, but a muttered word from Portia saw Silvana freeze in place with her own set of invisible bonds. She growled with frustration, but was clearly not in any pain. Meanwhile

Jason groaned as the pressure on him seemed to grow tighter.

"I've used this very spell," Desdemona growled, "to crush a man so absolutely that his body snapped clean in half. Test me further, if thou dares!"

She dropped him, and Jason collapsed like a ragdoll. He coughed and gasped for air. He lay on his back and clutched his core as his stomach muscles gave a horrible spasm that seemed to last for an eternity.

"We shall offer no further assistance," Desdemona said. "You may deal with thy immortal stalker however thou choose." No one dared question her as she walked towards Portia, took her hand, and the whole world seemed to rush towards them in a swirl of impossible dimensions, before revealing only empty floor where they had been.

Jason laid still. The spasms had finally died down, yet the pain didn't seem any lesser. He shut his eyes and felt Silvana kneeling beside him. "Darling, you ok? Jason?"

"I'm ok," he wheezed.

"Oh thank God. You shut your eyes and I…shit, I've already seen two husbands die… Here, let me help." She opened his bathrobe slightly and checked his stomach. "Just keep breathing."

"Silvana?"

The voice came from the door. Jason opened his eyes, mostly to check the robe still covered his nakedness. Both Silvana's aunts stood in the doorway, with the two older knights entering a second later. Phillip had his sword drawn, Nicholas his magnum, and the two vampires had red eyes.

"The Vigiles were here," Silvana said. "They attacked Jason."

"Without provocation?" Emberline growled.

Silvana winced. "Not exactly."

"Who cares why they did it!" Lisbeth yelled, rushing to Jason's side and kneeling next to him. "Jason, my dear, are you ok?"

Jason groaned, "Oh yeah, I'm fan-fucking-tastic!" He gave a thumbs up, though he couldn't help smiling at seeing Lisbeth doting on him. "I ask Desdemona by what right she entered our home without permission. She responded by picking me up with magic and squeezing my ribs."

"Jason was brave," Silvana said. "He didn't beg for mercy or anything. He stared her down until she gave up."

"That's my boy!" Nicholas cheered and holstered his gun. "Those Vigiles are gone now, right?"

Silvana confirmed with a nod.

"But why were they here in the first place?" Phillip asked.

"Oh, we should have come sooner!" Lisbeth cried over top of him. "I heard banging ten minutes ago, but I assumed you were…uh, otherwise occupied."

"Uh…" Jason muttered, "yes, you are correct, and I appreciate you not coming in then." He could feel his cheeks heating up, and he pulled his bathrobe even tighter.

"What did the Vigiles want?" Emberline insisted.

Jason clutched at Silvana's hand. He gave her a meaningful look. He knew she would want to please her family and tell them exactly what they wanted. *Don't tell them about Khadija. You know what they'll say. Our family will lose a powerful ally and justice will never been done. Please Silvana!*

She opened her mouth and paused. She studied him a moment more. "They said someone had been spying on us with magic," Silvana said, staring back at him with an intense look of her own. "But they were too busy to investigate."

Holy shit. She understood my look! We've come so far!

"Damn it," Emberline said. "I knew this would happen. It's because of that Al Khalifa woman. Her enemies are watching us. We have to prepare for an attack."

"I don't..." Jason started, but Nicholas cut him off.

"She's right. From now on, everyone needs to stay on the premises. You must go armed wherever you go. And stay with your partner at all times. No exceptions." He clutched his wife by the shoulder and held her close. "I'll message the Imperium and request protection. Maybe they'll send help."

"Good," Silvana said. Jason finally sat up against the bed, focusing on keeping his bathrobe closed.

"I'll need to go to work on Monday morning," Jason said.

Nicholas nodded. "That should be fine, if you go armed at all times. Silvana will have to stay near one of us during that time."

"Silvana," Phillip said. His tone was gentle. "It might be best if you carry Jason's sword until he's able to stand."

She stared at him for a moment. "Thank you for that suggestion, Phillip. I agree that it's a fine idea." She grabbed Jason's sword from the wall and strapped it over her waist.

Well look at that. He's learnt not to give her orders. That's progress.

The family all agreed to Nicholas's plan, then went their separate ways. Silvana shut the door, and growled when it wouldn't click back into the lock after the Vigiles had blasted it open. She blocked it with a chair instead. Then she came to Jason's side.

"I hope you don't consider this emasculating," she said as she picked him up with ease and laid him on the bed.

"It's actually kinda hot."

She smiled as she checked him again. "You'll have a lot of bruising. I'll get some ice packs. That'll hopefully keep the swelling down. You'll be sore for a couple of days, but I don't think you'll have any permanent injury. Just..." she sighed, "...maybe no strenuous activity."

Jason growled. "Fucking wizards."

Silvana left the room for a few minutes and came back with cool packs. She placed them around Jason's middle and slid them under his back. It ached at first, but then the pain began to ease. Silvana sat on the bed next to him and began stroking his forehead.

"I hate how powerful wizards are," Jason growled. "And I hate that I haven't even seen their true power."

Silvana kept patting his head with steady movements. He let his breathing calm down as the last of the panic began to fade. She whispered, "I'm sorry I didn't do anything for you."

"It's ok. You definitely shouldn't have tried to fight Desdemona."

"No, I mean… I had every intention of… paying you back. You know."

He smiled at her. "Right! Hey, it's ok. I feel like this was payback for last night. Now we're even." She cupped his cheek as a smile lit her face like a sunrise. "On second thought, you are pretty gorgeous. Give me an hour." He chuckled, and immediately clutched his ribs in pain. "Oof…maybe no jokes for a while."

"Why didn't you want me to tell my family about Khadija?"

He blinked. "What?"

"I saw that look. You wanted me to hide it."

"Oh. Well I knew what they would say. Report her to the Imperium, give up our chance of an ally."

"It's true." She sighed. "You know this could backfire, right? If we start working with Khadija, we'll have to hide it from our family. It could really anger them if they found out. And it could put a target on us within the wider Immortal community."

"Yes, I know. But this could also fix all our problems. And further the cause of justice."

"Maybe." She snuggled in closer and nestled her head on his shoulder. They rested silently for several moments. "Whatever happens, we're doing this together."

Jason held her hand and squeezed. "Together," he said.

Chapter 15

"Good morning, Captain."

Kader looked up from her computer screen. Her hair was in a neat bun and her uniform had been ironed to perfection. Yet her face was creased with lines of tension.

"Uh…happy Monday?" Jason chipped.

She grunted. "That was some report you sent me last night," she said as she gestured for him to enter the office and shut the door behind him. "A murder at a gala, and the killer had to be one of the guests. Didn't this happen once on the Orient Express?"

"There was no explosion in that one." He sat on the chair opposite her desk and folded his hands in his lap.

"But the murder was almost impossible, as if magic was involved."

"Ah. I don't like thinking about how many unsolved murders might have an Immortal behind it. That sort of thing keeps me up at night." He shivered. "So, any questions?"

"Yes, to say the least," she drawled. "First, did you have any time off on the weekend? Between two murder attempts and recovering from an injury."

"Two attempts?"

"I count that Vigile woman as one."

Jason grinned. *She's right about that, nasty little demi-god Desdemona.*

"I had lots of time with Silvana. That was nice."

Kader smiled at him. "Things are going well between the two of you?"

"Yeah, they really are. Which surprises me. I don't have a lot of experience with relationships. I've been with Silvana for six months, and it's already my longest relationship. All I know is how to treat people. Most of that I learnt from therapy."

"Well, I can't give you advice there," Kader said. "Been a single mum for ten years." Jason gave a formal salute, and the captain chuckled warmly. "I'm glad it's going well for you. You deserve to be happy. I just...forgive me for saying so. But I hope you'll keep your guard up."

"Captain?"

"I know you love her, and I know her family have formally accepted you now. I just think it's still wise to be watchful. There's a lot about them you still don't know."

Jason knew she was just being cautious, so he played along and nodded. "That's fair."

Kader looked relieved to hear him say it. "Now, on to this report. You know what really stands out to me? You saw a Dryad." He frowned at her. "The Fae. The tree spirit woman on the serving staff. And you found out that they apparently ruled the world before wizards and vampires even showed up. And you don't seem completely in awe of that."

Jason shrugged. "It was ancient history. The Fae are lower class citizens now. I don't think they have much chance of overthrowing the Imperium, if that's what you mean. They've had thousands of years to do so."

"But it changes everything we know about human history! Everything!" She laughed at him. "Have you not considered the implications? What that could mean to religions, historians, archaeologists?"

Jason could only shrug again. "No, I haven't. I'm investigating an active case. The Fae are basically a cold case."

"So practical." Kader sighed. "Fine. Let's talk about the murder victim. Samantha Kennedy. You said she was from House Kennedy?"

"That's right. No idea if it's the same one as JFK."

"You don't think it's a coincidence? Think about it. The Kennedy's had two major assassinations, and neither were solved in a particularly satisfying way."

"Two?"

"JFK was the first. Then his brother Robert, six years later. It's lesser known now. But they blamed the first one on a Russian who hated America, and blamed the second on a Pakistani who hated America." She sighed deeply. "And we know what police are often like when the suspect is a foreigner. Neither investigation was particularly well-handled."

"So you think the Imperium were involved?" Jason frowned. "You think JFK and his brother could have been anti-Imperium, like Samantha?"

"They were both progressive for their time. Meanwhile, the Imperium is all about holding onto ancient power structures. Surely, you can see room for conflict."

Jason ran a hand through his hair. "I guess. But the Imperium doesn't even have opposing politics of left and right wing. They're a monarchy. If someone gets in their way, they can kill them without repercussions."

"That might be more like mortals than you'd think," Kader said dryly. "Look, I'm trying to say that I agree with Khadija. I think it's very likely that the Glucksburgs, not the Imperium, are the ones trying to kill her. Those two men were offended by the mere suggestion of being homosexuals. So I think Khadija has enemies on the conservative side of the political fence."

He frowned in thought for a moment. "I don't know if I'd consider that a motive. Kill someone because they vote differently?"

She shook her head. "It's more than that, Jason. One thing you'll learn if and when you become a detective is that *any* belief can be used to justify murder. It doesn't matter if it makes sense to anyone else. It doesn't matter if the murderer even understands their own beliefs properly. If they believe it, they'll act on it. That's the thing about humans. We can use any belief system to justify evil."

Kader leaned further over the desk and lowered her voice. "So it doesn't matter if these Glucksburgs are conservatives or progressive, right or wrong, logical or illogical. In their mind, their belief could be an excuse to justify whatever they like."

Jason nodded. "So, any time in detective work I find someone with strong beliefs, I should be warry? It sounds almost prejudicial when you say it like that."

"Detectives can't afford prejudices, rookie," Kader said. "But yes. Any strong belief is a potential motive."

"Even if it doesn't make any sense?"

"Especially then."

"Alright," Jason said with a nod. "I'll start my investigation into the Glucksburgs."

"Not just yet." Kader smiled. "You remember what Lynch said on Friday? Today you're working with the detectives on the tax fraud case."

Jason blinked. "What?"

"Don't worry, you'll be working both cases in tandem. But most of today will be spent on the local case. Maybe you can find time to continue your Immortal case later this afternoon. If it helps, I have some time today. I'll do some preliminary work on your investigation to help you out. You'll still be the primary."

"Captain, surely my Immortal case is a higher priority."

"Not at all. Lynch and Cole are going to teach you how to do detective work. You need the experience." She stood up, and Jason reluctantly mimicked her without arguing further. They exchanged salutes. "Good luck, rookie."

"Thank you, Captain."

"Dismissed."

The bullpen of the Plymouth police station was quiet and the half dozen desks with their computer screens and stacks of files were unoccupied. The kitchen was full of officers muttering in low voices. Jason smiled to himself. *It'd be nice to join them. I could use some normality after such a fucking weird weekend.* He found all three uniformed officers crowded around the coffee station. Douglas's large form was shaking as he gave a jovial laugh. Next to him was Martin, a middle aged woman who was tall and thin. Last there was Wilson, thirty years old, short, squat, and loved talking about his two kids.

"Hey, there he is!" Douglas cheered when he saw Jason. "Our very own vampire hunter. How goes it, killer?" He slapped Jason on the shoulder.

"I'm not a vampire hunter," Jason said. "I'm dating a vampire. It's a bit offensive to…"

"Alright, vampire fucker. How's that?"

Jason sighed. "Actually I have to admit that sounds kinda cool."

They chorused with laughter. Jason didn't mind, but he wished they took it a bit more seriously. They had all glimpsed the supernatural stuff six months ago at Silvana's mansion, when they'd fought a wizard and his Immortal allies. But they were all still deep in denial, much like the detectives.

"Big news, Jase," Wilson said abruptly. "Now that you're all here, I can tell you all at once. Ready?" He smiled broadly, and when he did, Jason could glimpse what had made this man attractive to his wife. "Mel's pregnant! We're having a third kid!"

"Shit, man!" Douglas cried, spilling his coffee in excitement. "Do you ever get off that woman?"

"Bloody hell," Martin groaned. "Your poor wife's vagina. I couldn't do it after our third. Hope you can handle never having sex again."

"Guys!' Jason cried. "What you're meant to say is *congratulations!*" Everyone laughed as he shook Wilson's hand firmly. The other two quickly added their own well wishes.

"And there's more," Wilson said, reaching into his pocket.

"God, not twins," Martin cried, wincing and holding her stomach in what appeared to be an act of sympathy.

"No! We're having Millie's first birthday party and you're all invited." Wilson held out little invitations for the three of them. No one reached for the cards.

"Uh…" Douglas said. "I'm busy."

"You don't know when it is!" Wilson snapped.

"Shit. Spoke too soon."

Wilson waved the invites at Martin. "Come on, it's really just an excuse for adults to hang out. She's only one! She won't even remember."

"But I'll have to find a babysitter," Martin groaned.

"What about you, Jason?"

"Uh…I'm not sure it's a good idea. I was just at a party where a wizard friend of mine was attacked by shapeshifting velociraptors, and I'm a little worried they'll come for me next."

Everyone stared at him. He stared back.

"At least Douglas and Martin had the decency to lie *well*," Wilson huffed.

God damn it.

"Come on, guys. There'll be free beer!"

"Oh, well, if I must," Douglas growled and took an invite. Martin and Jason did so too.

"Hang on," Martin said looking at the invite. "This says the party is Saturday, the weekend after next."

"Yeah? Oh, don't tell me you've got something on."

"Wilson, that's the same week we're doing our office Christmas party."

"What's this now?" Jason asked.

Martin sighed. "Next week, Wednesday night. We're all doing dinner and drinks in the town. Captain Kader is paying up to forty pounds a head. Spouses are invited. Don't any of you read the emails?"

"Think I deleted that one on sight," Douglas grumbled. Jason snorted with laughter.

Martin rolled her eyes. "My point is we're going to be seeing a lot of each other outside of work that week. Wednesday night, then again Saturday morning? We're all going to hate each other by the end."

"If not the start," Douglas muttered, making Jason laugh again.

"Ok well please RSVP," Wilson said. "And don't change your mind last minute. I'll be buying beer and food if you say you're coming, and that costs money, and we've got a third child on the way now."

"Alright buddy, I'll try to be there," Douglas said, waving the invitation in the air.

"Me too," Martin said. They all looked to Jason.

"I'll try to catch the velociraptors by then." Everyone laughed. Jason ground his teeth together.

"Hey rookie," Douglas said, "Check it out. I think the detectives have finally showed up." Lynch and Cole had indeed entered the office, strutting through the main doors like they owned the place and dropping bags on their desks with loud bangs.

"You still working with them today?" Douglas asked.

"Oh Jase, I didn't know!" Martin said as she patted his arm. "How exciting for you. Finally going to shadow the detectives, hey?"

He tried not to wince at Martin's overly friendly touch. "Yeah. Apparently it's a tax fraud case. Lynch chose it for me cause he says it's the most boring case possible." He grinned. "I'm actually still really excited."

"Rookie!" Lynch called out. He and Cole were collecting folders and bags from their drawers. "We're heading straight out. Come with!"

Jason gave a quick nod to the officers, and left as they cheered out 'best of luck' and various other clichés. He felt almost sad to leave them for the day. Less than a year ago, he'd been a little disappointed by what a real police officer was like. Since then he'd seen them in action against vampires and grizzly bears without any Immortal powers of their own. They were normal people, and yet braver than most. There were few people who he respected as much as them.

He watched Lynch and Cole flicking through piles of paper, and shoving folders into laptop bags. Cole saw him watching. "Need something, rookie?"

"Just wondering if I should bring anything."

"Lunch, if you have it," she answered. "We'll be gone most of the day."

He got his lunch bag from the fridge and his work laptop, and followed the detectives outside. They piled into the detectives work vehicle – a plain blue sedan – with Lynch in the driver's seat and Jason in the back. He deliberately sat behind Cole for the extra leg room, but she made no move to adjust her chair. *She could dance the can-can up there.* He knew it was all part of initiation. He wasn't going to ask for room first.

"So, rookie," Lynch said in a chipper voice. "What do you know about Kennedy and sons?"

Jason felt a sudden jolt like a slap in the face. "Uh…Kennedy and sons?"

"Apparently nothing," Lynch drawled. "They're an investor company. People from all over the world give them their money, and they invest it as they see fit."

Kennedy. Is this the Immortal House of Kennedy? Jesus Christ. This could be far more serious than I expected. "So they're like, accountants?"

"Something like that," Cole said. "If they see shares in one company going up, they move their pool around. People go with them because they don't just drop your shares in one place and wait around. These guys actively sit there with their finger on the pulse and watch for opportunities."

"Just think," Lynch said. "A bunch of maths nerds coning people into giving them their money for their own use. Quite brilliant."

"It's legitimate, most of the time," Cole said.

"Uh huh. Anyway, someone made a whistle-blower complaint about these guys. Apparently some super up-tight control freak did the maths themselves and found they came up a few extra dollars short. Complained to the police about it. Now we have to investigate."

Jason frowned. "So we're looking through books? Don't they have professional auditors for that sort of thing?"

"They've already come and gone. They found nothing," said Cole. "Now we are investigating the case as cops."

"It's super boring," Lynch groaned.

"Actually, it's very intuitive. Our job is to cross-examine, apply pressure, and see if anyone cracks. We're here to check the *people*. Lynch thinks this case is perfect for you cause it's all numbers and spreadsheets. But *I* agreed to it because I think this is a better measure of a detective. Their EQ. I want to see where your emotional intelligence is at, and your ability to spot liars." She grumbled. "Also, yes, I complain about Lynch a lot. Get used to it."

"Cause she's jealous."

"Cause he's a dick." Lynch laughed at her. "But I will say this for him. He reads people like a telepath."

Jason suddenly pictured Lynch back in that mansion six months ago, waving his gun around, screaming like a lunatic and threatening to kill him, all because a telepath was messing with his mind.

The car went quiet and became very uncomfortable very quickly. It seemed everyone was having the same memory. Cole cleared her throat. "Sorry. Poor choice of words. He's…got good people skills, is what I mean."

"Yeah," Lynch muttered. "And as you can see, Cole needs some help in that department."

"Piss off." Lynch chuckled again, and the tension broke effortlessly.

He did that on purpose to put us at ease again. He IS good with people. But that also means when he's being an ass, he's doing it on purpose.

Still, they rode the rest of the way in silence. They drove through the main district of Plymouth town, passing serious looking office and government buildings, heading towards the waterfront. The sky was only slightly grey, which was about as good as it got. They found a tall silver-blue office building eight stories high. Lynch parked on the street only a short walk from the entrance, and they approached the main doors on foot.

"Now remember, rookie," Cole said, "just watch and listen. We really don't need your input today. If we need something, we'll ask. If there's no asking, there's no speaking. Got it?"

Jason grinned. "'Actually it's better if you don't speak at all, Peregrin Took.'" Cole stared at him. "Sorry. Got it," he finished.

Inside, the concierge area was a wide open space where every word and footstep echoed against white floors and silver pillars. A young woman with pink hair and dressed in a suit greeted them at the front desk. Lynch announced himself politely, and they all received access passes for the lifts and instructions to ride to level two. Once there, another receptionist guided them to a conference room filled with pot plants and bright windows that looked out over the waterfront. A large TV lined one wall and several sound boxes were positioned around the room.

"They've got a bit of money to spare on gear," Lynch muttered. He sat in the middle of an eight-seater table. "Jason, sit next to me. I want us all on one side of the table." They took their positions. The detectives arranged a few folders on the table before them. Jason sat back in the chair with his hands in his lap and waited.

After a few minutes the door opened and their first suspect walked in. Jason practiced his observation techniques. *Male, Caucasian, in his thirties, dark navy suit, short haircut shaved on the sides, blue eyes and defined jawline, clean-shaven.*

"Mr Christopher Jones, have a seat," Lynch said.

Jones sat opposite them. "Thank you for coming here to see me," Jones said politely. "It's a busy day today, and I didn't have time for a trip to the station."

"We're glad we could help," Lynch said, and Jason almost believed he meant it. "Everyone's busy these days. It's good to accommodate where we can."

"You guys don't seem that busy." Jones grinned with his perfectly straight teeth. "No offense, of course. But you're investigating a situation that has already been audited and proven harmless. You must have a lot of spare time on your hands if you can afford to waste it on this dead horse."

"Just trying to stave off retirement," Lynch said. "Now, you're the general manager of this location?"

"Not just Plymouth. I'm GM for the British branch of Kennedy and Sons." The smug look on his face was insufferable.

"Bit young for a major position."

"My youth makes me ambitious."

Lynch looked to Cole, and she put forward a single sheet of paper to read from.

"Your whistle-blower," said Cole, "was very specific about the maths, Mr Jones. According to their calculations, their shares were each worth a full five cents less than they should."

"Oh is that all?" Jones chuckled. "I've got twenty quid in my pocket. She can keep the change. Are we done here?" He chuckled again.

"Five cents per share," Cole went on. "For a client with twenty thousand shares, losing five cents per share means losing one thousand pounds. All this is just one client. Tell me, how many clients do you have in total?"

"I am unable to give out any information regarding our clients as it goes against our policy of protecting our clients' privacy."

"Uh huh." Cole ruffled the paper, reminding him of the facts of the case. "It's a few thousand, right? With tens of millions of shares in total. Sounds to me like you're siphoning off a few million."

Jones thumbed the side of his nose in flippant dismissal. "According to one amateur individual's calculation based off their limited file. The auditors spent months combing through here. You know, real financial experts with full access to all our records. They all confirmed that every cent was accounted for." Jones smiled. "Unless you have any further evidence, there's not much more to discuss, is there?"

Cole was silent. Jones had a polite, smug half smile on his face, and Jason had half a mind to slap the look off his face. The silence stretched, and Jones's expression never wavered.

"You make a lot of money for yourself here, Christopher?" Lynch asked. "I couldn't help but notice your living address. You own a waterfront property. At thirty one years old." He let the silence grow, and Jason noticed Lynch wasn't just running out of things to say. He was deliberately controlling the silence.

"That's not a crime, is it?" Jones said with arms outstretched and palms up.

"Your parents paid for your education in full?" Lynch said.

"Hey, hang on," Jones said, sitting up and losing some of the smugness that lined the corner of his mouth. "Please don't start telling me how privileged I am, like I'm single-handedly responsible for world poverty. Yes, my parents paid for my education like any good parent would choose to do if they could. But I also did all the work myself. I studied hard and got good grades. And when I graduated, I got this job on my own merits. So, yes, I got a head start in life. But I also made the most of it. I didn't waste my opportunity. I think you'll find it would be more disrespectful to the less privileged if I did nothing."

Lynch looked slowly over to Cole, then to Jason, and gave a dark chuckle. "You seem a bit defensive about that, Mr Jones. Do you feel...embarrassed for being rich? Like you're a little ashamed for how you got that wealth?"

Jones said nothing. He just inhaled a long, sharp breath. He forced his mask of a smile back on his face. "I try not to flaunt it. Cause I know how it upsets certain people." He looked at Jason, his eyes lingering on his uniform. "But I'm not ashamed. I just have the decency to avoid bringing up my two million-pound home, and my two investment properties in London, and my BMW, and my soon-to-be purchased holiday home in Valencia." He smirked again as he continued to look at Jason. "It tends to make street cops uncomfortable about their minimum wage pay."

Jason didn't react at all, and Jones seemed to lose his enthusiasm.

"Well, I think we've seen enough," Lynch said in a chipper sing-song voice. "Thank you for coming in, Christopher. Please, send in your boss when you get a chance."

Jones stood up, adjusted his tie and nodded. "Thank you for your time, detectives," he said, and left the room with a noticeable strut.

"That went well," Lynch said. His tone was flat, so Jason had no idea if he meant it. "Notice how he got defensive about wealth, then took a shot at the rookie to deflect. He's feeling guilty about something, even if it's not related to the case. You did alright not to react, by the way. Some guys will try to get under your skin to avoid you getting under theirs." Jason nodded.

"He didn't give us anything useable," Cole said.

"But he was being difficult," Jason said. "I know he cooperated, but surely that's still suspicious behaviour?"

Lynch sneered. "Just means he's an asshole. And sadly there's no law against that."

"Don't know why *you'd* find that sad, Lynch," Cole said.

Lynch chuckled as he looked to Jason. "How do you feel about helping out with the next one?"

"Oh. Sure. What do you need?"

"We'll still lead, but if you feel ready, just ask a question or two. You saw what we did with the last guy. Ask similar questions and try to catch him in a lie. Go with your gut."

"Trust your instincts, padawan," Cole said with a wink. Jason smiled broadly, and offered them a nod.

Ok. Act tough, and fully confident, and ask some basic questions in a flat voice. See if you can catch him off guard. Remember what Nicholas taught you. Don't freeze. ACT.

The door opened, and another man walked into the room. Jason studied him. *Middle aged man, late fifties, Caucasian. White hair, medium height, pudgy stomach. Dressed in deep black suit with gold cufflinks.*

"Gene Conroy, CFO," Lynch said. "Thank you for coming. I understand it's hard to find time in your busy schedule of delegating work to everyone else."

Conroy didn't react to Lynch's dig at him. He took a seat across from the detectives, tugging his jacket forward, and sat with his hands cradled in his lap. "I've already been very generous with my time," Conroy said. "Do you have any new evidence to present?"

Lynch ignored the question. "How long have you been CFO here?"

"Detectives? Do you have any new evidence to present?" He spoke in that same polite tone.

"We're conducting an investigation on personnel," Cole said. "Kennedy and Sons is an international company with four branches over the world. Yet you, the CFO, operate in Plymouth, the smallest branch. And you've been here for…five years now?"

"This isn't new evidence," Conroy said. "I've already answered your questions. Now, do you have any more evidence, or am I free to go?"

What a fuckwit.

"Have you ever fired anyone?" Lynch asked. "Forced them out of a job through coercion? Someone who may be smart enough to do the maths on your books and find out inconsistencies?"

"You're speculating. Have you got any more *evidence?*"

Jason couldn't help shaking his head. The man's tone was so polite. He hadn't even raised the volume one decibel. Jason was ready to change tactics and go on the offensive, but he let the detectives lead.

"Mr Conroy," Cole said, "is there a reason you won't answer any of our questions?"

"You won't answer my question. Have you got any more evidence?"

Lynch's jaw clenched. "You ever worked in law enforcement, Mr Conroy? You ever run an investigation? Cause if you did, you'd know what a fool you sound like right now. To be honest, I'm rather embarrassed for you."

Conroy didn't flinch. "It sounds to me like you don't have any new evidence, and you're just here to waste my time. What's the matter?" He turned to Jason with a friendly smile. "Intern couldn't find anything else to investigate?"

Now's my chance. "Sir, you're impeding this investigation," Jason said in a firm voice. "You need to cooperate with the detectives, or you can be charged with obstruction of justice."

The CFO turned to him. "Do you really think I'm obstructing justice?" He paused for a long time. Jason squirmed beneath his gaze.

"Yes. You are."

"How am I an obstruction?"

Jason inhaled sharply. He forced himself to come up with an answer. "You have refused to answer a single question."

"When did I refuse?"

The detectives were watching him. Jason had to swallow. "Just now, in this very interview."

"I don't mean to be rude, son, but is this your first investigation?" Jason's mouth opened, but nothing came out. "Oh, I thought so. Sounds like you might be a little out of your depth. Have you ever read an audit report before? It's over a hundred pages of university-grade analysis. Do you think you understand the investment process enough to comprehend it?"

Jason felt a wild urge to get up and leave the room. He forced himself to stay, yet it felt like his mind had shut down. He couldn't think of anything to say. "Answer my questions," Jason insisted.

"What questions?" Conroy said with a smile. "You haven't asked any."

Conroy's eyes were boring into him. Jason couldn't breathe, couldn't think. *God, what am I doing here? I don't know what to do!* Again, he felt the impulse to get up and leave. It was overpowering. *Fuck! I'm stronger than this! Why can't I think of something to say!?*

"Well, this has been enlightening," Lynch said, cutting into the silence, and Jason nearly cried out in relief of being saved. "You really seemed to enjoy yourself just now, laying into my rookie. But that's low hanging fruit. You haven't actually proven your innocence."

"Innocent until proven guilty," Conroy said. "It is in fact *you* who have something to prove, not I." He smirked again. "Now unless you have any new evidence, then I'll be going now." He stood up.

"Sit back down," Cole growled. "We're not finished with you yet."

"Do you have any new evidence?"

Cole's lip twisted like she was ready to snap, but Lynch cut her off. "If we have any further questions, we'll be in contact." He glared at the CFO, who stared back smugly at the detective. He left the room without a backwards glance.

Jason could only stare into the distance. His mind still felt like a weight was pressing down against him, making thought difficult. Lynch started talking to him, but every word seemed to flitter through his mind without actually landing. It took a second for Jason to actually process Lynch's words.

"You got rattled, rookie. Happens to all of us sometimes. Don't worry. That guy was a real piece of shit. Not your fault."

Jason made a feeble humming sound. His mind was still blank. All he could feel was numb terror.

"But you know where you went wrong?" Cole said, coming over to stand beside him. "You started trying to answer his accusations. That's when he took control of the conversation. It's tempting, especially when they're being a dick, but you can't get caught up in what they're saying. Focus on what you're saying. Don't get swept up in their reasoning. Stick to your guns, alright?"

Jason could only nod. A minute had passed, and he was still in a state of panic. *What the hell is wrong with me?* His mind was so slow to respond. He tried to form words, but they wouldn't come out.

Lynch patted him on the shoulder. His grip was stronger than expected. Yet the simple action helped to stir Jason into full consciousness. "Come on. Let's get some food and coffee. Then we'll look over the numbers side of things. That's the real fun stuff anyway."

Chapter 16

They spent the rest of the morning at a café across the street. Jason had a coke. He normally avoided soft drink, but he knew the dose of sugar would help calm his nerves. No one talked about his freak-out, which he both appreciated and hated. They spent their time silently going over the reports from the auditors. When lunch time came, the detectives ate as they worked, so Jason did the same.

In the afternoon they went back into the corporate office and conducted two more interviews. This time, Jason stayed silent. The two witnesses were also older males in management positions, and both were just as unhelpful. Yet neither seemed to rattle Jason as much as the CFO.

Around three o'clock they went back to the station. The other officers were all there, the captain included, and were very excited to hear how things went. Jason told them everything, sparing no detail. They all agreed Gene Conroy was an asshole, and it felt good to hear them say it. They all had dozens of suggestions for what Jason should try next. Yet no one seemed to understand just how affected he had been.

Before long he was summoned into the Captain's room again.

"Afternoon, Detective Turner," Kader said with a grin. "Solve the case yet?"

He gave a fake laugh. "Did you find out much about the Glucks-burgs?"

"We'll get to that in a moment. How did you go with that CFO?"

He stared at her. She stared back. *She knows.*

"It wasn't good," he told her plainly. "I completely froze. I don't know what came over me. It's not like he was yelling, or swearing or anything. He was polite!"

"They often are."

"And I knew he was wrong, and I was right. But I just couldn't think of what to say." He gave an exasperated huff. "It's been five hours, and I still feel tense. Like there's something wrong with my brain." His voice started raising. "I've fought wizards and vampires and grizzly bears! Why couldn't I look that bastard in the eye?"

He suddenly realised he was standing up. He didn't remember deciding to. He forced himself to breathe deep and calm down.

"What did the detectives do?" Kader asked.

"Lynch told me the guy was an asshole. Cole pointed out that I let him take control of the situation, and I shouldn't have addressed his arguments."

Kader shrugged. "Those are good points. But that's not why you reacted like you did." She offered him a smile and spoke gently. "Jason, you did nothing wrong. Do you understand? You had a reaction and it was completely involuntary. It wasn't your fault."

He felt his mind start to return to normal. His body relaxed, and the tension in his shoulders gave way. "What happened to me?" he asked.

"Jason, you had a trauma response."

He frowned at her. "What? It wasn't traumatic. I told you, he was polite."

"Exactly. You know how to identify aggressive behaviour. That's why you were able to fight the wizards and vampire and grizzly bears. Because you know how to respond to violence and abuse. That is familiar to you. What you don't understand is the *passive*-aggressive. The gas-lighters. Those who get inside your own head and convince you to doubt yourself."

"That's not as bad," Jason said. "I've dealt with much worse."

"It IS just as bad, Jason. That's why you're afraid." Kader looked away from him and stared out the window as a light shower of rain began to trickle down the glass. "Your brain is telling you there is a threat and to expect pain. But you can't see a tangible threat so you don't know how to react. That's why you freeze. The part of your brain that creates fear will take over the part of your brain that controls speech."

"That's true. I couldn't speak."

"Your brain is literally shutting down in self-defence. It's not your fault. It's something your body has learnt to do in order to survive something so horrible it nearly destroyed you."

Jason nodded. "I hate that this affects me. I mean, I understand it better, but I'm still anxious right now. How do I stop this from happening?"

Kader stared at him, and he was surprised to see…*something* in her eyes. Not tears. But some heavy, unidentifiable emotion there. "You practice being familiar with the trauma. Remind yourself of how it felt, then replace your thoughts with the truth. You say, 'I know I'm scared, but this situation is completely different to the old one. I'm stronger now, and I can handle this.' Do that enough times, and your body will start to believe it."

Jason stared at her. "What happened to you, Captain? What did you go through?"

She smiled back. "Some other time, rookie." She sat back in her chair. "Now, I have some information on the Glucksburgs, if you still want to hear it."

She was obviously deflecting from his question. But since she wasn't comfortable talking about it, he accepted her change in topics. He was feeling calmer, after all. "What did you find?"

Kader opened her laptop screen and clicked several times with her mouse. "Here we go. Glucksburg is the royal family of Norway. By all accounts, they're good guys. Not much political power. One of the most affluent royal families in the world. Estimated net worth of thirty million." Kader looked up. "That's not *that* much, compared to modern billionaires."

"It's still more than Silvana's family."

"They have a famous castle named after them. Considered one of the most beautiful castles in the world and a major tourist attraction."

"Any mention of Wilhelm and Ingolf?"

"Not within the immediate royal family. I had to stop using google and start using the police database for this. Turns out the Glucksburgs do have a cousin called Wilhelm." She turned the screen around. The picture was of a man in his early forties. He was gorgeous. Piercing bright blue eyes, short hair and sculpted thin beard. Besides that, he looked pretty normal. Though his thin cheeks and strong chest suggested a high level of fitness. *A mortal knight.*

"That said, there's no mention of Ingolf anywhere." She turned the screen back and clicked several more times. "Not since the seventeenth century. Ingolf, eldest son of the king at the time, abdicated due to poor health." She rolled her eyes. "My guess is he gave up the throne to learn wizardry. However all records of him disappear when he died at the end of that century."

"Anything suspicious in Wilhelm's life?"

"No. He's a lawyer, and apparently a pretty good one. However, I did find one interesting fact. Apparently, the Glucksburg family has had some financial setbacks."

Jason frowned. "What do you mean, apparently?"

Kader clicked over to a web browser to show a newspaper headline. It was in Norwegian. "It says 'Glucksburg penniless'. This article was published in a major newspaper. It suggested the family lost a lot of money in bad investments. However, no other company reported the story, and no follow-up story was published. This is a one-off."

"Sounds more like sensationalism. You know how the media is with royal families."

"Yes, constant smear campaigns and rumour-mongering. That's a distinct possibility. Or it's possible the Glucksburgs put a gag order on them to cover it up." Kader sat back in her chair again. "Unfortunately, that's all we've got."

Jason frowned. "I think I need to investigate further." He looked up at his captain. "I might need to go to Norway."

"Oh no, rookie, you're not vying for a government funded vacation."

"Well I doubt we will get any more information here"

Kader shook her head. "No, Jason. You're not going."

"What? Why?"

"Several reasons. You're a local cop. If you go to Norway to work an investigation – even off the books – it can cause a whole bunch of problems at Interpol and complicate international relationships. Especially if you investigate members of the royal family."

"I've got to do something."

"I understand that, Jason. But what would you really do in Norway? Wander around the streets looking for clues? Door knock on the royal palace and ask to speak to His Royal Majesty?"

Jason stuttered. "No. I'm technically a distant relative. I could request a meeting."

"Didn't Silvana's aunt and uncle fail to get a meeting at the gala?" Jason's posture wilted. "Face it, Detective Turner. You don't have the authorisation to work this case. If you want to take this further, you'll need to pursue…alternative avenues."

"Do you mean criminal?"

Kader's mouth dropped open in bewilderment. "What? Why would I mean criminal? No, rookie. I mean use your connections in the Immortal world."

"Oh. Right."

Jason slunk down in his chair. He'd never imagined he'd hit a dead end so soon. Still, Kader was right. He could ask Silvana's family for more information. Better yet, he could try to contact Khadija and hopefully get some more clues. Maybe even contact the friends he made at the gala; Edward the Alchemist. And the Asian couple, Hana and Mikeru. Yes, there were other avenues. He'd start there.

"Thank you, Captain. And thank you for your help with the other case as well."

"Of course. I'm happy to talk about this more if you need help. My door's always open."

"Thank you, Captain." He lowered his tone, struggling to speak with such vulnerability but knowing it was necessary. "I mean it. I really appreciate that I could talk to you about this."

Kader smiled back, like she knew how much he meant it. "Any time, Jason. And keep practicing how you react to trauma. Remind yourself, you are not who you once were. You're not a child. You are a grown man, and a police officer."

"And a Knight Templar," he added and smiled. "You're right. I can do this. Thank you Captain."

Chapter 17

Silvana clutched the papers to her chest and took a long breath. *This time. I know it will work this time.*

She knocked on the door. "Uncle Nic? You in there?"

"Come on in, love."

Nicholas was sitting in an old leather chair with a high back, reading a small paperback novel. A fire was crackling in the hearth nearby, and an old record player was playing a 1950's big brass number at a low volume.

"Sorry to interrupt. What are you reading?"

He held up the cover proudly. "*H.G Wells, War of the Worlds*. That man was a genius! They'll never write anything this good."

Silvana smiled politely, yet inwardly she wanted to cringe. *Doesn't he ever enjoy anything from this century?* "You know, if you like science fiction, I could recommend a comic series. *The Kree-Skrull war* is particularly good. And it's fifty years old, so it's perfect for you."

"Oh, I don't buy into those comic books. I don't need pictures to enjoy a good story." He smiled up at her and placed his book face down on the arm of the chair to hold his place. He clapped his hands together. "What can I do for you?"

This is it. Keep a straight face.

"I've been thinking about how to help our family. And I've decided

I want to go back to school." She held up her papers. "It's been fifteen years since I studied nursing, and I have to do additional study to catch up with modern advancements. It will take four years. But once I've done it, I can actively begin work as a doctor. You'd be surprised how much money a doctor can make these days."

"Ok," Nicholas said, his tone unsure.

"I've done the maths, and if I start work as a general practice doctor in four years' time, then in the fifth year I can make a six figure income."

"Really?"

She smiled. "So I need to fill out some forms to re-enrol in this course. I need a non-immediate family member to witness—"

"Say no more. Where do I sign?"

Silvana blinked. "Uh…what?"

"I was busy reading. I'm proud of you and all, but can I just sign this thing and get back to it? The Martians are approaching London and nothing can stop them."

Silvana stared at him for a moment. *I just wasted a perfectly good lie. I could have walked in and said 'sign here' and he would have done it!* Then she realised she'd paused too long. "Thank you, Uncle Nic."

She set down the forms and handed him a pen. She had several tabs marked for signature and turned to the first one. Nicholas signed without reading. She turned to another page.

"Sure are a lot of these things."

"It's a big form." Nicholas nodded and kept going. *God this is so easy.* Still, her heartbeat was racing. If her aunts had been there, they would have heard the thumping in her chest and grown suspicious. Nicholas signed the last one and grabbed the paper. Silvana held her breath as he folded it back to the front page. He handed the forms to her without reading the title.

"Thanks Uncle Nic."

He smiled so wide it made his whole face crinkle. "Why do you keep calling me Uncle Nic? I was just telling Jason the other day how you never call me uncle."

She frowned. "I'm just being nice. Why were you telling Jason about it?"

"Oh. Um…he asked why you call your aunts 'aunts' when they call you daughter."

She studied him a long moment. She could hear his heartrate increasing. "You told him about my adoption."

Nicholas's mouth fell open, before grimacing. "Don't be mad. I was surprised he didn't already know, and…"

"You had no right to tell him about that."

A silence fell between them. He stared up at her with a pained expression. But he offered no excuses. He set his jaw firmly and bowed his head. "I'm sorry."

Silvana breathed out sharply. Now Jason knew she was a war orphan with an unknown ancestry. He would know why her aunts never trusted her, because she wasn't their true child. And he hadn't even heard the truth from her. *I'll be lucky if he ever believes me again. In fact, now he'd probably start trying to fight her family more than ever. This would cause so many problems.*

"When did you tell him?"

"Saturday morning, during training."

She frowned. That was right before he'd come into her room, and they'd shared a bath. He'd been perfectly normal. She hadn't suspected anything. Had he been hiding his new revelation out of pity? Maybe that was why he'd insisted on fingering her to completion. He'd been so generous because he felt sorry for her.

Her train of thought cut off. *Or maybe he knew…and just didn't care.* She breathed a little calmer. Maybe she was just overreacting and she should show him a little more trust.

Still, she glared at Nicholas. Now she felt a little less guilt about deceiving him and thought it best he kept thinking he was in her debt.

"I will forgive this, since you helped me today," she said. "But I won't forget it."

She left the room without waiting for a reply.

Outside in the hallway, she marched straight towards the garage. She hadn't driven the car in months, and she hadn't driven it all the way into town in years. Her heart was racing at just the thought of getting behind the wheel. *It's necessary. I can't back down now.*

She sat in the driver's seat of an old Rolls-Royce, and started up the engine with a turn of the key. She steadied herself with a breath, her body alert with nervous tension. Still, she pushed down the pedal and began to move forward.

* * *

"Well, Mrs Clarke, everything seems to be in order," said the banker, a stout man with a bald head and a rather large, toothy smile.

Silvana smiled sweetly. "Thank you, good sir, for all your help." She brushed down the hem of her dress to smooth the creases. It had remained folded in the backseat of the car for too long, but she couldn't stand before Nicholas while wearing her most luxurious gown. It would have given everything away.

"With this form, I think we can finally get your loan approved," said the banker. "The sum of five million and fifteen thousand pounds, to be paid into your account. A fixed rate of four point seven six percent interest compounded monthly." He looked up from his computer with another toothy smile. "You'll achieve great things with this sum,

I'm sure."

"Thank you." She brushed her hair back over her ears. The man's eyes followed the motion. He was smitten with her, as planned. "And how soon will the money appear in my account?"

"In a hurry, miss?"

She gave a polite blush. "My investment opportunity has a short window."

The banker leaned down on the table. "Sounds like a real goldmine you've got there. Care to share the secrets to your success?"

"I think you'll be benefiting enough already from the interest on my loan."

"I couldn't make the rate any lower."

"Too bad."

The banker gave a rough laugh. "Alright, keep your secrets. You'll have your money within the hour."

She stood up and ran her hands through her hair one last time for good measure. "Thank you again, good sir. I am, as it were, in your debt." She winked, and the banker roared with laughter far more than necessary.

Silvana marched out through the bank with her arms by her side and her eyes glued ahead of her. Her posture was upright and proud. Several heads turned as she passed through the waiting room and outside. She went back to the carpark and sat down inside the Rolls Royce. She checked that no one was nearby to watch.

Then she burst into tears.

Five million pounds of debt. And I committed fraud to get it. Oh fuck, what have I done?

She pressed her forehead against the steering wheel and gripped it with tight hands. She gritted her teeth together with each sob.

"Oh God…" she whispered.

Yet the emotion passed as suddenly as it had come. Soon, Silvana sat up and began to breathe deeper. She moved the rear-view mirror to check her makeup and paused when she saw the look in her own eyes. Hard, angry eyes, full of disgust and hatred at this whole situation.

"I have to do this," she whispered to herself. "It's the only way to save our House." Then she slammed her fists into the steering wheel a half dozen times in a frenzy. "Damn you! Damn you all for making me do this. You could have just listened to me. Just respected me like I *deserve* to be respected."

She forced herself to take a long breath and steady herself. Thankfully, she hadn't left any dints in the wheel. She pulled out her phone and checked her bank account. Nothing yet. So she swiped the screen over and over to refresh the page, waiting for it to update. She cleaned up her face and reapplied the makeup smeared by tears. A faint tremor of hunger ran through her. The blood in her system was low and Jason wasn't due to share blood for another week. She'd spent more than normal this month. He had offered her more blood, but it would be unfair on him to take more. She'd have to last.

She checked her phone again. And there it was. Five million pounds.

Here we go.

She took out the business card in her gown's pocket, and dialled the number. It began to ring. She waited while staring at her face in the mirror. *You can do this.*

"*Konichiwa?*" said the voice of a young woman. There was no further information.

"This is Silvana. I'm calling to speak with Hana."

"Ms Hana is not available," said the girl in perfect English with only the slightest accent. "I will tell her you called."

"Please put me through to Ms Hana," Silvana insisted calmly. "This is Silvana of House Romanov, and I will speak to her now."

"There is no one else here for you to speak with, ma'am, no matter where you come from. You can tell me your problem."

Silvana nearly crushed her phone in her vampire grip. She forced her voice to go higher into an extra sweet tone. "Ms Hana invited me to make a business deal. So you can tell her to call me back. I will only deal with her."

"Ma'am," a tightness crept into the woman's voice, "even if you did get to speak to Ms Hana, she would only tell you to come back to me. I am her representative for dealing with these issues."

"I'd like to hear that from her, if that's alright with you."

A pause. "Let me see what I can do."

Music started playing over the receiver. Silvana's mind started racing. What if Hana was only mocking her by giving her the business card? She still didn't know what house she was from. Even the receptionist had avoided giving out that information. What had Emberline said? *You can't trust people who hide their House. They're all cheaters and con-artists.* Silvana stopped that train of thought. She still had all the investment options she'd researched earlier, all six different options. If Hana didn't work out, she had backups. She'd be ok.

The phone clicked back on. "Hello?" Silvana blurted.

"Hello, Miss Silvana," said a male voice, the accent thicker, and the voice deep.

She startled. She knew that voice. What was the name? "Mikeru?"

"Correct."

"Where's Ms Hana?"

"You are as close to Ms Hana now as you will ever get. Now, let's not waste anymore of my time. What do you want?"

She swallowed and steeled her voice. "The deal that was promised me. I'm ready."

Mikeru gave a slight hum of satisfaction. "Buy in price is five million pounds. Are you capable of that?"

Silvana froze. She thought they would ask for one or two million. But this was nearly her full amount. There would be no chance to diversify her portfolio. All her eggs would be in one basket. It was the riskiest of ventures, and all she knew about it was that Hana was building skyscrapers in city districts. It was all too vague.

"I didn't think so," Mikeru said.

I've paused too long.

"Actually, it won't be a problem for me. I just want to hear the specifics first, regarding the return on my investment."

"I see. This is a rapid growth investment. You can expect at least an eight percent increase each month. Possibly more."

She did the maths in her head. *The interest on the loan was 4.76%, compounded monthly. The investment gives an 8% increase, at least. That's enough for a profit.*

He huffed with amusement. "Need me to spell out the maths?"

"Actually, I was wondering if you could spell out 'asshole.'"

The line went quiet, and Silvana clapped a hand over her mouth. *Oh my god! What did I just say!?*

"Such wit, Miss Silvana. I'll just text you the portfolio information instead for you to look over." *Oh thank God.* "You live in Plymouth, England, correct?"

"What of it?"

"You're in luck. We have a Plymouth branch of our enterprise. I'll text you the address too. If you're happy with the portfolio, you can go in person to get started today. My staff will answer any further questions and they'll set up the transaction. Good enough for you?"

"Absolutely. Thank you for your time, sir Knight."

The phone hung up. Silvana bit her lip. It wasn't a friendly partnership, but it would work. She stopped thinking about Mikeru and opened up her phone's calculator and an online loan calculator.

4.76% interest on my bank loan, minimum 8% return on my investment. So I pay the bank $28,545 a month back, but I'll make $38,601 a month from the investment. That's $10,000 profit each month with no work required. If I put that profit straight back into the loan, that means I'll be able to pay off the loan completely in...15 years 3 months. Probably quicker, since I'm making 8% minimum. After 15 years, I will own five million pounds of shares outright. Then I'll be making the full $38,601 as cash in hand each month.

Her mind spun a little, but she did the maths four times to check. It came out the same way every time. This was it. This would actually work.

Best of all, I could just pay the bare minimum on the loan and put the $10,000 a month into other investments. Build up diversity in the portfolio from there. Make more money. Then pay off the bank loan when it's more comfortable.

Her phone buzzed. She got the address, and started driving.

She could imagine the look on her family's face when she finally told them the truth. She could pay to fix that damaged wall in hallway, and set up a nest egg to keep the House alive indefinitely. And only after she had saved the Romanov House would she explain how she got the money, when she had proof of its effectiveness. Her family may not understand right away. Aunt Emberline would definitely try to undo it. But they would finally understand how to make their money work for them. And they would finally show her respect.

Silvana arrived at her destination. By now, she was smiling.

The office building was by the waterfront. The girl at reception had pink hair and a black suit. Silvana was led to a conference room filled with luscious green pot plants and high tech TV and digital equipment. And she waited with a smile.

"Hello, Miss Clarke?" said a stout man in a black suit as he came into the room. "My name is Gene Conroy, I'm the CFO of Kennedy and Sons. It's an honour to have you here."

Chapter 18

Portia sat on the castle floor, sprawled out with her legs to the side. It always unnerved people to see a Vigile so relaxed, without a care in the world, as if there were no power that could threaten them. Her host – the vampire Hana – knelt opposite her in a refined pose with her feet tucked underneath her and hands in her lap. Hana was rigid, definitely not as in control as Portia.

The door opened and Portia flinched with alertness. Her will hardened into battle readiness as a spell began to form on her lips.

It was just the Knight. Mee…Mekerro? Some foreign and weird name that Portia had no interest in learning. *Ok, maybe I am a little tense,* Portia admitted to herself.

The Knight bowed low as he spoke. *"Gomen'nasai, Hana-san. Kyuketsuki."*

"Yoku dekimashita," Hana replied, then turned back to the Vigiles. "My apologies for my knight's delay. He had important business to attend to. I believe you were asking me some questions?"

"I was asking questions of both of thine," Desdemona said. The older Vigile did not sit like Portia, instead standing motionless in the corner of the room with her hands at her side. She gestured towards Hana, indicating that the Knight should sit next to his mistress.

"With respect, great mistress, Mikeru is my Knight. He will stand guard at all times."

Portia openly laughed at her in that sweet voice others found so infuriating. "Really? And how would the mortal knight guard you from us?" She looked at this…Mikeru. "Sit your ass down, *dobber*, before I throw you down." The knight glared at her as he crouched down into the lotus position. Portia flashed a bright smile, and was thrilled to see his glare intensify.

"These are lovely quarters, Hannah," Portia said.

"My name is Hana," she insisted quietly, pronouncing it *'HarNar.'*

Portia only smirked again. "Is this your family's home?"

The old castle was oriental in theme and design. The floor was made up of old wooden boards that make strange creaking and whistling sounds when someone moved on them. It was impossible to sneak up on anyone here. Several paintings and woven tapestries hung from the walls, depicting elephants and tigers that had clearly been drawn by someone who had never seen one before. Hana wore a white and pink kimono with a sash tied around the middle. Her knight Mikeru had his legs crossed under his black combat robes.

"The castle has been in the family for some time, yes," Hana said simply. "But I doubt you came all this way to ask about my home."

"Thou art most astute," Desdemona said dryly. She took a slow, deliberate step as she began to pace around the room. "On the night of the gala, you were both in attendance. Did thou make any business transactions?"

"Not one," Hana said. "It was a most disappointing evening."

"Didst thou speak with the host? Any member of the Al Khalifa family?"

"Sadly, we did not have that pleasure."

"Then what were you doing all night?"

Hana pressed her lips tighter. "Well, if you must know, my knight found my attire to be…irresistible."

Portia raised an eyebrow. "So you were fucking that whole time? For over an hour?"

"He is most skilful."

Portia stared at the two of them, and neither showed even the slightest emotion. Mikeru's face was like a death mask. *Good poker faces. But not perfect.* "Right then. I would like to see proof. Start fucking now, please. I'll time you."

Hana's eyes widened. "Excuse me?"

Ha! Not so poker-faced now, are you?

"My partner jests," Desdemona said, turning on her heel and pacing back to her starting position. Her path took her within reach of the vampire, as if flaunting her lack of fear. "For now, let's say I believe thee. Why wouldst thou make such a poor use of thy time?"

"We thought we had more time to spare," Hana said. "We had no idea of the interruption that would come. Or how lax the security would be."

Desdemona glanced at Portia. *I know that look,* Portia thought. *That's the look of not giving a single fuck.*

"Where were you at the time of the explosion?" Portia asked.

"I was bent over a handbasin," Hana said.

A smile broke over Portia's face and she erupted into raucous laughter. "Oh, very well done!" she cried.

"Which handbasin?" Desdemona cut in, her heels clopping with each step. "Specifically."

"Bathroom on floor one hundred and four."

"Guests weren't allowed up that high."

"We bribed a servant. We wanted privacy."

"Can you name that servant? We'll need someone to verify your alibi."

"Why would I bother to learn the name of a servant?"

Portia smirked. *What a bitch. I like her.*

"Then tell me," Desdemona said, stepping towards the couple and tilting slightly to lean over them. Her long braids swayed within centimetres of their faces. "If thou was on the hundred and fourth floor, then how was thou able to locate one of the Skinwalkers, and decapitate it?"

"After all," Portia sneered, leaning back with her hands behind her and wiggling her feet. "You were so eager to show off that dinosaur head to the High King. Almost like…oh I don't know…you set up the whole thing to curry His Majesty's favour?"

Hana looked to Mikeru. The knight spoke in a low gravel. "We came running downstairs to investigate. We saw crowds of people in the stairwell, all of them running down. But two people were running up the stairs towards us. It seemed suspicious. I stopped them and demanded an explanation. They were both dressed as wait staff. One man, one woman, both black skinned and young. They tried to force their way past me, so I drew my sword. The woman said I was only a mortal and shapeshifted into a demon. That's when I decapitated it." He looked at the Vigiles expectantly, but they gave no praise. He finished, "The man turned into a bat and flew past me up the stairwell. I didn't see where he went after that."

Portia stared at the knight. He stared back, meeting her gaze.

"Couple of questions," she said. "You're telling me you heard an explosion and ran *towards* it. Seems unusual. Second, you stopped a pair of random *wallopers* who happened to be the assailants and decapitated one for rudeness? And third, you pick up the dinosaur head and brought it with you to show the High King?"

"Wallopers?" Hana said. "I do not know this word."

"My partner is Scottish," Desdemona sighed, like someone who had been putting up with this for a century. Portia smirked.

"To answer all three of your questions," Mikeru said with raised chin. "I did my duty as a Knight of honour."

Portia stared at him blankly. *His duty? Either this guy's very naïve, or very psychopathic.*

"Tell us about the shapeshifter man," Desdemona said. "You saw his face."

"He was medium height. Dark skin, lots of black hair. Very young, maybe a teenager still?"

"Wait," Portia cut in. "Dark skin? Can you be specific? You know there's a wide spectrum of skin tones besides white."

Mikeru shrugged. "What's the difference? They all look the same."

Portia's mouth widened into a full smile. "Oh mortal knight, you should not have said that in front of my mistress." She looked to Desdemona, and her eyes – vacant of all emotion – were locked on the Knight.

"I apologise for my Knight," Hana said. "He spoke without thinking. I will punish him later in private. There's no need for—"

"*Tab Izī.*"

An open flame appeared in Desdemona's hand, floating an inch off her skin and casting red shadows that danced over her face. She glared at the knight. "Thou should show more respect for dark skin, boy, lest I darken thine own skin through fire."

Mikeru's eyes widened. The red light of flame flickered in his eyes.

Reluctantly, Desdemona made a fist and snuffed out the flame. *God I love that woman.*

Portia gave a sweet laugh and flicked her hair again. "If you saw this Metamorph man again, would you be able to identify him?" Mikeru nodded. "Good. We'll be back with a picture soon." She reached towards her mistress and placed a hand on her shoulder. Then, with an effort of will, she bent the world around them with a spell.

"*Śilaürudu.*"

The universe folded. A sudden plunge jolted them, before they landed on plush, velvet carpet. Portia always sighed with relief upon returning to their office.

The Vigiles worked out of an old Victorian era library that had been refitted with modern conveniences, like electric lights and air-conditioning. The walls were made of granite stones, with mahogany bookcases placed in front with high shelves reaching to the roof. Several workstations filled the centre of the room, laden with the fastest modern computers money could buy. Security screens showed camera-feeds of the area around the property. Portia could tell at a glance that the five miles surrounding their old castle was vacant.

"Thou best find that list soon," Desdemona whispered. "The High King grows impatient."

Portia sat down at the nearest station and loaded up a screen. "Al Khalifa had hundreds of workers employed as staff. This may take some time to find someone who matched the knight's description."

She scrolled quickly through a list of profiles. "*Alisha Black, London born, Fae Dryad. Jo Karas, Greek Isles, Witch.*" She stopped reading out loud. There were a lot to get through.

"I still fail to grasp the connection," Desdemona muttered to herself. "Al Khalifa was an ally with other Royalists, according to our Skinwalker friend in captivity. Even allied with Erickson, allegedly. So why would they come under attack? Is this some internal dispute between rebels?"

"Could be loyalists," Portia said, "trying to preserve the Imperium."

"My love, there art no loyalists. Only opportunists."

Portia looked up from her screen. "So you do suspect the knight? I was just messing with him when I called him out."

"He cuts the head off an assassin and displays it to the High King. It could not be clearer."

"But why? What's the end goal?"

Desdemona gave a sharp huff, and nearly two hundred years of partnership told Portia exactly what her mistress was thinking. *She has no idea, but she will never admit that.*

"We'll find out," Portia said. "Together. We always do." Portia kept scrolling through the profiles.

"Erickson wanted to overthrow the Imperium," Desdemona kept muttering, and Portia had to stifle a huff of annoyance of her own. *I'm trying to concentrate. Must she talk out loud?* "That's the Royalist plan, to overthrow the High Kings and rule in their stead. Restore the monarchy and rule the mortals in open displays of power. Ah, the audacity of youth! Secrecy and ignorance has always served the Imperium better. But why would these rebel Houses turn on each other?"

"Maybe they didn't," Portia said, giving up on her search. "We could have received false information from our captive. We also don't know who hired the Skinwalkers. When we do, we'll be able to understand the picture better. Now, may I continue my search?"

Desdemona eyed her, as if surprised to find her in the room. "Well of course. Best get right to it. No time to waste." Portia gave her an annoyed grin in return. It was the closest her mistress would ever get to an apology.

She scrolled through more names and faces, searching for anyone that matched the description the knight had given. Her eyes were already struggling to focus. Everything seemed to be blurring together. The room seemed to spin. *That's weird, I haven't been working that long. Am I dizzy?*

"Portia!" Desdemona cried. The sudden urgency in her voice jolted her alert.

The room truly was spinning. Folding around itself. Folding around them, in a teleportation spell.

"I'm not doing this!" Portia cried.

"Neither am I!"

Portia threw her mind against the magic growing in the room. She pressed her will against the change to stop it. And nothing happened. Her will had no impact whatsoever. The power was unstoppable.

"Mistress!" Portia screamed. She thrust a hand towards her and Desdemona reached back out. Maybe if they combined their will, they could stop the spell. But the space folded between them, and suddenly they were light years apart. Portia dropped as the floor was removed beneath her feet. She kept falling. She screamed and flailed her hands and flung her magic towards the ground beneath her desperately. *Nothing's working! Why won't my will do anything?*

She hit the ground. Hard.

Portia groaned as she lifted her face off a stone slab. Someone was moving next to her. She sensed her mistress reaching for her. Their hands clasped together.

"Touching," said a deep, male voice. Portia looked up.

The High King, Reynold the First, was sitting on his throne directly above them.

They had been transported directly to his throne room and Portia found herself sprawled on the ground at the High King's feet. *No wonder we couldn't stop the spell.* Every inch of Reynold's throne room was covered in gold plating. The light from his jewels and crown made him appear too bright to look at. Behind the throne, a massive painting overlooked him, depicting dozens of angelic beings playing trumpets and harps. In the centre of the painting was a giant Jesus Christ with a golden halo, looking down on the High King in approval.

Reynold was smiling in a very self-satisfied way. His weathered face had sunken red splotches under his eyes and black marks on his cheeks. He wore a simple golden crown with a red and blue fur robe. It was less formal attire than he'd worn at the recent gala, but still enough to mark him as Lord.

"Thank you for answering my summons," Reynold said.

Portia's body was flushed with fear and adrenaline. *He summoned us here. He snatched us with his mind, teleporting us from across the world, directly to his feet. My God, I thought that was impossible!*

"I desire an update on your investigation," the High King said. "What have you, so far?"

Desdemona adjusted her posture into a neat bow. She pressed her face to the floor, so Portia copied her exactly. "My King," Desdemona said. "We have a witness description of one of the attackers. We were just cross-referencing it with the list of staff working that night. Once we've identified the attacker, we can determine their whereabouts. It shouldn't be long before we know who was responsible for their presence."

"Good," Reynold said, his tone surprisingly warm and gentle. "I expected as much. I want confirmation of which House is behind this as soon as possible." He smiled. "And now that you've been to my palace, I expect you to teleport yourselves back here as soon as you have news."

"Yes, your Majesty," Desdemona said, and Portia echoed her. "My Majesty, if thy servant may be so bold, hast thou suspicions regarding the attack?"

"Of course," Reynold said, bemused. "But that is my information to hold."

"As thou wishes it, sire. Thy servants shall return to thine service, master," Desdemona lifted herself to her feet. Portia copied her, feeling relieved to be getting out of here so easily. She was not a sycophant trying to ingratiate herself with the powerful. It was safer to keep her head down and avoid their notice altogether. Portia didn't even look at the High King. She just reached for her mistress' hand to teleport the hell out of there...

"A moment," the King said.

Portia looked up, to find his withered old face staring directly at her. His eyes were just like any other man's, and yet somehow far more terrifying. She did not like those eyes focused on her. She felt like her thoughts were exposed.

"What is it you wish, your majesty?"

"You're…Scottish, yes?"

Portia bowed her head. "That is my heritage, yes."

"You barely have an accent."

"My mistress taught me to use the more familiar British accent." The King nodded in approval. She relaxed and reached for her mistress's hand again.

"Strip for me."

She froze. Her mouth was hanging open, but she couldn't speak. She only stared up at the High King. *Surely he did not just say that. I must have misheard him. He couldn't have...*but she saw that look in his eye. That leering look that only men could have, so monstrous, and so unapologetic for their desires. Reynold had that aura of entitlement, as if Portia should be grateful for his predatory attention.

"Thy Majesty," Desdemona said in a perfectly polite voice. "Our work for thee is of the uttermost importance, and time is pressing. We best not waste time."

The High King was silent, ignoring her. He kept staring and staring at Portia.

"I'd prefer it to be done by your will, and not mine," he said. "In fact, I think you and I would both prefer that."

She understood then. If she didn't act, he would force her with his magic, violently if he so chose. She'd already fought against his mind when he'd teleported them, and both her and her mistress had been unable to even nudge it. He was too powerful. There was no fighting this. She might even lose part of her magic if she tried. Or even her life.

Maybe this will be over quickly.

She slipped her tuxedo jacket off her shoulders and let it drop to the stone floor. Immediately, her hands begun to shake with nervousness. The cold air was already biting at her half exposed flesh. Her thin collared shirt did little to keep off the chill emanating from the cold stone walls. She untucked her shirt, but her fingers fumbled against the tiny buttons. She had to pour her magic into her own body to force it under control. She wanted to undo the buttons at a medium pace and stare him in the eyes the whole time, but those terrifying eyes kept staring…staring… and she had to look at the ground as her fingers rushed to open her shirt. She half paused when it came undone, as if hoping for him to grant her permission to stop. But no order came. So, she unhooked her bra and let it fall from her arms.

He stared at her chest. Portia forced her hands to her side. He looked at her, and tilted his head in question. The meaning was clear. *Why did you stop?*

Fucking hell. She unbuckled her belt and kicked off her heeled boots. She saw Desdemona flinch towards her, as if she wanted to intervene. Yet she made no further move, unwilling to challenge the High King. Portia pushed the last of her underclothes down to her ankles, and kicked them off with a small flick of her ankle. She stood with her legs together and her arms at her side in what she hoped was her bravest pose. Tiny goosebumps dotted her body, the air painfully cold on her exposed skin.

"Truly," Reynold said, and Portia found herself bracing for something really fucking creepy. "Women of the north are always the most beautiful. The fairest of creatures, the most like Mother Eve." He nodded and smiled at her, and his look couldn't have been any clearer. He expected her to thank him for the praise.

"You are most gracious, sire." Her voice came out no more than a whisper.

"Come closer," he ordered, his finger curling in a gesture for her to step towards him.

Portia's legs wavered as she walked to the side of the throne. She could feel the old king's eyes on her bare skin. The cold was covering her flesh in more goosebumps as an uncontrollable shiver racked her body. She stood within arm's reach. Reynold stared at her middle. In fact, she realised with disgust, he was staring at her crotch.

"Closer," he ordered.

She swallowed the bile in her throat and stepped closer until she was up against his seat. Now, he leered at her breasts. "I see you are as excited as I am," he said.

Portia glimpsed down. The cold air had made her nipples harden. *He thinks I'm aroused? What the fuck...*

His hand gripped her breast, and it took everything in Portia to stop from crying out. Reynold was breathing hard through his open mouth, with rasping breath and gross 'gluck' sounds from the back of his throat. His thumb kept digging into her at a sharp angle.

"Lift your leg," he said and patted the seat next to him.

Portia's eyes started to sting with unshed tears. She looked away and pressed her lips together to stop them from trembling. She refused to let a tear fall in front of this man. *I am a wizard. A Vigile of the Imperium. I fear no man.* Yet she felt a twinge of fear deep in her belly as she obeyed her High King, and he began to touch her between the legs.

It went on and on. His fingers kept thrusting. He began to speak grand compliments of her beauty. Portia felt her mind detach from her body and retreat into a dark corner of herself. She was far away. She was somewhere else. On a mountain. On a vast cliff side looking out over the sea, with bristling cold wind stinging her face to make her feel alive. She was home in another age where nothing could harm her.

A jolt of pain brought her back to hell. He had thrust harder. Why was he even still going? What was he possibly…

Oh my god. He's expecting me to climax.

She saw the lecherous gaze in his eyes and the eagerness in his movements. He was waiting. God, couldn't he even tell how dry she was? Beads of sweat dripped down his forehead and the jowls on his neck jiggled with his every hand movement. He was panting hard, like even this was strenuous for him. But he would not stop. There was only one way she was going to make this awful ordeal end.

She clutched his shoulder and his wrist and let out a loud gasp. She made her knees shake, though thanks to the freezing cold it was easy to let them shiver. She bent over, closer towards him, where she could smell his musky stench.

"Good girl," he whispered in her ear. He withdrew his hands, and Portia forced herself to calmly step back. "Let this remind you of the gifts God gives us when we follow His will."

What? He thinks this was a gift for me? Instead of saying anything, she forced herself to bow.

"Are you not grateful?" he asked, a slight warning tone in his voice hinting at his disapproval.

Portia's face was pointed to the floor, so she allowed it to twist in rage. She forced her voice to sound calm as she whispered. "Thank you."

"You may go."

Portia jolted in surprise. He'd said it so casually. Yet within an instant she drew up her will and folded the world around her faster and stronger than she'd ever done before. She was in such a hurry to be rid of the High King's company that she left her clothes behind. A mere second later she was back in the castle, by the desk she'd been sitting in only minutes ago.

Her lip trembled. Her eyes started to sting. She blinked back the tears and moved towards the closet by the door.

"Portia," Desdemona said her name from behind. It wasn't to get her attention, or to start a conversation, she was simply saying it for the comfort of hearing her name spoken by a loved one.

"That fucking creep!" Portia hissed as she opened the closet. There were multiple uniforms hanging in neat rows. She pulled one off the rack and started dressing, not caring to replace her undergarments.

"Thou art correct," Desdemona said. "Yet the High King rules the world with his will. He is above every law. He does as any man would with his power."

"Then no one should have his power!"

The words burst from her in a scream. Portia felt a stab of disgust at her own body and the fresh clothes that were now touching it. She roared, *"Tāb Izī!"* and burned the clothes off of her. She all but ran to the bathroom and into the shower. Her hand slipped on the nozzle and she let out a sob as she struggled to turn on the water. She plunged into the freezing cold and cried out wordlessly as she waited till the heat came through. She then let herself burn under the hottest water she could tolerate.

Desdemona was standing next to her. She saw the look of calm on her mistress's face.

"Forgive me, mistress. I am under duress."

"Rightfully so," she said gently. "Thou art right to be angry. But thou must also remember thy place."

"So I deserved that?"

"Of course not. Tell me, why do we serve the Imperium?"

Portia sighed. "Because power creates truth."

"That's right. The Imperium is stronger than us. The High Kings could overpower even us, as thou saw. We serve them because that is where we are safest. To challenge them is to die. Established power gives protection to those who serve. But only if they serve."

"Is that what the High King wanted to prove?" Portia said as water ran down her lips. "That I'm his servant?"

"Possibly. More likely it was his own desire. At least we can be grateful for his advanced age, limiting what he can do."

Portia couldn't help laughing, the sound was shrill and delirious. Tears spilled from her eyes as hysteria filled her voice. She tested her will and felt the building around her starting to shake. The ground rattled. Her power was still intact and ready to be unleased. She would crush everything in her reach. She would burn anyone near her. She would destroy anything she wanted.

A hand touched her gently on the shoulder. It was a testing touch. A question.

"Please," Portia said to grant permission, and her mistress's arms slipped around her middle. Desdemona stood in the water fully clothed, her head nestled down on the back of Portia's shoulder. She gave just the faintest squeeze and Portia felt her breathing settle. Her mind calmed. She ran her hand along Desdemona's arms and held her close.

It didn't completely remove the terror. But it helped.

Chapter 19

"Is no one gonna address the elephant in the room?"

Jason looked in the rear-view mirror. Freddie looked right back at him. "What?" Jason asked.

"The velociraptors!" Freddie through up his hands.

"What?"

"How come no one is talking about the velociraptors?"

"What?"

Freddie put on his best Samuel Jackson impression, "Say what again! I dare you, I double dare you, motherfucker, say *what* one more goddamn time!"

Silvana burst out laughing. Jason glanced at her in the passenger seat and rolled his eyes. "Alright, Freddie. *What* velociraptors are you talking about?"

"The ones at the party, in Dubai." Freddie leaned forward, popping his shaggy head through the gap in the chairs and gripping the shoulders of the front seats. "You've been telling me for the last hour about all the Immortals you met and the murdered wizard and the High King, yet you breeze right past the part where a bunch of shapeshifters turned into velociraptors. I feel like that's a pretty big deal!"

Jason drawled, "They're shapeshifters. They shifted shape. Pretty straightforward."

"But how did they become velociraptors? Doesn't that raise questions for anyone else? Hello?" He put on a John Goodman impression, "Am I the only one around here who gives a shit about the velociraptors?"

Silvana laughed again, and this time Jason had to join in. "I wasn't worried about it. Do you know how much weird shit I've seen in the last six months? I don't bother with questions like that anymore."

"But think about it. If the shapeshifters were able to turn into dinosaurs, doesn't that imply they could turn into other extinct animals? Or does it imply that raptors aren't really extinct? Does the Imperium keep T-rexes in an exclusive Immortal zoo somewhere? Or does this mean a shapeshifter could turn into fictional creatures? What about dragons? Or Balrogs?"

Silvana had been giggling all through Freddie's rant. She even had to wipe tears from her eyes from laughing so hard. Jason squashed down the part of his mind that felt jealous. *Freddie is funnier than me, and that's ok. I'm glad Silvana can laugh so much.*

It was a dreary Saturday morning with the sky completely covered in grey clouds which gave not a drop of rain. Yet despite the gloomy weather, Jason was grateful to just be outside. He'd spent all of the last week cooped up at the police station trying to research the Gluckburgs and coming up with next to nothing, and the tax fraud case wasn't going any better, much to Lynch's satisfaction. It was all a lot of work without any real progress.

But today would be different. They were driving to Swansea to meet Edward the Alchemist, and Freddie could not be more excited to have been invited along. So far they had spent one hour on a three lane highway with minimal traffic, driving past open farmland and plenty of green fields. They had just passed the city of Exeter, which meant there was still two hours left to go.

"Silvana?" Freddie asked. "What do you think? How could they shapeshift into dinosaurs?"

"I only know a little about Metamorphs," Silvana said. "They have to study each animal before they can shapeshift into it. That can take months or even years just to learn one new form. Then they can add it to their repertoire. The older Metamorphs can do heaps of creatures."

"That's disgusting," Freddie said. "No one should *do* heaps of creatures." Silvana laughed so hard she snorted. "So do shapeshifters need a master to teach them each form? Or can they self-teach?"

"I think they need a master, I'm not certain. But as for your question, I think it's possible the ancient Skin-Walkers saw dinosaurs of some kind, and just passed on the teaching in an unbroken chain."

Freddie sat back in his chair and hummed in thought. "Interesting. Do you think they could shapeshift into my dad? Cause he's a dinosaur too. Still has a landline and a chequebook." Predictably, Silvana kept laughing.

"Damn it, Freddie, stop being so funny," Jason said sarcastically. "We've got two hours of driving left, not including the trip back, and I can only laugh for so long."

"Relax, Jase. I'm pretty sure I can 'keep it up' the whole time. Ey? Ey?" He nudged the back of Jason's chair.

"That's it!" Jason cried as he turned the music on and cranked it high. Old school Judas Priest was playing.

Freddie yelled over the music, "Joke's on you! I'm into that shit!" And proceeded to do his best impression of Rob Halford's high pitch shriek, which only made Silvana laugh more than ever.

"Alright already!" Jason cried and turned the music back off, just as Freddie started a particularly off-pitch howl.

Freddie lowered his voice, his tone growing sombre. "Seriously man, I can cool it if I'm being annoying."

Jason suddenly felt silly. "No, you're great. I'm just…" he couldn't find the words for it. "I guess I'm trying to be funny too. Uh, how am I doing?"

"Brilliant mate!" Freddie said. Jason knew he was just being nice, but he smiled anyway.

"You always make me laugh," Silvana said.

Jason drawled, "Yeah, but not like Freddie."

"Hey don't compare yourself to me. Cause if we started making comparisons, it would just make us both miserable." Freddie patted Jason's upper arm, then paused with his hand on Jason's bicep. "Jesus Christ, mate. You could pick up Mjölnir without being worthy."

"Come off it," Jason said, but he was blushing openly now. "You know you could join me for a workout any time."

"Nah. Sounds hard." Silvana laughed some more. "Besides. I'd rather be funny."

"Me too," Jason said mournfully. "I barely know how to talk to most people. This week at work, I tried to interview a suspect and I completely botched it."

"Hey," Silvana interjected. "You knew how to talk to Edward. You're the reason we're on this road trip."

"I just know how to be nice. I don't actually know how to charm people or smooth talk. Why do you think Phillip and Emberline can't stand me? Cause I can't speak without offending them."

"Look mate," Freddie said, patting Jason's arm again. "This whole being funny and charming and stuff? You don't know it cause you grew up as a foster kid. I'm not saying that to discriminate, it's a legit reason. You were too busy trying to survive every day. You never got the chance to learn basic social skills. Don't blame yourself for not being a social master."

Jason felt a brief stab in his chest. He had to focus on the road and lock down the emotion building in his throat. "Thanks man." His voice stayed steady.

"Besides, you don't want to be me anyway. I'm only funny to help me cope with the constant anxiety I live with every day."

"Oh really? What are you anxious about, Freddie?" Silvana asked.

"How should I know? It changes every three seconds."

He said it like a joke, but Silvana took it seriously. "Ok. What is it most of the time?" she asked.

Freddie actually stopped and thought about it. Jason watched him in the mirror as he stared out the window at the passing forestry.

"Mostly that I'll make a mistake," Freddie said. "That I'll do something wrong, hurt someone without meaning to, or just do anything less than perfect. It's my stupid dad's fault. Everything's always got to be perfect with him. Perfect grades, perfect behaviour, perfect wording of every sentence." He growled, "Gah! Yes, I know how it sounds. The stereotypical disapproving Asian father." He put on a terrible Asian accent, more like a western parody than an actual accent. "What's this? You only got an 'A'? 'A' very bad. 'A' plus or nothing! When you doctor? Give me grandchildren!"

Jason snorted, trying to hold in his laughter. "It's alright, Jase," Freddie drawled. "It's not racist when I do it."

"My aunts are the same," Silvana moaned. "I mean, not the Asian part. But they always want me to act the same way, speak the same way. They get mad when I wear jeans instead of ballroom gowns."

"Right? That's why I'm a gamer who smokes weed. I mean!" He cut off and patted Jason's arm again, "*Don't* smoke weed. Yeah." Jason rolled his eyes. "Cause I can't stand the pressure all the time. It's easier to not even try, instead of aiming for perfection in every little bloody thing. And the few times I did try, I failed spectacularly. Such as when I joined the Monster Hunters. Remember that cult? Stupidest thing I ever did, and I was just trying to get my dad to see me as a big tough man. But I just keep making stupid mistakes.

That's why I avoid trying most times."

"I wish I avoided trying," Silvana said. "Instead, I just kept doing everything my aunts told me, even though it made me miserable. I married who they wanted. Dressed how they wanted. I thought eventually they'd be happy with me and treat me like an equal. But it was never enough for them. They'll always treat me like a child."

"Seriously?" Freddie cried. "But aren't you like, a hundred years old?"

"Hey! I'm only ninety-two."

"Oh geez, sorry. Well you don't look a day over fifty." Silvana laughed. "But seriously. You're ninety-two, and they still treat you like a child?"

"Yep. Sucks."

Freddie was quiet a moment. Jason checked him in the rear-view mirror. "You ok, bud?"

"Yeah…I just had an epiphany." He leaned forward, poking his head into the front row of seats again. "It doesn't matter if I do everything perfectly, like my father wants. Cause I could live to be ninety-two, and it still wouldn't be enough for him. So why the fuck would I waste my life trying to please him? It's impossible!"

"Yeah!" Silvana cried.

"God," Freddie groaned. "I should just live however I want, and not give a shit what he thinks."

"Hell yeah!" Jason cheered.

Freddie laughed. "Geez. Good thing I didn't wait till I was ninety-two to figure that out." He cut off. "Uh…sorry, I didn't mean it that way."

"No no, you're right," Silvana tried. "Better late than never. But I'm getting the hang of it now, that's for sure." She smiled to herself proudly, and Jason patted her hand.

The conversation lapsed into silence, which Jason appreciated. He loved Silvana and liked Freddie, but three hours of talking would be too much for his introverted brain to handle. They spent much of the next hour dropping in and out of small talk without latching onto any firm topic. They changed music a few times, and all burst out singing when the Proclaimers came on with 500 miles. After losing a vote two to one, Jason reluctantly had to pull into a McDonalds outside of Bristol just to get everyone Sundaes.

"So Silvana, you're ninety-two," Freddie said abruptly as he finished his last mouthful. "How old were you when you became a vampire?"

Jason forced himself not to flinch. He'd never asked Silvana before. He still hadn't told her what Phillip and Nicholas had told him, about her origin. He couldn't let her find out that he already knew.

"I was twelve," Silvana said casually. She offered no further explanation.

"Is that the normal age for being turned?" Freddie asked.

"No. Normally it's much younger."

"Ouch. That's sounds brutal."

"It's actually a kindness. When a child is turned, it changes their physiology completely. Even changes their brain chemistry. It can be quite traumatic. That's why it's better to do it young. The younger a child is, the more adaptable they are. They haven't had time to get used to the mind and body of a mortal. The change is less harmful. If it happens too late, the vampire can become savage, almost bestial. They can lose their humanity altogether."

"Huh…" Freddie softened his voice. "So your change into a vampire…was it really bad?"

Jason held his breath. He glanced at her from the corner of his eye, while trying not to look like he was watching her.

"Kind of. All that happened to me was I lost my memory."

What? All that happened to her? Jason studied her, while keeping his own face blank. She had a calm, neutral expression. *Is she lying? Or does she genuinely believe that?*

"Wait," Freddie said suspiciously, "how much memory?"

"All of it."

"Geez…and did you get it back?"

"No."

Freddie frowned. "But did your family tell you what happened?"

"No. I was turned right at the beginning of World War 2. In all that chaos, I was separated from my family. My aunts found me and adopted me. I don't even know how I was turned." She paused to lay a hand on Jason. "I'm sorry I've never told you this."

"That's ok. I never asked. I figured you would tell me if it was important."

She clutched his arm tighter. "So you know what this means? I'm adopted into this family. I'm not a true blood relation to any of my aunts and uncles. I may not even be from any Immortal family originally. I could just be a very unlucky mortal. I have no idea where I came from, or who bit me, or why."

I see. She thinks she's telling the truth. She doesn't know that she went savage for years. She doesn't know she killed people. And her family have kept her ignorant.

Silvana kept talking, and Jason realised he'd been quiet for too long. "I'm sorry if this changes the way you see me."

Jason simply shrugged. "So you're kinda like a foster kid too, hey?" He clutched her hand in return and squeezed. "You have nothing to be ashamed of."

He glanced at her again, and saw tears in her eyes. "My God. How did I ever get so lucky?"

"I'm the lucky one," he said.

"Blargh!" Freddie cried and started fake vomiting.

The final hour of the trip was spent with Freddie trying to ask Silvana for information about the Immortal world, to which she had to repeatedly tell him she couldn't say anything to an outsider. "Our whole world is bound to secrecy," she said. "I could get in serious trouble for telling you anything."

"Then just tell me how to find out more," Freddie said. "Point me in the right direction. Give me a website. I'll find out myself from there."

"It's too dangerous. Jason's been with me for six months, and he's nearly died…I want to say three times now?"

"I'm not counting," Jason said.

"So cool," Freddie whispered.

"It's not cool! Jason's a trained professional. You'd be at risk. Just be content to be friends with us. I've never had a mortal friend before who wasn't connected to an immortal house. This is really cool for both of us."

"Are you saying let's just be friends? But Silvana, I love you." They both laughed, and Jason couldn't help the strange mixture of feelings at hearing Freddie say that to Silvana. "Alright I see your point. It's just crazy that you have access to all the secrets of the universe and I can't ask you about it."

"I don't know any secrets, Freddie. I'm unimportant among my people. We're like, lower class plebs. It's the Vigiles who know all the secrets."

"The what?"

Silvana groaned.

"I can't blame you, Freddie," Jason said. "You're curious. You're an investigator, like me."

"Exactly!" Freddie cried.

"But that's the thing about being an investigator," Jason said in a low voice. "You don't always like what you find."

They finally turned off the highway as they approached Swansea. It was a relief to their ears to hear the engine grow quieter after so much time on the highway at a high rev. Jason turned up the GPS on his phone and starting following instructions north of the town and through the suburbs towards Edward's address. They drove past acres of high grass, brown and dry, yet tall enough to block any view.

"Any idea what type of place we're looking for?" Jason asked.

"I've never been here before," Silvana said. "We do all our transactions via mail."

"Seriously?"

"Hey. He's like a hundred and forty. And we're going to help him learn how to use the internet. He's going to be behind on a few things."

Freddie was looking at his phone. "So you said this guy's got autism, right? Cause I've been researching how to talk to people with autism. Do you know there's actually a huge difference between how it shows in men and women? And that there are 'categories' of autism?"

"Yeah it's a spectrum, mate," Jason said. "Every case is unique."

"Any tips, Jason?" Silvana asked.

"Yeah. Just let him go at his own rate, don't force him to go at yours. If he wants to talk for ten minutes about mushrooms or quantum physics, just listen. Let him know he's safe to be himself."

Freddie hummed. "Doesn't sound so hard. What about your investigation? Are you going to ask Edward about the attack at the gala?"

"Maybe. But I won't push that hard. He may not be comfortable with me right away." He cut off as the GPS announced their destination up ahead.

They were heading up the side of Black Mountain, just north of Swansea. Large cliff faces of grey stone were topped with empty green fields of grass. There were no properties in the area, and the roads were narrow and bendy.

"I can't see his place anywhere," Jason said. "Are we at the right location?"

"Maybe it's invisible," Freddie asked.

"Invisible?"

"Hey, how the hell should I know what's possible? Silvana, do you have invisible houses?"

Silvana put on a gruff voice. "Damn it man, I'm a vampire, not a wizard."

Freddie laughed. "Ha! Nice."

"Ok, but I still don't see Edward's house," Jason reminded them. "I think we've made a wrong turn somewhere."

Silvana checked Jason's phone. "Google says we're in the right place. According to the map, it should be just there on the right."

"Don't suppose we can call Edward?"

"No. We correspond by mail."

"Right. Geez…"

"Hey!" Silvana suddenly cried out, pointing in front of Jason's face and causing him to slam on the brakes. He turned, and saw what she meant.

A large two-story Victorian house sat sure and steady inside an empty green field.

Jason stopped the car in the middle of the empty road. He stared at the house, or rather the mansion. It had purple wooden walls and a black tiled roof. The second story railing had coiling steel in the grates. There was no fence, no yard, and no property perimeter. Just a single mansion in the middle of nowhere.

"I swear that wasn't there a moment ago," Jason said.

"I swear that too," Silvana said, staring wide-eyed at the mighty structure sitting just by the edge of the road. Freddie was silent. As one, the couple in the front turned around to look back at him. The young man's face was white. "Freddie?" Silvana asked.

"I was…" he swallowed. "I was looking right at it when…it just appeared. No flash of light or anything. Just suddenly there."

It was a very subdued trio who parked the car. Jason's legs ached as he stood for the first time in three hours. He wrapped a thick coat over his shoulders, but the cold British air still stung his face. He could almost feel the mansion's presence looming over him.

"Are we sure about this?" Freddie said. "I don't think this guy is just playing with a chemistry set. He might be a true mad scientist."

"A magical mad scientist," Silvana said.

"Easy, guys," Jason murmured. "Edward's a good man. I'm sure we can trust him."

They walked up to the front of the mansion and came under its shadow. The lawn was cut short. The front door was a plain white wood with an adorned golden handle and knocker. Jason stepped forward and knocked three times.

The door opened without a second's pause.

Edward stood on the other side, dressed in a suit with a grey jacket and brown pants. He looked like someone in a Sherlock Holmes movie with his white shirt and a fluffy plume on the clavicle, and even a black top hat. Jason blinked in surprise. Was this what Edward wore every day? Or was he putting in extra effort to welcome his guests?

Or maybe, this is how people dressed in the Victorian era, when he was born.

"Hello," Edward said. "Welcome to my home." His voice was strained, like he'd practiced the words several times.

"Hi Edward," Jason said. "Thanks for inviting us. It's good to see you again."

"Hi Edward," Silvana echoed.

"This is our friend, Freddie," Jason said, his hand on Freddie's shoulder. "He's my roommate."

Edward nodded. "Homosexuals. I understand."

Jason cut off. He stared at Edward for several seconds. "Oh! No, sorry Edward. Freddie and I are just roommates. That's not code for us being in a relationship. It just means we share a house and live together."

"Yeah. Saves a lot of money," Freddie added.

Edward nodded again. "Defensive. That's normal."

Jason stopped and frowned again. This time he just looked at Freddie and shrugged. Freddie gave a very suggestive wink back. Jason rolled his eyes.

"Freddie is an expert with technology."

"You might say I'm a *wizard* with IT," Freddie chuckled, then cut off when no one laughed. "Uh, I brought my laptop." He lifted up a small bag he wore slung over his shoulder. Edward made no comment.

"I like your suit," Silvana said. "Looks like authentic Victorian era."

"It is Victorian era," Edward corrected.

Jason blinked again. He was wearing a suit that was over one hundred years old? This might be the worst case of 'man holding onto clothes for too long' he'd ever seen.

"I hope you don't mind that we're not dressed up," Silvana said, gesturing to her attire. She was wearing jeans and a captain America t-shirt under her thick jacket. It had been a reference to their conversation at the gala, and Jason had thought it a very thoughtful gesture.

"Oh I just like this suit," Edward said as he tugged on the lapels of his jacket. He seemed very proud of it.

Jason smiled. "It looks great."

"I wish I had one," Freddie added with a smile.

A silence spread over the group. Edward kept staring at their feet, his hand on the door. Jason exchanged a glance with the others, then worked up the courage to be direct. "Uh...can we come in?"

"Of course," Edward said, but he made no move to step out of the entranceway.

Jason hesitated, then politely squeezed past him through the narrow gap. Up close, Edward smelt of old cotton and…some kind of strawberry shampoo. *Not what I expected.* The others followed into the hallway.

The inside of the mansion had a long hallway that ran from one end of the house to the other, with a single red and brown carpet running along the wooden floorboards. The scent of old wood and musk was overpowering. Yet the house seemed much cleaner than Jason had expected. He could feel fresh air on his face from the other end of the house.

"The basement is off limits."

Edward had said it out of nowhere. Jason couldn't help the feeling of suspicion that clung to him. He wrestled the thought down and just nodded. "That's ok. Um… could I trouble you for some water?"

"I have water!" Edward declared and started jogging down the hallway.

A few minutes later the trio found themselves sitting around an old Victorian table, each with a wine glass filled with water in front of them. Edward sat opposite them, staring at the empty chairs. Jason politely sipped the water. It was too-small a serving. Edward had clearly filled it like it was a small taster of expensive wine, instead of water for rehydrating. Jason had to resist the urge to gulp it down and ask for more.

"So," Silvana said, brushing her hair back. "Do you live here with anyone?"

Edward shook his head.

"You could get a roommate," Freddie suggested. "I mean, just a friend to live with for company."

"Well, sometimes I think I would like company," Edward said. "It's a big house and I have more space than I need. I can never keep it clean enough." Jason stared at the immaculately clean kitchen and dining room, but decided not to say anything. "I wouldn't mind someone living here to help with the cleaning. But they would make their own mess. I guess I don't like change. I like things to be in the same place as I left them. Especially with my lab. I have ingredients that could do a lot of damage in the wrong hands. Better I don't risk it."

Jason smiled as Edward kept explaining his reasons for living alone at length. The alchemist had clearly put a lot of thought into this and was happy for the chance to explain himself. He also knew this to be a common autism trait of focusing on a particular train of thought, even repeating themselves several times for self-assurance. It was best to just listen. Thankfully, Silvana and Freddie seemed to be following his lead.

Eventually Edward went quiet again.

Silvana said, "This is a beautiful home." She waved a hand at the small dining room. Several open shelves were built into the walls, displaying spices, cooking utensils and several household plants. For an old home, it had beautifully modern interior.

"It was my father's," Edward said.

"Was your father an alchemist?" she asked.

"Yes."

Freddie sat up a little straighter. "Oh, actually I'd like to understand that better. How do Immortals pass on their…immortality? Is it random? Like a wizard can have a non-wizard baby, or vice versa?"

Silvana glanced at Jason, a concerned look on her face. Jason understood her right away. He thought Freddie was a little too eager.

"There's no elixir of eternal life," Edward said.

"Oh sure. I just mean, how does someone become an alchemist?

Are you born that way?"

"You have to be born with the aptitude. But the skills are learnt from your parents."

"What's the aptitude?"

"Extreme focus, attention to detail, patience for long processes and unwavering attention. Also belief in the process is vital."

Freddie nodded. "And does it still count if you use stimulants for help?"

"Uh, Freddie?" Jason said, trying to slow his friend down.

"There's no elixir to teach you alchemy quickly," Edward said. "You have to learn it through years of study."

Freddie chuckled. "I didn't mean that kind of stim…you know what? It's cool." He looked at Jason with wide eyes, as if to say '*help me*'.

"So, Edward," Jason said. "I heard that you helped out Silvana last weekend, after the explosion. Thank you for that."

"She hired my services." He looked at Silvana directly, showing a rare moment of eye contact. "Thank you for your on-time payments."

Silvana smiled back. "Glad I could do it. You really came to my rescue that night."

Jason frowned. *How did she get money to pay for that?* Still, he wasn't worried about it. He had just noticed that Edward had made eye contact for the exchange. Maybe he was growing more comfortable. Or he found Silvana pretty. Either way, this was going well.

"I heard you put out the fire. What did you use?"

"A vortex of ice."

Jason blinked. "How…uh…how does that work?"

"Super-charged bomb of sub-zero temperatures, concentrated in a self-contained ball of air. After all, cold is just the absence of heat. When cold appears, heat rushes in to fill the void. The vortex pulled the heat into itself to neutralize the excess."

Freddie gasped. "Wait. That's not magic, that's chemistry. Absorb the heat." He frowned in thought. "And the vortex is actually a vacuum that would suck in air, right? Deprive the flame of oxygen and starve it on both fronts."

Edward nodded several times. "The real challenge is the off switch. The vortex is set to automatically turn off once the flames are gone, otherwise it could keep sucking in heat until it wipes out all life on earth."

"Well by that point it would form a gravitational pull, and we'd have bigger things to worry about!"

Edward laughed loudly, and the sharp bark made Jason jump. "I hadn't thought about the gravity! I wonder if it could become a black hole!"

Freddie grinned back. "It would certainly fix the fire, that's for sure."

Edward barked out a laugh again. "You're really funny," Edward said.

"Thank you. You're really smart," Freddie said.

"Do you want to see my lab?"

Freddie burst into smile. "Absolutely!"

The two men leapt to their feet and sprinted from the room, leaving Jason and Silvana sitting in silence.

"Well," Silvana said. "I think it's fair to say that bringing Freddie was a good idea."

"Right?!" Jason said, and they chuckled. He took the chance to cross to the kitchen sink and fill his glass with more water, then drained it twice. He sat back down a moment later and took Silvana's hand. "You were doing really well."

"Really? I barely said anything. I didn't know what to say."

"But you listened. That's important."

"Yeah," Silvana said, trailing off in thought. "It's funny. I always thought Edward was rude. But he's not actually that rude. He's just very direct and blunt."

"He just doesn't understand social cues. It's everyone else who sees rudeness where none is intended."

Silvana nodded eagerly. "But that's just it. He's not stupid either. Cause sometimes things go over his head, but he *knows* something happened. He just doesn't know *what*."

"Absolutely. He's very smart. You hear all that stuff he said about science? I didn't understand any of it."

Silvana laughed. "Me neither. And I studied medicine!"

"The black hole thing was concerning though."

"I'll say."

The sounds of Edward's laughter came from upstairs, and they both giggled in response.

"You started asking about how he helped me at the gala," Silvana said. "Was that you trying to start a subtle interrogation about that night?"

"Kinda. That attempt ended pretty quickly. I think Edward will focus on different things. I may have to be more direct."

"Can I help?"

He grinned. "I'll let you know. For now, we should probably go join them."

"Oh. He didn't invite us?"

"I think that was just an oversight. We'll knock before entering."

They stood up and wandered through the halls until they found the spiral stairs leading upwards. Jason scanned the upper floor. It was almost a mirror of the lower floor with a long hallway down the centre. Yet it was shorter, cause at the end it turned into one giant alchemist laboratory.

It was huge to the point where Jason checked the outer walls to make sure this room wasn't somehow bigger than physically possible, like the inside of the TARDIS. There were rows of IKEA shelves on the outside, and dozens of work stations spread throughout the middle. Each station had rows of tools, vials, jars, boxes. Cauldrons were everywhere. Some sprouted black smoke, others bubbled and splattered little drops of green goo.

"Hey guys," Freddie called. Jason had to tear his gaze off the room towards the people.

"Don't touch anything," Edward said. "Just stay by the stairs there."

Jason nodded. "Ok, sure thing."

Silvana glanced at him. "He wants us to just stand here? That's a bit much."

"I think we'd stress him out if we came in. He's watching Freddie very carefully." Silvana sighed, but seemed to accept it.

Edward was showing Freddie a cauldron and explaining the order of ingredients. Jason struggled to hear them, and even what he heard was hard to comprehend, so he just looked around. There was plenty here to see.

The lab was perfectly ordered. Jason had expected something this big to be chaotic. But everything was stacked neatly in the shelf. Even jobs in progress had materials positioned to one side. Jason noticed everything was labelled. Every vial, jar, workbench, had a little white label. Even the extensive shelving was labelled in a numbered system like a library.

Yet something felt off. Jason couldn't put his finger on it. But he was getting a strange feeling. An instinct. A gut impression. Something made him uncomfortable. He kept searching the room. *Containers of wax, herbs, oil. Cloths for cleaning, empty beakers for measuring, dishes beside several sinks, drying. Something...*

He looked back at the cloths. The fabric was not folded neatly. It was scrunched together. *Is that all I was worried about? One messy thing in a room of perfect order?*

One of the cloths was black. It looked like a different material, like an item of clothing that should be worn, like pants or a suit jacket.

In fact, it looked exactly like a suit jacket. Made of cheap synthetic polyester that had a noticeable plastic glisten on the surface.

That's my cheap suit jacket. Mine! The one I gave to...Samantha Kennedy.

He felt a chill creep up the back of his neck. Why did Edward have that jacket? Had he collected it like some sort of souvenir? Had he taken it off her dead body? Or was he investigating it for clues on orders of the Imperium?

Jason didn't know. And he knew it was unfair to start making judgment calls about Edward. The jacket was circumstantial evidence at best. In a court of law, it wouldn't hold up to anything.

But what if...

"Hey," he said in a cheerful voice. "Let's go back downstairs."

Silvana agreed instantly and took his hand. She must have sensed something was up. They glimpsed at Freddie and Edward, and ducked back downstairs without a word.

"Your heartrate went up significantly," Silvana said when they got to the first floor. "What happened?"

"He has my jacket. The one from the gala. It was on Sam Kennedy's body when she died."

Silvana's face went even more white than normal. Jason had forgotten she had seen that body. A reminder could bring up trauma. But a moment later Silvana seemed to push through the shock. "He could be part of the official Imperium investigation."

"Or the official cover up." Jason grimaced. "I know this is going to sound bad, but I want to check the basement."

"The one place he said we..." Silvana cut off. "Actually, that makes sense. If he was hiding anything, it'd be there. But he's an alchemist. I don't know what he's capable of. If he decided to fight us, I don't know if I could take him."

"Then let's be quick."

They moved down the hallway and started checking every door for a stairwell. Every room was just as tidy as everything else, but also normal looking. Nothing indicating an Immortal person lived here. Just a study, living areas, library room, and lounge rooms. Yet as normal as it was, it still looked like a set for Downton Abbey, designed with a different era in mind.

"I don't know what we're looking for," Jason said.

"Hurry," Silvana hissed back. "He's talking quieter, like he's listening for us."

Jason huffed in frustration. *Should we even be doing this? Edward has shown trust. We could just ask him. No, I'll ask him after we've seen the basement, so we know if he's telling the truth.*

They came back to the dining room they'd been in before. "That's everywhere," Silvana whispered. "The basement must be hidden. Oh, why did he even tell us we couldn't go there? We'd never know there was a basement without that!"

"Can you still hear him upstairs?"

Silvana listened. "Yeah I can…" she cut off. She turned sharply to Jason. "I can hear airflow." Jason shrugged at her. "Airflow *beneath* us, Jason."

He gasped. "You're a genius."

"Ssh," she held up her hand and started listening. She tiptoed out of the dining area and back down the hallway. Jason followed her on silent footsteps. She suddenly stopped still. He tried not to breath. Then she reached down and pull back the old rug that ran down the hallway.

A trapdoor sat beneath, with an old black gripper and ancient hinges. It folded into the wood so that you could stand on it without finding it.

"Brilliant!" Jason said.

Silvana started to lift it slowly, and stopped immediately. "What if it squeaks?"

They froze for a moment. "No, Edward is super clean. I'm betting he would oil the hinges so they don't squeak."

She frowned. "Are you sure?"

"Certain," he lied. "Let's go."

She set her jaw and lifted. The trapdoor shifted…and *creaked* slowly. Silvana flinched and held still. She glanced at the ceiling. "We're good." She glared at Jason. "I believe the word you used was 'certain.'"

"Sorry!"

She huffed and lifted the trap door open all the way in one smooth motion. The creak was over quickly. The room downstairs was dark, and a set of grey stone steps led below. Jason leapt forward to go first. He placed his hand on the trapdoor edge for balance, and found a rubber seal along the edges, like he'd seen on the side of fridges. Yet the air wasn't cold. *What's that for?*

He crawled into the darkness and felt each step with his feet. He pulled his phone out and hit flashlight, then he went down the steps carefully. He shone the light around the room. Just rows of boxes for storage. Old furniture, all with plastic sheets covering them. He aimed the light higher, towards the back of the room.

Something lay on a table. A plastic sheet over top. It was shaped like a person.

"Oh my god."

Jason ran across the room and Silvana followed. He held the light up high. His footsteps thundered in the closed space. He reached the table.

It was human.

The person was under a white plastic covering, just clear enough to show the colour of skin underneath. They were naked and almost certainly dead, judging by how rigid and motionless they sat.

"Do you think…" Silvana said.

Jason reached for the face and pressed down on the plastic to smooth it out.

It was Samantha Kennedy.

"Oh no," he whispered. "Why is her body here?" He turned to face Silvana. Her eyes were wide. "Is he like a mortician for immortals? Is he doing an autopsy?"

"Or is this a creepy sex thing?" Silvana winced.

He looked back at Samantha. Her body looked strange. The skin was…coloured. He thought it'd be white and pasty.

"Oh my god," Silvana whispered. "Where's her wound?"

Jason looked at the neck, shining the torch on it. It was fine. The wound was gone. "Edward must have sewn it…"

The body lurched up.

"Fuck!" Jason cried and stumbled back. The body sat upright. The arms reached out. "Holy Jesus!" he cried and turned to run.

Edward was right behind him.

Jason and Silvana froze in place. Edward stared at them with a blank face, blinking from the bright light of Jason's phone. He held a vial in his hand. The stopper was unplugged, and purple fumes rose upwards.

"What are you doing in my basement?" he whispered.

Behind them in the darkness, the body of Samantha Kennedy let out a raspy cry.

Chapter 20

Silvana was ready for a fight.

Edward was staring at them, his eyes settling just below their faces. But Silvana was more concerned about the inhuman moans coming from Samantha's rising body.

"Is she a zombie?" she asked.

"Of course," Edward responded as if it were the simplest of questions.

Samantha was trying to move her arms, but the plastic sheet pinned them to her sides. She moaned loudly and thrashed around, her legs kicking out and her torso wiggling like a fish on land. It was too dark to see clearly, yet that only made the thrashing shadows more terrifying. Somehow, she pierced through the sheet and began ripping her way clear.

"Edward, what is going on here?" Jason yelled. "You turned her into a zombie? You can't just do that."

"Yes I can."

Hell, he chills me when he does that. Says everything so matter-of-factly. Silvana clutched Jason's arm and stood shoulder to shoulder with him. "You're going to let us out of here, Edward," she said in a warning tone. Edward just stared back at them with a vacant expression.

The zombified Samantha moaned again. Her mouth ripped clear

of the sheet as she lurched forward and fell off the table. Silvana jumped back, and brushed up against Edward who was still standing in the path of the stairs.

"Let us out," Silvana demanded. Edward said nothing.

"Then tell us, is she dangerous?" Jason said. "Will she bite us? Infect us?"

"She won't be a zombie for long."

"What?" Silvana cried.

Edward clasped his hands to his ears and cried, "She won't be a zombie for long." Then louder. "She won't be a zombie for long!"

"Let us out, Edward!" Silvana screamed.

He screamed back, "She won't be a zombie for long!" Samantha's moans grew high pitched and savage. Silvana crouched low and prepared to launch at Edward. *I have to get that elixir in his hand first. I will....*

"Hello? Eddie?"

Edward went quiet. "Freddie?" he cried, still clutching his head in duress.

Freddie came running down the steps and stopped at Edward's side. He spoke in a gentle tone that lowered the volume in the room drastically. "Hey, it's alright, Eddie. Nothing to worry about." He frowned. "Except the naked chick going crazy. That's concerning."

"She won't be a zombie for long," Edward said.

Freddie nodded. "Uh-huh. Zombie, hey? You made a zombie? That's cool, I think." He turned to Jason and Silvana. "What are you guys doing in the basement? He asked us one thing."

"He has a zombie in here," Jason said.

"Probably why he said don't come down here. And didn't you hear him? She won't be a zombie for long. Hey," he turned to Edward. "Mate, are you resurrecting this woman? Bringing her back to life?"

"The zombie state is part of the process," Edward said again.

"Hey, that's awesome! I didn't know you could raise the dead."

"That's necromancy. No one can do necromancy. I can just bring back someone from the dead if they've only been dead an hour."

Jason slapped his forehead. "Your elixir. You told us about that at the gala. I never even thought about it."

Samantha moaned again. Her face was fully clear of the sheet now. Her eyes were crazed and alien, almost glowing in the darkness. There was no conscious mind behind them. She placed her feet underneath her and stood.

Edward suddenly jerked forward and shoved Silvana aside. She fumed, but bore the disrespect without reacting. Edward took the elixir in his hand and with the other, seized Samantha's jaw. He shoved the elixir down her throat without spilling a drop. Her eyes widened before she started growing quieter. Her muscles went limp, her head lolled to the side, and she seemed to fall asleep within seconds.

"I need to get her on the bed," Edward said.

"I'm on it, Eddie," Freddie said and crouched beside him. They lifted Samantha back up and laid her down on the table. Edward took another plastic sheet from under the table and laid it across her like a tablecloth.

Edward turned around and looked at the ground. "She'll probably wake up tonight. She'll be like a child at first, but her brain's capacity will return over several days. This time next week, she'll be herself again."

"You're trying to save her," Jason said.

Silvana was sick to her stomach. Edward's vacant face did not show any hurt or sadness, but that was surely what he was feeling. *God, what have I done? Did I assume the worst of him because of the autism? Am I prejudice?*

"Edward," she whispered. "I am so sorry."

"Yes, me too," Jason said. "This was a terrible mistake, and it was all my fault. I saw my jacket upstairs. Samantha was wearing it when she died, and I had to know what was going on. I should have just asked you. I'm sorry I disrespected you like this."

"If there's anything we can do to make it up to you," Silvana said, "please tell us."

Edward just blinked at them. "No harm was done. And Freddie's still going to teach me how to use the internet, right?"

"Right, man."

"Then there's nothing to fix."

Edward climbed back up the stairs and left without another word. Silvana felt like her heart was breaking. *He wasn't angry. Not even a little. What a beautiful soul.*

"Well," Freddie said dryly. "I hope you're happy."

"Freddie, please don't," Jason started.

"Excuse me, you invited me as your guest. Was I just a distraction so you could break and enter?"

"It's not breaking and entering if you're already in the house."

"Well thank you, Officer Turner," Freddie drawled. "What about all those tips you gave us? On how to treat Edward properly?" As Freddie grew louder, his faint Korean accent grew thicker. "Maybe you forgot to add, 'don't lie to him and deliberately do things he asked you not to do'. Cause I heard that might piss off people with autism. For regular people though, it's totally fine."

"Freddie…"

"Come on man!" Freddie took a breath. "That guy was telling me so much about alchemy, then he gets scared and starts running."

"Hey," Silvana cut in. She lowered her voice to a whisper. "Freddie, are you trying to find immortality?"

He shrugged. "Are you offering?"

She glared back. "You've been asking about this a lot. I hope you're not just using Edward in the hopes he teaches you magic…"

"Oh please," Freddie said. "Me using him? I've already given him a nickname. Didn't you hear me call him Eddie? He fucking loves it! I told him we are Freddie and Eddie, the dynamic duo. He must have repeated it back to me twenty times he loves it so much. So no, your royal vampireness, I'm not using him to find immortality."

"Are you sure?" Jason said. "I know you're a good guy, Freddie, but you seem really fascinated by Immortals. I'd hate for you to go to the dark side."

Freddie's temper seemed to ease off then. "Ah. Cause I joined a cult last time. That's a far concern, I guess. And only a true friend would call me on it."

"You're…welcome?" Silvana made it a question.

"Don't worry, I won't go to the dark side. How about I make it an exchange instead? He introduces me to immortality, and I'll introduce him to internet porn." He grinned. "Hey hey?" No one laughed. "Fine. I'll be careful. And I suggest you two follow your own advice. Now, I'm going to teach that hundred and fifty year old coot how to use a keyboard and mouse. Please stay out of trouble." He turned around and climbed back up the stairs.

Silvana looked at Jason. He just sighed. "We should probably get away from this zombie infested basement." He looked back at Samantha with a frown on his face. "But I think we need to stay in this house until she wakes up."

"I don't understand," Edward said. "How can all the computers talk to each other if they don't use magic?"

"It's wireless technology," Freddie explained. "Just think of it as computers can talk to each other over a distance cause they have super loud voices that only computers can hear."

Edward nodded. "Why didn't you just say that?"

"Cause it's a terrible metaphor, bruh."

Silvana had listened to them talk around the kitchen table for hours. Edward kept asking the same questions over and over for reassurance, and Freddie had limitless patience for him. Silvana wished she could say the same about herself.

"I can't believe we broke into his basement," Jason whispered.

Silvana leant back in her couch. The lounge room was comfortable if a little sparse, with multiple couches arranged in a U shape and zero decorations. It was the best place to wait out the day until Samantha woke up, and they could keep an eye on 'Freddie and Eddie' in the other room. Meanwhile, Jason was sulking, and Silvana was trying to get him out of it.

"I encouraged you," Silvana said. "You were just being suspicious because of the jacket. I was the one being prejudice."

"But I should have known better," he said. "I betrayed a friend's trust. I never do that."

Silvana almost sighed out loud. Sometimes Jason seemed to forget that she was about four times his age. Not to mention that Immortal culture dictated that, as her mortal knight, she was the master and he was the servant. They didn't hold to that principle at all, but still. In a legal sense, she was the one responsible for big decisions.

Like your massive investment plan. It had been a week, yet she was still nervous. The man at Kennedy and Sons seemed trustworthy and good at his job. Her money was in good hands. It was just hard to trust herself. It seemed every two seconds she flipped between utter surety and crippling self-doubt. She couldn't help being nervous about all her decision making. She would feel better once the first payments came through. One day soon, she'd rub her money in her aunt's faces.

"This is all new to me," Silvana said. Jason stared at her silently.

"We both want me to be more independent. I think we're doing that. But it means I need to start making decisions, and making your own decisions in life is hard."

"That's true."

"It's like sometimes I get so worried that I'm not moving fast enough. So I sprint ahead and end up going too fast."

"Yeah. But it was my idea too, ok?"

Silvana blinked at him. It took her a moment to realise he was still talking about the basement, not her investment. *Maybe I should tell him about the money. Would he be mad at me, or proud? He might be furious that I broke the law and committed fraud with Nicholas's signature.* She should trust him either way. Open up and admit what she had been doing. He had backed her up on everything so far. Surely he would support her on this.

"It's not your fault," Jason said.

She just smiled back sweetly. "Thank you, Jason." He accepted it, and leaned back in his chair. She added nothing further.

Freddie's voice grew louder in the other room. "We've got to buy you your own laptop, then get an internet connection installed in your house."

"Why can't I just have your laptop?" Edward asked.

"Whoa man. That thing is my child, ok? It's precious to me."

"I can buy it off you."

"Bro, it's a gaming laptop. It was pretty expensive."

"How's a hundred thousand pounds? Is that enough?"

Freddie went silent. There was a long pause.

Jason shouted, "Freddie, you cannot sell your laptop for a hundred thousand pounds!"

"Come on, Jason. Let's not be hasty."

"Freddie!"

A loud sigh came from the kitchen. "Fine. Eddie you can't give me a hundred thousand pounds. I bought it for nine hundred pounds, alright? Nine zero zero. But we could get you the same make and model so you're comfortable with it."

"I don't like going shopping," Edward said.

"Hey, I can teach you to shop online. Get stuff delivered to your house. You'll never need to leave again."

"That sounds amazing! I can't—"

A chair squeaked on the floor and Edward's voice cut off. Footsteps thudded from somewhere below.

"Eddie?" Freddie called. The alchemist hurried past the doorway to the lounge. Silvana and Jason leapt up and jogged into the hallway to follow. Edward had rushed to the trap door and thrown it open. He looked up. His eyes met Silvana's.

"The wizard is awake."

Then he disappeared down the basement stairs. Silvana stared at his retreating form, unable to make herself follow. "Eddie!" Freddie shouted and ran down the trapdoor after him without hesitating.

"Well, there's a fine thing," Silvana said. "A mortal runs underground, when an Immortal dares not? Oh I'd never hear the end of it." She laughed wildly, though Jason's answering laugh had a tinge of nervousness to it. *I think I'm hysterical with fear*, she thought absently.

The basement was dark but for the flickering light of several candles. Silvana could hear raspy breathing from ahead, the sound too soft for human ears to pick up. Fingers scratched against plastic and wood. A breath became a murmur, which in turn became a whimper. Silvana's eyes adjusted to the dim light and the faint outline of dark silhouettes emerged from the wall of black. One lay on the table. The other two crowded around them.

"Samantha Kennedy," Edward said. "You are waking up. Do not be alarmed."

A loud "Mmmm!" came from the wizard.

"Eddie? What can I do?"

"Hold her down. She might injure herself."

Silvana approached the table. She could hear Jason's heartbeat from beside her. She saw Samantha lift her head, her eyes frenzied with panic. Her gaze locked onto the two men holding down her arms.

"Do not be alarmed," Edward said. "You are safe. I have raised…"

"*TAB IZI!*" the wizard screamed.

Silvana let the blood surge within her, and with superhuman speed she grabbed Edward and Freddie and yanked them back just as a wall of flame burst from the wizard. The roar of the passing fire was like the howling wind of a cyclone. Heat seared the front of Silvana's body as the basement lit up with red. She covered her face and pressed her body against the floor. The flames died off as Samantha gave an animalistic snarl and stood over the fallen trio, still wrapped in her plastic sheets.

"Where am I?" she cried. "Khadija? *Khadija!*"

"You're in England!" Jason cried, standing a few steps away and keeping his distance. "You are Samantha Kennedy. I am Jason Turner, we met at the immortal gala at the Burj Khalifa. I gave you a jacket. You and Khadija are our friends."

What are you doing, Jason? She's a weapon of mass destruction, and she's crazy. It'll only take a hair-trigger to set her off. Silvana clenched her fists. *I should rip out her throat and save us all…*

Samantha let out a whimper. "Where? I don't…" she muttered and a white light spread out of her hand. Silvana blinked at the sudden blinding effect. The others were holding up hands to cover their eyes. Samantha had become invisible, almost transcendent, behind a luminous wall of light. "I don't know any of you."

"You died," Edward explained. "It's normal to experience memory loss."

"Died?" Samantha cried. "No no no," she began to whimper. "I can't…who killed me?"

"We brought you back," Jason cried. "You're ok now. We're going to help you."

"*Who killed me?!*" she screamed.

The sudden noise made them all cower. Jason was on his knees now. Freddie was covering his head with his hands. And Edward had just pulled a clear vial out of his robes. *What is he planning to do with that? Is he thinking the same thing I am? That we have to take her down? This might be our only chance.*

"We don't know who killed you," Jason said. "We're investigating. I was hoping you might remember—"

"I don't remember anything!" Samantha cried, her hands clenching fistfuls of her hair. "The last thing I remember…John? Do you know John, my great nephew? No, he was shot, wasn't he? That was years ago."

"Samantha, you need to calm down," Jason said. "You're among friends. We're here to help you. Just sit back down on the table and we'll check…"

"Where's Khadija? Is she safe?"

"She's safe," Silvana said. "She came to see us. She's fine. She doesn't know you're here."

"Did Khadija say who killed me? Does she know?"

Silvana glanced at Jason. Khadija had given them a name to investigate. Should they tell her? Probably not, right? She might do something terrible.

Samantha growled, "Too late. *Śuhür!*" Suddenly Freddie lurched up into the air with a scream and floated directly into her outstretched hand. The hand that shone with white light was cut off by Freddie's struggling body. His scream was cut off by choking gargles.

"Freddie!" Jason cried.

Silvana launched herself in Samantha's direction. In a flash she crossed the room and stretched her hands towards Samantha's throat.

"*Haš Edün!*" she shrieked, and an invisible force struck Silvana down mid-flight. She slammed into a rack of shelves and hurtled the whole thing sideways, landing and rolling onto her back as dozens of items scattered all around her. Silvana cried out in pain. *Damn it! I waited too long to attack.*

"Who killed me?" Samantha screamed. "Who did Khadija say killed me? Tell me now, or I'll burn your friend to ash."

Freddie choked, "Jase…"

"Glucksburg!" Jason cried. "She thought it was the Glucksburgs. You two interviewed them. The Knight Wilhelm and the wizard Ingolf. Khadija thought they might have turned on you, but we don't know for sure. It's just a suspicion! I'm in the middle of investigating them. I'll find something. But right now we need to think about this calmly. Now please put my friend down."

Instead, Samantha lifted him higher. His legs kicked out wildly. The wizard raised her other hand towards Silvana.

"Those murderers!" she shrieked.

Edward threw the vial. It splashed at Samantha's feet, and a pink mist quickly spread out and covered the entire room.

The wizard dropped Freddie, letting him fall to the ground gasping. Samantha held her hands to her head and moaned. "Nooo…" she cried. "What are you doing to me?"

"Edward," Jason moaned, holding his head. "What is that? It's…"

"Jason?" Silvana clutched him. She breathed in the powerfully scented cloud. It smelt strong, like hospital grade cleaning products, yet it didn't affect her.

"It's a Regrowth Potion," Edward said. "It should speed up her brain's recovery. She'll remember who she is quicker this way."

"Uh… buddy? What's in that potion?" Freddie said, and Samantha began to sway on her feet.

"Bat wings, snake scales, crushed worms," Edward started listing. Yet the whole time, the room began to shake around them. Samantha rose off the ground and floated in the air, her body twitching, light flickering from her hands. "Panax ginseng, hyssop, marjoram, and rosemary."

"What does that even mean?" Freddie cried.

"Should work like a healing elixir. But I added a few things to speed up her brain, making the healing faster."

"Faster?" Freddie yelled. "Oh mate, I know that smell. It smells like crystal meth!"

"That's what I added."

"What?! Are you telling me you've just put her into a drug craze?! And all of us too?"

"It'll be quicker this way."

"EDDIE!"

Samantha's eyes were growing bloodshot. She kept wiping at her nose as she jerked and twitched in little spasms.

"Edward!" Silvana cried. "You need to fix this."

"I can't reverse it."

Samantha shrieked, and the ground itself began to shake. Silvana braced herself as the house rumbled. Shelves fell over and debris spread across the floor. The wizard threw out her hands as flames danced along her arms and shredded the plastic covering wrapping her body. A second later fabric and cloth came rushing towards her from around the room. A blanket unravelled into individual threads that rewove themselves into clothes. In seconds Samantha was covered in a long brown wizard robe with a cape, a deep hood, and low wings under her arms. The white light from her hand flickered like a strobe in the darkness.

"GLUCKSBURG!" she screamed.

The world began to shift. The shaking room began to fold in on itself, the walls and roof crossing over each other at impossible angles. The white light and flames emanating from Samantha's body flickered into the opening void of space.

"She's teleporting us!" Silvana screamed.

She tried to dive at the wizard again, claws out, ready to slash her throat. But the world seemed to drop out from underneath her. She fell into open space. Stars flashed by her at light speed and whisked away into the infinite blackness. The wizard's appeared before Silvana, and she reached out a clawed grip, only to grope helplessly at emptiness. She waved her arms wildly as she fell into the void.

Ground appeared from out of the blackness. She spun so she could land on her feet. Instead she ploughed into freezing cold water.

The shock made her breathe in a mouthful of dirty water. She tried coughing and spitting the water back out. It tasted of dirt and pond-scum. Everything was dark. Silvana forced herself to calm her nerves and looked for the surface. *There.* She thrust upwards with powerful strokes and broke the surface.

Everything was just as dark as it had been underwater. The air was cold here. Much colder than Swansea England. There were stars in the sky. *Stars? It's night-time? My God, we've teleported into a different time zone!*

Samantha Kennedy was high above the water, shrieking with rage. The air was swirling around her in a vortex until it was roaring as loud as the wizard's own cries. A tornado formed over the water, churning up the pond into the sky. Silvana searched the bouncing waves for signs of the others. She caught a glimpse of a pristine white castle, lit up with spotlights, resting on the far side of the lake. Above, Samantha's wizard robes and blonde hair were billowing out behind her, a dark shadow spreading across her beautiful face. Despite the fear clawing at Silvana's insides, the scene was awe-inspiring, leaving her senses overwhelmed.

"Jason!?" she cried. No one else had reached the surface. And no one answered her. Silvana dived back beneath the surface.

Everything was black and murky. She had to call on more power to enhance her eyesight, and she could feel her reserves of blood beginning to dry up. She saw movement below. A man was struggling against the sludge and underwater plants that had wrapped around his arms. It was impossible to tell who it was. Silvana swam down, clutched them to her chest and dragged them to the surface.

"…the fuck!?" Freddie spluttered between gasps for air.

"I'll be back," Silvana said with a pat on his shoulder and immediately dived under again. Another form wiggled nearby. She swam forward and caught them around the middle. They thrashed hard against her grip as a hand clawed at her face. *Edward. He's panicking.* She nearly let go, but instead worked against him to pull the alchemist above water.

"Get back! Don't touch me!" Edward screamed.

"I'm trying to save you…"

A high pitch scream cut them off. Samantha had a fully formed water spout spraying over the castle. A black cloud seemed to form in the centre of the storm, humming with energy and slowly rising higher in pitch. Samantha flung her arms out and the storm launched at the castle. Silvana watched as windows were smashed open and half the roof was ripped from the walls.

"Silvy!" a man's voice cried. Silvana saw Jason bobbing on the water nearby. She swam to his side and clutched him around the waist.

"I couldn't find you!" she cried.

"The others?"

"I found both of them while looking for you." She paused as he gasped for breath. "I like the nickname, by the way."

"Nickname?"

"Silvy."

"Oh. Truth be told, I was trying to say your name, but I choked before I could finish."

"That's what she said."

Jason stared at her. "Really? Now?"

Another shrill scream cut them off. Samantha was levitating across the water and moving towards the damaged castle. She suddenly plummeted down and touched the earth. The moment her feet came into contact with the ground, it began to shake. A huge rumbling sound of grinding stone seemed to fill the whole world. Trees swayed and bent, before being ripped out of the ground by their roots, a chorus of sickening cracks of branches and trunks. The water rippled violently. Flakes of paint and wood crumbled off the castle walls and floated down like pieces of confetti.

"Is she causing an earthquake?" Jason said while treading water.

"We need to take her down, before she hurts someone."

They swam towards Freddie and Edward through the choppy water. The alchemist was struggling with the waves. "I don't think he can swim," Freddie said.

"I can swim. I just haven't done it for a hundred years."

Silvana sighed. "Let me help you. We've got to reach Samantha."

"Don't touch me," Edward growled.

"Eddie, she needs to touch you in order to help." Freddie had to shout to be heard over the earthquake. "It's just until she gets you to the shore. Then she'll stop touching you, ok?"

Edward let out a moan, but didn't say anything, so Silvana took that as permission. She threw his arm over her shoulder and began to swim. She kept both of their heads above the water. "How do we stop her?"

"We cannot fight a wizard," Edward said.

"But we have to stop this rampage."

Jason shouted, "What about the other wizard? Glucksburg's wizard Ingolf. He might kill Samantha before we can intervene."

"Well that's good, right?"

"No no no," Edward cried. "She must live. All my work cannot be for nothing."

Silvana stared at his face from up close. He was avoiding her gaze. "Who hired you to save her?"

"No one."

"Edward!?"

"We can create a sleep draft. That castle should have a kitchen. Get me there. Give me five minutes, and I can brew a potion to knock Samantha out."

Silvana growled as they started swimming. "Fine. Sounds like a pla—"

The front doors of the castle swung open and a man stepped through. The spotlights kept his face cast in shadows, but Silvana could see the long wizard robes billowing out behind him. A second man stood at his side, a two-handed long sword in one hand, and a shotgun in the other. One of the men shouted something in another language. Samantha responded by making the earthquake grow in intensity. The waves on the lake thrashed against the side of the castle.

A flash of light came from the male wizard as a wall of flame ten stories high surged towards Samantha. The earthquake was cut off and a tornado burst up in front of her. It sucked in all the flames until the turret was a dark red that splashed out little tongues of orange. With a backhanded wave, Samantha sent the firestorm rushing towards the wizard and knight. The entire landscape was suddenly covered in thick black smoke and embers. Little pools of flame sprung up across the building and grounds. Even Silvana could only see the outline of figures now.

It seemed inevitable that the firestorm would fall on the castle and shred it apart. Instead, it jerked to a stop. The storm began to shake violently, tilting one way and then another, as the two wizards battled their magic against each other for control.

A spark of gold lit up the night. Silvana watched as it came again, and she recognised the shotgun blast. The knight had sheathed his sword and was charging at Samantha with his shotgun firing. Samantha seemed momentarily stunned. Then she spoke something inaudible over the sounds of the firestorm, and at her spoken command, the earth opened up and swallowed the knight. But the act distracted her, and the male wizard seized control of the firestorm and ripped it apart in a spray of red. The smoke cloud settled and visibility returned. Samantha had levitated away from the castle and towards the nearby township. The male wizard waved his hand and pulled his knight back to the surface of the ground, and together they charged after her.

Silvana finally reached the castle, still dragging Edward through the water. There was no ground here. The castle had been built entirely over water. However, Samantha's attacks had created a gap in the wall, so Silvana hoisted Edward up into the gap and onto solid ground. She followed a second later, then turned around to help Jason and Freddie climb up as well.

"Jesus, did you guys see that?" Freddie cried. "An earthquake and a tornado! They're fucking gods!"

"How can we stop this?" Jason said. "Fuck me, do we even have a chance?"

Edward stood up and made hard eye contact with him. "I can make a potion to put her to sleep, but I need five minutes and a well-stocked kitchen." He was repeating himself. "Freddie can help me.

You two have to keep her alive until then."

"Alive?" Silvana growled. "Why alive? She's a massive threat right now. She could kill innocent people and expose the Immortal world." Jason stared at her, open-mouthed. "What? Call me ruthless, but it'd be safer to stop her."

"She must live!" Edward shouted. "She must survive! You saw what happened when the knight attacked her. She cannot face the wizard and the knight alone. She must be supported."

"Then you can support her, alchemist!"

"I can't, I have to make the sleep potion to end this. You must ensure she survives."

Silvana nearly screamed back, but Jason cut in. "We can't go up against those two. We're unarmed. I don't have my gun, or even my sword."

"Uh, mate?" Freddie said and pointed. "There's a sword on the wall behind you."

Everyone turned to look. Silvana hadn't taken in her surroundings till now. They were standing in a medieval style lounge room, with a stone fireplace and a coat of arms hanging on the mantle piece above. Two genuine swords of fine craft where sheathed through the display. Jason sighed as he ripped a sword from the wall. It was a sabre, long and slightly curved, sharpened for slashing and stabbing.

"Fine," Jason said. "Silvana and I will try to support her. But only if talking doesn't work. You two just be damn quick with the potion."

"On it, mate," Freddie said and patted Edward on the shoulder. "Come on, Eddie. We have to save the freaking day." The duo left the room at a sprint, and Jason turned to face Silvana.

"Are you sure?" he asked. Something about his tone was off. He was vulnerable. "We don't have to do this."

"Jason? We can't just leave. There's a whole town over there, with people who could get hurt if..."

"What if *you* get hurt?"

She saw it now. He wasn't afraid of the wizards or their powers. He was afraid of losing her. Silvana hesitated a moment. Then she stood up straight. "Sir Jason," she ordered. "You are a Knight Templar, sworn to protect your charge. Now stand by my side as we go into battle. That is your place."

He stood up straight to match her, the glow of pride in his eyes. "Yes, my love." He eyed Silvana, and the second sword in the mantelpiece. "You want one?"

"I trust my strength," she said.

"Right. Let's do this."

He held the sword at his side in one hand and dived into the water, swimming towards the town where the wizards were battling. Silvana took a moment to watch him with pride in her eyes. Yet the same fear played in her mind. *What if he gets hurt?* Silvana flexed her hands into fists. She wouldn't let that happen. Then she dived into the water after him.

Chapter 21

They reached the shore at the same time. Jason was glancing back at her longingly, the same fear of loss burning in his eyes. They began running across grass and patches of wizard fire towards the nearby bitumen road. They crossed a car park by the lake's edge and sprinted towards the nearby buildings. Huge flashes of white light came from over the town. A shotgun could be heard in the distance, firing loud blasts. People were screaming. Several locals had taken to the streets and were running away from the sounds of conflict, covering their heads and clutching at young ones. Silvana couldn't see any injuries. A huge crack of lightning shot into the sky with a deafening roar, and for a moment, the night became as bright as day. Then the lightning faded, leaving an afterimage burned into the backs of Silvana's eyes.

Dammit. Maybe Jason was right, and I should be running away. How the hell can we fight that?

They ran along the street until they reached the first corner. The buildings were four or five stories tall made of old brick and stone. Silvana spotted movement just as a figure was blown through the wall of a block of units and out the other side, ripping a great hole in the structure at the same time. The wizard flung out her arms and steadied herself in mid-air. Samantha's blonde hair rippled out behind her from the force of the blow. Yet somehow, being knocked through a building only seemed to enrage her further.

"That should have crushed her," Jason cried. "How did she survive? Are wizards physically strong too?"

"They must have spells on their persons," Silvana said. "Like a magical shield to absorb attacks. There's no other way they're strong enough. Hell, that attack would have killed me."

The wizard Ingolf flew towards her. He raised his arm back and a mighty lance of blue fire and wind sprung from his hand. It looked like he held a tornado in a single thin column of air with flames swirling inside. People on the streets were screaming in terror. With a roar, Ingolf swung his arm over his shoulder. The tornado arched up fifty meters into the sky and came down like a hammer, swatting Samantha out of the air. But at the last second she raised her arms over her head and seemed to absorb the worst of the blow. She was forced down, but not all the way into the earth. Instead, she formed another column of air around her person and shot upwards as if out of a cannon, pushing through his attack. She collided with Ingolf and they both spun end over end as they raised further skyward.

"He's trying to force her towards the ground, and she's trying to stay airborne," Jason said. "The Knight Wilhelm must be below. He'll shoot her in the back while she's distracted."

"You're right," Silvana said, impressed. "We could restrain him, two vs one. And I'm a vampire, so I count as two."

"It still won't be easy. He's a fully armed and trained knight. And if we succeed, we'll still have to stop Samantha. Though how we can stop a wizard is beyond me."

Silvana stopped short in the street amidst debris and rubble. Jason ran on a few steps, before realising and turning back. "Silvy? What are you..."

"We need another wizard," Silvana said. "Of course. We need to call Khadija."

Jason's face lifted. "But how? She's on the run. It's not like we can call the royal family of Dubai and ask to speak to…"

"She gave us her card!" Silvana cried and drew it out of her back pocket. "At the gala. She gave us her contact details."

"Oh." Jason frowned. "You just carry that card with you?"

She rolled her eyes as she searched her pockets. "Damn, I don't have my phone."

"Right." Jason focused on a person running past them. He intercepted them with his hands raised. "Hey hey, I need a phone." He gestured to his ear for a phone. The local man said something in what sounded like Danish. Jason fumbled. "Call the police? You know, um…" He badly imitated a European police siren. But it worked and the man handed him a mobile before sprinting away.

Jason passed the phone to Silvana, just as huge chunks of a nearby building were ripped apart and flung up into the sky. One of the wizards smashed them apart, and fragments of concrete rained down on the street.

Someone cried out in terror. Three people were nearby, two adults and a child, directly in the path of falling rubble. Jason was closer to the young girl, so Silvana sped to the parent's side and shielded them with her body. Blocks of concrete struck her back and shoulders and she grunted in pain, her knees buckling with the strain. The rain of debris ended. Silvana ached as she stood up straight. As expected, Jason had shielded the child in his arms. Neither appeared harmed. The parents shouted their thanks, nodding and clasping their hands together, before they grabbed their child and ran.

"You ok?" Jason asked.

"My back took a hit," she said. "I'll be ok."

"You need blood?"

"After this." Silvana still held the stranger's phone and Khadija's card, which she noticed now was laminated. *Good thing, or the lake would have ruined it.* She read the number and dialled with super speed. She glanced around. The streets had started to clear already. Either people had cleared the area, or they had resolved to hide in their homes. This was good. Now she could focus on the wizards.

The phone rang only once before a woman answered in Arabic.

"Khadija?" Silvana cried. "Khadija is that you?"

The voice switched to English. "Who is this?"

"Silvana. You gave me your card at the gala."

"I gave my card to many people. Please be clearer."

A sudden crack came from the sky, and Silvana lost all patience. "Samantha Kennedy is alive! She's attacking the Glucksburg palace. She's fighting Ingolf right now. You need to come help her!"

The phone was silent a moment. Then, "Give me your exact address."

Silvana froze. Something in the cadence of her voice was different. It sounded lower than it should have been. Was Khadija nervous? Or maybe…*this isn't Khadija.*

"Where is Khadija? I need to speak with her," Silvana snapped.

"Khadija is a criminal and has no part of the Al Khalifa family. If you have any dealings with her, you need to turn yourself in to the Immortal Imperium right away." The voice sneered. "Bloody mosquito."

Bloody mosquito? Silvana blinked. "Portia?!"

The receiver filled with the sounds of a woman's laughter. "Don't worry, she guessed," Portia's unmasked voice said to someone in the room with her. Something brushed against the mouthpiece, and a second voice replied in a tone of cold iron.

"Is thou an ally of a criminal, Miss Romanov?"

Silvana scowled. "Desdemona." Jason recoiled back, his lips curled in revulsion. Silvana knew her own face looked the same.

"Thy behaviour art most suspicious. Doth thou wish to confess anything now and save thyself further suffering?"

"There are wizards fighting in a public place. They'll expose the Immortal world. You need to help us."

"I need do nothing," Desdemona growled.

"But it's your job! The Vigiles are supposed to cover up our world."

Desdemona snapped, "Thy place is not to give orders!" Her voice lowered into an icy purr. "Perhaps thy dear knight needs another taste of the crushing grip of a Vigile."

Silvana inhaled deeply, ready to scream. Then remembered who she was talking to. "Fine. We'll handle this ourselves." She hung up. "Khadija isn't coming to help. I don't think the Vigiles care either."

"Crap."

A brilliant flash of lightning lit up the town. A half second later, thunder roared loud enough to shatter glass windows. Silvana covered her ears, yet it still felt like the world was splitting apart. Something hit the ground in front of her.

Samantha Kennedy. The bolt of lightning must have knocked her out of the sky. She was laying right in front of them. Her eyes were vacant and dazed as she stared up to the starry sky.

Jason dived on the wizard before she could act. He dropped his sword and knelt on Samantha's arms, pinning them at her side. He stuck his hand over her mouth to stop her casting spells and wrapped his legs around her middle in a wrestlers move, locking his feet in a grip to keep her down.

Silvana merely watched, considering. *I could slice her throat and be done with it.*

A second later, a wizard swooped down out of the sky and stopped two meters off the ground. Silvana moved to shield Jason with her arms.

"Wizard Ingolf of House Glucksburg!" she screamed. "I am your cousin, Silvana of House Romanov. We're no threat to you. This was a mistake."

The wizard stared at her. Up close, Ingolf looked to be in his late forties. He was clean shaven and handsome, and his hair was long enough to reach over his ears. His eyes were a piercing blue as they narrowed in on her face, and they flashed with the same rage that had summoned lightning just moments ago.

"This woman attacked my home," he said in accented English. "By rights, her life is forfeit. Step aside, or I will destroy you too."

"There's no need," Silvana said. "This wizard is under the influence of a drug. She's not in her right mind. Please, just let us take her from here. We will owe your House a great debt."

"Look what she did to my castle." Ingolf gestured at the white castle by the lake, and even at this distance they could see the chunk blown off the corner and the burning scars across the entire façade, coated black with soot and dust. "Glucksburg castle is a national heritage. This bitch has damaged something priceless. Her life belongs to me now. Stand aside."

Jason let out a growl. Silvana turned to see him struggling against Samantha. He was barely keeping her under control. His legs pinned her body down. His left hand was over her mouth, and his right arm wrapped around her head in a vice. It was a perfect grip. Yet still he struggled.

"Look at her!" Silvana cried. "She's like a savage animal. Surely you can tell she's under the influence."

Ingolf growled, "She belongs to me! Now fuck off, you filthy vampire whore, or I'll rip out your innards and burn them while you scream."

Silvana gasped. "I'm your family. We share blood."

"Please. You think I'd ever acknowledge a vampire as my own?" He spat towards her with an exaggerated head movement. "Stupid bitch. Your relatives spent the whole gala harassing me with their lower class desperation. I could practically smell the poverty on them. Don't you realise your family is powerless? I could do whatever I wanted to you right now," he leered at her body as he said it, "and no one would dare challenge me."

Silvana felt a cold chill at the pleasure in his eyes.

"Bastard!" Jason roared between struggles. He was glimpsing the sabre at his side, as if thinking of picking it up.

"You dare speak to me, mortal scum?" Ingolf growled. "You are but an insignificant fly, alive today and dead tomorrow. I shall enjoy swatting you from this earth." He raised his hands towards Jason and Samantha, fire beginning to form in his palms.

"Please!" Silvana cried. "We can trade for her. How much do you want for her?"

A gun cocked behind her, and Silvana spun on the spot. The knight Wilhelm was standing behind her, the shotgun aimed at her back. The knight was so handsome it was jarring, his body fit and muscular, and his arms were flexed in readiness.

"Do you wish to die with them?" Wilhelm growled. "Your choice."

Silvana froze. She could shield Jason with her body, but it would only spare him for a second before the wizard simply attacked again. She couldn't take the Glucksburgs on her own. What could she even do in this situation?

From the corner of her eye, she saw Jason nod at her. Then he deliberately weaken his grip over Samantha's mouth. Samantha squirmed out of his grasp and screamed.

"Haš Edün!"

The spell sent out a shockwave that blew everyone backwards. Silvana was thrown off her feet and spun as she flew. The sound of the shotgun cracked once. *Jason!* Silvana twisted mid-air to land on her feet. Jason was ten meters away on the ground, unharmed, and

Ingolf and Wilhelm were scrambling to their feet.

Silvana launched at the knight. She caught him from behind, raised the shotgun in his hands, and fired it at the wizard. Ingolf grunted and dropped to the ground.

Wilhelm shifted, and a sudden pain exploded in Silvana's side. The knight had pulled a knife from his waist and stabbed at her hip. The pain was almost blinding. He tried to stab her again but her fear and adrenaline made her react fast enough to catch his wrist. He spun around while keeping his grip on the knife. In one move he dropped the shotgun and drew his sword from over his shoulder. He slashed at her head the moment the blade tip cleared his sheath. Silvana used her speed and put her hand on the flat side of the blade, then forced it sideways so that his swiped missed.

A crack sounded as Samantha rose from the ground and launched herself at Ingolf. The male wizard had been slowed by the shotgun blast, but was still ready for her. They both flew upwards and began throwing spells at each other with verbal shouts.

Silvana had to ignore them. Wilhelm had tried to swing his sword back for another strike even has he tried to yank his knife hand out of her grip. Silvana caught both wrists in a tight lock. She smiled at him from up close, baring her fangs.

He head-butted her in the face. It was enough to break her grip on both his wrists. She fell back, just as he grabbed the sword with both hands, already swinging down.

Jason appeared with his sabre in hand. Wilhelm had to adjust his swing to block Jason's attack. The swords shrieked as the metal scratched together.

Jason immediately went on the offensive and thrust the tip at his enemy's chest. Wilhelm had to step back and counter with a broad sweeping stroke. Jason kept on the attack, striking from multiple angles in rapid succession. Silvana saw now that Wilhelm's sword was thicker, a proper two-handed longsword. Jason's sabre was curved. It would likely shatter if he tried to match blows strength for strength. He was faster, but wouldn't last long if Wilhelm managed to get on the offensive.

Silvana poured all of her power into healing her stab wound enough to keep fighting. Meanwhile, Jason dodged a sword thrust and perfectly executed his own counterattack. He stabbed straight into Wilhelm's chest.

But the sabre didn't pierce anything. The knight was wearing a vest under his clothes and the tip wedged against the steel plate. Wilhelm seemed to expect this. He swung his sword right at Jason's middle, and Jason had to drop his own sword and fall backwards to avoid it. The sword clanged to the ground as Wilhelm charged at Jason.

Silvana dived forward. Wilhelm's shotgun was laying two steps back, unguarded. He saw her going for it and swung wildly. She dodged the sword then snatched the weapon by the handle. But he stood on the barrel and pinned it down. He swung the sword again. This time Silvana dived directly at him and tackled him to the ground.

They landed in a crumpled heap. Silvana climbed up and very deliberately headbutted him in the face, just as he'd done to her. But Wilhelm seemed to expect it and wasn't stunned at all. As a trained knight, he knew how to absorb a blow without flinching. Instead of weakening, he punched her in the jaw. Her vision filled with stars as he punched her again and again until, in desperation, she caught his hand between her teeth and bit down.

She tasted blood. He screamed.

Oh my god, what have I done?

She immediately released his hand from her jaws. She reached out to check on him, to see if he'd received any of her venom. To check she hadn't just broken Imperium law and turned him into a vampire…

Wilhelm hadn't frozen like her. He shoved her back, rolled on his knees, and seized the shotgun with both hands. He raised it at her head. She froze as the nozzle centred on her eyes.

"You bit me?" he growled. "Now I can legally do thi—"

Jason snatched him around the throat and jabbed his sabre against the side of his neck. "Touch her," he hissed, "and I'll run my blade through your neck!"

Wilhelm glanced over his shoulder. The tip of Jason's blade sent a trickle of red down Wilhelm's neck. Jason's eyes were blazing with an intensity Silvana had only see once before, in the moment when he had killed Peter Erikson.

Yet Wilhelm still pointed the shotgun at Silvana, like he was weighing his options.

"This whole fight was a mistake!" Silvana shouted. "We're just trying to help Samantha. Stand down and we can still—"

Silvana saw the muscles in Wilhelm's forearm flex. He was going to do it.

She put all her power remaining into a single burst of speed. She ducked and rolled, just as the blast went off. "No!" Jason screamed and thrust the sword in a killing blow. But Wilhelm thrust his head back into Jason's face and ducked under the sword.

Wilhelm turned to shoot Jason, but Silvana snatched the gun out of his hands.

Yet somehow the knight was ready for this too. He rolled aside, scooped up his two handed sword, and charged at Jason. *What is with this guy? How did he get this good?* Jason raised his own one-handed sword and parried the attack again. The knights moved into close combat, and even with the shotgun in hand, Silvana couldn't get a clear shot. Wilhelm clearly planned to use Jason's body as a shield even amidst the fight.

Yet even with all Wilhelm's skill, Jason was matching him blow for blow. *He's really doing it. He really is a Knight Templar.*

A woman's scream made Silvana look away. Samantha had been knocked to the ground. She knelt on her hands and knees, clutching at her ribs in obvious agony. Ingolf rose above her in the night sky. He held out his hands to the side, and two blinding white columns of lighting appeared in each fist. The threads of lighting were flickering everywhere, casting dozens of forks in every direction, yet the central column remained in Ingolfs hands. He snarled as he raised his hands higher, ready to strike.

Silvana froze. She glanced at Jason, locked in sword combat with Wilhelm, matching him strike for strike so far. She glanced back at Samantha, helpless and beaten on the ground.

God damn it.

She took aim, and fired the shotgun up in the air. Ingolf stumbled back from the impact and the lightning was ripped from his grasp. Without his control, it struck all across the town. Flames erupted at every place the lightning landed, including several buildings that exploded like fireworks. The wizard's flames devoured everything, casting shades of blue and crimson as they did.

Jason screamed in pain. Silvana spun around. He was still crossing blades with Wilhelm, but his shirt had caught fire across the shoulder. *Oh my god! He got struck by lightning!* She rushed to his side. She shoved the shotgun into the space where the swords clashed, and Wilhelm's blade wedged into the barrel and stuck.

Jason stepped forward – even as his shirt continued to burn – and sliced at the knight's gloved hands hard enough to make him roar and pull back. Jason followed up with a kick to the chest that sent him to the ground. Then he placed the sword against Wilhelms throat once more. The knight held up his hands in surrender and stayed still.

Finally Jason stood still long enough for Silvana to smother the flames on his clothes. Then Silvana aimed the gun at Wilhelm's prone form. As soon as she did, Jason collapsed onto his knees in exhaustion.

Silvana checked him. There was blood across his left shoulder and burn marks on his skin. There was also smoke coming from his foot from where the lightning had exited his body. The wound was severe, but not deep. He was still awake.

"Silvy?"

"Stay still." She peeled his shirt back to inspect the wound, while holding one hand on the gun pointed at Wilhelm. Jason's wounds were only superficial. "You had a faint heat rash. It didn't burn through your body, just across the surface. Where do you feel pain?"

"Shoulder," he mumbled. Then, "Foot hurts too."

Another scream made her look up. Samantha was at last rising to her feet and staring at the wounded Ingolf.

"You killed me, you bastard," Samantha cried. "I'll make you pay for what you did."

"I wasn't responsible for your murder, woman," Ingolf shouted back. "But I sure as hell will be this time."

Silvana growled. There was no stopping them. Wilhelm was watching her, waiting for her to lower her guard. But she couldn't leave Jason now. She was out of options. Those wizards would kill each other.

"Hey Morgan le Fay!" a voice shouted.

Freddie had emerged from the shadows, the light of burning buildings flickering on one side of his face and his long fringe obscured the other side. The mortal man looked like a hero out of ancient legend. Freddie threw a vial at Samantha's feet. It cracked open, letting out a thick green mist that quickly surrounded her, and she collapsed in an instant without a noise.

"Yes!" Freddie whooped. "Success! You did it, Eddie." He turned to the shadows as Edward appeared at his side, panting heavily and trembling. They seemed to notice Silvana at the same time. "Hey girl," Freddie shouted in a laugh. "You would not believe what we've just been through. There was some weird shit…" He froze in place as he seemed to finally notice the wizard opposite. "Oh. Hello there."

"Who are you?" Ingolf growled.

"Uh, buddy, that's not the traditional nerd reply when someone says hello there."

"Oh crap," Jason groaned.

"Freddie. I don't suppose you have two of those vials?" Silvana asked.

"No, just the one. Why?"

The wizard Ingolf flew up into the air again, snarling.

"Oh shit," Freddie cried.

Ingolf had splotches of blood on his clothes. Wilhelm rushed over to stand underneath his master. Both men were injured. Ingolf looked like he had shotgun pellets in his arm and side, judging by the blood streaks. Silvana felt a sudden jolt of pain herself. She checked her side, and remembered being stabbed there. The adrenaline had kept the pain at bay, until now. The cut was just above her hip bone. It had only pierced about four centimetres of skin and flesh, and her power had partially closed the wound. It could have been a lot worse. But now that she looked at it, her mind seemed to finally acknowledge all the pain she felt. She clutched it tight to stop the bleeding. Only then did she realise she was completely out of spare blood. *I've used too much of Jason's blood in the fight. I need to replenish.* She checked Jason, and he was clutching his shoulder wound. *It might be some time before he's ready to give blood.*

"Hey! Vampire!"

She looked up as Ingolf steadied himself, his lips pulled back in a vicious snarl. "You've crossed a line tonight. You wounded me with a mortal weapon. You attacked my knight without provocation. You defended our attacker." He pointed at Samantha. "You all deserve to die now."

"Wait!" she cried. "We just defeated your enemy for you. We did you a favour. Now you should reciprocate with a favour and let us leave here without further conflict."

"That's bullshit," Wilhelm growled.

"Indeed. We have every legal right to kill you now, and you just took out the only person who could stop us."

"You can't!" Edward shouted, as he, Freddie and Jason came to stand beside Silvana and Samantha. They faced the Glucksburg wizard and his knight with their heads held high. Edward went on. "You would break all Imperium law by killing us now. An Immortal cannot kill another, except in self-defence. We are all defenceless now."

"Right!" Freddie cried. "And I'm a mortal. Not even part of any family. For God's sake, I'm just here as *tech support!*"

"Doesn't matter!" Ingolf bellowed, and lightning once again flashed into his hands. "I don't care for Imperium law. I am a wizard! I am judge and king of my own country, not the High Kings. Here, my word is law, and I declare you will die now for attacking my home and my knight."

He raised his arms up high. Silvana desperately fired the gun at him once more, but it was too obvious an attack and this time the bullets bounced off some invisible barrier between them. Ingolf grinned wildly and hurled the lightning. Silvana glanced at Jason, wounded and leaning on Freddie for support. His eyes met hers.

White light flared all around them. The crack of thunder was deafening.

Yet Silvana was unaffected. They all were. The lightning passed through them without causing any damage. She searched for whatever had caused it.

A single figure emerged from the shadows of the broken pavement. A streetlight shone over them. They wore a hood, their face was in shadows. Yet Silvana recognised that scent. That posture, and those strands of long, black hair.

Khadija.

"Wizard!" Ingolf roared. "Show yourself. Tell me who dares to interfere in my judgement. I will—"

The figure remained motionless, yet suddenly the world shifted around them. The town buildings were covered by night sky, the road spun around to stand above them, and the world turned into a black void.

She's teleporting us!

Ingolf screeched in fury. A rush of heat flooded the air around Silvana, but too late. Her whole group dropped away into empty space.

Portia smiled to herself. *That was a close one.* The group of five people in the town square had vanished, plus the wizard who had saved them, leaving the Glucksburg wizard and knight standing in the empty street, shouting in impotent rage.

Only now did Portia finally step out of the shadows, slowly clapping her hands. The look on the two men's' faces was priceless.

"Oh, well done," she cooed. "A thrilling spectacle indeed. If there had been a bard here, the tale of your battle would become a song for the ages. Like the Illiad, or Beowulf. Truly, I did not know which way the fight would go."

"How long have you been there, Vigile?" the knight growled.

"Long enough," Desdemona said, stepping out from the opposite side of the street, her black suit and dark skin making her blend into the shadows, "to hear of thy disrespect to the High Kings and the Imperium."

The male wizard had fear flash across his face. Then he set his jaw. "So you saw that Kennedy woman attack me for no reason, only for you to stand by and do nothing?"

"Oh we would have stepped in," Portia said in her sweetest voice. "If she had killed you, we would have killed her to give you justice. Does that reassure you?" Both men scowled at her.

"I want justice done now," Ingolf said. "You saw those people with Kennedy? The Romanov girl and her allies?"

"They are known to us," Desdemona said. "But that is not why we art here."

The wizard and knight exchanged a glance. "What do you want?" the wizard asked.

"The truth," Desdemona said as she stalked forward, the light of flames dancing in her eyes. "Just tell me. Why did thou kill Samantha Kennedy?"

Chapter 22

Jason landed on concrete ground. His shoulder still felt like it was burning, and every few seconds his foot would flare up like he had stepped in something hot. It was an effort to sit up, stop focusing on his own body, and look around.

They were all on a rooftop. The sun was still in the sky here, just barely visible as it set over the horizon. Sirens were wailing in the distance. The air felt thick with smog and car fumes. Jason could see building skylines in the near distance, but he couldn't recognise the city. Judging by the distance between those buildings and Jason's rooftop, there were a kilometre or two from the CBD.

"Well that was close," Freddie said and collapsed down next to him. "You ok there, dark knight?"

Jason smirked. "Yeah, I guess."

"What happened to you? Looks like burns."

"It was lightning, actually."

Freddie was quiet. Jason looked up to see his friends eyes widen. "That…is seriously fucking hardcore."

"I know, right?"

"I wish I got struck by lightning."

Jason rolled his eyes. "I wish you did too."

"Ha! Nice."

"Where are we?" Edward cried, his voice agitated. "This isn't my house. We should be back at my house."

"Stay calm, my alchemist friend," a woman's voice answered. "We will return to your home soon. I'm merely trying to see if Samantha is still alive."

Jason shifted awkwardly so he could see the others. Samantha was lying still on the ground, her wizard robe torn and blood smearing her face. Leaning over her was Khadija Al Khalifa, wizard of the royal family of the United Arab Emirates, and fugitive of the Immortal Imperium. She was dressed incognito in jeans, sneakers, and a jumper with the hoodie pulled over her face. She was checking Samantha for injuries with a deep scowl on her delicate face. When she seemed satisfied, she held a hand to the sleeping wizard's face and brushed her cheek. There were tears in Khadija's brown eyes, and she blinked them back.

"Thanks for the rescue," Jason said.

Khadija gave a genuine laugh. "Glad I could help."

"How did you find us?" Silvana said.

"You called me."

"But you weren't there. The Vigiles answered the call."

"I know. I tapped my own line years ago." She grinned. "Most Immortals are too old school. They forget that modern technology even exists. But yes, I heard your message. Sorry it took me so long to teleport there. I hadn't been to the Glucksburg castle before."

That's right. Wizards can only teleport somewhere they've been before. Khadija can work around that because she uses thoughts to cast spells, not words, but it takes her more time to form the spell.

"I thought you met the Glucksburgs," Silvana said.

"Yes, but not at their castle," Khadija said. "A different social event." Silvana eyed her sceptically.

"Where are we now?" Jason asked.

"America. This is Brookline, just outside the city of Boston." Khadija smiled. "It's the birthplace of Samantha's great nephew."

"JFK?" Jason guessed.

Khadija nodded. "I first met Sam here, about one hundred years ago. It's one of the easiest places for me to teleport to, and we had to get out of there quickly. Now," she turned to Edward. "How is your patient doing?"

Edward cleared his throat. "After initial transport, patient spent a full week in forced coma and regeneration cycle. Cycle was interrupted once by outside disturbance, six hours before completion." He glanced at Jason. "Subject woke on schedule with a better cognitive function than expected. However, subject experienced unintended hysteria. Uncertain if a result of treatment or pure emotional response. Administered an accelerate to decrease recovery time. Later had to use a sleep potion to calm subject's agitation."

"But she's going to be ok, right?" Khadija smiled. Edward nodded, his eyes askew, and Khadija choked out a laugh. "You actually did it. You brilliant man, I can hardly believe it."

Jason blinked several times. The words had all sounded incomprehensible, but after a moment he understood the social dynamic at work here.

"You work for her," he said. "Don't you, Edward? Khadija is the one who hired you."

"Actually," Khadija said, "he offered to help." She smiled warmly at the alchemist. "He approached me after you left the gala. Said he had an experimental new potion that could reverse death. Asked for half a million dollars. I told him I'd pay him two million, but only if it worked. I honestly didn't believe him." She grinned. "I guess I better pay up."

"Wait," Jason said. "So Edward's potion that reverses death…is new? He's the only alchemist who can do it?"

Edward nodded.

"Then why isn't it available to everyone?" Silvana cried. "Every alchemist in the world would love a potion like that, even if it only works within an hour of death."

Edward just shrugged. "This is my first time testing it. And I'm not allowed on the alchemists guild."

Jason stared at him in disbelief. "You mean, they don't respect you cause you're different."

"Everyone always says I'm different," Edward said, his voice had a slight edge to it. "I've never understood why. It's everyone else who acts so strangely all the time. I have dozens of new potions that no one else knows about but they won't let me share it with the community. I'm always struggling to find clients. I barely make enough money to afford my needs. That's why I offered to help Khadija. I just needed the cash."

Khadija still had a bright smile on her face. "Well your staggering levels of altruism aside, I still can't thank you enough. I thought I'd lost her…"

"And now you're innocent," Edward nearly shouted in excitement. "Everyone thinks you murdered her. But you can't be her murderer if she's still alive."

Khadija just laughed. "Sure. That's exactly what was on my mind." She laughed again as she stroked the side of Samantha's head. Yet a sudden look crossed over her face. The tears dried up and she frowned deeply. "Oh my god," she muttered.

"What is it?" Jason asked.

She looked up. "I can't believe…" she trailed off. She buried her face in her hands. "Dear Allah, what have I done?"

"What happened?" Silvana asked.

Khadija covered her mouth with her hand. "I found the Skin-walker."

Jason's eyes went wide. "The one from the attack. The one suspected of killing Samantha." He stared at the horror on her face, and his worst fears were confirmed. "Khadija…what did you do to them?"

"I…" her lip trembled, so she squeezed her jaw shut. "I needed a confession from them. I had to find out who hired them, in order to clear my name. I…I was desperate."

"You tortured them?" Jason asked.

"I thought they murdered her!" Khadija suddenly cried, but Jason could see the denial behind her anger. "The Imperium wasn't going to do anything. They used it as an excuse to hunt me for my beliefs. They didn't care about justice. So I had to step in."

"That was not justice," Jason said.

"They were Skinwalkers. They were on my staff, and they betrayed me. They deserved what they got."

"Are you sure of that?" Silvana asked. "I found a young Skinwalker in your kitchen, wounded from the blast. I had to hide her to protect her from the wizards. Because they would have killed her on suspicion alone."

Khadija went quiet. "A young girl? Fifteen years old? Brown skin, dark eyes, and a thin face?"

Silvana's eyes narrowed into slits. "Yeah, that's her. How did you know?"

Then it clicked.

"You tortured the wrong person," Jason gasped.

"No! No, I didn't," Khadija cried, but her tone was shaky.

"That girl was innocent," Silvana said. "I found her in the kitchen. She was unconscious from the explosion. She was lucky to be alive. Then you seized her for no other reason than her race." Silvana barked a laugh. "I thought you wanted freedom from oppression. But you don't care about that at all, do you? You just want freedom for yourself. You're no better than the High Kings."

"How dare you lecture me," Khadija growled, standing up and facing off against Silvana. "You live in the middle of fucking nowhere. You have no idea what it's like in the spotlight. Your every action scrutinised. Your every word and gesture measured against you. My entire life of one hundred and eighty years has been spent suffocating under their rule. You've only just seen it for the first time *last week.*"

"I never tortured anyone," Silvana snapped.

"Cause you never had to choose," Khadija growled.

"Alright," Jason said and stood to his feet, his shoulder burning anew as he did. He came to stand between the vampire and the wizard while clutching his wound. "We need to move on. We can't stand on this rooftop and yell at each other." He gestured to Samantha, lying unconscious on the floor. "Edward, what do we need to do for Samantha?"

"Take her back to my place," he said instantly. "I need to monitor her state of mind over the next few days. Then I need to learn more about the internet."

Khadija frowned. "What?"

"Don't worry about it," Jason said. "Khadija, can you take us to Edward's home? Then can you take Silvana and myself to see the Skinwalker you captured? I'd like to ask her some questions."

Khadija stared at him. "You have some nerve making demands of me, knight. I don't see…"

"Samantha would be dead without us," Jason snapped. "Without all of us. I believe that puts you in our debt. Or have I misunderstood your customs?" She only glared back. "Excellent. Let's go."

* * *

Jason felt the world drop out from underneath him before he landed gently on solid ground.

He was in a warehouse. Silver moonlight was shining through the window and flicking with each turning of a ventilation fan. It squeaked with every rotation. The air smelt of dust and tin. Another smell came to him then, harsher and fouler. The stench of urine. Khadija stepped forward, her footsteps echoing off the walls, and a woman's voice responded with a faint whimper. Slowly, Jason's eyes adjusted to the dim light as he moved forward.

A figure was tied to a steel chair. Their hands tied behind their back and cuffs shackled their ankles to the legs of their seat. The skin around the point of contact had been rubbed raw and was now bleeding. A dark puddle rested under the chair. It smelt of blood and piss.

"My god," Jason cried. He stared at Khadija, her face obscured completely in shadow. "What possible reason do you think exists to justify this?"

He marched to the victim's side, and was relieved to see Silvana join him. The victim was indeed a young girl, exactly as Silvana had described. Only fifteen, not yet old enough for her Immortality to slow the aging process. Now her face was gaunt and haunted and covered in sweat. Her shirt had a streak of vomit down the front. When Jason approached, the girl pulled away with a cry. She shouted something in another language.

"Hey, it's ok. We're here to help," Jason said. She kept speaking in a language Jason didn't recognise, her tone frantic and begging. "It's ok. We're friends. Don't be afraid." It had no effect.

"I don't think she speaks English," Silvana said. "She only said a few words to me when I met her, all of them another language."

Khadija muttered, "Every Immortal speaks English. She's lying."

"Don't even start!" Jason hissed at her. He pulled out his phone and opened google translate. He set it to detect language and turned on the microphone. The girl's words were picked up and a moment later the translation appeared on his screen.

"Stop. Just stop it. I don't know anything. Where is my brother?" The language had been detected as something called Telugu.

Jason held the screen to Silvana, and her face hardened. "I want to speak to her," she said. Jason switched the settings to translate from English to Telugu. Silvana started, "Hello my friend. My name is Silvana, and I want you to know that I was the one who rescued you from…"

Jason cut her off, "Sorry, it's better to use short sentences. Google can translate individual words, but it gets weird with sentences. Shorter is better."

Silvana rolled her eyes. "Hello. My name is Silvana. I rescued you last week. After the explosion. We're here to help you." Jason gave a thumbs up and held the screen towards the girl. He pressed the speaker function. A computer voice spoke to her in a flat tone.

The effect was immediate. The girl's face lit up and tears streamed down her dirt-stained cheeks. She started speaking, and Jason hurried to flick the settings back.

"…know where is brother? This evil wizard wants him angrily. But I don't know everything. She won't believe me."

Jason and Silvana turned back to Khadija. "Release her," Silvana hissed. "Now."

Khadija stammered, "But she might shapeshift. I'm sure she wants to kill me. If I let her…"

"Now, Khadija," Jason growled, barely restraining his fury. "Release her."

The wizard clenched her jaw. The moonlight flickered over her face, illuminating the anger in her eyes. Jason braced for an attack, clenching his hands into fists. Something snapped behind him. He spun, and saw the cuffs break off the girl on the chair. She slumped forward. Silvana caught her and gently laid her down on the floor. She checked the girl for injury.

"There's no wounds," Silvana said. "There's blood, and definite signs of stress. But no injuries." She glared up at Khadija. "Were you hurting her, then healing her so you could hurt her more?"

"No, that would be sick."

"And this is so much better?" Jason said. "I know what you did. You used your telepathy, didn't you? You put horrors into her mind to break her psychologically." He pointed at the blood on the girls' face. "Do you see how distressed she was? Sweating blood. You've probably traumatised her for life."

"But…but…" Khadija stammered. "I didn't hurt her. I caused no injuries. I…I was being merciful."

"Mercy," Silvana snapped, "would have been talking to her like a human being."

Khadija was silent. Her mouth moved up and down. She turned suddenly and stepped into the corner of the warehouse, out of sight.

Jason turned back to the girl. "What is your name?" he asked through his phone.

"Aakriti Varma."

"My name is Jason. I am Silvana's knight. Can you answer some questions for me?" She agreed. "Why are you so scared for your brother? Is he in danger?"

"He disappeared after the explosion. I'm scared for him. He is seen with strange people."

"What kind of people?"

"Strange people."

Jason smiled. *"Other Skinwalkers?"*

"Sometimes. Other vampires. They were all strong physically."

"Physically enhanced," Jason muttered to Silvana, then asked the girl, "Do you know why your brother saw these people? What was he interested in?"

Aakriti gave a strained smile. *"He imagined being a king. Can you believe that?"*

Jason shivered to hear the word king. He turned to face Silvana, and saw the same tension on her face. She'd noticed it too.

"Royalists?" he whispered.

"Like Peter," Silvana whispered. "They want to bring Immortals out of hiding and rule openly as kings and queens again." She gestured to Aakriti. "Do you think she's correct?"

"It would make sense if Peter and his friends weren't the only ones. It could be an organisation. They could operate in cells. The real question is, did this group act alone? Did they carry out the attack on Samantha and orchestrate the explosion too?"

"Do you think someone else could have helped them?"

Jason sighed. "I don't know. But as a detective, you have to explore every angle, not just the one you suspect the most." He turned back to Aakriti and used the translator app. "Do you know the names of any of your brother's friends?"

She nodded eagerly. "Gerard," she said, not using the translator.

"Gerard…" Jason murmured. "Do you mean Gerald? The Skin-walker? I know him." *Hell, I fought him three times. Guy nearly killed me as a lion.*

She shook her head. "Gerard." She insisted.

He nodded. He remembered how he'd been unable to find any information on Gerald during his database search six months ago, even though he had found the other two Immortals he'd looked for. Perhaps that was why? Maybe his birth name was Gerard. It sounded French. "Do you know any others?"

"Just one. His name was Dorin."

"Dorin?" Jason looked up at Silvana. Her face was a perfect silver mask. "What do you know about Dorin?"

"*He's a vampire. He birthed in East Europe somewhere. I don't know exactly. He's big leader in the group.*"

"How do we find him?" Jason growled.

Aakriti grew agitated, but managed to answer. "*Please help me find my brother alive. He could take you to Dorin.*"

"Then where do we find your brother? Is he on the run after the attack?"

Aakriti scowled at them. "*I don't know where he is. Even if I did, I won't betray him.*"

"But if we find him, we could help him."

The young girl just shook her head, causing tears to spill down her face. "*If brother is not here, then he's safe. I just want to go home.*"

Jason sighed. "Ok. Thank you." He stood up and stepped away, Silvana at his side. Aakriti sat on the ground massaging her limbs as the couple moved away. "Dorin," Jason said. "The man who claims to know about your past. He could be someone important to you. And he's probably a Royalist."

"I don't want to find him."

"What?" Jason blinked at her. "You wanted to know him when you met him."

She smirked. "I was just being a bitch to Emberline. I don't actually want to meet him. Especially now that I know he's in charge of…" her voice grew louder, "…a fucking terrorist organisation!"

"Alright," Jason said slowly. *What is with her? Is she scared that she might find out the truth?* He didn't say that out loud. "Well, I think we should try to find Aakriti's brother. It could uncover the plot behind the gala, and lead us to Dorin and the Royalist organisation."

"I agree," Silvana said.

"Good. Now I need to speak with this wizard. Do you want to join me?" Silvana shook her head. So Jason walked over into the dark warehouse corner, while Silvana stayed with Aakriti.

Khadija's breathing was shaking as Jason approached. It might have been sobs. But when she spoke, her voice was steady. "What did you find?" she asked.

"I found someone broken by torture," he said flatly. "That girl is traumatised." He took a deep breath. He found his legs were shaking with the adrenaline. "Have you done this before?"

"No, of course not." He didn't say anything. Khadija raised her voice, "I swear. I've never done anything like this before. Jason, you need to understand. I was pushed to my very limit. I had lost everything. Samantha, my family, my place in the world…and I just snapped. I thought if I could break her, she would exonerate me."

"Then why did you keep going? When she clearly knew nothing, and couldn't even speak your language?"

"I thought she was lying!" Khadija cried. "Really, I genuinely believed that. By Allah, every Immortal speaks English! How could she not?"

"Maybe she never had your education," Jason growled. "Maybe she never had your hundreds of millions of dollars, or your magic, or your powerful family. Maybe she was too poor to learn English. Maybe she was busy just trying to survive. And maybe that's why she was working out back in the kitchen, instead of in the gala itself in front of customers. Because of the language barrier." Jason took a step towards her and hissed in a low voice, "but you wouldn't have a clue what that's like, would you? Mighty wizard, princess, and leader of the free world. You think you're so hard done by. Like you're the great victim of the world. You wouldn't have a clue what real misery is."

Jason's blood was roaring in his ears. He knew he was losing his self-control. In the back of his mind, he knew this was because of his upbringing in the foster system, one step away from homelessness, always scared he'd run out of money or food. He hated how everyone else had more opportunity than him, how teachers blamed him for not getting straight A's when he was busy trying to survive. *But damn it, I don't care if I'm being emotional. I'm still in the right!* He didn't even care if Khadija blasted him to hell for this. All he could think was how furious he felt, and how scared that little girl had been.

Khadija raised her voice to a shout. "Alright! I made a mistake. I'm not trying to justify that. I feel sick to my stomach about this. But that doesn't give you the right to judge me. You have no idea what I've been through, and not just in the last week. I've spent my life resisting the Imperium in every way possible. Sometimes I think I'm the only Immortal who even tries. So excuse me if I'm not perfect all the time."

Jason snarled. "This isn't a simple mistake. You kidnapped and tortured someone. By mortal laws, it's one of the worst crimes imaginable."

Khadija stepped towards him. Her face was covered in shadows and flicking moonlight. In this moment she was beautiful and menacing. "Everyone breaks someday, oh knight," she whispered. "Everyone has a limit. The only people who think they don't are those who've never been pushed beyond it."

"Don't," Jason growled. "Don't even start that crap. I am not like you."

"Oh really? Then imagine if I killed Silvana."

He launched forward and grabbed her by the scruff of her jumper, shoving her back against the wall. She let out a small gasp on impact. Her eyes flashed with fear, and Jason felt his rage surging in confidence.

And he instantly stopped himself.

"Ah," she whispered. "Just the thought of me harming her makes you unstable. You really think you would react any better if you lost the woman you love?" She pointed a finger at him. "You're lucky I didn't rip your head off by the way."

Jason bit his tongue. He noticed Silvana was standing nearby, her eyes red, and ready to strike the wizard down. He forced himself to release Khadija and step back, lowering his hands to his side.

"You will take all of us back to Edward's house," he said, unconcerned by the annoyance in the wizard's eyes. "That includes the girl. Edward will do what he can to heal her."

"Fine," Khadija said. "But let me remind you two, you have still not found out who is behind all this. Until you do, I consider you both under my employ." She stepped around Jason and turned her back to him without concern. "So I suggest you get to work."

Chapter 23

Jason woke some time later. The sun was high in the sky, but his surroundings were unfamiliar. All he could see through his blurry eyes was an old maroon curtain and four-poster bed he was lying in.

Where in the world am I? He stared at the wall. *My god, what kind of question is that?*

He rolled to the edge of the bed and nearly collapsed. His head grew dizzy, his stomach was painfully nauseous, and his shoulder was throbbing. He had to stay sitting until the ill feelings lessened. He took a deep breath, and recognised the faint scent of old musk and cleaning products. *Edward's house. I'm still in Swansea.*

Jason wandered down the hallway towards the sounds of voices. He found Silvana and Freddie sitting together in the lounge room. They both leapt up when he entered.

"Whoa big guy," Freddie said. "You ok? You've been asleep for fourteen hours."

"Huh?" Jason murmured, rubbing at his eyes.

"You had a healing elixir last night. Edward said you would be hungry," Silvana said.

"I think I want to throw up."

Freddie drawled, "That's hunger, genius. Just sit down, we'll get you something."

Jason fell into a chair. The world seemed to spin around him so much that he half expected to be teleported somewhere. Freddie handed him a Gatorade. "For the electrolytes," he said. "I insisted we do a trip into town just for this. Drink up, me hearties!" Silvana appeared with a sandwich. Jason stared at it.

"Did…five minutes just pass?" he murmured.

"No sweetie. I had this ready."

"Huh." Jason started eating and drinking, and soon found his mind coming back online. "Where is everyone?" he asked.

"Khadija left after dropping us here," Silvana said. "She's being tracked by Vigiles, so she has to stay on the move or they'll find her. She said she'll be back later tonight. Samantha is still unconscious. Edward's potion will keep her under for a few more hours. Hopefully she'll be more herself when she wakes. Right now Edward is trying to heal Aakriti."

"How's that going?"

"Not sure. He said he could heal her body's stress well enough. The mind is trickier. He'll do what he can."

"Right." Jason took a few more mouthfuls. "Are you two ok?"

They both nodded. "I'm miraculously uninjured," Freddie said. "Don't ask me how. Thought I was gonna die like six times."

"And Silvana, how's your blood supply? Do you need more?"

"I'm fine, Jason," she said with a laugh. "Really, you shouldn't be giving blood in your state anyway."

"But you said you needed more."

"Not right this second, Jason. Thank you."

"Hey!" Freddie cried. "I could give blood if you need it."

Silvana held up a hand. "It's against Imperium law. I can only take blood from my husband."

Freddie looked between them. "But you're not married. If you're already breaking one law, what's one more?"

Jason tilted his head and found himself considering it. Freddie made a damn good point. But Silvana was quicker to answer. "Thank you, Freddie, but it's not really something I'm comfortable with right now."

"Oh alright. Just trying to help."

Jason smiled to himself. He'd enjoyed a moment of peace with his closest friends. But he knew what they had to talk about. "Freddie," he said in a grave voice. "I want to apologise for what happened last night."

Freddie blinked. "Uh…did something happen that I don't remember?"

"I invited you here to teach Edward computers, and you ended up nearly dying." Freddie tried to protest, but Jason cut him off. "I was responsible for you, and I failed in that duty."

"Oh come on, Jase. I've been asking you to let me get involved in Immortal shit for months. I knew it might be dangerous. You are hardly responsible for all that…" he waved wildly, "I don't even know what you'd call what happened last night. But it was fucked. Not your fault at all."

Jason shook his head. "You didn't agree to fight a wizard."

"Jase, I'm also an adult who can make his own decisions."

"But we nearly died. I can't…"

Silvana held up a hand, and Jason paused at her assertiveness. "Do you think you are our leader?" she asked.

"Leader? No, I…"

"Exactly. You're not our boss. You're not our superior. We're all equals here. Which means we're all equally responsible. If you're taking on extra blame, then you're being unfair on all of us, especially yourself."

"Yeah!" Freddie insisted loudly. They both looked to him. "Sorry, that was all I wanted to say."

"Alright," Jason said. "I'm not trying to blame myself. It's just…" he found himself unable to speak. It wasn't just his tiredness. The words formed a lump in his throat.

"It's ok, sweetheart. You can tell us."

"Yeah mate, we're here for you. What's up?"

Jason took a deep breath. "I've lost people before. You know…my mum…" They both nodded. "I'm just scared to go through that again. I think that's why I don't have many people in my life. Now, I have you two. And honestly, you're probably the closest two relationships I've ever had with anyone. I only met Freddie six months ago, and already, you're my best mate."

"That's not weird, Jase. You're my best mate too." Freddie rolled his eyes at his own words. "God, so fucking cheesy, right?"

"So cheesy."

Silvana nodded, but she was hiding a smile. "It's too cheesy. I *camembert* it."

It took a moment, but both men got the pun and immediately booed her. "So bad!" "How dare you?" "Get out!"

Their laughter died down a moment later. "You know, Jason," Silvana said, her tone abruptly sombre, "I've lost two husbands before you. Something you learn as an Immortal, you cannot stop change. You will always lose the people you love eventually, given enough time."

"Well, that's a terrible thing to say," Jason said.

"But that's the point. Loss is inevitable. That means our time together is precious. You can waste that time struggling to hold on, or you can live with peace and acceptance, and treasure every day."

"Like Anakin," Freddie said. "He tried to hold on to Padme out of fear, and it drove him to the dark side."

Silvana pressed her lips together. "Sure. I would have gone with

Macbeth, personally. Cause fear of loss is a self-fulfilling prophecy."

"Oh yeah, that's probably better," Freddie said.

"The point is, you don't have to be afraid."

"Exactly. Just fucking chill, bro."

Jason just smiled even as he shook his head. "Alright. I don't mean to be so worried. In my defence, I'm not at my sharpest right now. I got struck by lightning, you know."

Freddie scowled. "Man, I wished I had been struck by lightning so I could win every argument." They all laughed.

"That's why I dived in front of the bolt. I thought, 'this will really piss off Freddie.'"

"I knew it!"

They laughed again. When the sound died off, a deep silence fell over them. Jason could feel their eyes on him, waiting and watching. Like he might break down into a heap the moment they left him alone. He clutched his hands together and turned his gaze towards the ground.

"Whatever happens next," he said, "we need to be careful of Khadija and Sam. They are allies, but they are not our friends. I don't think we can trust them just yet."

"Agreed," Silvana replied.

"I think we can trust Edward," Freddie said. "I can't explain it. Maybe it's a gut feeling. But I think he's friends with us now."

"He's a bit unpredictable," Silvana said. "Remember when he threw crystal meth at an enraged wizard?"

Freddie rolled his eyes. "Yes, I do remember. I was there. Literally less than one day ago."

"Alright," Jason said. "Something else. I think we can rule out the Glucksburgs in Sam's murder." They both frowned at him. "Ingolf fully intended to kill us all. He was bragging shamelessly. Guy was drunk on his power. Yet even then, he said he had nothing to do with

Sam's murder. I think if he was responsible, he would have bragged about it in that moment."

"I guess, but that's not exactly concrete evidence," Freddie said.

"It is a hunch. But I'm willing to bet on it. He was arrogant enough by the end that he would have said anything."

Silvana shrugged. "Then where does that leave us? The Glucksburgs were our only lead."

"Not our only lead. For one, there is Samantha. I would like to interview her when she wakes. I'm hoping she'll remember something about her murderer."

"Whoa!" Freddie cried. "How often do you get to interview the murder victim? That's gotta be the first time in history that's ever happened."

Jason sighed. "Ever heard of attempted murder? Or people surviving their wounds?"

"Oh." Freddie held up a finger as if in thought, then lowered it again. "Oh. Right."

Jason grinned. "The other lead is the last Skinwalker. Aakriti's brother. Either lead should be able to tell who is behind all this. We'll interview the Skinwalker again and see if there's anything more she can tell us."

"Edward's working on healing her," Silvana said. "They may be a while."

"Well. Guess there's nothing to do but wait." Jason sighed again. "Man, I want to drive back to Plymouth already. We're gonna be stuck here for hours yet."

They spent the afternoon mostly resting in the lounge room and slowly snacking on Edward's food. Jason couldn't believe he had work the following morning, and he was still in Swansea. He didn't have enough energy to update the Immortal Investigations, so he just slouched on the couch while cuddled up to Silvana. He tried to rest on her shoulder, but she kept shifting him to lay on her lap instead. It was perhaps less dignified. Still, he managed to fall asleep again.

He woke to the sounds of television at low volume. Silvana and Freddie were watching Countdown, and both were racing each other to guess the largest word. In their excitement, they'd grown louder and startled him out of a deep sleep. Jason smiled and kept his eyes shut a little longer, happily listening to their competition. It was a nice contrast to his nightmares of zombie wizards and firestorms burning through buildings and people with terrifying ease. It was much nicer to listen to Silvana and Freddie getting along so well. At some point, they found paper and pencil and were furiously writing down their answers with each round.

"Look it up, that can't be right," Silvana cried.

"Google confirmed. Removed from the dictionary in the 70s."

"Bullshit! This is so unfair!"

"Unfair? Excuse me, at least English is your first language. And you know tons of old words."

"Well, you're so much better at the maths."

"Cause I'm Asian? Wow, racist much?" They laughed. "But yes I'm good at maths. And it's a hundred percent because I'm Asian." They laughed again. Jason kept his eyes shut, but he couldn't help the deep smile on his face.

A door opened somewhere in the house.

Jason sat up straight. The others were already tense and alert. Multiple sets of footsteps came down the hallway, then Edward appeared in the lounge room doorway, Aakriti at his side.

The young girl looked much steadier on her feet. Her eyes were no longer flickering in paranoia. Yet she had a fragile edge to her, like a gust of wind would blow her off her feet. She smiled at Jason and held up her hand to her ear. "Fon," she said.

Jason blinked. "Oh, phone." He opened his translator app again. "How are you?" he asked.

"*Sad and less scared,*" the phone translated back. Jason grinned. She gestured to the phone, and he let her record again. "*Where is wizard?*"

"She's not here. She will be coming back here shortly. But you don't have to be afraid. She won't hurt you while we're here."

Aakriti shook her head. "*I don't want to be here with the wizard. I will go.*"

Jason and Silvana exchanged a glance. "You should stay," Silvana said. "We want to find your brother and help him."

"*I'm sorry. I never want to see that wizard again.*"

"But what about your brother?"

"*I will help him alone. I just wanted to thank you for saving me.*" She turned to go.

Jason and Silvana hurried after her, following her down the hallway towards the door. "How are you going to get home? You're in England. Do you need transport or money?"

"*I have forms.*" The translation seemed cryptic, but she relayed nothing more to them. Jason understood she probably meant shapeshifting forms.

Aakriti opened the front door and turned back to face them. She looked so young, barely fifteen, and Jason felt an irrational urge to hug her and shield her from this cruel world. She smiled at them, showing just a glimpse of the happy face that was nearly destroyed.

"*You are my friends. I indebted to you twice.*"

She held out her hand for the phone and Jason handed it over. She typed a mobile number and an email before handing it back and pointing at the phone. Jason turned it back to translate.

"*I can't offer much. I am homeless. Not many friends. But if you need me, I will help.*"

She held her hands over her head and clapped them together, then quick as a blink she turned into a blue feathered falcon. Her wings flapped powerfully to lift her into the air and within seconds she was airborne and moving at incredible speeds, climbing further out of sight.

Jason put the phone back in his pocket. "Well. That was no help at all."

"She's probably traumatised from Khadija's shit."

"I know, I know. It's still just really inconvenient." He found Silvana shaking her head at him. "What? It is."

"Just take a moment to be happy. We saved that girl and made a friend. That's still a good thing."

Jason rolled his eyes. "I guess." Silvana chuckled and patted him on the shoulder. They closed the door and turned to go back inside.

Khadija was standing behind them.

"Jesus Christ!" Jason hissed and took a fighter's stance. The wizard was pulling the hood off her jacket and shaking her long, wavy black hair loose. She eyed them in silence. Then she smirked.

"I didn't scare you, did I?"

"Fuck you," Jason snapped.

"I take that as a yes." She looked over his shoulder. "Where's the Skinwalker?" Silvana barred the front door with her body. Khadija sneered, "Oh, you're standing in my way? I guess there's nothing I can do about it now, is there?"

"Leave her alone," Silvana said. "That girl has been through enough. There was nothing more she could tell us."

"Samantha isn't awake yet," Jason said. "You can wait with us, but you need to be a guest, with all the courtesies that entails. Can you do that?"

Khadija sneered for a moment, then seemed to think better of it. "I didn't want to be like this, you know," she said. "This is me at my very worst. I don't mean to be so difficult. Losing Sam…it broke me." She avoided their eyes.

Jason softened his tone. "Come on. Let's go see her, then." He patted Khadija's arm to steer her down the hall. Silvana followed closely behind, watching. Jason led them to the lounge room, where Freddie was showing Edward something else on his laptop.

"Hey Edward," Jason asked. "Khadija is here. We were wondering when will Sam wake?"

Edward nodded. "I could wake her now."

"Please do."

"Come with me." Edward left the room, and Jason frowned. Did Edward mean just Khadija or everyone? Apparently, they all had the same question, as they all looked at each other. Jason shrugged and followed the alchemist, and everyone followed once someone else went first. Edward led them upstairs, down the hall, and into the bedroom at the far end of the hallway.

Samantha was lying on another four-poster bed, sleeping on her back with her hands folded over her belly. Her hair was splayed over on the pillow in the shape of a bright, golden V. She looked calm and not at all like the frenzied lunatic who had brought down half a township mere hours ago. Edward approached her side, opened a vial, and waved it under her nose. She inhaled the invisible vapours, and a second later her eyes flickered open. They settled on Khadija, and started watering.

"Dija?"

"I'm here, Sam."

The two wizards clutched each other's hands, tears mirrored in both sets of eyes as they pressed their foreheads together. Jason felt a pang of guilt for being so hard on Khadija, but it only lasted for a moment. Aakriti's terrified expression flashed in his memory, and Jason's guilt fled.

"How am I…" Sam drawled, her voice slurring. "My mind is…really foggy."

"You were dead," Edward said. "I brought you back. Your brain is still repairing itself. It may take another few days before you are yourself again. And there may be side effects too."

Sam blinked. "Side effects?"

"Shh," Khadija whispered. "The important thing is you're safe now. We've been taking care of you. You're going to be ok."

Sam nodded with a thoughtful expression. "What side effects?" she asked again.

Edward launched into a reply instantly. "I'm expecting gaps in your memory. And you'll probably struggle to remember new information for a while. You may also experience a shorter attention span. Probably changes in your personality." Everyone turned sharply to look at him. He shrugged. "Only subtle changes. You won't be a different person or anything."

"That's a relief," Freddie said. All eyes turned to him. "Well it is," he said uncomfortably.

"But you're alive," Khadija said. "We will get through the next challenges together. We always do." She clutched Sam's hand and squeezed it tight.

"Sam," Jason said to get her attention. "I am Jason Turner. Do you remember me? We met at the gala."

"I think so. You gave me…something important."

"My jacket. Your dress had been ripped."

"What ripped my dress?"

"That's not important. The point is I'm a friend, and I'm a police officer. I would like to ask you some questions about what happened to you. Do you feel ready for that?"

Sam nodded.

"What do you remember about the explosion?"

She thought about it. "Just a loud bang, then everything got smokey. I don't remember casting any spells. Or…maybe just one spell for air. I remember it was hard to breathe."

"Who was with you at the time of the explosion?"

"I don't know."

"Were you standing with Khadija? Or were you in separate rooms."

"Mmm…we were separated."

Jason frowned. "Do you remember anything about the people near you at the time? Anything about skin colours or dresses, or hair styles? What country were they from?"

"I remember they were hot."

Jason blinked. "Hot? Like, a good looking man?"

"A good looking *woman*," Sam corrected, with mock outrage. Jason smiled at her. *Mental note; Sam is gay, not bi like Khadija.*

He went on, "Did you see anyone else *after* the explosion took place?"

"Not really. I remember people running and shouting through the smoke. But I didn't talk to anyone. There was just a…" her voice rose sharply. "…a terrible pain. Awful pain. It was a…a blade. I just remember a blade."

Jason glanced at Khadija. She seemed just as surprised. "A blade?" Khadija asked.

"It came from beside me. Went right into…my neck." She trembled and squeezed her eyes shut. Her hand absently felt at the side of her neck, as if feeling the same pain all over again. "It was indescribable. I can't…the sheer pain of it was nothing like I'd ever imagined. I couldn't breathe. I couldn't speak any spells. Then they just…started cutting me. Over and over in my neck."

"They? I don't understand," Khadija said. "The Skinwalkers were shaped as dinosaurs. They were using claws."

"It wasn't a claw!" Sam suddenly screamed. Everyone jumped back from the bed. Khadija gripped Sam's hand as she started shaking. "They used a sword! A metal sword! They stabbed me through the neck, and when I fell, they slashed me over and over, and there was *nothing I could do!*" She started sobbing and clutching at her throat. "God, get it out! Fucking get it out of me now! Oh God I can't breathe!" She wheezed as she gasped for breath.

The room began to shake. The walls and windows rattled, and the light seemed to grow darker.

"GET IT OUT!" she howled.

Edward held another vial under her nose, and Sam started to go still. She twitched several times, before her head fell back onto her pillow and she drifted into a restful sleep.

The room went quiet again. Khadija checked Sam's face, even as tears streamed down her own cheeks. "Will she always be like this, now?" she asked.

"I don't know," Edward said in a flat voice. "She should stay here for a few more days. I'll monitor her progress. But you must admit. She is alive."

Khadija glared at him. "Are you seriously demanding payment? Right now of all times?"

"I just want an acknowledgement."

"Fine. You have your fucking acknowledgement. But she needs to be restored to her full mental capacity before she can testify that I'm not her murderer. Only then will I get access to my family fortune, which I need in order to pay you. So get to work."

Jason just stared at her. The interview had clearly shaken Khadija, who looked like she was straining to keep her composure. Her eyes suddenly landed on him. "Well, detective? What are you still standing here for?" she snapped. "Get to work and find Sam's killer!"

Silvana clenched her fists and crouched slightly like she was ready to attack, but Jason just held up both hands. "It's ok, Khadija. I'll get to work. Come on, guys."

He walked back downstairs into the lounge room, and was relieved to see Silvana and Freddie had taken the hint and followed him out. Edward stayed in the room with his patient. When Jason was far out of earshot, he sat back down on the couches and spoke in a whisper, "Well this sucks. We had two leads, and both haven't helped us at all. If anything, we're further from the truth now. Sam was killed with a blade? What does that even mean?"

"It means it wasn't a Skinwalker," Silvana said. "It was a knight. A mortal knight killed a wizard."

"Then what were the Skinwalkers even doing there? Why'd they attack you and Portia? Why'd they attack Khadija?"

Freddie shrugged. "Maybe they're unrelated."

Jason froze, before staring at Freddie in awe. "My god, you might be right. These could be two completely separate events. The Skinwalkers dropped a bomb then attacked Khadija, for whatever reason. Then a random knight saw their opportunity to kill an enemy in the confusion." He slapped his own forehead. "And the knight slashed at Sam's throat multiple times."

"To make it look like a Skinwalker attack!" Silvana cried.

"Exactly. You're right, Freddie. Two separate events."

Freddie was frowning. "Unless, they coordinated."

Jason blinked. "Oh I see what you're getting at. The explosion, the dinosaurs, all part of the distraction to let a knight surprise-kill Samantha. Hell, that would even explain why the velociraptors attacked Khadija, to keep her occupied."

"That's a really good point, Freddie," Silvana said. "You're pretty smart at this." Freddie blushed under her praise.

"Well shit," Jason said. "This is actually a complication. Now we have twice the work." He stood up and started pacing the lounge room while stroking his chin. "So the Skinwalkers were not there to kill Sam. They were just trying to kill Khadija. Unless that's what we're supposed to think? Except Silvana was in the wrong place at the wrong time and got in the way."

"I was also on the balcony when it blew up," Silvana reminded him.

"Right. So..." he spun sharply. "Maybe you were the target. Or at least *one* of the targets. A secondary goal, or the primary? Either way, the question is why? What do you, Khadija and Samantha have in common? What enemy would want both of you dead? Where's the connection?"

"We discussed some taboo topics, that night," Silvana said. "Our conversation could have made us look like anti-Imperium sympathisers."

Jason stopped pacing, and instead just ran a hand through his hair.

"So which do we investigate first?" Freddie asked. "The knight who murdered Sam, or the shapeshifters who tried to kill Silvana and Khadija?"

Jason looked between them. "I don't know. Guys...I don't have any leads left to follow. There are no more clues."

"That doesn't mean we give up," Freddie said. "We can hunt for more clues..."

Jason waved his hand at him. "If I had jurisdiction, I could go back to Dubai and investigate the royal family. I could ask questions within the Immortal community. But I don't have the authority to do any of that. I'm just an amateur. And I think I've hit a dead end."

Silvana shook her head. "Not yet. Just think about it more. You've got plenty of clues to work with. We know a knight killed Samantha. We might be the only ones who know that. Just consider this for a few days. You'll think of something."

"And don't tell Khadija any of that 'dead end' stuff," Freddie said. "She's scary, man."

They heard voices and movement in the kitchen, so the trio

marched across the rooms to find Khadija and Edward speaking in hushed voices around the table. They cut off when Jason arrived.

"We need to go home," Jason said. "It's Sunday afternoon. I have work in the morning, and I have a three and a half hour drive ahead of me."

Khadija said, "If I teleport you all home, can you use that time to work the case?"

"Oh. Well sure. But Silvana has to go to her house, and Freddie and I go to our house."

Khadija gave a coy smile. "Oh I see. Roommates, hey?"

"Why does everyone assume that?" Freddie asked.

Khadija sighed. "Fine. I can do two trips, as a favour to you all. I'll start with Silvana, since I've been there before. Then I'll need some time to prepare a trip to your place." She held out a hand for Silvana.

"Right. Just a moment please," Silvana said. She turned to Edward and gave a low, formal bow. "You have my deepest thanks for inviting us to your home. I ask your pardon for any offence, and hope to part from you today in friendship."

Edward looked at her, actually forcing himself to make eye contact. "Thank you, Silvana. We are indeed friends. You are welcome here any time." Then he stared at the wall once more. Silvana looked to Jason with a huge smile, her entire face alight.

She gave Jason a quick kiss on the lips. "Text me when you get home."

"I will. I love you."

"I love you too." She waved to Freddie. "We have to have a Countdown rematch."

"You are so on!" They shared a laugh. "I had heaps of fun, Silvana."

"Same."

The vampire took the wizard's hand. Magic bent the room around them, and Jason found he had become familiar with the bizarre sight of a wormhole opening up in the middle of a domestic kitchen and two women disappearing into it.

Jason found himself standing opposite Edward. He cleared his throat. "So, uh… thanks again for letting us stay the weekend. It was full of surprises." Edward smiled at him. "Would you like to visit us some time?"

"I don't really go out unless I have to."

"Just consider it, mate," Freddie said. "At home, I've got a big computer. Not just a tiny laptop. We're talking major firepower."

Edward paused. "Well, maybe."

Khadija reappeared. "Right. This will be easier if you hold my hand." She reached for both men.

"Should I click my heels three times?" Freddie asked. "Or would it help if I go out and pushed?" Khadija glared at him while Jason stifled a laugh. She started to concentrate, while everyone else stood around awkwardly.

Jason phone buzzed. It was a text from Silvana. *"Home safe."* He smiled. It was nice to have someone checking on him.

"Wait," Jason cried. "Edward, can I buy a healing potion off you? I just feel like it might be useful in the coming—"

Edward reached into his robes and handed one to him. "Just take it."

"Oh!" Jason grinned at him. "Thanks man. I appreciate that." He shrugged towards Freddie. "One of these really helped last time shit was going down. Figured it couldn't hurt."

"Hey, what's the deal with those healing potions?" Freddie asked. "Can they cure diseases? What about the common cold?" Khadija was grimacing in annoyance. She had her eyes shut in a meditative stance, but her lids flickered as she struggled to concentrate.

"The body has memory," Edward said. "It remembers how it should be when it gets injured. So the healing potion restores it to how it was. It's extremely effective on wounds but not so good with diseases. The potion restores organisms, and technically most diseases are organisms themselves."

"Ah, that's pretty cool." Freddie frowned. "Then what if Jason drank it now, and tomorrow I stabbed him."

"Freddie!" Jason cried.

"Would the potion heal him then?"

Edward got excited. "Oh I tested this! So the potion has a limited life span once ingested. If it's sitting in your stomach, you have about twenty minutes where it will heal a wound the instant it appears. Any longer and the potion won't be effective at all."

"Cool! So if Jason gets shot—"

"Freddie!"

"—he would heal?"

Edwards shook his head. "Elixirs cannot remove foreign objects. You'll have to do that yourself."

"Please stop talking," Khadija said in a strained voice. Everyone went quiet. A second later, they suddenly dropped into space once more.

"Bye Eddie!" Freddie cried as they fell away into darkness.

Chapter 24

Jason woke to his alarm blaring, alerting him it was seven on a Monday morning. He had work in an hour.

His mind was in such an exhausted fog it was hard to wake up properly. He rolled out of bed and groaned as he felt the fiery burn in his shoulder. He glanced down at his bare chest to where the healed skin around his wounded shoulder still looked pink and raw. The muscle felt painfully tender as he rolled out the stiffness in his joints. It was tolerable. He ate a simple breakfast and got dressed in his uniform. Then he picked up his car keys and went out to the garage to begin his drive to work.

The garage was empty.

He stared at the vacant space in front of him. He blinked several times and rubbed his eyes. The garage was still empty. *What the hell is going on? Did I park on the street?* He kept staring, as if expecting to see the car appear if he stared hard enough. *Did someone steal my car? When was the last time I saw it?* Then a single thought pierced the fog of his mind.

"Oh my god," he said out loud. "My car is still at Swansea."

He'd left it at Edward's house. He hadn't even considered it when Khadija offered to teleport him. He was just relieved to not have to drive in his exhausted state. Now he was stuck here. *And my car is three and a half hours away.*

Unless…

He pulled out his phone and dialled. "Hello, Khadija? It's Jason. No, I don't have any update on your case yet, sorry. I was just calling cause my car is still at Edward's place in Swansea. I don't suppose there's any chance you could teleport it here? Or just teleport me to work, if it's easier… Hello? Hello? Khadija are you still…"

He put the phone away.

A moment later he knocked on Freddie's bedroom door. "Whaaaat?" Freddie groaned in a sleepy voice.

"My car is at Swansea."

"So?"

"I need to get to work."

"Why is that my problem? I don't have a car."

"I know. But I need to get to work somehow, and you get by without a car all the time. So how do you do it?"

"Jesus Christ, man, just call a fucking *uber*!"

"Oh." Jason blinked. He slapped himself in the forehead. "Sorry, man, that should have been obvious. I'm a bit out of it this morning."

Freddie just grunted. "All good, mate," and went back to sleep.

"Officer Turner, you're late."

Jason just grinned. "Piss off, Douglas," he said and patted his partner on the shoulder. "How was your weekend?"

"Nice and quiet," Douglas said as he poured himself a cup of coffee. "You know my former daughter, Tracey?"

"Doug you don't have to introduce your trans son as your former daughter every time."

"I just want to be clear. Anyway, he officially goes by Timmy now. Turns out, having a son is awesome. We spent half of Saturday in the shed trying to fix my old Ford Cortina. Then we watched Scarface and drank beer." Douglas chuckled. "Honestly, things are so much simpler between us now. You want some?" He held out the coffee pot. Jason nodded, and Douglas poured him a cup. "It's strange, but these days I can't wait to get home and hang out with Timmy. We've never been this close. I wish he came out years ago."

Jason found himself staring silently. "What?" Douglas asked.

"Nothing. I just… I think I'm gonna cry."

"Come off it," Douglas groaned. "The coffee that bad?"

"What? No. Buddy, you're an amazing father." Douglas scoffed. "I'm serious. You accept your son and want to be with him. That's beautiful."

"Yeah yeah, I know. But I don't know why you'd want to cry about it. That's why I like having a son. No sissy stuff."

"Real men cry, Douglas."

The older cop shrugged. "Look, I've accepted a lot of strange new stuff lately, but that one's a little too strange for me, alright?" He grinned. "So how was *your* weekend?"

"Well I saw a zombie wizard fight another wizard. I went to Norway and America. Oh, and I got struck by lightning."

Douglas stared at him. Then he silently refilled his coffee from the pot and walked away.

Jason chided himself. It had been funny to mess with him, and yet Douglas was one of only two cops who believed him about the Immortal world. He shouldn't overwhelm him like that. *Gotta ease people into the crazy shit.* He sat down by his desk. He had barely touched his chair when the captain called him into her office.

"Morning Captain," he said. "How was your weekend?"

Kader looked up at him, and he immediately knew he was in trouble. "What did I tell you about the Glucksburgs, officer Turner?"

Oh no.

"To not investigate them."

"Correct. It was a pretty simple instruction, wasn't it?"

"Absolutely."

"So why was my TV, in the privacy of my own home, and on my weekend off, reporting a gas leak and explosions in the town of Glucksburg, Germany?"

"I…" Jason stopped. "Did you say Germany?"

"Yes. At the Glucksburg castle."

Jason frowned. "I thought that was in Norway. Isn't that where the Glucksburgs rule?"

Kader took a breath to calm herself. Her tone struggled to remain civil. "The Glucksburgs are a large family. Yes, they're the current rulers of Norway, but they also hold territory all across Germany, Denmark, Sweden, even Greece. Which begs the questions. Why would you assume you were at their centre of power?" She frowned. "How could you *not know* what country you were in?"

"Huh." He shook his head. "Captain, it's not what you think."

"I noticed your weekend report on the Immortal Investigations hasn't come through. Something keeping you occupied?"

"Captain…"

"And you seem injured. You wouldn't have been off doing something stupid without my permission, would you officer?"

"Ma'am, can I please explain?"

Kader finally seemed to slow down enough to go quiet, and instead sat back in her chair and gestured for him to speak.

"Ok so…things got weird." Jason recounted the weekend events to Kader in as much detail possible, leaving nothing out. When he finished, she stared at him a long time. He wondered if he should say more, or just wait patiently, as his mind imagined a dozen ways she might react. Then…

"That's the oldest excuse in the book."

Jason jerked back. "What?!"

"A wizard made you do it? Come on, Turner. You might as well tell me your dog ate your report while you're at it."

"But…but…surely you're not serious."

Her eyes glimmered. "I'm am serious. And don't call me Shirley."

Jason blinked rapidly. "Was that a joke?"

"Airplane," Kader said with a grin. "Leslie Neilson. You ever seen it?" Jason shook his head. "Too bad. Sorry, I just…" Kader gave a sigh. "Sometimes we have to laugh. What else can we do?"

It was a sobering thought, and Jason felt the last ebbs of joy fade away. "You're right. Captain, watching those two wizards fight was like watching hurricanes collide. They were forces of nature. One caused an earthquake. I mean…they wield so much power. It's terrifying. One wizard just teleported me across the world without my consent. It was completely disempowering."

"You can explain it all in your report," Kader said. "I'm just relieved you didn't go to the Glucksburgs deliberately. Now moving on from the weekend incident, please update me on the case. It sounds like you learnt a lot of new information."

Jason briefly explained his current lack of leads. "So I know there were two aggressors at the gala. A mortal knight, and a trio of Skinwalkers. But I have no idea how to get more information about them. I don't have jurisdiction. If only Lynch and Cole believed me on this stuff, I could ask them for input. What do you think, Captain?"

She sat back in her chair and folded her hands in her lap. "I think crimes go unsolved far more often than anyone likes to admit."

"Really? You think this is unsolvable?"

"Not necessarily. I just want to prepare you for the possibility. If you ever want to be really depressed…"

"Why would I?"

"...look up some statistics on unsolved cases. That is a black hole. You know how many people go missing every year? How many rapes and sexual assaults go unreported, and how many of the reported ones go free? It's estimated that for every one hundred sexual assaults, only two lead to jail time."

Jason twisted his mouth like he tasted something sour. "Well that's fucked," Jason said.

"It is. The point is that all detectives are just humans. Sometimes our best isn't good enough. Doesn't make us failures. Just means the world is too big to solve on our own."

"Yeah...and at the same time," he shifted forward in his chair and whispered. "I have this hunch."

Kader leaned forward too and whispered, "Oh?"

"I don't know. A feeling. Like I have all the clues I need in front of me, and if I can just put the clues together in the right order, they'll click together."

She shrugged. "Maybe. Or you just need fresh eyes." She sat up straight and her tone became formal once more. "Today you're going to resume working the tax fraud case with Lynch and Cole. Focusing on something else will give you a break. Also, you'll be interviewing that asshole again, the CFO."

"Oh great."

"I know," Kader grimaced in sympathy. "Just remember what we talked about. Don't answer his accusations, and don't play his game. Don't let him control the conversation. You'll be fine. Then this afternoon, when you work the Immortal case again, I hope you'll have a fresh perspective."

"Do you want me to work overtime?"

"I can't pay you to investigate wizards. How the hell would I justify that? Also, I still need your report on the weekend."

Jason sighed. "Can't I have a day off? Did I mention I got struck by lightning?"

"Oh come on. My son's been using that excuse since he was five."

"*He has?!*"

Jason was squished up in the back seat of Lynch's car. Once again, Cole had not moved her seat forward.

"So, do we have any new angles to try?" Jason asked.

Lynch snorted. "Get your mind out of the gutter, rookie." He gave a dark chuckle. "But no. We're literally going to go back to interview the same people and harass them into confessing."

"But we don't call it harassment," Cole said. "In fact, we go to great length to avoid using that term and deny that's what we're doing."

"Even though it's essentially what we're doing."

Jason nodded. "Is this a common practice? If you run out of ideas, you just revisit old places and press for more information?"

"Yeah, but it's real bottom-of-the-barrel stuff. I know these bastards are guilty, and I know they've covered their tracks too well. And they know that I know. So my plan today is to annoy them into leaking something. That's why I bought you along, rookie."

"Cause you find me annoying?"

"Nice catch." Lynch chuckled. "But no. I brought you because today's going to be a shit show and I want you to see it."

Jason didn't bother arguing the point. He just stared at the window at the passing waterfront of Plymouth town. After seeing Boston, Dubai and Glucksburg castle all in the last week, his home town was looking smaller than ever.

"And this time," Cole said, "ask them annoying questions. If they try to ask questions of you, ignore them. Don't get flustered. Make them play to your tune."

"Yes, ma'am."

They parked on the same street as they did last week, outside the office complex. They were led again to one of the fancy conference rooms to wait for their guests. Jason felt his heartrate go up slightly. He remembered the way Gene Conroy had got under his skin. If the CFO tried that again, he'd be ready. *Hell, I just fought a fucking wizard. I can handle this little bitch.*

The door opened, and Gene Conroy walked straight in as if he'd been lying in wait for this exact moment. He wore a suit and tie, and his white hair was brushed back. He looked at Jason, and immediately Jason's chest constricted. *Fucking hell, I will not let this guy affect me again.*

"Am I under arrest, or am I free to go?" Gene said, still standing in the doorway.

"Please take a seat, Mr Conroy," Lynch said, gesturing to the chair across from him.

Gene didn't move, instead he took a relaxing leaning pose against the door frame. "Am I under arrest..." he repeated.

"You are here for an interview. Now sit down."

Gene smirked. "So I'm not under arrest then, am I?"

Jason had an idea and spoke without thinking. "That's a nice suit, Mr Conroy. Where did you get it?"

Gene paused. Then he smirked again. "No point telling you. It's out of your price range anyway."

Jason couldn't help smiling back. *He thinks he just landed a blow. But he actually just answered my question, on my terms. Let's keep this going.* "So you do a lot of shopping for suits? Or do you have people to do that for you?"

"How is this relevant?" Gene demanded, still holding the door open.

"It just seems like you have a large disposable income. Where did it all come from? You're still on a set salary, even as a CFO."

It was a slightly dumb question, but it did the trick. Gene entered the room and leaned over the table towards Jason. "Isn't this perfect. A rookie cop on an entry level salary wants to investigate a CFO on financial matters. As if you could even comprehend the mathematics behind what I do. Your tax return is probably as simple as uploading your annual statement and clicking submit." He scoffed, and the sound reminded Jason of a snorting pig.

"My…" Jason stopped himself from explaining that his tax return was indeed that simple. *Don't play his game. You ask the questions.* "I would like to know how you do your tax returns. Isn't that the reason we're here?"

"The reason you're here is you're a dumb cop who doesn't know any better. Why don't you save yourself the embarrassment and just go run a speed camera. That's more your skill level."

Jason started to freeze up. *He's right, I am a dumb cop. Hell, I left my car in Swansea.* His confidence was waning, and his heart was pounding. *Come on! I can do this. Nicholas taught me not freeze.* He blurted out the first thing that came to mind, "I doubt you'd get many speeding tickets. You'd need a hell of a lot of horse power to haul all of you around." And he suggestively eyed Gene's mid-section.

It was a low blow. Jason wasn't proud of insulting the guy's weight, but it clearly hit a nerve. Gene scowled darkly and went still. "So am I under arrest, or am I free to go?"

Jason eyed Lynch and Cole, as if to pass the lead back to them. They both stared at him. *Crap, they want me to keep going.* He was starting to get shaky. But he forced a smile. "Do you find me annoying, Mr Conroy?"

"Am I under arrest…"

Jason talked over top of him. "I think that's a yes. I must be very annoying to you. A dumb cop who doesn't know anything, daring to question you, the big Chief of an oh-so-important institution."

"Am I under arrest…"

"How much money did you scam out of your clients? What was the amount again? Five million pounds?"

"Am I under arrest…"

"What did you do with that money, Mr Conroy? Buy lots of suits? Reinvest it somewhere else?" Jason raised his voice, "Cause clearly, it wasn't a gym membership."

Gene went quiet. Jason paused to see how he'd react. A strange smile crossed the CFO's face. "Actually, now that you mention it," he said and pulled out his phone. "We did receive a rather curious investment recently. In fact," he laughed, "I can't believe I didn't think of it before. I mean, you all claimed that we lied about… how much exactly?"

"Five million pounds," Jason said. "Give or take."

"Right. Cause this whole case got me thinking. If I did hide money, I would absolutely reinvest it. Hide a leaf in a forest as they say. Well, we actually had a client show up the other day and would you believe it, they invested five million pounds exactly!" He laughed again. "It was so precise! Almost as if they were dumb enough to embezzle it and reinvest it to the same place."

"Who placed that investment?" Lynch said, leaning forward and pointing a finger at the table before him. "Give us a name."

"I'd be happy to. It was a beautiful young lady, blue eyes, very white skin. Had an old-timey name. Was it Samantha? Or Savannah?"

Gene Conroy looked at Jason and gave a malicious grin. "Oh no no, I remember her name now." He leaned forward and whispered. "Her name was… *Silvana.* Yes. Silvana Clarke. Perhaps you know her?"

"You're lying!" Jason shouted, rising out of his chair and clenching his fists. He immediately regretted it. Lynch was beside him with a hand on his chest, and Gene was chuckling to himself as he held out his phone screen. Jason barely scanned the words. It showed an investment document, with Silvana's name and the sum of five million pounds.

"Oh, did I hit a nerve?" Gene chuckled again. "Good heavens, why son? Do you know this girl?"

"Turner, look at me," Lynch warned.

"Or maybe you only *thought* you knew her," Gene said. "Maybe you don't really know her at all."

Jason saw red. His mind was flashing with rage, and suddenly all he could see was his mother's body, swinging from the belt around her neck, and his father mocking her and blaming her for everything. This powerful man in a suit was mocking Silvana in just the same way. Jason wanted to leap the table and punch this man's teeth out. It would be so easy…

"Bastard," Jason growled as he forced himself to step away from the table and turned his back on the group. He forced himself to breath steadily, but the sound of Gene's laughter made his rage burn even hotter. *I need to bash him. I need to fucking kick his skull in, that fucking asshole! How dare he go after Silvana!*

"Detective," Cole said in a calm voice of command. "Wait for us in the car."

Jason left the room without another word.

"So," Lynch said a few minutes later. "Seems your girl is flushed with cash."

Jason stood on the street corner, leaning against the bonnet of the car. The doors were locked, and Lynch had the keys, so there had been nothing to do but wait for his colleagues and calm the rapid beating of his heart. The late morning traffic was rolling past, and pedestrians walked by with their inane chatter.

"Between the two of you," Cole said, "I assume she wears the pants? Cause you seem like the emotional one."

"I'm sorry, detective."

"I know you're new at this, but that's no excuse to be so temperamental. That's twice now you've let that guy unhinge you."

Lynch cleared his throat, "Look that's a bit unfair. He was doing alright for a while there. And Conroy played really fucking dirty."

"Yes, then Jason had to be held back from attacking him physically."

"To be fair, you've held me back before."

"Shut it, Lynch!" Cole snapped, and both Jason and Lynch took a step back from her. Jason had never seen Cole this angry before. She took breeches in professionalism very seriously. "The point is you lost your shit, rookie. Big time, in front of a civilian. There is no excuse for that. Ever. I don't care what triggers you have in your past."

Jason inhaled sharply and turned on her. Up to that point he'd been expecting a dressing down. But that was too far.

"That's none of your business," he growled.

"It is my business when it bleeds into your work," Cole snapped back. "You need to act like a professional. You represent all police when you act like a hot-headed dumbass. Your behaviour needs to be above reproach."

Jason bit back his reply. He had half a mind to explain just what horrifying image had appeared in his mind when he had lost his shit. But somehow he knew it wasn't important. Cole was angry, but she was still trying to teach him something. "Ok," he said. "I'm sorry. I'll try to do better."

"Damn right you will," Cole said. "Cause we're about to go pay a visit to your girlfriend, and bringing you along is a major conflict of interest. So you better fucking behave."

"Yes, detective."

Cole hopped into the front seat. Lynch gave Jason a pained, sympathetic smile before getting behind the wheel and starting up the car. Jason climbed into his usual tight space on the back seat and they drove away.

"So what happens next?" Jason said over the hum of the vehicle.

"We interview Silvana," Lynch said. "Find out her story. And while we're on the way, access her files and bank records." Cole pulled out a laptop and started typing. "We'll see what the official story is, regarding where all that money came from. When we talk to her, we'll see if she tells us the truth."

"Unless you can tell us anything?" Cole said.

"No. I know nothing about Silvana's financial situation."

"How shocking," she said.

Jason ground his teeth, but said nothing.

"Hey Turner," Lynch said. "This probably goes without saying, but I don't want you texting your girlfriend to tell her we're coming."

"Yeah, of course."

"To be sure, hand over your phone," Cole said and reached her hand around the back of the passenger seat.

Jason let out a growl, but gave his phone to her without a word. *One of these days, Cole...*

They drove out of Plymouth town without encountering any traffic and entered the northern suburbs where the signs of civilisation faded and the land became a thicker shade of green. Cole was able to find the bank records she was looking for in that time. "Apparently she took out a loan, and invested everything."

"What?" Lynch said. "Loans incur debt. Even I know that."

"It was a low interest loan from the bank, with a high interest investment. She would have made enough to stay ahead of the loan repayments and make a profit."

"How'd she get a loan for five million?"

"She used the mansion as leverage. Apparently Nicholas Clarke signed off on it."

"Oh my god," Jason groaned. "Oh my god, Silvana." He shook his head. "I know what she's done. I was there when she talked to her family about it. She suggested this very thing to the family as a way to make money off their assets. We voted on it. Everyone was against her."

"Except this Nicholas Clarke, right?"

"No. He voted against her too."

Lynch and Cole exchanged a glance. "Do you think he changed his mind in private?" Lynch asked.

"Or is it possible she committed fraud?" Cole asked.

Jason sighed. He couldn't answer.

Chapter 25

Jason and the two detectives pulled into the cul-de-sac in the dead forest with piles of scattered leaves. The trio approached the mansion on foot. Jason remembered coming here once six months ago with Peter, his then roommate, to chaperone him on a date with a vampire. Now he was leading yet another enemy straight to her home. Was it possible that since then he'd only had a negative effect on Silvana's life? Would she be better off without him? *Don't think like that. Focus up.*

Lynch knocked on the front door. "Don't make a scene," he said. "Stay professional and don't get all crazy."

"I won't."

"I was talking to myself."

Jason blinked at him in confusion. *Right, last time he was here, a telepath messed with his head.* He decided not to say anything.

Lisbeth opened the door, wearing a long blue gown and her hair up in a tight bun. "Oh hello Jason…and officers," she said nervously. "What's this about?"

"We're here in an official capacity," Lynch said. "Is Silvana Clarke here? We would like to speak to her."

Lisbeth looked to Jason. "What's this about?" she repeated.

Lynch answered instead, "I think it best we speak to her first."

"Oh. Well, ok then. She's just…"

"What's this about?"

Phillip appeared in the doorway and immediately stood between the officers and the entry. Jason nearly groaned out loud.

"Sir, we're here to speak with Silvana Clarke."

"Why?"

"They won't say," Lisbeth said.

"Really?" Phillip drawled. "Well, unless you can tell us what you want, we don't have to let you into our house."

"Phillip," Jason groaned. "Come on, man. Don't do this. This is important."

"Oh really? So important you can't tell us anything? Sounds suspicious to me. In fact, it sounds like you've done something wrong and now you're trying to get Silvana involved."

"Phillip, I'm trying to help this family."

Cole raised a hand. "That's enough, officer." Jason bit his tongue.

"Please," Lynch said, "we're asking politely. We just want to interview Silvana first to get the full story, then we can explain everything to you. Trust me, this will keep everyone happy."

"No," Phillip snapped. "If you want to speak to Silvana, then we'll get the whole family together and you can speak to us all at once."

Jason groaned again. "Phil, I'm telling you, that's a really bad idea."

"Don't care. Those are the options. Unless you want to take several days to come back with a warrant."

Lynch glanced at Cole, and while neither reacted in any discernible way, an understanding seemed to pass between them. Lynch answered confidently, "We agree to that."

"Lynch," Jason started, but a glare from Cole cut him off.

Phillip stepped aside and finally granted them entry to the house. He called out to the others in the household to come downstairs as the police stepped inside. Silvana appeared out of the east wing.

She smiled brightly when she saw Jason, but her face showed a brief flash of fear at the sight of the detectives. That, more than anything, confirmed to Jason that Silvana knew she had done something wrong.

"Sweetheart," she said with a noticeably forced smile. "How are you?"

"I'm good, Silvy," Jason said. "The detectives need to talk with you."

She nodded casually, though a little too casually. "Aunty, I'm happy to talk to the detectives first while you get the others."

Phillip answered for Lisbeth, "We'll be speaking to them together. As a family."

Silvana didn't react. "Actually, there is one small thing I'd like to check first, if you don't mind…"

"No, Silvana. Do not talk to them," Phillip snapped. Silvana stared back with frosty eyes. She glanced to her aunt, but Lisbeth avoided her gaze. So she locked gazes with Jason. He took a slight step towards her, and instantly Lynch moved to cut him off while shaking his head. Jason flexed his fists.

He was helpless to protect her, and that was the feeling he hated the most.

They all followed Phillip and Lisbeth towards the dining room table. The residents took their usual seats. When Lynch went for the head of the table, Lisbeth stopped him with a polite cough and hand gesture towards the opposite end. Jason tried to sit next to Silvana, but Cole was watching him hard enough to change his mind. The police all gathered at one end.

A few moments later, Emberline and Nicholas arrived. The two of them were touching by gripping each other's forearm, and for a second Jason wondered at seeing them paired together. Then he saw Nicholas's limp. The old man was panting from the exertion. His wrist was shaking.

"Sir, do you need help?" Jason said and leapt to his feet.

Nicholas held up a hand. "At ease, son. I'm being helped." He put on his best smile as Emberline pulled out the chair at the head of the table. But his smile turned into a wince as he moved to sit down. All signs of pain were gone a second later. He clasped his hands together.

"Sorry to worry everyone. It's that damn pain in my wrist again. You remember Jason?" He did remember, from when he accidently fired his magnum. No wonder he wasn't explaining it fully in front of the detectives. "Well it seems to have caused a bit of pain to flare up everywhere else. It's crazy, but it's almost as if all my body parts were connected."

Jason tried to smirk. "Who knew?"

Nicholas grinned back at him. "I'll be back to full strength after a few days of rest. Then you and I can have that wrestling match we keep putting off."

Jason couldn't help smiling for real. "Maybe we should wrestle *before* you're fully recovered, so I might have a chance."

They chuckled again, until Lynch pointedly cleared his throat. "So," Nicholas said, his tone more formal. "Welcome to our home, officers. Is there something you'd like to talk to us about?"

Lynch took a breath. "Yes. We've encountered some unusual financial activity. At this stage we'd just like to ask a few questions. No one is under arrest. Also, we really just wanted to speak to Silvana, but Mr Phillip insisted we speak to everyone."

The instant Silvana's name was uttered, Emberline's head whip-lashed to look at her. *She's like a shark smelling blood,* Jason thought. He grimaced. *No. Like a vampire smelling blood. God that's so much worse.* Silvana was ignoring her aunt's gaze, but Jason could see the cracks already appearing in her mask.

Lynch cleared his throat. "So, Miss Clarke. What do you do for a source of income?"

Silvana smiled. "I'm a student. I'm about to begin studying

medicine. I'm hoping to begin work as a doctor in four years' time."

"Really? Cause we did a background check on you. I didn't see your name in any university enrolment."

"I haven't enrolled yet. I only just submitted the application."

"Yes," Nicholas said. "I only signed the guardian permission form for her last week."

Lynch and Cole shared a glance. *Oh crap.*

"Did you have a good long look through that form?" Cole asked.

"Didn't need to. Nowadays it's all terms I don't understand anyway."

"Right." Cole looked to Lynch, and he continued.

"So Miss Clarke, you're twenty-three years old?"

"That's right."

"You graduated university over two years ago with a nursing degree. Did you just have two gap years back to back?" Jason knew she'd actually studied nursing fifteen years ago, but mortal records had been updated to hide her immortality.

"No. I've been doing art. I draw. I like comic books, and I was hoping to make it as an artist. But it's taking too long. Thought I would continue in medicine instead."

Lynch looked to the family. "And this house. A rather nice place. How did you all afford it?"

"It's inherited," Phillip said.

"By you?" Lynch asked. Phillip just scowled back at him.

"By me," Nicholas said. "Phillip is my brother-in-law. I'm happy to share my home with my family."

"And who does Silvana belong to?"

Lisbeth gave a sweet smile and nod. "She's my adopted daughter. From an earlier marriage."

Lynch eyed her, then slouched back in the chair and sneered. "What was wrong with the first husband? Mansion too small?"

The table went quiet. Emberline sat up rigid and clenched her fists, but Lynch only slouched further. Jason understood then that Lynch had been offensive on purpose, to test the waters. He could see everyone sitting just a little more upright. Lisbeth took just a little too long to reply.

"It was his coffin," she said, and her flat tone gave Jason the chills. "His coffin was too small."

"So the family fortune," Lynch said, unaffected. "It's all yours, Nicky. Is that right?"

Nicholas stared back. "Yes."

"Is it a big fortune?"

"Big enough."

"Really? So how do these assets make you money? You have investments somewhere, perhaps?"

Nicholas raised his chin. "I'm a steward. I inherited this land from my father, and I will pass in onto my son one day in a better condition than I found it."

"Ah. That's what I thought. In other words, you're broke." Lynch shrugged and gestured at the dining space, the chandelier, the fireplace. "You've got a nice place, but it's just gathering dust. You need the money badly, don't you?"

Nicholas blinked rapidly a few times. "What is your point, detective?" His voice shook slightly.

"My point is on the surface you look rich. But in truth, this family is in dire straits. And desperate times call for desperate measures, don't they?" He looked at Silvana. "Don't they, Miss Clarke?"

Emberline rounded on her daughter again. "What is he talking about, Silvana?"

"If there were no legal options available to you," Lynch powered on, "you would have to turn to illegal options. Such as fraud. Perjury. Extortion. Tax evasion." Jason blinked. *Tax evasion? Is he just saying random terms now?*

"I don't know what you're talking about," Silvana said.

"Really? Does the number five million mean anything to you?"

She flinched. Everyone saw it. She immediately brushed her hair back and tried to smile. "Is that how much I won in the lottery? Is that what this is all about?" She laughed, and no one joined her.

"Tell me, how long have you been working for Gene Conroy?"

Emberline's eyes widened. "Who the hell is Gene Conroy?"

Silvana stuttered, "I know he's the CFO of some investment company, aunty. I was going to use him for one of the investment plans I told you about a few days ago."

"Or was he going to use you?" Lynch said. "Here's what I think happened. Mr Conroy is being investigated for tax fraud. We suspect he siphoned off five million pounds from the investors in his company without their knowledge. Then here you come, Miss Clarke, with exactly five million pounds, ready to invest it back into his company. I believe you did it on his instructions."

"Five million?" Emberline cried. "What are you talking about? We never invested anything like that. There's no…"

She suddenly went quiet, looking down at the table and frowning as the gears turned in her head. *Here we go. She's figured it out. Brace yourselves everyone.* He looked at Silvana. She knew it too. And there was nothing Jason could do to protect her from what was coming.

"Oh my god," Emberline said. "No. No way. There is no way you could be that stupid."

"Emberline," Lisbeth warned.

"We said no to your idea. We all voted and agreed. Surely you did not go behind our backs and do it anyway. Surely not."

Silvana said nothing. Emberline looked between her and Nicholas. "And the enrolment forms you got him to sign. They were financial statements. You…" She looked at Nicholas. "You blind old fool."

"Emberline, that's enough," Lisbeth said.

But she paid no attention. She looked at Silvana, and snarled, "You foolish girl. You fucking idiot."

"Emberline!" Lisbeth shouted, at the same time Jason shouted, "Hey!" and Lynch pleaded, "Mrs Clarke, please."

"I can't believe you would be this stupid," Emberline said. "How could you do this? You borrowed five million pounds against our wishes? You tricked your own flesh and blood out of his money, then threw it all away…"

"I didn't throw it away!" Silvana snapped. "I *invested* it. I explained to you in plain simple terms why we had to start investing, and you ignored everything I said because it wasn't your idea!"

Emberline slammed a fist down on the table as she stood up. "We *did* listen to your bloody idea, and it was *wrong!* We emphatically forbid you from doing it."

"Someone had to save this family!" Silvana said.

"Then get a damn job!" Emberline snapped back. "We've begged you for years to help us with our art. We've trained you in oils for decades!"

"Decades?" Lynch quizzed.

"But no," Emberline went on. "You insisted on drawing those worthless, childish stick figures."

"Comic books are not childish!"

"They make no money!"

Silvana nearly screamed. "If you'd watched a movie in the last fifteen years, you'd know comic books make more money than all other movies combined!"

"Uh, ladies?" Lynch asked.

Emberline spun to face the police, and fixed her eyes on Jason. "This is all your fault, you egregious little shit." Lynch and Cole stood to their feet in an instant, ready to defend Jason by force if necessary.

"You show up in our lives and start telling us how we should live. You dare tell us how to treat our own daughter."

Jason held up his hands. "Hang on, Emberline, I'm not really involved…"

"I bet you told her to do this. You, whispering in her ear and filling her head with dark ideas."

"Ideas like we should respect her?" Jason growled, the words bursting out of him. "Show her basic courtesy?"

"You shut your damn mouth, zounderkite," Phillip growled. "Don't you dare talk back to my wife. You've caused enough trouble already." Jason inhaled, ready to fire back.

"That's enough, everyone," Nicholas said. His voice was quiet, almost a whisper, yet it broke through the rising tension in the room. The detectives sat back in their chairs and everyone went still as Nicholas turned his old weathered eyes upon Silvana. "My dear," he whispered. His eyes were squeezed together in obvious pain. He struggled to get the words out. "Is it true? Did you…deceive me?" His voice was shaking.

Silvana stared up at him, tears pooling in the corners of her eyes. "Uncle Nic…" she whispered. Her mouth hung open as she tried to get the words out. She stared around the room, as if searching for a single friendly face. Then she looked Nicholas in the eye. "Nic…" she whispered.

"Is it true?" he asked again, as if begging her to say it wasn't true.

"I'm sorry, Uncle. I'm so sorry." Silvana covered her face with her hands.

Nicholas recoiled back from her. Suddenly the words burst from Silvana in a torrent.

"It's just that you don't understand finance," she cried. "Things don't work the way they used to. If we didn't act soon, we would lose everything. I was trying to protect you." Nicholas said nothing. He just squeezed his eyes shut, causing twin tear drops to streak down his cheeks. "Uncle Nic, please. I wasn't trying to steal from you. I wanted to help you. And this will help! This investment will make us money! In just three weeks, we'll have ten thousand pounds in cash. You'll see, we'll be able to fix the wall in the parlour room…" she trailed off when he opened his tear-filled eyes. Jason could see her hold her breath as Nicholas stared at her.

"If you had just asked," he whispered, "I would have given you *everything.*"

Silvana froze. A single sob burst from her throat and her eyes filled with tears. Jason found his own vision blurring and had to rub his eyes to keep them clear. He couldn't bear to watch Nicholas anymore. Couldn't bear to see the heartbreak in his eyes. Or the pain in Silvana's either.

"So that's it, then," Lynch said in a business-like tone. "You admit to committing fraud, Miss Clarke, and tricking your Step-Father out of his money. I'm going to have to place you—"

"NO!" Nicholas roared, and his sudden fury made them all jump. His eyes flashed at the detectives, even through his tears. "I will *not* press charges on my daughter! If you take this to court, I will claim I did this willingly. I will not testify, and you will not get a conviction."

"You cannot lie under oath," Cole said.

"Damn your oaths!" Nicholas growled. "She's my daughter. Everything I own was going to her anyway. It's as good as hers. She had every right to do what she did. You will *not* arrest her for this, or so help me, I will use every connection I have to fight you."

Silvana buried her face in her hands. She squeaked a few times as sobs burst through her control. Jason could only stare at Nicholas in awe. *This man calls me son.*

"If that is your wish," Lynch said, "then we will not press charges. But there will still be consequences." He looked to Cole, and she nodded at him. Lynch went on. "Her investment has gone into a company that is being investigated for fraud. Therefore, her finances are suspect. We will have to seize those assets until such a time as we can corroborate your story."

Silvana looked up, fear in her eyes. "What does that mean?"

Lynch swallowed, and it was the only hint he gave at the discomfort he was clearly feeling. "It means that your money will be held by the government for the duration of our investigation."

"But…" Silvana cried. "That cash is a loan! I need the investment to keep up with repayments. Without the investment returns, I'll be out of pocket twenty eight thousand pounds for this month alone." Emberline clicked her tongue, but Silvana went on. "How long will you hold it? A week? Two weeks?"

"It might be a lot longer than that. Maybe six months. Maybe a year."

"A year!" Silvana cried. "But I can't afford that much loan repayments. We'll forfeit the house if you hold it that long!"

"Don't you have cash on hand?" Cole asked. "Surely you didn't invest the full amount of the loan into one place…" she trailed off when Silvana winced with shame.

"My god," Emberline growled.

Lynch could only sigh. "I'm sorry. All I can promise is that we'll try to work this case as quickly as possible."

"Detective, please." Silvana's voice had become hysterical. "We'll lose everything. I swear to you, I'm not working for Gene Conroy. I did this all independently. I'm not involved in anything…God, please! Just let me invest it somewhere else instead! Anywhere else!"

"I can't do that, Miss Clarke."

"Lynch," Jason cut in, just as Silvana collapsed back in her seat, clutching her head in her hands. "Surely you know Silvana didn't do this."

"It doesn't matter what I know, Turner," Lynch said. "I'm a detective. I don't have the luxury of following my beliefs. I have to investigate all possibilities. That's the job. You'll understand one day."

"But this could ruin them."

"That was the risk they took when they invested all their money in one place." Silvana let out a whimper. Lynch sighed and went on, "There is still a very real possibility that Gene Conroy siphoned off money to Silvana and tricked her into investing it for him. If we can link it back to him, we can stop an evil son of a bitch from stealing millions more. Until we can rule out that possibility, we have to do this."

Jason looked around the table. Everyone was looking down, avoiding each other's eyes. *They are my family too, and this has ruined them.* If only he had found some other way to beat Gene Conroy in his interrogation. Maybe he could have prevented this, somehow?

Lynch and Cole stood up from the table. Lynch said, "Miss Clarke, we'll need to see all financial statements for your loan and your investment. You can send them to us whenever you're ready, though I recommend all haste." He handed her a card.

"Thank you all for your time," Cole said. They turned to go, and Lynch stopped to put a hand on Jason's shoulder.

"If you want to stay for twenty minutes," Lynch said, "we'll keep the car running."

"Thanks, Lynch," Jason said. Lynch patted him once more and left, his footsteps echoing through the hall until the front door slammed shut.

Jason sat back in his chair. Now he was on the opposite end of the table, with no one beside him. He waited for someone else to speak first. He fully expected Phillip to call him a zounderkite any second now. But the older man was sitting quietly, his hands clutched together and held still. For once he didn't look angry. He looked like he'd given up.

"Before we discuss what Silvana has done," Emberline said in a slow voice, "and before anything is said about her betrayal of this family," she turned to face Jason, "this intruder needs to leave."

"Emberline?" Jason said. Lisbeth let out a gasp. Everyone was staring at Emberline with mixed reactions of surprise and disgust.

"You have brought nothing but misery to this family," she hissed in a quiet voice. She stood back from the table and clutched her hands behind her back as she raised her chin. "You've filled my daughter's head with ideas. Encouraged her to reject our advice. Ever since you came here, she's refused to listen to me. You are a danger to her. I want you *out* of here."

"That's enough," Nicholas said in a calm voice, yet he leaned forward in readiness. "Jason is my son. You will not send him from my home."

"It's not your home anymore, don't you get that?" Emberline growled. "It belongs to whichever Immortal house owns the banks. Silvana saw to that. Jason cannot be your son because he cannot be your heir, because there's nothing left for him to inherit."

"I don't care," Nicholas said. "You will not force Jason to leave."

Emberline's eyes turned a dark shade of crimson. Her pupils disappeared entirely, and she glared at Jason across the table as she whispered, "What if I slit his throat right now?"

"Aunt!" Silvana snapped and leapt to her feet. She moved with vampiric speed and blocked Jason with her own body. "You will not touch him!"

"Whoa, hang on everyone," Jason said, giving his best reassuring smile and standing up as well. "Let's all take a deep breath, ok? There's no need for threats of violence…or threats of murder."

"Shut up," Emberline hissed, her eyes unchanging. "Shut the *fuck up.* Everything you've ever done has made life worse for our family.

If you will not leave, I will make you."

"I'd like to see you try," Silvana growled, her eyes flashing red.

"You are in no place to stop me, daughter."

"I would stop you also, sister," Lisbeth said, raising to her feet as well.

Emberline blinked and stepped back. "Sister? Surely you can see the danger he has been."

"Silvana still needs his blood," Lisbeth said.

Jason rolled his eyes. *Cold, but efficient.*

"My love," Phillip said. Emberline stared down at him. His face was blank. "I love you. But you're wrong here." She glared at Phillip with blackened eyes, but he didn't back down. "This is not Jason's fault. Besides, he's a part of the family now. By Imperium law, you cannot kill him."

"Huh. Thanks Phil."

"Shut it, zounderkite."

Jason smiled inwardly. *And there it is.*

Emberline inhaled. She looked around the table once, and her eyes seemed to throw daggers at Jason. "Fine," she said. "But there will be a punishment for this. From now on, Silvana is not allowed to leave this house. Jason will be allowed to visit only with our expressed permission. And she *will* join us in painting with oils. Our only hope to save this family now is to finish our painting as soon as possible, which will require every skilled hand available. If we are lucky, we can sell it with maximum profits. Maybe then, we can stay ahead of these loan repayments long enough to get our money back and return the loan. And Silvana, I expect you to work day and night until you have paid off this debt to the family. Rest assured, your next husband will be chosen by my hand only. No more marrying unconnected mortal plebeians. You will marry who I choose, when I choose them, and you..."

"No," Silvana said.

Emberline inhaled sharply. "Things are bad enough already, Silvana. Do not make it any worse for yourself. If you want to stay in this family, you will…"

"I'm leaving."

The room went quiet. Silvana stepped away from the table. She turned to look at Jason for a moment, and straightened her shoulders back at the sight of him. She gave him a nod.

"You're not leaving until I've finished what I have to say," Emberline growled. "You will…"

"I'm leaving this *house*," Silvana said. "I'm moving out. Right now."

"Don't be ridiculous. You will not be this selfish. You will stay here and fix your mistakes."

Silvana shook her head. "I am sorry for what I've done. I'm sorry I hurt you all. And I will do everything I can to fix this problem." She held her head higher. "But I will *never* let you speak to Jason that way again. And you will *never* choose the man I marry."

"Silvana," Phillip growled. "You need to do what she has asked. Without your painting skills working alongside your aunts, this family is likely doomed."

"I will find Khadija's attacker," she said. "I will work the case with Jason and gain her financial favour. So no, I am not abandoning this family. I will fix this. But I'm not living another second under your control."

"Foolish girl!" Emberline hissed, and Silvana immediately spun and walked away. "Don't you see? That's exactly the reason we're in this mess to begin with!" She followed after Silvana, as Jason and Lisbeth raced down the hall after her, leaving the two old knights behind. "If you had just done what I asked of you, this wouldn't have happened. I'm two hundred and seventy years old! I know so much more than you do. If you weren't so arrogant, you would let me help you. Instead you're being a stupid, headstrong child…"

"Shut up!" Silvana shouted.

"…you refuse to do what you're told. Just once, just one bloody time, I wish you would do what you're told!"

Silvana stopped in the hallway. She glanced towards her room, as if considering going there and collecting some things. Instead she walked past it altogether and went to the front door. She opened it, and paused.

"Don't you step one foot outside that door," Emberline growled. "You are banned from leaving this house. If you go outside, I swear to God I will call the Vigiles and have them restrain you."

She ignored her aunt, and looked at Jason. Her eyes were red, but not from vampire blood. She held her head high and spoke in a calm voice. "Can I get a ride with you?" she asked.

"Yeah," he said. "You can stay with me and Freddie as long as you want."

"Thank you."

Emberline shoved Jason aside like he was nothing and block the doorway with her arms on the frame. "Don't you dare try to steal my daughter away. She belongs to me."

Jason's rage burned so hot within him that for a moment, he almost forgot Emberline could rip him apart. "I didn't steal your daughter," he snapped. "You drove her away. You have no one to blame but yourself."

"How dare you," Emberline hissed, stepping right into his face. She was half a foot shorter, but that didn't matter when her eyes were dark pools of blood. "How dare you speak to me that way? I should teach you some respect."

"What would you know about respect?" Jason growled. "You've never shown respect to anyone else a single day in your life."

Emberline inhaled, and suddenly Lisbeth was between them. A

gentle hand resting on her sister's chest. "Let them go," she said. "Peacefully. It's the only way you might ever win them back."

Emberline snorted. "Them?" She leaned towards Jason and snarled.

"If you ever come back here, Jason, I will kill you."

Then she launched away, moving down the hall with a vampire's speed and silence. Jason watched her go, and felt his hands trembling. Emberline had meant those words.

Jason stared at Lisbeth a second. "For what it's worth," he said, "I really am sorry about all this." Lisbeth's mouth was open, but she said nothing, like she couldn't find the words. Jason moved past her towards the door. He took Silvana's hand in his.

"I love you, mum," Silvana said.

Lisbeth nodded, and the movement made tears spill down her face. "I love you too, Silvana. And Jason…" she hesitated, her porcelain doll face glistening. "I should have said so earlier. But you are my son, and I love you too."

Jason froze in place. This woman called him son. It had been twelve years since a woman had said that to him. Yet before he could say anything, Lisbeth closed the door without waiting for an answer. The lock clicked into place with a solid thud.

Chapter 26

Silvana pressed up against Jason's shoulder in the back of the police car. She was determined not to cry while there were strangers in the car. But she couldn't stop the tears from flowing. The detectives had been reluctant to drive her, something about a conflict of interest. Jason had intervened for her. *Thank God for you, Jason. You're the only family I have left.*

"So, Miss Clarke," the large dark-skinned man said. She couldn't remember his name. "I'm sorry to ask, but where to?"

"My place," Jason said and gave the address. "Technically, I'll have to get Freddie's approval, and he'll need to get his father's approval for anything long term. But it'll do for now."

"Sure," Silvana managed to mumble. The car was silent for a few minutes, and Silvana was grateful. She wasn't up for conversation. They drove through the forest surrounding her family's estate and onto the main road, heading into the suburbs of Plymouth.

"Look, Miss Clarke," the man said again. "I hope you know there was nothing personal about all this. Just doing our jobs. For the record, as a person I think it's unlikely you did anything knowingly criminal."

"Except the fraud," the woman said.

"Yes, thank you, Cole," the man grumbled. "But like I said. We have to do our jobs. We have to protect people from corruption."

"I understand." Another silence followed her words.

"For what it's worth, kid," the man said again. She almost begged him to stop. "I know what you're going through. I'm gay, and my parents could never accept it. So I know what it's like to be rejected by your own parents." The words struck a nerve. *Rejected by your own parents.* That was exactly what had happened. Silvana squeezed her eyes shut as the tears flowed anew. "It sucks. There's few things in this life that hurt as much as that. But at the end of the day, it's the parent's choice to do that. It's not your fault."

"Thank you, sir," Silvana said.

The man seemed more enthusiastic. "I mean hell, I've seen murderers whose parents still visit them in jail. It's like, if anyone had good cause…"

"Lynch," Cole said dryly, still looking out her window without expression.

"Right. Sorry. The point is, you'll be ok."

"Smoothly done, Lynch," Jason said.

"Yeah alright. It wasn't my best." The conversation ebbed and stilled again. Silvana did feel a little better. Yet she thought to herself. *At least murderers didn't betray their family, like I did.* She stared distantly out the window as the world past around her.

The car slowed down, and Silvana was surprised to find herself already outside Jason's house. It had only felt like seconds. She finally stopped leaning on him and undid her seatbelt. "Uh, thank you both. Jason, I'll see you…"

"Actually, Turner," Lynch said. "If you want to clock off early, it's cool. We'll support you. Unless you need to pick up your car from work?"

Jason snickered. "I caught an uber to work. Thanks guys. If you're sure it's ok?"

"Take care of your woman, rookie," Cole said. "We'll tell the boss you're working from home. Detectives' honour."

"Cool. Hey, thank you both."

Silvana and Jason stood on the curb as the car pulled away. They waited there a moment with his arm around her. She noticed he was holding his work bag. She chuckled and pointed to it. "I think you now own more stuff than I do," Silvana said.

Jason looked at his bag. "Uh, yeah. Sorry about that."

"No, I'm joking."

"Oh, right. Uh…it was funny."

She took a long breath. "I've lived in that house for nearly seventy years. I feel like my life has ended."

He squeezed her shoulder, and his warm, firm hands acted like a lifeline in a storm. "Come on. Let's get you inside." He led her towards the door. "I can get you a beer, or order some takeaway as a treat. Or if you need some blood, I'm feeling much better today so you can have some early. Just tell me what you need."

"I'm fine, thank you."

Jason didn't push the issue. He opened the front door for her, and she could smell a strong musky scent inside. She raised an eyebrow. "Does Freddie just smoke weed a lot, or does he never fully stop?"

Jason grumbled. "I think I need to kick my landlord's ass." He stepped inside. "Freddie?!" he called out.

"Shit!" came the reply. A second later a door opened and Freddie shouted through the house. "Damn it man, can you text me when you're coming home early? It's best for everyone if you do." He stepped into view, shirtless, his hair frazzled, and his boxes low on his hips. "I'm trying to be accommoda…" he saw Silvana and trailed off. He pulled up his boxes. "Silvana? What…what happened?"

"Can she stay with us?" Jason asked. "We don't know how long. Maybe indefinitely. Things are just a bit…"

Freddie interrupted. "Hey no, of course you can stay, Silvana. Me casa es tu casa, god why am I Spanish all of a sudden? We've got a spare room. I can set up a bed for you. Or if you want Jason's room…" he blushed. "Sorry. I just mean you're welcome here. Of course." He looked between them. "Is everything ok, guys?"

Silvana shook her head. "I had to move out. My family…" she couldn't get the words out.

"Oh shit, I'm sorry," Freddie moved to her other side and put a hand on her shoulders. With him and Jason surrounding her, she felt safe. In an act that surprised her as much as them, she pulled them both into a tight hug. She wrapped her arms around their necks and shoulders and held them close. They held her back without hesitating. They stayed like that, until she realised they had both relaxed their grip.

"Sorry," she said and let them go. They both blushed and told her it was fine. "I'm just going to sit down for a moment. Jason, can I use your room?" He agreed, but she didn't really hear him. She just went into his bedroom and shut the door, where she collapsed down on the bed and laid on her back, staring at the roof, letting the inner void take her.

"What was that all about?" Freddie said in the other room, where she could hear him clear as day.

"Her family just had a big fight. Come on, I need a beer." She heard their footsteps recede into the kitchen. The sound of running water masked what Jason was saying. He was probably doing it on purpose as he started to explain. Still, she heard the words, "bad investment", and "tricked out of his fortune".

She tried to block them out. She kept staring at the roof, too numb to feel anything. All her thoughts were going too fast for her to process anything. She felt too many feelings to name a single one. "God, what am I going to do?" she said out loud, and it seemed to sum up exactly what she was thinking. She lay there for a long time. Ten, fifteen minutes passed in silence. She thought she had come in here to cry. Instead she just stopped everything.

"Crap," she thought. "I'm poor now." She started to laugh at the absurdity of it all. Apparently that's what she needed right now, because the deep chuckle seemed to build in her chest and just kept coming out. It broke through the numbness and after a while, she felt like herself again.

She tried to sit up, and a sudden stabbing pain flared up in her waist. She lifted her shirt. The stab wound from the knight Wilhelm was still on her hip. It wasn't healing. She was out of blood. She'd put it off too long. She had to ask Jason for blood.

I don't deserve his blood.

She'd been thirsty ever since the explosion at the gala in Dubai. Her thirst had only grown more extreme since the fight with the Glucksburgs, yet there was no way she was going to take his blood early. He'd suffered enough because of her. He was still suffering now. Here she was, taking over his home, his bedroom, his life. She couldn't possibly inconvenience him in any other way. Not without risking losing him, like she'd lost everyone else.

Someone knocked on the door. She sat up and was about to say come in. But her mind processed what she had heard. The knock had come from the *front* door.

She stepped out of the room. Jason had poked his head out of the kitchen. "Was that the front door?" he asked. She nodded. "I'll get it," he said with a sigh, his opened beer bottle looked like he'd barely touched it. He padded softly down the hall and swung the door open.

Two women stood there, wearing black tuxedos.

"Oh shit," Jason gasped.

Vigiles. Oh fuuuuck...

Jason recovered first. "Vigile Desdemona, Vigile Portia. Welcome to my home," he said. Then he frowned. "How did you even find this place?" His voice rose. "How did you even *get* here?"

"We went to the mansion first," Portia said. "Your family informed us you weren't there anymore. They left a forwarding address." Then she winced. "We had to call a cab. It was most galling. The driver kept trying to talk to us."

"That is the worst," Jason agreed.

Portia smiled as she leaned towards the doorway, staring past Jason, her red curls bouncing with the movement. "This might just be the smallest house I've ever been to," she said. "Is this how most mortals live?" There was something strange about her tone. She didn't have her usual teasing sweet voice. She sounded…normal.

"You think this is small," Jason said, "you should have seen my last place. Two bedroom apartment…"

Desdemona cut in, "Thy lack of size doth not impress us."

"Right. Sorry. Uh…how can I help you?"

"We desire to enter thy abode."

Jason looked between them. "You want to come in?"

"Just to check on thy safety. We know thou hast been in contact with a known fugitive, Khadija Al Khalifa. I wish to check thy home for lingering spells." She made to step forward.

"Whoa now," Jason said. The Vigiles glared at him. "I mean no disrespect, but I'd prefer if you did not come into my home. I know you can teleport anywhere you've been before. So I don't want you appearing inside my home while I'm sitting on the toilet or something. You can teleport to the front door and knock, like all my other guests." He blinked at that. "Ok, maybe not like *all* my other guests."

Portia tilted her head at him. "Are you wounded?"

"What?"

Her voice was soft, almost tender. "Your chest. It radiates magic. It must have been a serious wound."

"I was struck by lightning." Silvana noted the smugness in Jason's tone. *Bloody show off. That's the third time I've heard him mention it. Bet he was telling everyone at work too.*

Portia leaned through the doorway. "Let me take a look at that," she said, reaching out a hand. "I could probably heal it better..."

Silvana understood. She summoned her speed and launched to Jason's side, pulling him a step back out of Portia's reach.

They all looked at her. She smirked. "I know what you're doing," Silvana said. "You want to put a tracer spell on him, don't you? Like the spell you had on us at the gala that allowed you to teleport directly to our sides during our fall. I bet you can only put that tracer on us when you physically touch us." She glared at Portia. "You want to put another tracer on him now. Am I right?"

Desdemona glared back, her dark eyes seemed like caverns. "We are not behest to grant thee an explanation. I should think thy wouldst be more grateful. The trace saved thy lives but recently."

"It was a violation of consent," Jason said, now wrapping a hand around Silvana in appreciation. "You should have just asked."

"Oh sure," Portia said. "May we put a tracer on you so we can follow your every movements?" She raised an eyebrow at their silence. "I thought so. Fine, you want honesty? You two are our new top suspects in the murder of Samantha Kennedy."

"What?" Silvana cried. *God, why this on top of everything else?*

Jason was frowning. "Hang on. Samantha Kennedy is still alive. The alchemist Edward brought her back, on Khadija Al Khalifa's orders. We can't be suspects in a murder case if no one was murdered."

"Actually, someone *was* murdered," Portia said. "It wouldn't matter if they did come back to life. The act of murder was still committed."

"That's..." Jason stopped. "...a really good point. Damn, even mortal law would agree with that."

"Exactly. Now be a good boy, give me your hand, and accept the tracer. Otherwise it'll look like you have something to hide."

"Jason, wait," Silvana said. "You don't have to accept this. There are legal grounds for your refusal."

He shook his head. "No, I'm a cop. I can understand this. It's just like an ankle bracelet." He held out his hand and Portia cupped it gently between her own. The movement was stiff, as if she didn't want to touch him. She moved her lips without making sounds.

"Your hand is really warm," she said.

"Watch it," Silvana warned.

Portia rolled her eyes. "Relax, girl. It was just a comment." She grimaced. "Jason, my apologies, but it'd be easier if I could just..." she gestured towards his forearm. He nodded, and she clasped both hands around his arm just past the wrist. She seemed to squeeze once before releasing him.

Jason lowered his arm. "I assume you finished?"

Portia scowled. "Oh what a gentleman. He cares if I finish." Her words seemed like a joke, but her tone was dark, full of spite. Her eyes even flashed with anger.

"Is everything ok?" Jason asked. *Ok, so he sees it too. Portia is definitely acting weird.*

The younger Vigile tried to give a smile, but only managed to squeeze her lips together. Her eyes had just the slightest hint of a wince, like she was hiding pain. "We will be monitoring your movements during the course of our investigation," she said flatly. "I know mortal law enforcement would normally say you can't leave the country. We have no such complaints. There's no place you can go that we won't find you."

Jason sighed. "This isn't going to work because we're not hiding anything."

"They all say that," Portia answered.

"Listen to me," Jason said, holding up his hands. "This is silly. The four of us should be working together." Everyone stared at him blankly. "I'm serious. I thought you two Vigiles were just enforcers. You know, beat cops. But you're detectives too, aren't you? You're investigating. So are we. We should compare notes. Exchange information. We can help each other."

Desdemona only shook her head. "Thou art our top suspect. Thy words are poison."

Jason merely rolled his eyes. "We've looked into this case as much as we can, but we're out of leads. And since you're now investigating us, it looks like you're out of leads too. What's there left to try?"

"We couldn't trust anything you say," Portia said.

"So? You're investigators. You already know every time you interview someone they could be lying. It's the same thing. At least hear our side."

"There will be no exchange of information," Desdemona said with a tone of finality. "I am four hundred and seventy-three years old. Thou art what…sixteen?"

"Come on. I'm twenty-four."

"Thou might as well be two. We do not need the help of an amateur." She turned as if to leave, and Portia began to follow.

"Wait," Jason said. "You're not even going to ask us questions?"

"What would be the point of that?" Desdemona said. "We merely need to watch thy movements. We'll be in touch—"

"I have a lead!" Silvana shouted. All eyes turned to her. She had been surprised herself to hear the words tumble out of her own mouth. But she knew they were true even as she said them.

"Thou hast merely a distraction," Desdemona said.

"No, listen!" Silvana insisted. "I was set up by a vampire couple. Hana and Mikeru." She saw it. The slightest head-tilt from Portia. Only a vampire would have seen it, but it was enough to know she had their interest. "We met them at the gala and they suggested I invest in an opportunity of theirs. But they tricked me. I invested the money into a company called Kennedy and Sons, just like they told me to. Except the company was being investigated by local police and all my money has been frozen. It could bankrupt my family."

The two Vigiles exchanged a glance. "Mere politics," Desdemona said. "That is nothing more than business as usual within Immortal families. Thou seeks only revenge on thy enemy by setting them up as a target for us."

"But Mikeru was the one who killed the Skinwalker at the gala. We all thought he was a hero, but now I see that he is a liar. He's untrustworthy."

"My dear," Desdemona said with a chilling grin. "Welcome to Immortal culture. We are *all* untrustworthy." She took Portia by the hand, and the fabric of the world swirled around them until they disappeared entirely.

"What..."

They turned around. Freddie was peering out from behind a bedroom door, his face white. "...the fuck...was that?!" he finished.

"Wizards," Silvana said.

Freddie nodded. "Yeah, yeah I get that. But who the hell were *those* wizards, and why do they look like the Men in Black, but women?"

"They're Vigiles. They're like wizard police for the magical world," Jason said.

"And why are they at *my house!*" Freddie cried. He threw up his hands before they could answer. "You know what, I'm sorry Jason, but I have to do this. I like you a lot mate, you're a great guy and an awesome roommate. But bringing wizard police to my front door has decided it. You've left me with no choice."

Silvana and Jason glanced at each other. "What are you gonna do, mate?" Jason said nervously.

Freddie shouted, "Smoke a shit-ton of weed!" Then he went into his bedroom and slammed the door.

Jason sighed in relief. "For a second there, I thought he was gonna kick us out."

"Me too!"

"And I don't even care about the weed. I keep telling him it's legal." He frowned and his tone shifted. "Hey, did you see that look Portia gave me?"

Silvana glared at him. "What?"

He held up his hands defensively. "Not a flirting look. At the end there, when Desdemona said all Immortals are untrustworthy. Portia looked at her."

"I didn't see it."

"Ok. Well, I could have sworn she was annoyed at Desdemona. Like maybe she was listening to us and agreed. I don't know, maybe I'm just hopeful." He finally took a long swig from his beer, right there in the entryway to the house. He looked to her and his eyes narrowed. "So you invested that money because of Hana and Mikeru?"

The world grew silent. A wave of fear seemed to crush Silvana under its weight. Jason seemed to be standing on the opposite sides of the world, and a gulf lay between them. How could she reach him now?

"Yes. I did."

He nodded. "Ok." He nodded again. "Ok. Right. Well."

"Are you mad?"

"Uh…no. Just not sure what to do." He sighed. "I want to show that I'm here for you, but I also don't want to pressure you to talk about it. But I think maybe you should talk about it? I don't know. I'm not good with this stuff. I was gonna wait until you were ready to talk." He winced. "Uh…what do you want to do?"

Silvana realised her heart was racing with anxiety. She thought she better start talking before Jason got mad. Things would only get worse if she waited any longer…

She stopped herself. *Oh my god. I'm assuming he's going to hit me. Like Arthur.* The image of her late husband came to mind, drunk and furious, lashing out to hit her with no warning or provocation. His clumsy hand would hit her face too softly to cause any physical pain. Yet she felt the humiliation of it. Every time.

"I'm sorry," she said. "Please don't be upset, but… I keep thinking you're going to hit me."

"What?" Jason cried, before his face softened. "Oh. Like Arthur."

"Yeah."

"You know I would never hit you. You know that right?"

"Yeah I know. It's just…if ever there were a good reason to hit me, it would be…"

"Stop," Jason cut in. "Just stop. There is never a reason good enough to hit you. Never. Do you understand? There's never an excuse for that."

"But what I did was so bad!"

Jason went quiet a moment. "Alright. I think we're both feeling a bit anxious right now. How about we sit down and have a good talk about all this?" She nodded, and he led them to the couch in front of the TV. They sat facing each other with one seat in between them. Silvana tucked her feet underneath her. Jason took a deep breath. "So I'm feeling nervous. You know how my greatest fear is I'll become like my father?" She nodded. "Well, I'm worried I'm going to say something really dumb right now and I'll hurt you in some way."

"Ah," Silvana said. "You're scared of your dad, I'm scared of my late husband." She gave a black chuckle. "What a pair we make."

"I'll make you a deal," Jason said. "Let's leave those two bastards out of this conversation. It's just you and me here. Deal?"

"Deal," she said. She took his hand as her anxiety faded and her heartrate slowed. She was ready to talk about things now. "You remember when my family refused to even consider investing with Hana and Mikeru?" He nodded. "I knew it was the wrong decision. I knew I would never get them to see the truth. So I acted on my own. I told Nicholas I was re-enrolling in university, and he signed the forms to let me take out a loan in his name."

Jason nodded along. "And why did you act alone?"

"I had to. I couldn't tell anyone. Not even you. You saw how horrible Emberline was to you today. If you got in trouble with my family…" she trailed off. "But it was supposed to be such a safe bet. The numbers were infallible. It should have worked. I never expected the police to get involved."

"Yes but…what gave you the confidence to act so independently?"

She blinked at him. "You did."

He squeezed his eyes shut and turned away from her. "I thought so," he whispered.

"Wait," she blurted. "Are you thinking this is all your fault?"

He shrugged. "Well, think about it. I push you and push you to not live under your family's rule. We avoid getting married and we work at letting you speak your mind. Then you go way too far to the other extreme. How is this *not* my fault?"

"Uh *excuse me?*" she cried. Jason flinched back in surprise. "You want me to be my own person, right? That means I get to make mistakes like everyone else. You can't say I'm responsible for myself, but you're responsible for my mistakes."

"I'm not saying that," Jason tried to cut in.

"Cause then you'd be in control of me, in just the same way my family were."

Jason went quiet, and Silvana felt a stab of panic. *What did I just say? God, I am becoming too independent.*

"You're right," he said.

"Huh?"

"If I blame myself for your mistakes, it's because I assume I'm ultimately in control of you. And that's bad." He sighed. "I'm sorry."

"Oh. Thank you."

"But that means this is one hundred percent your fault."

"Oh. I forgot about that part."

Jason laughed. "Ok. As a cop, I'm angry that you committed fraud and lied to Nicholas. But that's up to Lynch and Cole to investigate you now, and it's not really my business. As for the act itself, I'm only mad that you didn't talk to me about it. Of course I'd be on your side."

"Really? You would have supported me?"

"Well, not exactly. I probably would have tried to stop you from lying about it. But I would have helped you. That's why we have people in our lives. They stop us making mistakes." He took her hand. "I'm not mad. Really. Just tell me the whole truth next time."

She studied his face. The sincerity of his words – the earnestness in his eyes – made her believe that somehow, Jason really meant it. He was completely honest. So she had to be honest with him. Yet being honest with someone she loved felt like the scariest thing in the world.

"Then I have to tell you something else," she said.

"Oh?" Jason tried to smile. "Another investment?"

She sat up straight on the couch. She lifted her t-shirt and lowered the waist of her jeans. They were sticky with blood and scabs as she peeled them off her skin, revealing the oozing wound beneath.

"Jesus!" Jason cried. "You're hurt."

"I know."

"Who did this to you?" He gasped. "Was it Emberline? Did she attack you on your way out?"

"No of course not."

"Did the Vigiles somehow…"

"It was the knight Wilhelm. He stabbed me during the fight."

Jason's eyes widened. "But that was two days ago. You should have healed by…" he trailed off, and abruptly his eyes flared with real anger. "You're out of blood, aren't you? You've been out of blood for two days and have been living with a goddamn stab wound, rather than asking me for blood?"

She winced. "Um…not exactly."

"Not exactly? What does that mean?" his voice was rising.

"I've been almost out of blood…since the gala."

"What?!" Jason snapped, and Silvana felt her blood freeze in her veins. He had never yelled at her before. It didn't matter that she was three times his strength. It still made her want to run out of the room as quickly as possible.

He held out his hands, palms towards her, and took several long breaths in an effort to calm himself down. Silvana could hear his heart pounding against his ribcage and his breathing growing more shallow and rapid.

"Ok, sorry for snapping there," he said in a calmer voice. "I did say I wanted you to tell me the whole truth next time. Well, if I want you to do that, I can't get mad at you when you do. So…" he swallowed. "Thank you for telling me the whole truth. I'm sorry I reacted poorly."

"It's ok," she said gently.

"It's just that I offered you my blood multiple times. I know I specifically offered you blood after the gala. And again after our fight with the Glucksburgs." He started talking quicker, more frantic. "Why would you turn me down every time if you were out of blood? Why do it when you are wounded and not healing? What was your plan? To just ignore it for another week until it was scheduled again?"

"I wasn't planning on it. I'm sorry, Jason. I was just scared."

"But you were in pain. How could you think that was ok? How

could you think I would want that?" He choked on his words, and Silvana's heart broke when she saw real tears in his eyes. He struggled to speak in a steady voice. "You know I'm terrified that I'm going to lose you. That I'll just walk in one day and find you dead, like my mother. Now you've shown me a wound you've had for days, and you admit you've been dying of thirst for over a week. It's…"

He stopped. He was struggling to breathe now. "God, I'm having a panic attack."

"Oh shit," Silvana cried.

Jason stood up and marched out the front door, banging the handle loudly with his movement and slamming the door against the door stop. Jason rushed outside, his shoulders rising and falling in rapid succession as he tried to get his breathing under control. Silvana followed him at a safe distance, wary in case she upset him further. Jason was bent over his knees, trying to take long breaths in the fresh outdoor air.

He needs me. Silvana approached him slowly. She stood at his side and gently patted his back. It took several minutes for him to work through it, and he looked like he was going to lose control several times when sudden sharp breaths broke his calming rhythm. But he held on. He got his breathing back under control each time and the colour returned to his face. He stood up again and sighed with relief.

"Well, that was fun," he muttered.

"I'm sorry," she said. "I didn't even think of how this would affect you. I didn't mean to scare you."

He waved his hand. "Not your fault." He gave a half-hearted laugh. "Fuck me, I haven't had a panic attack like that in years. I used to have them all the time after mum died. I think seeing you injured just triggered that memory in a big way." He took her hand in his. "I'm sorry I freaked out. I didn't mean to yell at you like that. I'm really sorry." He offered her a smile. "I just need to know. Why didn't you ask for more blood?"

She sighed. "I felt guilty. I thought if I asked too much from you, you'd get tired of it and leave me."

"Oh." He nodded in understanding. "That makes perfect sense. When you've got a family that just takes and takes from you, it feels selfish to ask for something yourself. So you learn not to be an inconvenience to anyone." He shrugged. "As a foster kid, that was my life. Everyone thought I was so polite, but it was only because I couldn't bear to accept anyone's help."

"So you understand?"

"Yeah. I understand. I still don't want you to do that again."

"Ok. I won't."

"Please, promise me you'll talk to me about your problems. Don't keep them to yourself."

"I promise."

She stepped forward to hug him, and instead he shoved his wrist against her mouth. Right there in the front of his lawn. He stared at her expectantly while standing outside their suburban house in the late afternoon.

"Please," he whispered.

She hesitated. But only for a second. Then she bit down.

His blood touched her lips, and exploded across her tongue with the power of life. Immediately her body absorbed it deep into her core. Power filled her like an electric current, warmth flooding through her arms and legs like she was being consumed by fire. The sharp pain in her waistline finally began to ease and the fogginess that had clouded her mind for days was stripped away, replaced by mental clarity. The blood was like an inferno that raced from her core into every extremity, healing every tiny wound and fatigued muscle it could find. Her body responded with heat of its own.

She pushed back his wrist. She had been biting longer than she intended, and he was trying to hide the tension around his eyes. "I'm ok," he said. "You feel better?"

"Yes," she replied with a big sigh. She looked up at his face, and noticed the absolute gorgeous masculine line of his jaw. "We're going to go inside," she said. "I'm going to patch your wrist. Then I'm going to rock your world."

He grinned like an idiot. "I just gave blood, Silvy. I might not have enough left for what you have in mind."

"You leave that to me." He let out a cheeky giggle as she took his hand and led him back inside.

Chapter 27

Jason smiled to himself. Things were good with Silvana. Really good.

Things were bad with the case.

Jason was working late at the office. He knew he had a beautiful woman at home waiting for him for the first time in his life, and he had been thinking of her all day and how amazing it had felt to resolve all the tension between them. How they felt closer than ever. *And how she fucked my brains out after drinking my blood.* He smiled ear to ear. Then realised his attention had lapsed again. No, he couldn't go home yet. He had to work this case.

Kennedy and Sons had allegedly hidden five million pounds from their financial reports, then Hana and Mikeru told Silvana to invest the exact same amount. How were the two connected? Where did the vampire and knight fit into the picture? Lynch and Cole wouldn't consider the Immortal angle, so it was up to Jason. If he could just find the connection, he could stop whatever they were up to, save his family fortune, and heal the rift between Silvana and her family all in the same step.

But there was no connection.

He had looked through the names of every single person who had ever invested with Kennedy and Sons. He had checked the names of every staff member who had ever worked there, and every person involved in the company's creation. There was no Hana or Mikeru. He had at least learnt that these were Japanese names, and even which kanji symbols to use when spelling them. Yet there weren't any Japanese names among Kennedy & Sons clients or employees. Which left the possibility that there were false name or details off the books.

If only the Vigiles had shared what they knew. If I just knew what house Hana and Mikeru came from, it would help my search so much.

He pulled out his phone and dialled Khadija's number. It was his fourth attempt that day. She finally answered.

"I'm not teleporting your damn car!" she snapped.

"I'm not calling about that," he snapped back. Then he lowered his tone. "Is everything ok?"

There was silence for a moment. "Sam is not herself," she whispered.

He made his tone serious and gentle. "I'm so sorry. What's going on?"

"She's severely traumatised. We think the damage is entirely psychological." Khadija gave a dark laugh. "You ever gone through something horrible and traumatising?"

"Yeah."

"Well, I bet it wasn't as horrible as literally dying. People don't think about it. But the act of being murdered – the sheer horror of it – would destroy a person's mind."

"Well. That's fucking dark."

"Yeah."

Jason grimaced. "I've got to ask, is it possible she could heal with more time? I've been traumatised and I learned to live with it after a few years. And Samantha's got a lot more time than I do, right?"

The phone was silent. He heard the slightest intake of breath. *Is she crying?* "Thanks Jason. That's actually just what I needed to hear." She went silent again. *If she is crying, she's obviously trying to hide it. I should let it go.*

"Good. I was actually calling about the investigation."

"Oh! Did you find the killers?"

"Not yet. But I'm onto something. There were two guests at the gala called Hana and Mikeru. A vampire and her knight. Do you know them?"

"...maybe. Was he the guy who decapitated one of the Skinwalkers?"

"Yes. Do you know what house they are from?"

"No I don't. But my family would know. Every name was on the guest list. If you solve this case and get me back in with my family, I could tell you."

"I see. So if I solve the case, you can give me the names I need to solve the case?" They chuckled in unison.

"Why do you suspect them?" Khadija asked.

"Long story short, they just tricked Silvana into a bad investment. I'm trying to see if it's connected to Sam's murder and your attempted murder."

Khadija's voice hardened. "Jason, it sounds like you're working on a completely different case."

"What? No I really think there might be a connection."

"I think you're working on a personal vendetta cause your wife got tricked and you're hoping it's connected. You should focus on my case. Besides, if you solve my case, I'll pay you enough to bail you out of the bad venture."

"I hear you, Khadija. But you should trust me on this. One thing you learn as a detective is tug on every string. I need to see what's behind this. I legitimately think it's all connected."

"Alright, tell me how?"

"Well, consider that the couple didn't share their last name, then they set up Silvana from a tax fraud claim, and the knight heroically kill one of the attackers. It's circumstantial, I know, but it's highly suspicious. It's all too convenient."

Khadija's tone was softer, but she sounded like she was speaking with a child. "I admit it's possible. But I think it's unlikely. I have no personal connection with them. I can't even remember what they look like. Why would they be the ones trying to destroy me? What's their motivation?" Jason couldn't answer her. "It's a good try, but you should look elsewhere. Even if I did know who they were, it's not the answer."

Jason sighed. "Do you have any other ideas? Any enemies?"

"Yeah. The whole bloody Imperium. Start with the Vigiles. Better yet, start with the High Kings."

"Oh. Ok then."

"Cause I've been thinking. It'd be just like the Imperium to hire Skinwalkers to kill Sam, then frame me so they can legally kill me too. They love finding legal grounds to kill their enemies. It's like poetry to them."

Jason remembered what Sam had said, how she had been killed by a blade, not a Skinwalker. *It's much more likely that it was a knight.* But when he spoke, he kept his voice flat. "Sounds like a great idea. I'll let you know how I go."

"Great. Thanks."

They hung up, and Jason swore under his breath. "It better not be fucking Vigiles, or I'm screwed."

He scrolled though names and profiles of Kennedy and Sons employees. He started opening them one by one and looking at their pictures, hoping to recognised any of them. Eventually a voice called out to him. "Detective Turner." He looked up. His captain was leaving her office.

"Hey Captain."

Kader shook her head at him. "Do you realise what time it is?"

"About five o…" he saw the clock. "About six o'clock, ma'am."

"Exactly. Go home. Try again tomorrow." She came and stood beside him. He could look at her eye to eye even when he was sitting. She lowered her tone. "Look, I read your latest report. That's really crappy what happened to Silvana. But overworking yourself isn't going to solve anything. Go home, get some sleep. Keep your mind fresh."

He nodded. "Yes captain." He pulled out his phone and started typing.

"What are you doing, Turner?"

"Ordering an uber. My car is still in Swansea."

She rolled her eyes. "Come on, I'll give you a lift."

"Oh. Thank you, captain, but I don't want to be an imposition."

"Then don't fight me on it. I'm giving you a lift and that's an order."

"Yes ma'am."

A minute later Jason found himself in the passenger seat of Kader's family car. She was silent as she strapped in and adjusted the aircon. She asked for his address, then entered it into her GPS and started driving.

"Where are the boys?" he asked.

"I've got a friend who watches them Tuesdays and Wednesdays. I watch their kid on Fridays and the occasional Saturday. It's definitely in my favour. They watch two extra kids, I only watch one."

"Nice. Do they live near you?"

"Same school."

Jason's intuition perked up. She was being secretive. She'd even used the gender neutral 'their' when referring to them. So he asked pointedly, "Is he handsome?"

She went still. Then snorted in laughter. "You're such a fucking child, Turner," she said and shook her head.

"You're smiling. I take that as a yes." She only smiled more. "Would I think he's cute?"

"Don't you dare steal him. I like this one."

"Alright. I won't tell anyone."

"Gee, thanks." She kept shaking her head, but Jason could see the smile lines on her cheeks. "Listen, I wanted to ask something about Silvana." She weighed her words. "I'm a bit concerned by her committing fraud. I know her step-dad covered for her, but she still knowingly committed a crime. I just wanted to check if you were worried about her."

"Are you concerned that she's wrong for me?"

"Uh…maybe. I don't know much about the two of you as a couple. And I know it's not any of my business, I'm your boss not your life coach. But I don't know if anyone else is going to ask. So…"

"Yeah, that's fair." He thought about it. "She definitely knows it was a mistake. I can understand why she did it though. But she won't do it again."

Kader nodded. "Can I ask? Is there ever a time when she seems unconcerned about following the law? Other crimes she seems likely to commit?"

"That's a fair question, but no she's not like that."

"So you're not afraid for your safety?"

"What?" Jason almost laughed. Then he saw the sincere look on her face. "No. I am perfectly safe with her. I'm positive."

"Ok." Kader nodded. "Ok. I just couldn't bear the thought of you being stuck with someone you were too afraid to leave."

He glimpsed at her for a second. He wondered if he should ask the question on his mind. Finally it just burst out. "Is that what happened to you?"

Kader was silent. The GPS announced his home was close. He wondered if she would just avoid answering. "It did for a while. My children's father was a scary man. But I left him eventually, and it was the best thing I ever did." She smirked at him. "So no. That is not my big secret."

"Alright. You can't blame me for asking."

He wondered again what had happed to Kader. She had cried, "*I couldn't save him,*" to the telepath. Who had she failed to save?

The car arrived at his house. "Thanks for the ride, captain."

"Don't forget our after-work drinks tomorrow," she said. "The whole squad is coming. Plus one's are welcome."

"Oh. I had forgotten."

"Well make sure you show up. Lynch is bringing his boyfriend, and I'm curious to see if he behaves better or worse with him watching."

Jason chuckled. "Ok. See you then." He waved as he got out, then walked up to the front door. He paused, checking the front steps for any signs that the Vigiles had been back even though he knew there was no point to checking. They could just teleport directly to where he stood, and it wasn't like they left marks behind. But it made him feel safer to look first before he went inside.

Silvana and Freddie were sitting on the couch, talking between each other. The lights were off, and the TV was flashing bright colours with sounds of gunfire and explosions. Jason checked the screen. "You guys playing Halo?" he asked.

"Nope. Just watching it," Freddie answered.

"What?"

Sure enough, neither held controllers. It was just a video of someone else playing. Sudden gunfire rang out through the house, and both Silvana and Freddie screamed at the TV as the player died. "That was bullshit!"

"Hacker!" Silvana cried.

"Fucking noob!" They roared with laughter.

Jason just stared at them. They both seemed to realise at the same time and hit pause. The silence made his head ring. "Sorry to interrupt. Any news?" he asked.

Silvana cleared her throat. "Yeah, actually. Aunty Lisbeth and Nicholas visited us today."

"They did?"

"Yeah. It was really rough." She gestured, so Jason sat next to her, with Freddie on her other side of the couch. "Aunty wanted me to come back. I kept saying that I couldn't go back until Aunty Emberline had accepted you. I mean, she threatened to kill you! I can't believe her." Her face looked ready to break like a dam wall. "Lisbeth couldn't guarantee what Emberline would do, so I stayed."

"Also," Freddie added, "she just summarized about three hours of back and forth conversation."

Jason shuddered in sympathy. "Yikes. You ok?" Silvana nodded. "What about Nicholas? What did he want?"

"He wanted to talk to you. When I said you were at work, he spent about two hours at your desk writing you a letter. I actually barely spoke to him."

"He wrote me a letter?"

"He's an old soul," she said with a smile. "Said only you could read it. He left it on the kitchen bench."

Jason looked between the two of them. "I best go do that."

"Any news on your end, mate?" Freddie asked.

"Bloody nothing. A whole day of dead ends."

"Shit, man. That sucks. But I did a grocery shop this morning, and there's an absolute shit ton of beer in the fridge now."

"You did buy other things too, right?"

"Oh yeah! I bought wine. In case we had fancy guests."

"Freddie…"

"Hey, it came in handy with your aunt and uncle today! On the same day I bought it too. Can't argue with that."

Jason rolled his eyes and went into the kitchen. Sure enough, there was a two-page letter, hand written in cursive script. *Oh Nicholas. You could have just called me.* He sat down at the dining table and began to read, while the sounds of Halo gameplay resumed with Freddie and Silvana's commentary. Jason tuned it out.

My dearest son, Jason,

Words cannot describe the heartbreak I feel right now. As I have said to you before, you are the son that I have waited all my life to have. I have cared for my father's house, and his estate, all my life just so that one day I could pass it on to you.

Now I can no longer do that. I am so sorry.

Jason had to stop reading. His eyes were starting to sting and he had to press his lips together to hold back a cry. He breathed deeply and blinked to try and clear the tears that were blurring his vision and obscuring the words.

But that's not why I'm here today. There was something important I needed to teach you, as part of your training as a Knight Templar. I should have mentioned it much earlier. But the time must be now. There is great risk if I wait any longer.

Do you know why there are no Knight Templar in the mortal world today? Do you know their history, and what happened to them?

They were originally an organisation that operated within the mortal world for over a hundred years. There were ten thousand of them at the height of their power. Then in 1307, King Phillip the fourth of France owed them too much money. So he made a slew of false accusations against the organisation. King Phillip said they were blasphemers. Devil worshippers. Homosexuals. He used his power to rewrite truth itself, just to avoid paying back the money he owed. That's how he justified the capture, torture, and execution of thousands of knights. So many died in his mad witch hunt that the Knight Templar ceased to exist as an organisation.

Jason blinked. "What the fuck, Nicholas?"

That's when we decided on a very important part of Templar doctrine. We had to admit that all the knights in the world, no matter how numerous, would always be at the mercy of the rulers of this world. There would always be kings, and High Kings, that could wipe us out on a whim. That's why we have a very important rule.

The Rule of Coexistence.

We protect our family at all cost. But we must also coexist with the powers that be.

I say this to you because I know about your investigation. I know you want to protect this family by discovering the attackers at the gala. But this is not coexisting.

Any time you take bold steps within the Imperium, you will attract attention. Any attention can be dangerous to your family. Remember, you don't actually have to do anything wrong to become an enemy. You just have to exist in the view of someone with the power to destroy you. They can, and they will.

This is why I have kept our family where they are in Plymouth. I have risked our fortune by staying out of the way. This is how we have continued to survive, when so many other Immortal families on the fringes have disappeared.

I know there are many opportunities out in the wider world. Opportunities for power and fame, for privilege and wealth. I know the Romanov family could become great again. But every time we forget the Rule of Coexistence, we risk utter destruction.

Please do not judge me too harshly. I know this may seem like the coward's way. But in a world with High Kings who wield the power of creation itself, it is also the ONLY way.

Please, my son. Come back to the mansion. Talk with us as a family. We will find a way out of this mess one way or another. I only ask that you do not draw the attention of the greater houses to ourselves through your investigation. Let it go. Whatever comes, we will face it as a family.

All my love

Nicholas the Third

Jason lowered the letter and stared at the wall. The ongoing sounds of Halo gunfire and Silvana and Freddie's friendly chatter all faded into white noise. Everything Nicholas said made perfect sense. Jason thought of the wizard brawl between Ingolf and Samantha. It had felt like the apocalypse, like he was watching the end of the world. He couldn't imagine any human trying to challenge a power like that. Even modern military would be hard pressed to challenge one wizard. Nicholas had summed up perfectly the despair in Jason's own mind when he considered what he was up against. He was just one man. A mortal knight.

Part of him wanted to give up. Everything he did seemed to make things worse for Silvana and her family. Was he playing with fire trying to go further?

But at the same time, he couldn't give up. He couldn't bear the thought of letting evil people walk around unchecked, just because they were too powerful to challenge. He was a police officer. He was a law enforcer. He'd made an oath to protect people. *From villains like my father.*

He folded the letter up and put it in his pocket. Then he moved to the lounge room to sit on the couch, this time in the centre seat between Silvana and Freddie.

They both eyed him. "Everything ok?" Silvana asked. He nodded. "What was in Nicholas's letter?"

Jason thought about it. "It's hard to explain. But I guess you could sum it up by saying, he still loves me like a son."

Freddie patted him on the shoulder. "You're a lucky guy, Jase. Just remember you can still talk to us if you need to."

"Thanks guys." He tried to change topics. "You know, Silvy, I still have that workplace party tomorrow night. Did you want to come to that?"

"Oh…I don't know. I'm not sure I want to be around people at the moment."

"That's fine. Well, it's just at a bar down the road from the station, and it'll only be for an hour or two. It's just that the captain is encouraging everyone to bring their plus ones. Apparently it's good for morale."

"You can bring me?" Freddie offered. Jason eyed him. "What? You said it was at a bar. I like bars."

Jason found himself blushing, and tried to act nonplussed. "It's just that people might get the wrong idea."

Freddie blew a raspberry. "You should be so lucky." He elbowed Jason in the ribs, and Jason's laugh was just a little too strained for his own liking.

"What if we both came?" Silvana said. "Both me and Freddie?"

"Oh…sure. I don't think anyone would mind," Jason smiled.

"Great. Now that's settled," Freddie said and gestured to the TV. "We're missing the best part." He turned up the volume, and the sounds of stylized sci-fi battles filled the room. Silvana snuggled up to Jason, and he watched with a smile on his face, even though he had no idea what was happening on screen.

Or in his life, for that matter.

* * *

Jason spent all Wednesday working on the case. Lynch and Cole went on-site again to speak with the auditors who originally looked into the Kennedy and Sons financial records, but neither detective invited him. They seemed happy for him to investigate on his own.

The other officers were about the station today. Douglas made him a coffee at one point. Wilson came over to triple check if Jason was coming to his one-year-old's birthday on Saturday, and Martin kindly led Wilson away again. They all supported him working in silence in their own way. Kader came over once to offer help, but they both knew there wasn't much she could do. Mostly, everyone let him work.

Today, Jason looked into the history of Kennedy and Sons.

Founded in 1923 by George Kennedy and his sons Michael and Hanson in New York City, there were approximately eighteen locations around the world, including one in Tokyo. They had seen massive growth in the fifties, and another burst of growth in the 2000s. George had died in 1961, and his two sons died in the eighties. Yet Jason couldn't help the feeling that this information could be falsified. After all, Silvana was legally known Silvana Clarke, aged twenty three. It was always possible that Immortals could overwrite legal document. Was George Kennedy any relation to Samantha?

He wished he could speak to the Vigiles. Or more accurately, just Portia, the least scary of the two. But that wasn't an option. Even calling Khadija would only make her mad at him for not investigating the Vigiles as potential leads. There was not enough access to information.

He knew he was scouring through dead ends. Yet somehow, his detective's instincts were optimistic. His gut told him he was getting closer to an answer.

He started looking up powerful families in Japan. Maybe he could get an idea of which families were actually Immortal houses in disguise.

The first one he found was the Emperor and his family from the house Yamato. It was one of the longest running ruling families in history, with a rule spanning eleven hundred years.

He also found another twenty powerful family names with little effort. Takeda, Minamoto, Imagawa, Oda, all of whom had a rich history spanning centuries and ruling different lands and commanding vast arrays of wealth. Jason slumped down in his chair. *God, there must be an absolute fuck-ton of Immortals in this world.* He sighed. Hana and Mikeru could be from any of these. It didn't narrow down his search at all.

The day began to pass by without him making any real progress. He had over thirty tabs open on his browser, and each one was a different desperate attempt to find clues. He ate lunch at his desk. He only stopped to stand up and stretch a few times, and each time he kept his eyes glued to his screen so he could keep reading. But his earlier optimism was starting to fade.

He tried re-reading his notes in the Immortal Investigations, retracing his steps. There were several factions in play. The Imperium, led by the High Kings and enforced by the Vigiles. There were Khadija and her sympathisers, which Jason knew little about. And there was the potential of more extremists who wanted to bring back the royalty and rule over the mortals in the open, like this mysterious Dorin figure. Or there was the simple fourth option: literally any other Immortal family who saw an opportunity and took it.

Fuck...

He went into the kitchen to get a coffee and check his phone. He had a text from Silvana. *"Hey sweetheart. Freddie and I are catching an uber into town. We'll see you when you get there. Love you."*

He checked the time. It was after four. *Damn. The whole day gone, and nothing to show for it again.* He even felt a pang of jealousy towards Freddie for getting to spend the day with Silvana. Or maybe he was jealous of Silvana for spending the day with Freddie? He immediately pushed both thoughts away. *They both need more friends in their life. I'm glad they're getting along.*

"Heeey!" Lynch shouted as he stepped back into the office with a wide grin and a fist held in the air. "Who's ready for drinking?" Douglas and Wilson whooped in excitement.

"You still have to wait thirty minutes," Martin said, a smile on her face, "You bloody alcoholic."

"Come on, let's leave early," Lynch jeered back. "Who votes we should leave early and go to the bar now?" He held his hand high. Douglas immediately joined him.

Wilson looked uncomfortable. He said, "We can't leave the station early. What if there's an emergency?"

"That's exactly *why* I want to leave early," Lynch said. Cole appeared at his side and punched him in the ribs, and he made an 'Oof!' sound. It didn't bring down Lynch's mood at all as he turned towards Jason. "What about you, rookie? Surely you could do with a break?"

Everyone looked at him now, just as he started pouring his coffee. "I'm loading up. Gotta make this last thirty minutes count."

"Come on, you're not going to have a breakthrough in the next half an hour," Cole said.

"You don't know that."

"Yes I do! Take a break, Turner. A beer will help your brain relax."

"Or it could damage his brain cells further," Lynch said.

"Gee, thanks," Jason drawled.

An office door opened, and Captain Kader entered. Everyone went silent. She looked around the room with a commander's gaze. "Are you all planning on leaving early?" she said with an angry undertone. "Leaving this entire station unmanned for half an hour?"

Douglas stuttered, "Uh…yes?"

Kader shrugged. "Great idea." Everyone cheered. "Besides," Kader said in a loud voice. "We could all use an extra drink before we have to meet someone crazy enough to be Lynch's boyfriend."

Everyone laughed, Lynch most of all. "You guys are going to love Steven! He's not as funny as me, but he's much more polite."

"The bar is low," Cole drawled.

The entire office started packing up. Jason sighed as he tried to think of ways he could stay back for an extra half hour. But he knew anything he said would just bring a barrage of peer pressure down on him. The only way he could hold his head high was to agree easily. He poured his cup of coffee down the drain and packed up his gear. He glanced at his computer screen one last time. He saw the name. *Yamato.*

He closed the screen.

Chapter 28

The bar was packed full of people, which seemed strange at four fifteen on a Wednesday afternoon. Patrons were lining the counter in wait for their drinks, or gathered around the tables, speaking in half shout voices. The room was dimly lit and smelled faintly of old wooden chairs with a strong undertone of beer. There was even a middle-aged bald guy playing acoustic guitar and singing Pink Floyd's '*Comfortably Numb*'. The performance was…ok.

The cops found a two-sided bench with about fifteen seats. Jason took a random seat, and Martin immediately sat next to him and pressed up against his arm, while Lynch and Cole sat opposite. *There is literally no seating arrangement possible that would be more uncomfortable.* Still, the mood improved when Kader announced, "First rounds on me!" That got a big cheer. Two beer jugs arrived seconds later and Jason started pouring.

"How's the detective work going, Jason?" Martin asked.

He shrugged. "Well it's strange. I've worked on two cases, and I seem to have become personally involved in both of them almost by accident."

"You're enjoying the work, right?"

"Eh…" He saw Lynch watching him with a smug smile. Jason smirked back. "Loving every minute of it."

"Oh fuck off," Lynch said with a laugh.

"Alright, being honest, mate?" Jason said. "It's nowhere near as boring as you made it out to be."

Cole waved down Lynch's protest. "Enough shop talk. Let's talk about something less divisive."

"Great idea," Lynch said. "Hey, who's everyone voting for in the next election?" Everyone booed him, and Douglas threw a coaster. Lynch just laughed at them all.

Martin and Cole started a conversation about their children while Jason sat quietly and listened in. Apparently Cole was raising two teenage girls, which surprised Jason. But then, she'd always been a very private person and who kept her personal and professional lives separate. He and Lynch just sipped their beers and listened to the ladies share anecdotes back and forth about their children's shenanigans. Nearby, Kader, Douglas and Wilson held a separate conversation about sports teams. Of the two topics, the one about family and children interested Jason more.

"Who do you support, Jason?" Douglas asked.

He grimaced. "Sports has never been my thing."

There were several scoffs, and Douglas muttered something about Jason being 'un-English'.

Jason's phone buzzed. Another text from Silvana. *"We've just arrived. Where are you?"* He stood up tall and spotted Silvana and Freddie at the entrance. They each wore jeans and a baggy tshirt with their hair down and slightly messy. Yet they could have been models for how attractive they looked. Jason noticed for the first time that they were the exact same height. He waved them over, and all the cops looked up in excitement.

"Everyone, this is my girlfriend Silvana, and my housemate Freddie who invited himself. He's a menace and I apologize in advance." That got a round of laughs.

"Hi everyone!" Freddie said with his usual extroverted cheer.

"Wait, you brought two people?" Martin said playfully. "It was supposed to be plus one."

"Hey, don't judge," Lynch said. "They're obviously a throuple. That counts as plus one."

"Hang on," Jason said, but the conversation ran away from him.

"What's a throuple?"

"It's a three-person relationship."

"I think it's really sweet."

"Maybe my wife would like to try that," Douglas said with a laugh.

Jason had to shout over the top of them. "We're not a throuple!"

Freddie put a hand on his shoulder. "It's ok, my love. I'm not ashamed of who I am." He stroked Jason's cheek.

"Piss off!" Freddie just laughed.

Silvana was smiling shyly and gave a polite wave to everyone, though she kept silent.

"Hey, welcome mate," Lynch said and gestured at Freddie. "Don't mind us. We just love to take the piss …" he trailed off. He stared at Freddie with sudden intensity.

"Lynch? You good man?"

"Hey I know you!" Lynch said to Freddie. "You're that punk who I caught dealing at the university!"

Freddie held up both hands. "Allegedly dealing. I was only in possession of."

"Freddie!" Jason cried.

Freddie gave an obviously fake smile.

"Relax son, I'm off the clock," Lynch said. He turned to Jason. "You sure know how to pick em. First vampires, now dealers. You have terrible taste in friends."

"That's why we're friends, hey Lynch?" Jason grinned widely, and Lynch just gave an unimpressed shake of the head.

"You know," Freddie said. "This wouldn't be a problem if the government just legalised it."

Lynch glared back. "Why didn't I think of that? And while we're at it, just legalise murder. Now we've solved every unsolved murder case. Brilliant." He growled under his breath. "Fucking smart ass."

"Alright guys," Jason said. "No fighting." He noticed Silvana still hadn't spoken. She was looking at Lynch and Cole. "Silvy? You ok?"

Lynch looked between the three of them, and seemed to guess what Silvana was thinking. "Hey, Ms Clarke. I'm sorry again for your family situation. But I'm off duty now and I'm just some guy. Is that ok with you, Miss…sorry. Silvana?"

She looked like she wanted to say something, yet at that moment the bar musician interrupted loudly announcing the next song, before launching into 'Whole Lotta Love' by Led Zeppelin. A few people around the bar cringed as the singer clearly missed several notes.

"Heey!" Lynch shouted and cut through all the chatter. His face lit up in the most genuine smile Jason had ever seen. Another man was approaching the table, medium height, wearing glasses and slightly balding. Lynch turned to the newcomer and planted a firm, deliberate kiss on the man's mouth, and held it for several seconds. He turned to face the group with a massive smile. "Everyone, meet Steven. "

The table all gave their welcome. Steven himself blushed and looked at the ground, but tried to put on a brave smile.

A second later, a woman entered the bar, and Jason caught himself staring at her obvious beauty. The woman was middle aged and blonde haired. She also wore tight exercise clothes over her toned figure, like she'd just come from her third gym session of the day. Jason tried not to stare. The woman walked up to the table and put a hand on Cole's shoulder. Jason understood a moment before it happened. The woman kissed Cole on the mouth and whispered something to her.

"Everyone, meet Amanda," Cole said.

Huh. Both detectives. What are the odds?

Everyone welcomed the newcomers and started shuffling seats to make room. Jason soon had Silvana and Freddie on either side of him. He watched Lynch sit with his arm around Steven, and Cole holding hands with Amanda.

Interesting. If I were being shallow and judgemental, I would say Lynch is a handsome man who's dating someone plain looking, and Cole is a plain looking woman who's dating someone beautiful. He smiled towards them both. He noticed Cole had gone quiet. Maybe this was her first time showing her sexuality to her colleagues. He decided to try and be welcoming.

"So, Amanda," Jason said. "How long have you two been together?"

She smiled at his question, and he nearly forgot how to breathe. She really was stunningly beautiful. "Well that depends on how you count it. We've been openly a couple for about seven years now. But before that, we were just 'roommates.'" She did the air quotes. "It's hard for some people to be open about it."

"Jason gets it," Lynch said. "He brought his roommate with him tonight."

"What is with everyone and the roommate thing?" Jason cried. But Lynch and Freddie laughed together, with Freddie elbowing Jason's ribs.

"He's so defensive," Freddie said. "See how ashamed he is of me?" Lynch laughed again.

"Do you have kids?" Silvana asked. The question was a bit blunt, but Amanda seemed to appreciate it.

"We've adopted two girls," Amanda said.

"That's wonderful. I've always wanted to adopt children," Silvana said.

"Really? How long is 'always'?"

"Like a hundred years." Amanda gave a genuine laugh. Though the detectives shared a worried expression. For a moment, Lynch and Silvana made eye contact, and both immediately looked away again.

"Adoption is a beautiful thing," Cole said, finally speaking up. "People put too much stock in biology. As if all you need to be a good parent is the same DNA. That's actually the least important part of parenting."

"I agree," Jason said with gusto. "DNA means nothing."

Cole nodded back. "And with adoption, you can't accidently get a child. You have to make the choice. When you adopt, I think it's more likely the parent is actually ready for the job."

Cole looked at him. "Are you two thinking about adoption?"

Jason and Silvana blushed. "Uh…" they both said.

Amanda patted Cole on the arm. "Too soon, honey."

At that point Steven came to their rescue. He spoke in a gentle, polite tone. "I guess you two are still pretty new together?"

"Six months," Jason said. Cole and her girlfriend shifted away and started chatting with the captain, so Lynch and his partner leaned in closer to Jason's side of the table. The bar grew a bit louder as the musician started up The Beatles, *'A Hard Day's Night'*, and strained to hit the notes of the chorus. Everyone talked louder to drown him out.

Steven said in a near shout, "Six months is still pretty good. You can know what you want for your relationship long term, even if you're at the beginning stages. It's good to have goals." He rubbed Lynch's shoulder. "Although, if you don't mind a bit of unsolicited advice, before you raise a child together you should travel."

Freddie chuckled, "Do you mean see the world? Before you're tied down?"

Steven shook his head. "Not exactly. Travelling is all about navigating strange new places and unexpected challenges. That's half of what parenting is." He smiled at Lynch. "Or so I'm told. I'm childless, myself, and quite happy that way."

"Which makes us the experts on parenting," Lynch said with a loud laugh.

Steven just shook his head. "Jonathan!" he said affectionately. Jason recoiled. Was that Lynch's first name? Jonathan? He'd never even asked.

"Where have you travelled to?" Silvana asked.

"Oh we've gone through Europe a few times. Italy is always gorgeous."

Lynch chuckled. "But we can never decide on our next trip. I want to go to the Caribbean, cause that's where my grandfather originally immigrated from. It would help me explore my heritage. But Steven wants to go to Japan, cause he 'just likes it'." He said the last words with as much scorn as possible.

"Ha ha," Steven drawled. "You just like the nude beaches."

"Hey, the nude beaches in Spain are cheaper to fly to, but you don't hear me suggesting that."

"Sounds like you just did."

Jason found himself laughing again. They were a cute couple. He liked how effortlessly they ribbed on each other in such a playful way.

Lynch gestured to Freddie. "You would understand going back to your country of origin, right? You ever been back to Japan?"

Freddie just stared back. "I'm Korean."

"Oh. Geez, sorry mate."

"I know we all look the same."

Lynch held up his hands. "Alright, we get it."

"Now you have to buy me a beer to make up for it." Freddie looked away, and side-eyed Lynch expectantly.

Lynch started laughing. "You bloody punk," Lynch said as he stood up. "I'll get you a beer."

"Can you make it Asahi? I love Japanese beer."

"Goddamn it!" Lynch was literally wiping his eyes as he walked across to the bar. A few moments later a waiter placed down three separate bowls of hot chips and the rich scent of heated potato and salt caused everyone to start digging in. A round of 'thanks captain' went across the table.

Steven leaned in and whispered like a conspirator. "I'm sorry about Jonathan. He loves to shit-stir. I thought I would train him out of it eventually, but alas." He got a round of smiles for his effort.

Jason shrugged. "Yeah, he's a bit of an ass, sometimes. But he's a good man." Jason grimaced. "Sorry, I didn't mean to insult him."

Steven grinned. "Nah, you summed him up perfectly."

Lynch came back with two glasses of Asahi and handed one to Freddie. "Hey tell me, Stevie," Lynch said. "You love Japan so much. Why they call it the land of the rising sun? The sun rises everywhere."

"It's the royal family," Steven said. "They believe the first Emperor came down from the sun to rule the country on behalf of heaven. That's why the royal family's name is Yamato. The name has many meanings in Japanese, but one of them literally means 'sun.'"

Jason went quiet for a moment. Lynch put his arm around his boyfriend and grinned. "See how clever this man is? I swear he's like an encyclopaedia sometimes. Go ahead and ask him a random question."

"Jonathan!" Steven said, blushing.

"Oh my god," Jason whispered. "The rising sun. Could it be that simple?"

Half the table turned to look at him. Silvana put a hand on his shoulder. "What is it, sweetheart?"

"The case," he muttered. "I can't believe it. The answer was right in front of me. And it's so stupid too!"

"What, rookie?" Lynch said. "Spit it out. Did you just solve something?"

Jason laughed and slammed his palms down on the table. "It's all in the name. Kennedy and sons. It's a play on words! It's Kennedy and *suns*."

Everyone stared at him with blank expressions. "Wait," Silvana said, "you don't mean sons, like male offspring? You mean suns, like the stars?"

Jason laughed, the sound coming out louder in his growing excitement. "Don't you see? Kennedy and sons is a co-owned venture between America and Japan, between House Kennedy and House Yamato! The name is a goddamn pun."

Lynch frowned. "That seems a stretch."

"But think about it! The founders were George Kennedy and his sons, Michael and Hanson. Those are clearly English names. But you know how you would pronounce those names in Japanese?" He turned to Silvana. "Mikeru and Hana!"

Her eyes widened. "They were in business with Samantha Kennedy!"

"Exactly! That's why they killed her. They were removing their business partner, so they could take complete control of their company. That's a net worth in the hundreds of millions of dollars."

"And Samantha was killed by a blade!"

"By the knight Mikeru, yes!" Jason tapped his finger on the table. "It all makes sense. They wanted to kill their partner. So they set off the bomb to break the enchantment to stop violence. Then the three shapeshifters that *they hired* attack Khadija and anyone else they encounter to create chaos. While everyone's distracted, Mikeru kills Samantha. But once the shapeshifters have done their job, Mikeru kills one so he looks like a hero and makes him seem above reproach."

"That's how he got close enough to kill them," Silvana said. "I thought it was strange that a mortal knight could kill a shapeshifter. But they knew him. His attack was a surprise. He probably meant to kill all three, or at least ensure they died in the attack. No loose ends."

"What are you two talking about?" Lynch said. "Who are these people you keep mentioning?"

Jason waved his hands in the air, nearly bumping some strangers walking past the table. "It's an Immortal Japanese couple, a knight and vampire. They were involved in a murder of a wizard."

"Uh…what's this now?" Steven muttered. Lynch rolled his eyes, but Jason cut him off.

"That's where the missing five million pounds went!" He slapped his forehead. "They siphoned it off themselves. That's why we couldn't find it. It's not tax fraud. It's embezzlement!"

Freddie hummed in thought. "I don't understand. What's the difference?"

Jason was nearly jumping up and down with energy now. "Tax fraud is where you lie on your records about how much money you made. But now we know the Yamatos own the company, so that means they stole the money from themselves. That's embezzlement! So that means they didn't lie. The money truly existed, but it passed through completely different channels into their back pockets." He pointed at Lynch and Cole. "Get the auditors back. I bet if they look for embezzlement, they'll find exactly what they need."

"It's worth a try," Lynch said, eyeing Cole, who shrugged.

"But wait, wait," Silvana said. "Why did they send the Skinwalkers to attack me and Khadija? It's too deliberate. Cause Khadija was implicated in the murder, and they tricked me out of money. There was clear malicious intent towards us."

Jason shrugged. "You're right. It had to have been deliberate. But I don't know why. It could be…" he stopped. "Hang on. Remember when we met Hana and Mikeru? At the gala?" He pointed at Silvana. "They asked if we were the ones who…" he trailed off and glanced towards Lynch, "…defeated Peter Erikson?"

"Right. They asked after him by name."

"They could be targeting you for revenge."

Silvana let out an 'Ah' sound. "They're doing a good job of it too. Our family are basically ruined now." She looked at Jason, frowning. "Do you think they must be part of Peter's organisation?"

"The Royalists."

"Exactly. And if they're Yamato, they're already part of a royal family. It would make sense why they're obsessed with monarchies."

Lynch turned to Freddie. "What are they talking about?"

Freddie shrugged. "Vampires and wizards, dude. Try to keep up." Lynch scowled at him.

"We still don't know why they targeted Khadija," Silvana said.

"I have a thought," Freddie said. All eyes turned to him, and he squirmed for a moment before talking. "I don't think they actually wanted to kill Khadija. They wanted to frame her. By attacking her, yes, she was distracted and couldn't help Sam. But she also got roughed up and now it looks like her and Sam had a big fight. No one knows they were a couple. The attack was less about destroying Khadija, and more about presenting someone to blame. And it makes sure Khadija doesn't come after them for revenge."

Jason pointed at his friend. "Freddie, you're a genius." Freddie blushed. "We've got it now. It's definitely the Yamatos." He cupped Silvana on the shoulder. "We're going to stop them and save your family at the same time." Silvana's face flooded with relief.

At that moment the music ended as the song finished. The singer stopped to take a drink, and the volume of the bar dropped considerably. Jason lowered his voice. "We need to go after them right now. Can you call the Vigiles and tell them what we know?"

"Vigiles?" Silvana said. "They'd never listen to us. We should call Khadija."

Jason shook his head. "We can't trust her either. She'd probably try to kill Mikeru on sight. You saw what she did to that girl Aakriti."

"Yeah," Silvana said with a wince. "But the Vigiles would be just as likely to turn on us. At least Khadija wants us to succeed."

"But imagine if we didn't tell the Vigiles, and they track us. They would be pissed if they found out. I'd prefer to play it safe with them."

Freddie cleared his throat. "Uh just a suggestion, but what if you told both of them?" Jason screwed up his face in confusion. "Tell the Vigiles and ask them to take you there. But tell Khadija as well in case you need a rescue."

"Oh no!" Jason said. "I am not risking another confrontation between wizards."

"Fucking hell," Lynch muttered to himself.

Jason put his face in his hands. "God, either option is so damn risky." He looked up. "But we have to do something. Silvana, this is your world more than mine. What do you think?"

She hesitated a few moments. Then nodded to herself. "You were right, Jason. We should tell the Vigiles. The risk of not telling them is too great."

"Ok, thank you, Silvy." He stopped. "How the hell do we tell them? Do they have a Vigile hotline or something? Triple nine?"

"Or triple six?" Freddie added dryly.

Silvana shook her head. "They do. But we need to speak to Desdemona and Portia directly, not any random Vigile. Oh!" she cried. "We can call Khadija's number. You know, her *home* number. The Vigiles answered last time."

Jason pulled out his phone. "You're *brilliant,* Silvana!" he cheered. He pulled out his phone and redialled the number from several days ago.

A woman answered in Arabic.

"Portia, is that you?"

"Ah, my dear Jason," Portia answered in her sweet sing-song voice. "How is my number one suspect?"

He figured he better play along. "I'm great. How are you?"

Her voice took on a sensual tone. "Oh, just itching to punish some lawbreakers. Thinking of all the fun things I could do."

My god, she's terrifying. How is she the less scary of the two? "Well, do I have some good news for you."

"Oh? You're ready to make a full confession?"

"We figured it out. It was Hana and Mikeru from House Yamato." Portia was quiet on the other end. Using the correct last name seemed to have done the trick.

Unfortunately, at that moment the bar musician announced his next song by yelling into the microphone, then started playing Pink Floyd's *Wish You Were Here*. Jason had to shout over the noise. "They co-owned a company with Samantha Kennedy, then killed her so they could absorb both halves of their business venture. They also hired the Metamorphs to attack Khadija and implicate her in Kennedy's murder. That's why Mikeru killed one, to set himself above reproach. Then they tried to set up Silvana in revenge for taking down their ally, Peter Erikson. We believe Hana and Mikeru are Royalists, just like Peter was."

"Huh," Portia muttered. "So you know about the Royalists too?"

"Of course. I'm a good detective, Portia." Lynch rolled his eyes, and Jason poked his tongue out at him in a decidedly childish manner.

Portia was quiet for a few moments. Jason coughed politely. "Uh, Portia? You still there?" More silence. "Hello?"

Lynch gave a wordless shout. Everyone on the opposite side of the table recoiled backwards in fear. Others turned around to look, only to leap away with cries of terror. Jason breathed deeply as he turned, half knowing what to expect.

The room was folding in on itself. Customers and serving staff were pushed aside. Several people cried out in terror. The music cut off with the painful dissonance of a missed chord. The walls and floors disappeared and glimpses of star constellations flickered through in their place. Then it all fell away, and a single woman emerged from the darkness of space. She wore a tight black tuxedo, but without the jacket, so her long white sleeves were visible underneath her black vest. Her long red hair swayed as she looked around the room at the cowering occupants. Her face sneered at their terror.

"Jason Turner," she cooed softly, her soft voice filling the silent bar.

"Alright that's enough!" a voice shouted. Lynch had drawn his handgun and pointed it at Portia. "Put your hands up! Right now!"

"Lynch, wait!" Jason screamed.

"Hands up, or…"

His gun was crushed into a little ball. He was left holding the handle and trigger, still intact, while the rest of the weapon had become a useless lump of metal.

"Consider yourself lucky, mortal," Portia said. "My mistress would have simply engulfed you in flame."

Lynch backed away with wide eyes. His boyfriend Steven was hiding behind him, his hands on Lynch's shoulders.

"Alright, calm down, everyone," Kader said, stepping into the centre of the room and speaking to every occupant of the bar. "People, there is no danger. We apologise for the scare. This is police business. Everything is fine now." Several strangers left the bar immediately, while other's took their seats in a calmer posture. Everyone continued to stare.

Kader turned to the police at the table. "No one do anything stupid, you understand? Also Lynch, why the fuck were you carrying at an office party?" Lynch gave a sheepish grin.

Portia looked at Kader with a smirk. "Ah, I remember you. The woman in charge. Glad someone around here has some sense."

Kader nodded her head. "Forgive my detective. He got attacked by a telepath last time we met but doesn't believe it really happened."

"He sounds emotionally stable."

"I'm working on it."

Jason cleared his throat. "Uh, hey Portia. Good to see you. Suppose I can hang up now." He pocketed the phone with unnecessary sass. "Where's your mistress?"

"Elsewhere," Portia said, her tone flat. "Now, I want you to look me in the eye and tell me the truth. How did you know they were Yamato?"

"It's in the name of their company. Kennedy and Sons. It's a play on words for 'suns', as in land of the rising sun. Also the founding sons were Michael and Hanson, a play on Mikeru and Hana."

Portia stared at him hard. "And you figured it out from a bad pun?"

Jason shrugged. "I'm not proud."

Portia smiled coyly. "How simple." She studied Jason a moment longer. "Very well. I will take you both to the Yamato castle. You can help me find evidence that will convince my mistress of what you say."

Jason and Silvana exchanged a glance. "Why isn't Desdemona with you?" Silvana asked.

Portia's lips parted, but no words came out, and the look in her eyes was vacant and far off. When she spoke, her tone had none of her usual sass. "My mistress has a weakness," she said. "She is unable to admit when she has made a mistake. She thinks it will limit her power."

"Of course," Silvana said. "But what mistake has she made?"

"Miss Al Khalifa is innocent. We all know it. I suspect even

Desdemona knows. But if she gets involved, she will target Khadija without hesitation. Our only chance is to take down the real culprit before my mistress gets involved."

Jason eyed her. "Why do you want this? You don't have to find the true culprits."

Portia stared past him into the middle distance. "Cause I want to see justice done. I want to see the guilty pay. Surely you can understand that?"

He did. There was clearly more to what she was saying. Still, he let it go. "Alright. But I need to arm up first. My sword is at my house, and my gun in at the office."

"Wait," Kader said. "I'm coming too."

"Captain," Jason started.

"That's an order," Kader snapped. "You're under my charge. I will not let anything happen to you."

"With all due respect, madam," Portia said, her words purring with amusement, "you are not coming. You're not a member of an Immortal House, and therefore have no place in our business."

Kader glared at her. "Do not challenge me, wizard. I am not afraid of you."

"You think you are the first to die bravely?"

Kader stared at Portia, and for a second her eyes shifted as if she were about to snap. Jason could see her straining. *This upsets her. This relates to her secret, somehow.* But just as he was about to step in, Kader seemed to come to her senses and back down.

"Then Jason, you can at least take my gun," she said and took the belt off her waist.

"Hey!" Lynch cried. "You were carrying too? What the hell?" Kader gave him a wink as she handed the belt and holster over. Jason took it and tied it around his waist. He looked to Freddie. "Are you cool to stay?"

"Oh shit yeah," Freddie said. "I'm curious, but not that curious. Just…be careful, you two."

Jason patted him on the shoulder, and Silvana gave him Freddie a firm hug. Jason turned to his captain. "Thank you," he said. "I'll be safe."

"You better," she warned. "Keep a level head. Watch your back."

"I will." He turned to the others at the table. "Uh…see ya later?"

"It was nice to meet you all," Silvana said. "Another time?" Everyone just stared back silently. Jason and Silvana held hands, then each took hold of Portia.

"Can we pick up my sword from my house?" he asked.

Portia nodded. "Then we'll take on the Royalists, and whatever surprises they have waiting for us." Her magic warped the bar around them and they teleported away.

Chapter 29

Jason marched down a long throne room, his sword hanging from the left side of his belt, Kader's standard issue Glock 17 from the right side, and a vial of Edward's healing potion concealed in his pocket.

Silvana moved on his left, her eyes red with blood and her power at its height. Portia walked on his right, brimming with authority and magic, clothed in a suit and menacing expression.

Around them, the grand hall was lined with silk tapestries of samurai, tigers, great battles, and cherry blossoms. The roof was so far above that Jason would struggle to touch it with a stone's throw. The floors were wooden, so that every step made a squeak like chirping birds. The walls were lined with servants with painted white faces and wearing kimonos of purple, blue and silver. Several men wore black vests with loose pants. Soldiers stood at the corners with modern tactical gear with medieval Japanese armour spliced over top. They half raised their weapons towards Jason, but stopped with furtive glances towards Portia.

At the end of the hallway, Hana sat on a throne, dressed in a pink kimono and wearing her hair up in a bun, the perfect picture of cold beauty. Next to her was Mikeru. His handsome face was lined with hard edges. He held himself with the relaxed stance of a warrior ready to strike.

You're mine, Mikeru, Jason thought to himself.

He walked down the hall with his head high and his sword ready. He swore he could feel the power emanating from Portia, and the rage from Silvana.

"This is it," he said to himself.

Hana called to them in a voice that echoed through the throne room. "Why have you come to my home? I did not invite you in. You have no right to be here."

"I have the right of an Imperium Vigile," Portia called back. "I am here because you broke Imperium law."

"Then why have you brought these belligerents?"

"We're here," Silvana said, "to see that justice is done."

The trio stopped at the foot of the throne. Jason kept his hand resting on his sword. He noticed Mikeru eying him with a mirror pose. *I can take him. Just remember what Phillip and Nicholas taught you. Do not hesitate.*

"We know the truth," Jason said. "I am a detective, and I've been investigating you. I know you are from House Yamato. I know you are co-owners of the investment company, Kennedy and Sons. I know the deed to the company is under an alias."

"I suppose you think that was hard to learn," Mikeru sneered.

"I know you killed Samantha Kennedy to remove your rival."

Hana and Mikeru shared a glance. *Yeah, take that you bastards.* Hana shook her head.

"Our animosity aside," she said, "I must assure you that we had nothing to do with the death of Samantha Kennedy."

Jason didn't flinch. "I find that hard to believe," he said. "Here's what I think happened. You hired three Skinwalkers to work the kitchens at the gala. They set off a bomb under Silvana and myself to try to kill us, because we killed your Royalist friend Peter Erikson."

Both of them stiffened slightly. Jason grinned. "Then the Skinwalkers stormed the party and attacked Khadija Al Khalifa, merely to keep her occupied. And during all the confusion, Mikeru attacked Samantha and cut her throat with his sword."

"Ridiculous," Mikeru said.

"I know, because Samantha Kennedy is alive." The couple visibly recoiled. "That's right! She was brought back from the dead by a powerful alchemist. And she remembers a blade cutting her throat."

Mikeru glared at him. "Then look at my blade." He drew his sword, a proper katana with a black handle. "There is no blood here. Have your vampire whore smell it for traces."

Silvana inhaled sharply, and Jason thought she was about to attack. Instead she whispered. "He's right. There's no blood."

"Then you simply used a different sword."

"That's enough," Hana said. "All your evidence is…what's the word…circumstantial. There is nothing that ties us to this crime. I demand that you leave immediately."

"You are somewhat right," Portia said, with a tone of finality. "The evidence is circumstantial. But you will come with me all the same. I will discover the truth of what happened here. And you will cooperate with my every instruction."

"We will do no such thing," Hana declared as she clenched her fists and leaned forward on her throne.

"You dare to challenge me?" Portia said, and an aura of haze began to shimmer around her. "You have no authority here. You will come with me and aid in my investigation."

"Or else what? You'll destroy us here and now?" Hana sneered. "I know you won't do that. Vigiles always travel in pairs. Where is your mistress, Portia? Why are you acting without her permission? I think it's because you're acting in an unofficial capacity." She smiled again as Portia remained silent. "You have no real authority here.

You will not touch us."

"Thankfully *I* have no such qualms."

Jason spun around. Crossing the hall towards them was Samantha Kennedy in a grey pant suit with a long black trench coat. Her long golden hair fell loose over the collar. Beside her, Khadija Al Khalifa wore more traditional Arabic clothes, a long black dress that was so large it hid her figure, and she wore a red headpiece that wrapped around her shoulders and covered most of her hair. Both women looked ready for battle. Samantha in particular had a wild, frenzied look in her eye.

How did they get here? Just as he thought that, he saw Khadija nod towards Silvana. *She must have messaged them. Damn, but I can't say I blame her.*

"I have no care for legality anymore," Khadija said and pointed at Hana. "You two tried to kill me. You successfully killed my dearest friend. So I suggest you go with the Vigile, before I kill you both here and now."

"No Immortal may kill another!" Hana shouted. "You know this."

"You tried to kill me first, and implicated me for murder. That would make my actions here self-defence." She smiled. "So go ahead. Try me."

"Yes, give me an excuse," Samantha hissed. "I still remember your blade passing through my neck. You have no idea what that feels like. But I'll make sure you do before the end."

Portia held out a hand in warning. "Easy, my fellow wizards. We're not going to turn this into a fight. Hana and Mikeru will come quietly now, lest I abandon them to these two fine wizards for their own devices."

Hana and Mikeru stared at each other. He was still holding his sword out. Jason could see the question on the knight's face, waiting for his mistress to give the order. He held his breath. Then Hana stood up from the throne. She adjusted her gown and held her head high.

"Very well," Hana said. "We will come with you and prove our innocence."

"You have made a wise choice," Portia said, and Jason breathed a sigh of relief.

Then the air started swirling. The world began to bend over and around itself between Jason and the throne. An instant later, a single figure emerged at the foot of the stairs, wearing a black tuxedo that matched her skin and long braided hair.

Desdemona.

The room went completely still. Jason felt his entire body go cold, like a kid with his hand in the cookie jar. Desdemona spun around slowly, leisurely taking in the sights of the room without a concern. She seemed to glare at Jason in particular, like her eyes could read his thoughts. Then she settled on Portia with a partial smile.

"Vigile Portia," she said. "Attend me."

"Yes Mistress," Portia said without the slightest hesitation as she moved to stand next to her fellow Vigile. The message was clear to everyone in the room. Whatever had happened before now was irrelevant. Portia would do whatever Desdemona told her to do.

"Now," Desdemona said calmly. "What is the story here?"

"Vigile," Hana shouted first. "These people have intruded on my home and threatened me with violence. I request that you deal with them."

"She's a murderer!" Samantha shouted back. "Her knight killed me in an unprovoked attack. You must arrest them!"

"I *must* do nothing," Dedemona said.

"Vigile Desdemona," Jason said, "If I may." She merely stared at him in silence. "I have been investigating this case. I believe Hana and Mikeru killed Samantha to take over their joint business venture.

And they tried to kill Silvana and I in revenge for defeating Peter Erikson."

"Enough," Desdemona held up a hand. "I do not require thy assistance, mortal knight. This investigation is my own. Last I checked, thou were our prime suspect, followed by Miss Al Khalifa here. Yet here thou art, invading another's lawfully owned property. Therefore, I will be detaining both of thee until such a time that I consider my investigation satisfied."

"Oh, bullshit!" Khadija snapped. "You don't like that Jason figured it out first. This is just to satisfy your pride."

Desdemona merely raised an eyebrow. "I care not for thy tantrums, girl. Thou wilt submit to my questioning, and I alone will ascertain the truth in this circumstance. I will deal justice."

"Liar!" Khadija growled. "You have no intention of finding truth or justice. You'll use all of this as an excuse to execute me without trial. I have seen Imperium justice, and I know exactly how foul it is."

"Mind thy tongue, insolent girl," Desdemona said, "lest I remove it from thy mouth."

It took Jason a moment to understand. Wizards couldn't speak spells without their tongue. Removing it was as good as removing their magic altogether. It may not apply as well to Khadija, but it was still an extreme threat.

"The four of thee wilt come with me," Desdemona said, pointing towards Jason and Silvana, Khadija and Samantha. "If I am happy with thy answers, I will investigate the Yamatos on thine behalf. But I will not suffer thou to overstep thy reach. Doth this seem fair to thee?"

Jason looked to Silvana, but he could only see fear and uncertainty on her face. She was just as clueless as he was. "Vigile Desdemona, please," Jason said. "I am certain of their guilt. If you would just…"

"We did nothing!" Mikeru growled. "I never touched the Kennedy whore."

"Liar!" Samantha shrieked. "You cut my throat, you bastard!"

"Now everyone," Portia said in a calming sweet voice, but it was instantly lost amongst the shouting.

"You want to feel my sword?" Mikeru sneered.

"I'll take that sword and ram it up your ass!"

"Oh, you'll feel my sword this time." He suggestively grabbed at his crotch and leered at her. "My sword will be deep inside you, coming in and out, over and over again. And you'll beg me for more."

Jason understood too late. "He's goading you!"

Samantha shrieked and hurled a bolt of lightning from her palm. Thunder clapped in the halls and a brilliant whiteness flashed.

The bolt disappeared in mid-air, fading into nothing. Desdemona had not even lifted a hand in gesture, but it was clear she had done it by the satisfied look in her eye.

"Thou darest challenge the Vigiles of the Imperium?" she whispered.

Samantha screamed again and raised a hand, but Khadija slapped it down. "Sam!" Khadija cried and shielded her friend with her body. "Your forgiveness, Vigile. She didn't mean it. She was provoked."

"You acted in direct violation on our wishes," Portia said. She and Desdemona took a step forward.

Silvana stepped between them with her hands out. "Vilgile, please! There is no need for violence. Samantha is suffering from extreme mental trauma. She's not in her right mind. Please show her mercy."

But Desdemona walked right up to Silvana's face and looked her in the eye. "Step aside," she said in response. "Final warning."

Jason could see the smirk on Mikeru's face. He'd planned this too well.

"Hey Kennedy," he jeered. "Maybe this time I can cut your lovers' throat too."

"NOOO!"

Samantha screamed and hurled a wall of fire in Mikeru's direction, with lightning bolts flaring in the midst of red.

Jason was too close. There was no avoiding the wall of death. The heat touched every part of his body and the light flared, forcing him to look away.

Yet some magical force shoved him aside with enough strength to send him sprawling. He looked up to see the four wizards pushing on the same fireball as it swirled in size to fill the whole hall. The servants screamed as they fled. Jason searched for Silvana. She was on the ground near him.

And beyond, Hana and Mikeru were charging at them.

Here we go.

Silvana was the first to launch to her feet and meet Hana's charge with a swinging fist. Yet Hana moved with skilled precision and caught the wrist, then followed up with an elbow to Silvana's face.

But Jason had no time to watch. Mikeru was upon him, his katana swung back, ready to strike.

Don't freeze. Act.

Jason came up into a kneeling crouch, drew his blade, and caught Mikeru's blow.

Their blades locked in place with a clang of metal. Mikeru pushed down with his weight and tried to angle the blades for Jason's head. Jason tilted to the side as the edge of the knights' blade twitched against his cheek. He pushed with all his strength. The blades began to rise away from him. *Yes! I am stronger than him.*

Mikeru kicked him straight in the face and sent him onto his back. Jason hit the floor and immediately rolled away. The sound of steel biting into wood echoed next to him.

Jason rolled up to his feet. Mikeru was already sprinting towards him.

Shit!

He barely had time to raise his blade and step back to deflect the blow. Something exploded nearby from the wizard's battle. Shards of wood sprayed across the throne room and Jason covered his face with his arm. It didn't stop Mikeru. He advanced through the debris, stepped directly into Jason's space and thrust his sword tip at Jason's chest. Jason could only avoid it by twisting his body. He was off centre and scrambling backwards. Mikeru kept coming, fully intending to strike a killing blow. He came in close again and swung for Jason's neck.

Jason dropped to the ground, rolled once, and came up with his Glock 17 in his hand, aimed at Mikeru's face.

But Mikeru caught the gun with the tip of the sword and swatted it aside, out of Jason's grip. Then he thrust the blade at Jason's chest once more. Jason twisted back. It was too slow this time, and the blade stabbed the top of his shoulder.

Jason screamed in pain. He could only cry, "Fucking bastard—" before Mikeru ripped out the sword and struck again. Jason barely managed to swipe the attack aside with his own blade and leap back out of reach.

A sudden bang filled the hall just as a flash of red fire went flying between the two knights and exploded on the wall nearby. Jason took the chance to glimpse at Silvana. Already her face was a mask of blood, and Hana looked completely unharmed. The Japanese vampire held herself in a crouch, wide stance, with one hand palm up by her stomach and another way out in front. She was clearly highly trained in martial arts and was having no trouble holding Silvana back. Meanwhile the two Vigiles were casting spells at Khadija and Samantha, the later pair barely able to deflect them in time. Each blow sent bolts of lightning, flames, and massive electrical charges shooting in all directions. The palace was being torn apart, tapestries shredding and burning up, cloth floating down from the roof like confetti.

Jason had to get to Silvana. There was no way they could win on their own. Mikeru was coming again, sword held high and already stained with Jason's blood.

So he turned and ran away.

He knew he was outclassed. He may be physically stronger, but Mikeru had far more skill with a blade. He couldn't last much longer. "Coward!" Mikeru roared, but Jason didn't care. He sprinted away from Mikeru towards the side of the hall, hoping to get around his opponent and move closer to the two vampires. As he ran, he grabbed a vial of blue liquid from his pocket and drained the contents. The stab wound in his shoulder began to heal. He threw the glass vial aside where it shattered.

You better be right, Edward.

Hana had just deflected another blow from Silvana, and responded with incredible speed. She jumped forward with a front kick from each foot, striking Silvana's chest and chin and forcing her back. Hana landed and threw herself into a powerful side kick. Her heel hit Silvana's stomach and knocked her flat.

Jason came up behind her. He had a clear shot at Hana's back. He raised this sword and slashed down.

But she heard him coming and leapt back with comfortable ease. It gave Silvana a chance to get up. Jason spun to put his back to her, just as Mikeru approached behind. He stopped when he saw Jason ready for him. Silvana pressed her back against Jason.

"You ok?" she asked.

"Yeah, you?"

"I've already used a lot of blood."

"Shit."

Hana and Mikeru stalked around the outside of them like predators around their weakened prey. Jason clutched his sword handle and wiped the sweat from his palms. He had to make this next attack count, or there would not be another chance.

A high pitch scream filled the throne room. A second later a chunk of the roof was torn apart. The lights went off and the hall was plunged into darkness as the night sky peered through the hole above them. The only lights were from bursts of wizard fire and cracks of lightning that flickered in jarring flashes. Samantha was floating in the air and thrust her hands down, throwing the piece of the roof she had just ripped free. Yet it bounced harmlessly off the Vigiles, reflected by an invisible barrier one metre off their heads.

Now the room was dark, and all Jason could see was the flash of silver from Mikeru's sword, and the red glow from Hana's eyes. *That's odd. Her eyes aren't just red, they're actually glowing slightly. Is she...an empowered vampire? Maybe just a little?* He had to play this right.

"I must admit," Jason said, "you are better than I."

Mikeru sneered. "Is that a compliment? Of course I am better. I've trained with the sword since birth. You are out of your league, nameless mortal from a bastard house."

"And you," Hana spat the words at Silvana. "You've never trained a day in your life to fight. You're a fumbling, pathetic shadow of a true Immortal. No wonder your line has failed."

"It hasn't failed yet," Silvana snapped. "I love my family, and you tried to destroy us. I would do anything to protect them."

Hana sneered. "Your love isn't going to save you."

A powerful crack came from the other end of the hall. The power of the wizards faded away as everyone turned to look.

Two more figures had appeared at the foot of the throne. One man wore a long robe and hood that covered him from head to toe. The other man wore tactical gear, a two-handed longsword on his back, and an assault rifle in both hands. Jason froze in horror when he recognised them.

The knight Wilhelm, and the wizard Ingolf, of the House of Glucksburg.

"Ingolf!" Hana screamed across the hall. "You took your bloody time getting here. Our enemies have come. Destroy them in the name of the Royalists!"

Ingolf bowed his head. "The House of Glucksburg is ready to help our Yamato allies," he said.

"Oh shit," Jason groaned.

Ingolf chuckled in his deep voice. He stepped forward, his knight at his side, and he grinned maliciously as he saw Jason and Silvana.

"My dear Romanovs," he said. "Time to die."

Chapter 30

Jason's heart was racing. He and Silvana stood in the middle of four Royalist enemies; two knights, a vampire, and a wizard. They had virtually no chance right now. He held his breath as he waited for his own demise.

"Vigiles!" Silvana shouted. "Surely you will not allow this. These two houses are Royalists. You know they are working against the Imperium."

"Shut your whore mouth, girl," Ingolf spat. Yet Jason noticed that all four Royalists were waiting. They were poised for battle, but none of them made a move. Clearly, they thought it possible the Vigiles would intervene, and none dared to challenge them directly. They were like dogs, waiting for their master's permission to eat.

"We've been helping you, Portia!" Silvana cried. "You cannot let them harm us."

Ingolf gave a scoff. "You severely overestimate your importance, girl." He raised his voice and declared, "We recognised the authority of the Vigiles of the Imperium. We will not interfere with your business, and we request the same courtesy in return."

Desdemona gave a laugh. "Thou art welcome to join this battle, short as it may be."

"Khadija?" Jason cried. He didn't have the words to plea. Yet he saw the hopeless look on her face. She and Samantha would not last much longer against the Vigiles. There was no chance of them helping him. Mikeru shifted his sword, as if miming plunging it into Jason and twisting. He gave a closed-mouth smile.

"I am asking the Imperium for help," Silvana cried. "One Immortal may not kill another."

"HA!" Desdemona barked. "And yet thou killed Peter Erikson. Do you know why we permitted it? Because Erikson invaded thy home. Well, now thou art guilty of the same offense. Whatever you think the Royalists have done, they have a right to defend themselves."

Hana gave a short laugh. "Accept your defeat, filthy quim. Your House is broken. You could never stand against mine."

Jason growled. He should have known he couldn't trust the Vigiles. He noted his Glock 17 was still on the ground nearby from where Mikeru had disarmed him. Did he even have a chance to reach it before Wilhelm's assault rifle cut him down? Could he…

He noticed something. "Wilhelm," he said in a soft tone. "What happened to your face?"

The knight had a massive patch of burnt skin covering the left side of his once perfect face. The flesh was crinkled and stretched thin, and a pink patch surrounded his eye socket. Flecks of white skin peeled away. Wilhelm only sneered back at Jason with a look of murderous rage.

"The price of failure," Ingolf said. "My knight will not lose to you again."

"Christ, man. You burned his face because he lost a fight? He's your own flesh and blood."

"He is my servant!" Ingolf roared. "And he will obey my orders."

Jason nodded to his fellow knight. "Why work for this piece of shit?"

"Because he knows his place," Ingolf growled, answering for his knight again. "All mortals will learn their place, at the feet of wizardkind. I am his king. I have ruled for four hundred years. You cannot even comprehend how much power I wield."

An idea came to mind, and Jason blurted it out before he even thought it through. "So much power, and yet you're scared of two simple women. Interesting."

Desdemona and Ingolf both glared at him. He could feel the full force of their fury, but he held his head high. "I am hardly simple," Desdemona growled.

"And I fear no man," Ingolf growled.

"Jason, what are you doing?" Silvana hissed.

Jason gave a fake laugh. "Really, Ingolf? Cause no sooner did you arrive than you were begging the Vigiles not to interfere. Sounds like you are afraid of them."

"I have no need to fight them."

"Or you know that you can't." Jason sneered. "Face it, Ingolf. You can be a king all you want. But when it comes to Desdemona, you are outclassed." He looked directly at Mikeru and winked. *Two can play at that game, you bastard.* Mikeru scowled back.

The Vigile gave a 'hmm' sound. "Flattery cannot save thee."

"What would the mortal know of a wizard power?" Ingolf growled. "A Vigile is strong, but they are no king. I have the divine power of God at my beck and call. I answer only to High Kings. While she is a servant, working at the behest of all."

Desdemona's eyes hardened and her glare turned towards the other. "Thou art confident in thy abilities, wizard. Too confident."

"Please," he barked a laugh. "I will one day soon become a High King. There are few with power similar to mine. I am nearly five hundred years old."

"Funny. So am I."

"And yet you are working class. I rule a nation. You are so far beneath my notice. I could not be bothered to fight you."

Desdemona turned her body to face him. "Bother thyself now."

Ingolf spun so fast that his robes twirled behind him. "Foolish woman. You have no idea what fate you are tempting."

"Glucksburg!" Hana snapped. "Stand down. The boy is goading you, can't you see? Put your pride aside."

"This won't take long," Ingolf said. "It's about time I remind the Imperium why they should fear me. I am lord and king of my country, and I tire of paying tribute." He stalked towards the Vigiles. "And this black bitch will remember why…"

The remaining palace roof collapsed and a monstrous beam of wood smashed down on Ingolf.

Desdemona was laughing, the sound echoing through the halls. "Thou fancies thyself my superior? Thou art a lazy," she took a step forward with each word, "fat, innocuous, mediocre magician." Ingolf groaned from under the collapsed wood. "Thou hast grown comfortable on palace cushions. I have forged myself in the fires of daily battle and combat. What wouldst thou do to challenge my power?"

"You fucking cunt!" Ingolf screamed.

She merely grinned back. "They all say that at the start."

A wave of power burst out of Ingolf, blasting the debris trapping him backwards. "Shoot the bitch!" he screamed. Wilhelm aimed his assault rifle. Yet with a flick of Desdemona's hand, it crumpled into a metal ball.

Ingolf roared and suddenly the dark hall lit up with a bright red flame. It took physical shape and formed into a massive draconic creature, a long serpentine body and two vast wings sprouting from its back. The flame beast opened its jaws, and the howl of wind was its roar. Desdemona answered his challenge with a wall of ice that congealed out of the air itself. Her ice formed jagged shards of razor sharp spikes. Fire and ice clashed and filled the throne room with steam. As their powers matched and contended for dominance, Khadija and Sam struck out at Portia with blasts of lightning. Yet the two of them had already been beaten down, and Portia seemed happy to match them on her own.

The wizards fight each other. We might just have a chance.

"That's enough of that," Hana growled.

Mikeru nodded in agreement. Jason prepared himself for the attack. Except the Japanese knight simply put two fingers in his mouth and whistled, then stepped further back. Jason watched him closely.

From the darkness, a monstrous shriek made the hairs prickle on Jason's neck. Several creatures came sprinting forward on two legs. They stood seven feet tall and moved faster than he could believe. They were covered in leather hide and feathers, with long talons tipping the end of each long finger and a large, curved claw on their feet that clicked against the ground as they stalked towards Jason and Silvana. The creatures let out an ear splitting screech that sent a rush of cold down Jason's spine. He knew these creatures all too well.

Velociraptors. Holy crap, the Yamatos have even more shapeshifters in their employ.

Silvana grabbed his arm. "Run Jason!"

He started running. Hana and Mikeru didn't even bother attacking, stepping back and sneering in satisfaction as their servants ran hot on Jason and Silvana's tails.

They sprinted from the darkness of the throne room and into a hallway where lights still shone, though they flickered menacingly. The wizards' magic had clearly done serious damage to the building's electricity. The creatures barked as they ran after them. Jason paid no mind to the expensive tapestries hung on the walls, or the squeaking wooden floorboards that announced their position. They just had to move.

There was a corner. Silvana reached it first. "Come on!" she yelled. The creatures were close behind. Jason held the sword in one hand and grabbed her in the other. She yanked him behind the wall just as a raptor snapped its jaws at his face. Jason spun, gripped the sword in two hands, and slashed down with a roar. The blade cut the creature across the muzzle. It let out a new sound, high pitch and sharp. Jason resumed running as more of them came after.

"It think there's four of them," Silvana yelled. "But there could be more elsewhere."

A loud rumbling seemed to shake the entire castle. It sounded like a long, drawn out roll of thunder that lasted several seconds. It came from deep underground. Jason could only imagine what the wizards were doing right now.

Another archway appeared ahead. Silvana grabbed his hand and dragged him towards the door. "It's a sliding door," he yelled. "You pull it acro—"

She smashed through the wooden door entirely.

"Sure, that'll do," he quipped. They raced outside and into a garden courtyard, with a gravel pathway twisting between long pools of water. Dozens of koi fish zipped away from them in a flash of red, orange, and gold. Silvana weaved through several bonsai trees, leading them deeper into the green foliage. She stopped ahead at a bamboo fountain in front of a stone lamp. She spun in place.

"Damn," she said. "We're still in the castle. We need to get outside."

High stone walls lined every side. The Yamato castle was like a maze, and Jason feared one wrong turn would mean their doom.

Silvana moved in a flash past Jason. He spun, just to see her collide with a raptor and be driven into the ground. Before he could help her, two more launched themselves at him.

He stepped forward and swung the sword up, carried the motion over his head, and struck back down. Both strikes missed, but successfully warded off the creature's attack. They stopped just out of reach and crouched low in readiness. Up close, he saw their snouts filled with teeth in a wide almost human smile. Their tails were raised high for balance. He kept his sword between them both, two hands on the handle, and tilted forward slightly. He widened his stance, ready for any move. Silvana growled and wrestled one of the creatures on the ground next to him. He had to wait. The moment he attacked one, the other would be upon him. Neither were moving.

In the sky above, flashes of red light went off like bombs, signalling the wizards' duel. Each flash lit up the creatures in front of Jason and made a loud crack resound a half second later. Still, neither attacked. Why were they still…

"Shit, they're stalling us," he cried.

Jason looked over his shoulder. Between one flash of magic and the next, Mikeru was right in front of him.

The katana slashed at his face.

Jason tried to duck, but he was too late. Something hot seared across his forehead, slicing deep into his flesh. He screamed as he fell back.

The pain was sharp and blinding. Blood pooled in his eyes from the gash on his forehead. He could hear Silvana screaming. He looked towards her, stunned and barely thinking. Silvana was surrounded. A velociraptor was on one side, and Hana on her other. But she was focused on them. She couldn't see Mikeru approaching her from behind, sword ready to strike.

"Silvana!" he screamed and ran to save her.

Mikeru's sword spun around. His attack on Silvana had been a feint. His blade suddenly thrust at Jason instead. He was too slow.

The blade plunged into Jason's belly.

"NOOO!" Silvana howled.

Chapter 31

Jason froze, hunched over the sword that pierced deep into his core. Silvana was screaming. He could see the blade sitting inside him. His mind trembled and threatened to shatter at the sheer horror of it. There was pain everywhere, so far beyond his capacity to handle that it overwhelmed his mind. Another explosion rocked the castle, and the night lit up like day as lightning struck nearby with a deafening crack. Jason couldn't move. He started coughing up mouthfuls of blood.

He looked up. Mikeru stood over him, with two dinosaurs flanking him, his face gleaming with sweat and a satisfied scowl. Silvana was behind him, screaming and clawing at Hana's petite frame, but Hana managed to hold her down in a wrestlers pose.

"Now we watch him die together," Hana said.

"Bitch! Get the fuck off me!" Silvana roared. "I'll kill you! I'll KILL YOU ALL!"

Mikeru put both hands on the handle of the sword. His eyes gleamed with pleasure, and he twisted the blade. Pain suddenly burst everywhere inside Jason, from his core to his head. Everything seared in agony.

"Guess we know who is better with a sword now," Mikeru said. "I must say. It suits you."

Silvana roared, "I'll fucking kill you! Fucking bastard, I'll tear your fucking throat out!"

"Shut up, whore," Hana growled, but her voice was strained. She was losing her grip. Silvana shrieked and thrashed in a frenzied state. Jason understood. *This is her vampire savagery. It's her berserker mode, like Nicholas and Phillip warned.*

Silvana got a limb free and elbowed Hana in the face with a crack. She broke free and slashed at Hana, spraying streaks of blood and sending her to the floor. Then she turned on Mikeru. The knight reached for his sword as if to rip it clear of Jason's body, but Silvana moved faster and leapt at his face. The shapeshifters roared as they defended their master. Silvana's shriek was inhuman. She didn't seem to care that there were half a dozen opponents. She went wild with rage. She drove Mikeru to the ground and reached for his neck. Mikeru screamed and pushed against her. Tooth and claw bit at her. Hana reappeared and struck at Silvana back and neck, but to no effect. Silvana was determined to kill him.

Jason looked down at the sword still in his belly. He remembered Edward's words. *"Elixirs cannot remove foreign objects. You'll have to do that yourself."*

Don't freeze. Act. He knew what he had to do. He gripped the handle in two hands.

Fuck me, this is gonna suck.

He counted down. "Three, two, one," and yanked.

The next thing he knew, he was lying on his side. The sword was still in his gut. *Damn, I passed out.* He saw Silvana still in the same pose, trying to kill Mikeru, everyone's attention on her. *You weren't out for long. Come on, Jason, get up!* He reached for the handle again and didn't think. He pulled. This time he felt the pain, and the sound he made was more animal than man. He felt the blade shift and squelch, but refuse to come fully out. His hands were shaking uncontrollable. He couldn't grip the handle properly. *One more.* He gritted his teeth, roared in readiness, and pulled.

It moved slightly, but didn't come clear. He had pulled the handle as far from his body as possible, still the blade was inside him. There was no choice. He had to grip the blade itself. The edge cut his trembling palms and blood ran down his enclosed fingers. *Come on, Jason.* He squeezed his hand and yanked.

The sword finally came out.

He collapsed onto his back with a cry of pain. A strange feeling of euphoria rushed over him. He lay in a pool of his blood, yet the searing heat in his stomach began to ease. He gasped in relief as his pain levels went down. His body shivered with cold even as sweat burst from his forehead. *I recognise this feeling. The elixir is working!*

Silvana was screaming. Hana had her head gripped between two hands. She was preparing to snap her neck.

Jason acted. Before he knew it, he was on his feet with Mikeru's sword in his hand. He charged past the dinosaurs directly at the vampire. Hana looked up. He didn't know how sturdy vampires were, so he swung with his fullest strength.

The blade hit her in the side of the head and slashed across her face. Hana screamed and clutched at the bloody wound as she collapsed.

"Hana!" Mikeru screamed.

The shapeshifters turned on Jason. He swung wildly and desperately to fend them off. Yet Silvana leapt on the back of one with a crazed shriek and *bit* down on the back of its neck. She lashed out at the next one with a kick. Jason managed to cut the third across the muzzle, and the fourth turned to flee.

Jason saw Mikeru scrambling on the gravel towards Jason's sword, still lying on the ground, where he'd dropped it. Mikeru grabbed the hilt.

Jason stepped forward and swung the katana in an upper cut,

severing Mikeru's hand.

The knight screamed and clutched at his wrist. Blood squirted from the wound, so he pressed his stump against his chest to stem the flow. The shapeshifters could see that the tide had turned, so all of them fled back into the castle.

"How?!" Mikeru screamed. He looked up at Jason with hatred in his eyes, his shirt soaking in blood. "How did you get up again!"

Jason lifted his shirt and showed the pink skin that covered where the sword wound had been. Blood stains pooled down to his waist, but the flow had stopped completely. "I took the time to befriend an alchemist," he said.

"Cheater!" Mikeru said. "Knights don't use elixirs in battle. You acted with dishonour."

"Don't fucking preach to me about dishonour," Jason growled. "You're a liar and a—" Something moved behind him. Jason spun around with his sword held ready to strike.

Silvana had dived on Hana. The Yamato vampire was dazed from the massive sword gash to the side of her head. Yet Silvana raised her hand back as if ready to kill her.

"Hey!" Jason yelled. "Silvana, stop. There's no need."

Silvana's face snapped up to stare at Jason with bright red eyes. "She's not here," she said.

Jason blinked. "What?"

"She's not here!" she snapped again.

He waited for her to explain, but she said nothing else. She just held Hana's limp form between her blood-stained hands, her chest rising and falling with each rapid breath, and her fist ready to strike. Jason watched her, and a sudden feeling of unease settled on him. He pointed his sword towards Silvana and spoke in a gentle tone.

"Who is not here?"

She smiled back at him, her teeth red with blood that dribbled over her lips and down her chin.

"*Silvana,*" she whispered.

A cold chill ran down Jason's spin. He saw it now. That wasn't her facial expression. The eyes were different. The look of mania, of a violent frenzy and rage. It wasn't her.

"Then who am I talking to?" he asked in his calmest voice.

A shrill, cold laugh came out of her then, and Jason felt his hands start to tremble. "I don't know why she puts up with you, cunt," Silvana spat. "You're twice as fucking stupid as she is, yet you boss her around. I would never put up with your bullshit."

Jason's mind was racing. What was he witnessing? His childhood visits to Anglican churches made him think of demonic possession, but he dismissed that. Was this the frenzy state Nicholas had warned him about? It could be some sort of vampire power. Maybe this was why the Imperium had such harsh laws about vampire control? Was this a darker side? An alter ego? Either way, he had to stay calm.

"I want to keep Silvana safe," he said. "Do you want that too?"

Silvana sneered. "Yes, not that the stupid bitch deserves it."

"Ok. Can we work together until she is safe?"

She finally dropped Hana roughly against the gravel path. She stood up straight, rolling her neck around with a sigh. "Like I need your help. You're such a fucking pussy."

An explosion rocked the world around them. It was so loud and bright that it took Jason a moment to comprehend what he was seeing; lightning had struck the ground only metres from where they stood. The burning white light still flashed in Jason's eyes every time he blinked, the image seared into his retinas. A bonsai tree was on fire, and blackened scorch marks spread along the walls. High above, the wizards who had cast it were still locked in combat.

"We need to work together," Jason said. "We still need to defeat the Glucksburgs. We cannot take them on our own."

Silvana tilted her head and walked towards him, each step making a soft patter on gravel. "And do you trust me, Pussy Knight?" Silvana asked.

He steadied himself. He wanted to ask questions, but now was not the time. "If you want to keep Silvana safe, then yes."

She smiled again and some of the blood had cleared from her teeth.

"Lovely," she purred. "Lead on, Pussy Knight."

He nodded and took stock of their surroundings. Hana and Mikeru were both still alive but unable to fight. Hana had regained consciousness and was clutching her face, but still breathing steadily. Her power was slowly healing her wound. Mikeru was tying off his own tourniquet. So Jason picked up his own sword again and sheathed it at his waist, while keeping hold of Mikeru's katana as well.

"That bitch is crazy," Mikeru growled.

"And I married her. So watch what you say to me," he growled back.

"Hey," Silvana snapped. She pointed at the katana. "Give me that sword."

Jason paused. "You said…" he stumbled, "Silvana said she didn't need a sword."

"Well I do," Silvana said. "I don't have my telekinesis, like last time. I need something."

Jason frowned at her. Like last time? Surely that was a reference to the battle with Peter, when Silvana had fought him in the empowered vampire state. Had that been…this version of her? But if it was, why did she have more power last time? What had awaked this state, if it wasn't the empowered vampire?

Silvana was still waiting. Jason set his jaw and handed over the katana. She smiled. "I promise not to probe you with it." Then she ran her tongue over her teeth and raised her eyebrows.

She moved at him with a sudden burst of speed. She snatched his head and shoulder and bent them apart. He saw her teeth coming for his throat. He screamed and struggled, but she was far too powerful to stop. She bit the side of his neck.

The pain was blinding. Jason could only let out a weak gasping sound. *Oh my god! She's killing me! What the hell is happening!* He tried to say her name, but nothing came out.

Then she released him. Jason gasped and clutched at his neck as he fell back. He felt blood on his hands. And yet, it wasn't that much blood. He checked it several times, but the wound was not deep at all. She had only taken enough blood to feed. She was licking her lips, and when she saw him looking, she winked back suggestively.

"What the hell was that?!" he growled.

"I needed to feed, you fucking idiot," she said simply. "Now I can keep Silvana safe in the battle. Isn't that's why you're here? As a walking refrigerator for her to snack from whenever she feels?"

"Not without permission," he growled, but Silvana only laughed back.

"I shouldn't have bothered. Your blood is shit anyway. The fuck is wrong with you?" she growled. Jason wanted to ask what was wrong with his blood, but she cut him off with an order. "Come on!"

She led him back into the castle. Jason checked his wound to confirm it wasn't bleeding too much. It wasn't healing, which meant the elixir was all used up. Jason followed after Silvana – or whoever this was – careful to keep his grip on his blade in case she tried something again.

They ran back towards the throne room and towards the sounds of wizard battles. Silvana ran much faster and this time made no effort to wait for him. Jason did his best to keep up. His body was exhausted. The healing from his impalement had taken everything out of him. Now he just needed food and sleep, if only he had the time. His mind and reflexes would be slower. He had to be more decisive than ever.

The throne room was filled with debris and patches of fire. The moon cast its pale light through the open roof, revealing two figures side by side, slumped down against the walls. Samantha was shielding Khadija with her body, but blood was smeared through her blond hair and one arm hung loosely at her side. Khadija was lying on her front, her headpiece loose around her shoulders. She was crawling on her elbows and trying to rise.

Portia stood over them. Her tuxedo was ripped in a few places, yet she looked totally unharmed. A wild torrent of air was whipping her hair up behind her and flaying it about.

"I…" Samantha shouted, "…must kill the knight. He deserves to die. Why won't you let me kill him?!"

"Just stand down, you lunatic," Portia growled.

Far above, a flash of red light filled the sky and exposed the outlines of several clouds. A burning pillar of flame fell towards the castle like Lucifer falling out of heaven, and the comet plunged into the ground. It was Ingolf, and he cast off his burning wizard cloak to stop the spread of flames. He growled in fury up towards the sky. "I'll kill you for this! Whore!" he roared.

Wilhelm came running to his master's side and lifted him up onto his feet. Both of their backs were turned.

Silvana saw her chance before Jason could act. She shrieked and hurled the katana faster than humanly possible so it spun on a vertical axis, flying straight at the back of Ingolf's head.

Wilhelm heard her cry and saw the blade coming. He tackled the wizard down and the sword flew past him with millimetres to spare.

Jason was already charging at the duo. Silvana following close behind him.

Wilhelm saw them coming and sat up. He drew a handgun from

a holster. Silvana got to the pair first and caught the nozzle of the gun between her blood soaked hands. She aimed it upwards as he let off a short burst of automatic fire. A flash of wizard lightning lit up Wilhelm's face. He was baring his teeth and snarling. Jason stepped into to strike with the sword, just as the wizard turned.

"Khad Nga!"

Jason was hit with the force of a solid wall. He felt himself twist in the air before hitting the ground hard and rolling, with bruises forming across his shoulders and legs. Silvana landed beside him a second later, growling and already lifting herself back up to attack again.

"Fool," Ingolf said. "You attacked the gun? You should have gone for the wizard." He summoned up a ball of fire in each hand. "Now you will burn."

Silvana responded with a full-throated scream. There was no time to move. No opportunity to counter-attack the wizard. Yet Jason noted that even now, Silvana was standing in front of him and shielding him with her body.

A figure came out of the darkness. One of the palace servants. Jason had half a second to glimpse a short, brown-skinned girl, before the servant transferred into a lioness. The massive four-legged beast let out a yowl and launched at the wizard.

What the hell?

The lioness bit down on the wizard's shoulder, and he screamed in wordless agony. The creature clung to his back, twisted its head and wiggled its jaw for a better grip. The wizard screamed too much to form a proper word for a spell. Wilhelm struck the lioness hard with his sword. It hissed at him and backed off, a red gash appearing on its shoulder. Wilhelm made to swing again, but Jason stepped in to block the sword with his own. He shoved Wilhelm hard enough to send him sprawling out on the ground.

The lioness shifted back into human form. She was bleeding down her shoulder and arm. Jason saw the girls' face now, and recognised her. "Aakriti?" he cried.

Aakriti pointed at Ingolf and shouted in her language. The wizard was propping himself up. Blood poured down his face. He tried to speak and coughed up blood. Ingolf looked at Aakriti, and opened his mouth again in a snarl.

Silvana leapt at him. She brought her fist down on Ingolf's mouth, and shattered his jaw.

He screamed again, but this time it sounded more like gargled choking. His bottom jaw was a jagged mess of bone and blood and tooth. There was no way he could speak a spell now. Silvana smiled. "Shall I tear you limb from limb?" she purred.

Wilhelm roared, "Don't you dare touch him!" He had his handgun free, aimed at Silvana. There was no way to block him in time.

Then he fell.

It was the strangest thing. But he tripped over and fell forward, seemingly for no reason. Jason pounced on him and kicked the gun out of his hand, before levelling the point of his sword at Wilhelm's throat.

And just like that, they had won.

Jason looked at Wilhelm's feet. Why had he fallen? Something was moving on the ground. It looked like a wiggling snake, shaped like a tree branch. It folded into the wood and disappeared back into the floorboards themselves.

He looked across the hall into the shadows. Sure enough, a servant man was watching from in the darkness. Jason understood. The man was a Fae. It was probably one of the two Fae men Silvana had saved in the kitchen at the gala. That's how he had tripped Wilhelm, by growing a tree branch out of the wooden floorboards. The Fae saw Jason looking at him, and gave a half nod.

Thank God she helped those servants.

"Jason?" Silvana asked. Something about her voice was different. She was standing over the injured form of Ingolf, staring at her own bloodied hands as if confused to find them there. She looked up at Jason. Her mouth curled up and a cry escaped her lips. "Oh Jason! You're alive!" She was suddenly on him, hugging him tight and squeezing. Her chest was shaking with sobs. "Oh my love! My dearest Jason!" She was openly crying now. "I thought I lost you!" She sniffed through her tears, her whole body trembling.

Jason could only hold her in stunned silence.

She pulled back suddenly and checked his stomach. "The blade went right through! I don't understand what happened," she cried.

"Edward," he said in a stunned, flat voice. "He gave me a healing elixir. I drank it before we came."

"Bloody hell, you should have warned me!" But she was smiling as she said it. "I was terrified. I..." she looked around. She seemed to slowly realise where she was. She noticed the Glucksburgs on the ground beneath them, and the bloodied mess of Ingolf's face. "What the hell happened?" she asked.

"You..." he trailed off. How could he possibly explain what just happened? He didn't even know himself what that was. He decided to just give a short answer for now and talk about it later. "You were pretty upset. We beat the Yamato's, and came back here to fight the Glucksburgs."

"I... I can hardly remember."

"It's ok. We're fine now." He felt like he was lying, even though it wasn't a lie. But he was only hiding the truth for now. He would explain everything later. *God, how can she not remember? Is she going to turn back into that other person again?* He resolved again to discuss it later. Now he simply wanted to enjoy the fact that the battle was over, and they were alive.

"Well," a voice came from above. Desdemona was floating back down from the sky, her tuxedo jacket flapping in the wind. "Thou hath done well to dispatch my opponent, weakened though he was."

"Mistress," Portia said. "I have kept these two wizards in their place." She gestured to the injured forms of Khadija and Sam, still largely in the same posture. They had well and truly lost their fight with the Vigiles. But they were alive.

"I am hardly surprised," Desdemona said. "So many wizards think they can challenge a Vigile. They will all learn their folly in time." Ingolf gave a wordless cry, his mouth too broken to speak words, and it only made Desdemona's smile widen. "Now, I think there should be an appropriate punishment for daring to strike a representative of the Imperium, don't you?"

"Stop it!" Silvana screamed. The Vigiles turned to face her. "Hasn't there been enough blood already?"

"Thou should know best, vampire," Desdemona said. "There is never enough blood."

"But you've been manipulated. Hana and Mikeru have used you to destroy their enemies. And Samantha only attacked you because she's not in her right mind."

Jason couldn't help cringe at hearing Silvana say the phrase 'not in her right mind'.

"That is irrelevant now," Portia said, a hint of regret in her voice. "Kennedy attacked us unprovoked, and Al Khalifa made a choice to join in."

"You bitch!" Khadija screamed.

"Indeed. She is also the prime suspect in Kennedy's death. Or should I say, her original death." Portia gave a reluctant sigh and looked to her leader. "I think her aggression alone is reason to believe her guilt."

Desdemona sighed as well, though there was clear eagerness in her manner. "Indeed. Let's end this, shall we?"

Aakriti shouted loudly, cutting off the Vigiles in her own language. The young Skinwalker was eyeing the wizard Ingolf in fear while she spoke. Yet no one understood her, and the Vigiles stared at her blankly. Aakriti hissed in exasperation.

"Chaitan!" she shouted.

There was a long pause. Jason looked around the outskirts of the destroyed throne room to a few servants waiting there. Finally one of them stepped forward. It was a man of medium height with brown skin and shaggy black hair. He stood in the centre of the hall and bowed low. "Mistress Vigile," he said, and his voice sounded just short of adulthood. He had a thick Indian accent that was only just understandable. "I am Chaitan Vamar. I am the Skinwalker who attacked you at the gala. I also attacked Al Khalifa, and the Romanov girl."

"Well!" Desdemona jeered. "Thou art braver than most. What compels thee to confess thy sins now?"

Chaitan looked to the others in obvious confusion. *He probably doesn't understand all the thee's and thous.* Portia addressed him, "Why?" she said in a clear voice. "Why tell us?"

He nodded in understanding and pointed at Silvana. "She saved my sister. I owe her." Then he pointed again at the throne. "My masters, Hana and Mikeru Yamato, snuck us onto the staff list. They ordered us to attack. They said they would kill my sister unless I attacked their enemies at the gala. I had no choice. But we didn't kill anyone." He pointed at Samantha. "She was dead when we found her. She," he pointed to Khadija, "fought us off. Then she," he pointed to Portia, "killed my friend. We ran away. We found our master to report to him. And he cut my other friend's head off. Only I escaped."

Portia was watching her mistress in silence, yet Desdemona only stared at the Skinwalker man. "Thou art irrelevant," she said finally.

"Al Khalifa and Kennedy still attacked me here in this hall. They will still die. Then I will deal with the Yamatos."

"No!" Jason screamed, but Desdemona suddenly flared as fire surrounded her in a raging aura.

"Try me again, boy! See what happens!"

"You can't just kill them!" Jason cried. "Khadija had probable cause. All of her actions have been self-defence. And Samantha should be able to plea insanity."

"Does thou wish to die as well?"

"Oh come on!" Jason screamed. "This cannot be justice. You've just had a confession from the assailant directly. You're only killing them now because of your pride."

Desdemona clenched her fists. "I am done with this game." The entire hallway started to swirl as magic bent reality itself.

Oh shit!

It affected everything within sight. The walls were shifting in circular patterns. Starlight flickered through the dark gaps, swirling constellations of giant space gas clouds passed before them. *Wait, this isn't an attack. It's teleportation.* He looked at Desdemona. *But that's impossible. The Vigiles need physical contact to teleport us.* Then he saw the wide-eyed fear in Portia's eyes, and the stoic hardness on Desdemona's face. *They're not the ones doing this! Which can only mean...*

Jason fell.

The ground was suddenly yanked out from beneath him and he dropped into empty space. His arms flailed for balance. He cried out for Silvana, but no noise came from his lips. There was nothing to grab on to. Nothing to do to save himself. He plummeted into nothingness.

Light flared. Something appeared before him, and he hit the stone ground.

His head blared in pain. His chest felt tight, and his wrist had a sharp stabbing sensation when he moved it. He heard others moaning in pain from their landing. Yet over it all, the raspy voice of an old man gave a satisfied hum.

"Well well well," he said. "By the grace of God, you all arrived in one piece."

Jason looked up and realised where he was. Another throne room, but where the Yamato room was pitch black, this one practically shone with dazzling bright radiance. Everything was gold and bejewelled, from the walls to the very ground. He saw the throne, one man sitting on it with a resplendent crown and ornaments on his garment. Behind the throne, a painting of heaven shone down with Jesus Christ front and centre.

"Welcome to my kingdom," said High King Reynold the First.

Chapter 32

The Vigiles were the first on their feet. "We serve thee, our King," Desdemona announced in a bold voice, though Portia seemed to be shaking. Her hands were clutched together to keep them steady, but Silvana could see that they were trembling. She appeared terrified of the High King.

Silvana looked around. Everyone who had been in the Yamato castle was here now. They all stood in pairs. Jason was at her side, also Khadija and Sam, the two Vigiles, the Glucksburgs, and even the Yamatos had been collected from elsewhere in the castle. In the centre was the shapeshifter girl Aakriti, and her brother Chaitan. Almost all of them were nursing wounds from the fight, and every single one of them were recoiling from the High King with looks of terror.

"Now then," Reynold said in a commanding voice. "I understand several of you just threatened the Vigiles, who art my most loyal servants."

The throne room was silent. Ingolf and Wilhelm were cowering with their faces low to the ground. Neither dared speak, though Silvana wondered what Ingolf might have said if his jaw were intact. Elsewhere, Sam and Khadija had wrapped an arm around each other and held on tightly. Khadija's eyes seemed to glisten in the light.

"But what I'd like to know," Reynold said, "is why my Vigiles were about to kill the wrong person?"

Desdemona bowed low with her arms outstretched. "My lord, to whom doth thou refer?"

"Do not lie in this holy place. You know I heard everything that happened. As God is everywhere, so am I. And I heard the Skinwalker confess his crimes. So why punish Al Khalifa?"

He heard everything? How? God that is terrifying.

"We…" Desdemona cut off and had to swallow. "She attacked us."

"Because she was threatened. Come now. You know who the real guilty are." He turned to Hana and Mikeru, and his weathered old face hardened into cruel lines. "The Yamatos."

"Your Majesty," Mikeru said, his voice strained. His right limb ended in a mass of bloodied cloth tied around his stump. "I know you are wise. Surely you know this is not true."

"We heard the confession from your own servant. He knows he doomed himself to say it. Why else would he, if not for the sake of justice?"

Chaitan stuttered. "Uh…doomed myself? But I never killed anyone."

"You attempted murder. Do you think your incompetence should save you?"

"But… Sire, please. Have mercy."

Reynold smiled, and Silvana felt her blood grow cold. "Of course, my son. Our God is just and merciful, therefore, I can be too."

What happened next was over in the space of a blink. One instant Chaitan was standing there with his hands clasped forward in a pleading gesture. In the next, he had shrunk down into a tiny ball of red and white. Now this horrid inhuman shape hung suspended in the air. It took Silvana a moment to comprehend what she was seeing. The ball was all that was left of Chaitan. He'd been crushed in an instant by the magic of the High King. There hadn't even been any sound. Reynold had not spoken a word or moved in any way.

Aakriti let out a piercing wail. She collapsed on the ground and sobbed heavily. Reynold seemed unaffected.

"Why grieve, child?" Reynold said. "He asked for mercy, and I granted it. There could not have been a quicker death. However, as for the Yamatos," Reynold's voice grew stern as his eyes fell on the vampire and her knight. "I'm afraid I cannot be so lenient."

"Wait! Sire!" Mikeru shouted. Silvana's heart was racing. She was about to witness their deaths. She couldn't bear to watch. Yet she forced herself to hold her head forward, so she saw Mikeru shuffling forward on his knees so that he shielded Hana. "It was all my plan. My wife had no idea about what I was doing."

"Mikeru," Hana cried, as if the word burst out of her. Yet she visibly steadied herself and spoke calmly. "He is correct. He planned the attack without my knowledge. I had no part in it."

"She tells the truth," Mikeru cried. "Please, your majesty. Spare this innocent servant."

It was almost certainly a lie. Or at least, a very skewed version of the truth. Yet Silvana could sympathise. In his last act, Mikeru was trying to save his wife. It was admittedly noble. Reynold stared at him with a blank face. Silvana held her breath. She felt Jason's hand clutch at her shoulder and gently try to turn her away. But she pulled back against him to show she needed to watch. These people had tried to destroy her family. And yet, Mikeru had shown true bravery. For both of these things, she would bear witness to their final breaths, no matter how sick it made her feel.

"Very well," the High King said.

It happened just as quickly, but this time they heard everything.

Mikeru was yanked high into the air, and in the same jerking motion, all four limbs went in separate directions.

Silvana screamed in shock, just as Hana let out a high-pitch wail. Mikeru did not scream out like Silvana had expected. He could only make a wretched agonised gasp. He floated in mid-air like a twisted starfish. Blood poured and squirted from the open flesh of his torso. Yet the blood didn't land on the floor. It landed on an invisible barrier of magic that surrounded him.

Oh my god. Reynold doesn't want the blood staining his throne room.

It was impossible to know how long Mikeru hung there. The shock of the scene made it seem to last for an eternity. Finally the broken knight slumped forward and his breathing grew jagged. At that point, his body and limbs were crushed back together into another ball of red pulp and white bone. This time, Silvana heard the crunch and squelch sounds clear as day.

"Justice has been done," Reynold pronounced. "The wrath of God has been appeased. Blessed be the name of the Lord."

The two balls of red that used to be Mikeru and Chaitan levitated out of the throne room doorways. Silvana didn't watch to see where they were disposed. She clutched her stomach and had to swallow down the bile. She dared not vomit in the High King's throne room.

"Now, Miss Al Khalifa," Reynold said as he faced Khadija. The wizard princess had tears streaming down her face and a furious hatred burning in her eyes. "By the power of God in me, I hearby judge you innocent of Samantha Kennedy's death. Also I absolve you for the crime of attacking my Vigiles, deeming it to be only committed under extreme duress and in self-defence. You may return to your wealth and titles. You may thank God for His mercies."

Khadija's mouth hung ajar. Then she clenched her jaw hard. The room was silent, and it was clear Reynold was waiting. Khadija tried to keep her face neutral, but her lip twisted on its own as she spoke.

"Thank you, my lord," she mumbled.

"Good. Perhaps you can show your gratitude by aiding this young servant here," he gestured to Aakriti, "find a new place of employment. I doubt Miss Yamato will wish to see her again."

The two shared an awkward glance. Aakriti didn't understand what had been said, but recognised that Khadija was now her mistress. She seemed to quiver where she stood. "Of course, my lord," Khadija said. She offered Aakriti a bow of respect. Somehow, it did seem to calm the grieving servant somewhat.

That was...surprisingly merciful.

"Kennedy," Reynold said. "While you attacked the Vigiles under similar circumstances, I sense by the wisdom God has imparted to me that you were not of sound mind. I sense your experiences have left you unwell of thought. Therefore, I must sentence you..."

Samantha let out a growl. It burst out of her, and she seemed to regret it immediately. Silvana and the whole room held their breath.

Reynold scowled. "...sentence you to an asylum for the sick. You will stay with the Vigiles, and they will take you there once you are dismissed. I suggest you commit to your improvement."

Samantha merely glared at the High King. Silvana couldn't help a sigh of relief. After Reynold had killed Mikeru so quickly, she was certain Khadija and Sam would go next.

"And Glucksburg," Reynold said, turning to Ingolf and Wilhelm. "For attacking the Vigiles without provocation, you will pay a fine to the Imperium. My aides will be in touch with the exact amount. I suggest you get some healing for that jaw. I pray the healing hand of God be at work in you."

"Thank you, sire," Wilhelm grumbled. He kept his arm around his master's shoulders, though anyone could see the rage in Ingolf's eyes at his humiliation.

Reynold smiled, and it caused his face to crease with countless lines of wrinkles. "I declare a mandatory peace period between Yamato, Glucksburg, and Al Khalifa. Bad blood leads only to strife and bloodshed. Better to coexist under our Lord's divine light. No house may take action against another for six months. You will swear to this now."

At this, Khadija, Hana, and Wilhelm all muttered their reluctant agreement. Silvana found herself staring at the High King. Why was he feeling merciful all of a sudden? After such an extreme response to Mikeru. What was Reynold up to?

"I hope you all find peace and wisdom during this time," Reynold said. "And I hope I don't have to intervene again." At last the High King turned to face Silvana. "Now, House Romanov. How in God's name did you end up so entangled in all of this? I can't help but…"

"It was you," Silvana said.

Reynold paused. "Did you just interrupt a High King? While he sits on the throne, before God and all mankind?"

Silvana pointed at him across the room. Her heart was pounding, but she didn't care. She finally understood. "This was you all along."

"Watch thy tone, girl," Desdemona hissed.

"I see it now," Silvana went on. Even Jason was staring at her with wide eyes, as if begging her to be silent. But the words burst out of her. "Every House in this room is an enemy to the Imperium, in one way or another. Yamato and Glucksburg are both Royalists that want to destroy the Imperium and rule in their stead. Then Al Khalifa and Kennedy?" She gave a harsh laugh. "They're merely free thinkers. Progressive and innovative. That line of thinking challenges the established powers of the Imperium. Naturally, you wanted to get rid of these enemies. But even you couldn't just destroy them for no reason."

She pointed at Reynold, her finger boldly aimed at his face. "So you turned your enemies against each other. It was easy. You simply paid Mikeru five million pounds in exchange for his service."

Jason let out a gasp as he finally understood.

Silvana spoke in a clear voice, growing louder with each sentence. "You invested it into his company, Kennedy and Sons, and he removed it to his private account from there. He was ordered to attack us at the gala. It didn't matter to you if he succeeded or not. All you wanted was for your enemies to focus on fighting each other." She spun around and announced to the room. "That's why the no-violence enchantment at the gala failed. We thought it was destroyed by the bomb, because it used non-magical violence. But we were wrong. High King Reynold simply removed it." She turned back to the old man on the throne. "You alone had the power to do it. You needed the violence to be permitted because you wanted your enemies to fight each other. That's why you came to a public event for the first time in years. To ensure your plans were carried out."

Silvana's heart was racing. Reynold was staring at her in silence. She kept picturing Mikeru being crushed into a ball, and knew that could happen to her at any second. Yet she had to finish. "That's why you were quick to kill Mikeru and his accomplice, so they didn't expose you. And that's why you spared Hana, as a reward to Mikeru for his silence. Isn't that right, your majesty?"

The throne room was silent. Reynold stared back with a blank face. And Silvana suddenly realised what a terrible mistake she had made. She could have simply kept her realisation to herself. But she had exposed him. And in front of the very people he'd been trying to trick. Now they all knew what Reynold had done, and they would all hate him for it.

"Sire," Desdemona said. "Doth thou wish the girl destroyed for her lies?"

Reynold merely shook his head. "All of you may leave. I will speak to the Romanovs."

The throne room filled with the swirling motions of magical teleportation, though it was unclear just who was making it happen.

Khadija gave them a parting nod and a sympathetic smile. Within a few seconds, everyone else in the room had gone, leaving only Silvana and Jason standing before the High King.

"Approach me," Reynold said.

Silvana started walking immediately, with Jason following, until she stopped at the foot of his throne. Up close, he looked like nothing more than an old man in a fancy costume. But she knew the power that mind held. She had seen how quickly he could rip a person apart with his magic. They could not fight him if they tried. Meanwhile Reynold just stared at them. He looked at Silvana, and for a long moment, his eyes wandered up and down her figure. She tried not to squirm under his lecherous gaze.

"I must say," Reynold whispered. "You're smarter than most, Miss Romanov." He grinned at her, but she felt none of the humour. "If God has granted you so much intelligence, answer me this. How do you think I have stayed in power for over nine hundred years?"

Silvana glanced at Jason. He was nearly panting from the fear. She tried to think about Reynold's question. Should she say it was his power? Or perhaps God's power in him? No, he had mentioned her intelligence. So it had to be a clever answer. She thought about his position in the Imperium. About what he'd just done in the last few weeks.

"You turn your enemies against each other," she said.

He grinned. "Obvious, isn't it? Miss Romanov, in the last nine hundred years, there have been plenty who have opposed me. False kings, bloodthirsty maniacs, and idealists. Some I have fought and destroyed myself. But most mortal happily destroy each other." He looked past her into the distance, as if seeing back across time. "That's why my brothers and I chose England, all those centuries ago. Why remain in the bloodbath of Europe with all the other kings contending for power, when I could carve out my own kingdom in the isolation of the isles? I let them kill each other, while I grew in strength. Then two hundred and fifty years later, I began the war with France, and none could stop my advance. That is how I rose to the position of High King. That is how you play the long game."

Silvana noticed something. He hadn't mentioned God in a while. Was this…his true self?

"Both the Royalists and idealists want the world to change," Reynold said. "Many people do and have done so. Yet why does it never change? Because they waste all their energy fighting each other. They never bother to fight me."

"The law of coexistence," Jason said. Silvana frowned at him. But Reynold seemed to understand.

"Exactly. They fight each other because I scare them. I'm too big a target. They'd rather attack something they can defeat." Abruptly his face grew hard and all his charm seemed to vanish. "Until you exposed my plans to my enemies, and undid all my work."

Silvana felt herself literally tremble before his wrath. She clutched Jason's hand for comfort. His palm was sweaty.

"I did not ask Mikeru to attack you," Reynold said. "He must have done that on his own as revenge for removing his ally. Up till now, I've had no ill will towards you. But you have drawn my attention today." Reynold scowled and tilted forward in his chair. His eyes seemed to burn through Silvana's soul. "I would advise you to not draw my attention a second time. Is that understood?"

"Yes sire," Silvana answered immediately.

"Yes, your Majesty," Jason echoed.

"Good. Because it is I who rule this world, as God intended." Reynold looked up to the roof of his palace and his eyes burned with fervency. "God Himself placed the burden of rule on my shoulders. I am the Chosen One, destined from birth to rule, as I have for nearly a millennium. As Christ was the Son of God, so too am I the next holder of that title. Greatest of His servants, firstborn of His children. My rule is His will." He glared back at Silvana.

Was that passion in his eyes, or mania?

"It is for the good of all that my rule not be challenged. If I am weakened, then God is weakened, and the Devil may yet bring all to ruin. We must not let that happen."

"No sire," Silvana whispered. *My god. He might genuinely be insane.*

Reynold turned and looked at Jason for the first time during the entire speech. He stared on and on for nearly a minute without a single word.

"The wizard slayer," he said finally. Then his voice became a near whisper. "Jason Turner, of Plymouth, England."

Jason's eyes widened as far as they could go. "Your Majesty is wise. I am honoured that you still remember me." Reynold only continued to stare. Silvana and Jason shared a glance, both looked as confused as each other. Yet neither spoke. They waited under the High King's intense gaze.

"Remember what I told you," Reynold said. "It is given to men to rule. Do not defy the heavens."

Jason bowed his head low, though Silvana could see him hiding the fury in his eyes. "Yes, sire."

"Good," Reynold said. "I will be keeping an eye on you, Jason Turner."

"You honour me, sire."

Reynold nodded his head. "God be with you," he said as a clear dismissal.

The world shifted around them, and Silvana fell away from the throne room of the High King, but not before seeing his eyes run up and down the length of her body once more.

Chapter 33

The instant Jason landed on solid ground, he turned to Silvana and gripped her in a tight hug. Something gave way in his chest, and he felt tears come to his eyes as heavy sobs burst from deep in his stomach. She hugged him back just as tightly. Her body was shaking. She had been just as scared as him.

"Is this a bad time?" Khadija said.

Jason was so numb with terror he could barely register the surprise he felt. He pulled back from Silvana and actually looked at where Reynold had sent them. It was a fancy bar and a suite in a high-class building. There were burn marks in the centre of the room. He saw Khadija standing nearby, and Aakriti just beyond her. Everything looked completely new, and yet somehow familiar.

"It looks different without all the guests," Silvana said.

"Oh, we're back here," Jason said. The Burj Al Khalifa, the place of the gala. Clearly, Reynold had not known or cared where he sent them, and so had returned them to the last place he had seen them. The room was now empty of furniture and decorations, instead lined with construction tools and wooden boards as repairs were undertaken. A half dozen staff members came running forward to see to Khadija's needs, all rapidly speaking in Arabic. She waved them off and faced Jason and Silvana.

"Listen, I've got a lot to sort out right now," Khadija said as she gestured to the servants. She started wrapping her hair back in a turban. "I have to make peace with my family and ensure my innocence is announced. But I promise, give me a day or two, and I will pay you back in cash." She tied her turban off around her shoulders and sighed. "I mean it. Thank you both."

"Oh right," Jason stammered. "Somehow I'd forgotten about the payment. Yes, that would be incredible." He looked to Silvana, and they each let out an elated laugh. "That will save House Romanov. Thank you."

"Is there anything we can do for Samantha?" Silvana asked. Jason finally realised that the other wizard hadn't been teleported back with them.

Khadija shook her head. "No. Reynold called it an asylum. But we all know medieval asylums were basically just prisons. Immortals get thrown in these places and disappear for decades. Dark rooms, locked doors, and everything." Her eyes teared up. "They didn't even let us say goodbye…" Then she growled in anger and seemed to force the tears back by sheer will. "I will start fighting for her release immediately. I won't rest until she is free."

Jason nodded. "If we can ever help, we will," he said.

Khadija looked at them both for a moment, ignoring all the other people in the room. "Before today, we were allies. Now, I consider you both my friends." She bowed her head low towards them in a sign of deep respect. Some of the servants seemed shocked, seeing a wizard bow to a vampire and a mortal knight.

Jason wanted to reply in kind. Yet he saw Aakriti hiding behind Khadija's shoulder and huddling in on herself. He remembered what Khadija had done to her. It wasn't something he could just overlook.

"We consider you a friend as well, but on one condition," Silvana said, clearly thinking along the same lines as Jason. "Promise us you will take care of the physically enhanced, and all the working class servants under your care. Do better this time." She nodded meaningfully to Aakriti, and Khadija nodded.

"I will," Khadija said. "You are right to demand that. I promise I will do better. I'll get her a good job here. I'll pay for all of their education." The staff members grew impatient and started speaking in Arabic, and Khadija finally turned to start arguing with them.

Silvana was already stepping towards Aakriti, so Jason followed. He watched as Silvana walked right up to the girl, took her in her arms and embraced her in a hug. The young Skinwalker began to weep softly. Silvana held her for nearly a minute and let the girl cry. "Jason, do you have your phone?" she asked. He pulled it out of his pants pocket, and was not surprised to find the screen had partially cracked. He loaded up the translator.

"Your brother was brave," Silvana said. "He saved us all. I'm sorry you saw it happen. But he loved you."

"*Thank you*," Aakriti replied. Then she pulled out of the hug. "*Will I be safe here?*"

"Yes. I promise you. Khadija owes us for our help. She has sworn to provide a job for you here. Will that be ok with you?" Aakriti gave a brave nod, and Silvana wiped a tear from Aakriti's cheek.

"I have to ask," Jason said into the translator. "Why were you here on the night of the attacks? You weren't involved, and you were injured."

"*I was scared to be alone at Yamato castle. My brother brought me here. He said stay in the bathroom. I should have listened.*" She started to cry again. "*Now I will always be alone.*"

Silvana gave her another hug. "You're going to be ok," she whispered. They stayed like that for a minute, while Jason stood around without anything to do.

Jason noticed the bar. He stepped away from everyone else to go behind the counter and pour himself a shot of whisky. He sipped it as he watched Khadija wave down the staff and gesture to the new guests she'd brought with them. The drink was sweet and burned on the way down. Jason felt his mind finally relaxing after all the terror of their battle. His adrenaline was still surging at just the right level to help him think clearly.

"You ok?" Silvana said as she came to his side. Aakriti was content to sit by herself nearby.

"Something bothers me."

"Should I even bother asking what? There were so many things."

He gave a short laugh at her. "Mikeru denied killing Samantha. Then Aakriti's brother, Chaitan. He said he tried to attack her at the gala, but she was already dead. That can't be a coincidence. Their stories matched."

"Mikeru could have just lied."

He raised an eyebrow at her. "I'm asking for your opinion, miss genius detective. I can't believe you figured out Reynold was playing us all. I didn't even think of it."

She gave a modest shrug. "Maybe you taught me a thing or two." She waved him down when he started to protest. "Alright, maybe being tricked by Mikeru has made me more paranoid. I was looking for the lie. Even so, I don't think it did any good." She sighed, and Jason reached over the bar to hold her hand. "It doesn't matter that I exposed him. Reynold's still in control. He arranged for the murders. He lied and cheated. Exposing him did nothing."

"No," Jason said. "Exposing him means that Hana and Ingolf will be just as furious with him as they are with us. Reynold has cause to watch his back now, thanks to you."

"Yeah. But so do we."

"I suppose." Jason took another sip. "We may have exonerated Khadija and got the money to save our family. But I still don't feel like I have the answer. I honestly don't know who killed Samantha Kennedy. It was probably Mikeru, but we can't be certain. Even if that was a good enough answer for Reynold, it's not good enough for me."

"Well, you two don't exactly have the same sense of justice," Silvana drawled.

"It doesn't feel right." Jason emptied his glass, then looked across the floor. "This is where it happened, isn't it?" Silvana nodded. "Can you show me where you found her?"

Silvana led him towards the burnt out area on the floor. "Just here." She pointed to an unmarked patch of floor. Jason stared at it for several minutes. He walked in a circle, crouched low and checked the distance to the exits. He nodded his head several times throughout his search.

Khadija approached them, breaking Jason out of his focus. "Sorry about that. I just realised, you two are probably stuck here, aren't you?"

"Yes," Jason shrugged. "I wasn't going to complain. Kinda just happy to be alive."

"We can catch a flight," Silvana said, but Khadija waved her away.

"I'll take you home. I have enough magic left for that. It's the least I can do." She smiled. "Is your family mansion a good destination?"

"Uh…actually, I'd prefer not."

"Wait," Jason said, holding up a hand. "We can go there." He pointed to Khadija. "She's tired, and the mansion is a place she's familiar with. We can just catch an uber from there."

"Oh. Ok."

Khadija put a hand on either of their shoulders. A moment later the world shifted around them, and Jason caught his final glimpse of Aakriti, sitting alone.

This time, there was no falling sensation. Apparently that only happened in a teleportation without physical contact. *That freaking asshole Reynold didn't care if we free-fell during transport.* Khadija dropped them off in Silvana's bedroom.

Jason saw her familiar bed and drawing desk. He felt a pang of longing for the many days when they had lazed around in this room together, sleeping in late, bathing and having sex without a care in the world. He sighed regretfully. Those days were gone.

"Thank you," he said.

Khadija nodded. "Thank you both. Any time you need anything, just give me a call."

"I'm sorry for your loss," Silvana said.

"Yeah. Me too," Jason said. "I'm sure you'll get Samantha back one day soon."

Khadija just stared into the distance. "I'll make those bastard High Kings pay. Every single one of them." She gave a full smile that failed to hide her pain. "But hey. You can also call if you want to just hang out. I haven't forgotten my offer to be your third."

"Goodbye, Khadija," Jason said pointedly. She gave a short laugh, before she teleported away again.

Silvana looked around the room. She moved to her desk and collected her art supplies, shoving them in a bag. Then she faced Jason. "Let's sneak out."

"Hang on," he said. "I want to talk to Nicholas about that letter he wrote me. Do you think it'd be ok if I went and saw him in private?"

Silvana hesitated a moment. "What time is it?"

Jason checked his phone. "Nine-thirty?"

"I guess that'd be ok. He's usually in his library at this time of the evening. He'll be alone."

Jason nodded. "I'll just be a few minutes."

He snuck out the bedroom door and crept down the hallway. He had a strange sense of déjà vu. He had once crept through this hallway at night time, chasing an intruder in the house, all because he'd been chaperoning Peter Erikson on a date with a vampire. So much had changed since that day. The world seemed more complicated now. But one thing had changed for the better. Now, he loved Silvana more than ever.

He guessed it had worked out for the best. Provided nothing worse happened in the future.

The library door was closed. Jason knocked on the door. "Come in," came Nicholas's voice, and hearing it made Jason feel like he had come home. He entered.

Nicholas was sitting in a reading chair, a paperback copy of H.G. Wells' *The Time Machine* in his hands, while old jazz band music played on a record player. Nicholas glanced up from his book, and his face lit up into a warm smile.

"Jason, my son! It's good to see you!"

"It's good to see you too, sir," he said, and meant it.

Nicholas put his book down and stood up with a groan. "Come here, son." Jason nearly objected, but Nicholas was adamant and grabbed him in a hug. He smelled of soap and musk. "Is Silvana here? Did you want to move back in?"

Jason smiled. "I just came for a quick chat. I haven't told anyone else I'm here."

"Oh." Nicholas sat back in his armchair. Jason took the chair opposite. "What did you want to talk about? Did you get my letter?"

"Yes, actually. I had a question, about the law of coexistence."

"Ah. That's natural. It's a rather complex topic. I've had many long discussions into the night debating details of that philosophy. What did you want to know?"

"Well, if knights are trying to avoid attention, then when is it ok to take action?"

Nicholas just chuckled. "It's simple, and complex. Basically, you take action when you know you can get away with it. Or, you take action when it's more dangerous not to. But it's complex, because it takes time and experience to learn to spot the opportunity. Remember, the original Knight Templar did nothing wrong. King Phillip destroyed them just to absolve his financial debt. You must make sure no one will benefit from your defeat. Does that make sense?"

Jason nodded. "Can you make peace *after* you've pissed someone off?"

"Oh yes. Usually just by staying out of sight and out of mind. Immortals may be long lived, but they can forget just as quickly as mortals. Good behaviour is the secret."

"I see." He studied Nicholas for a long moment. He couldn't bring himself to say what was really on his mind. He stared at the ground and sighed deeply. "I should thank you. Your training just saved my life. Two days ago I fought with the Knight Wilhelm of House Glucksburg. Tonight I fought Knight Mikeru of House Yamato. I bested them both in swordplay, thanks to your teaching."

Nicholas barked a laugh. "You're joking! Oh Jason, that's incredible! A Yamato? Jason, the samurais are the best of swordsmen. There's a reason the British only fought the Japanese with machine guns. No one is a match for them. How did you do it?"

"I cheated."

"Well naturally." Nicholas laughed. "Seriously, tell me."

Jason explained how he had pulled the sword from his own gut, then let the elixir heal him enough to strike back.

Nicholas mimed falling back out of his chair. "Incredible! I'm so proud of you, Jason. You didn't freeze! That's my boy." Jason tried to smile under the praise. Yet it only made him sick to his stomach. "My son, I can see something is troubling you. Whatever is wrong, you can tell me."

Jason let out a long sigh. "I don't want to."

"Please, my son. What is it?"

Jason looked up at Nicholas. He forced the words out. "I know the truth now."

Nicholas frowned. "What truth?"

"That you killed Samantha Kennedy."

The words hung between them like a widening chasm. Nicholas's face was blank, but he was blinking a little too quickly. He leaned over and pulled the needle off the record player. The music scratched as it stopped. He leaned forward in his chair and clasped his hands together.

"How did you know?" Nicholas whispered.

The words were a blow to Jason's chest. He had hoped in some part of his soul that he'd been wrong.

"The night of the gala," Jason said. "I ran into you getting drinks. I asked you if there were people who didn't like the High Kings, and you said it was treason to disagree with them. But you're a smart man. You knew I had just helped Samantha Kennedy after her run in with the High King. So when I came back asking about traitors, you figured out that Samantha Kennedy had tried to turn me against the Imperium. It was my own damn fault for bringing it to your attention.

"Then after the explosion, Silvana went back inside searching for you everywhere, but you were nowhere to be found. Which mean you didn't have an alibi." Jason shrugged. "That alone isn't a big deal. It could have been a coincidence. Though, it was curious that later that night when we had the family meeting, you explained how to kill a wizard. You specifically said it had to be by surprise." Jason shrugged again. "I thought you were referring to Erikson. But it was clearly on your mind, for some reason. Also, in that same meeting, you were opposed to me investigating this crime. You even wrote me a letter about coexisting, begging me a second time to drop my investigation."

Jason held up his hands in admission. "But again, that could all be a coincidence. What really gave me a clue was the next morning. You remember? When we were training with the swords."

Nicholas' squinted his eyes. "What about it?" he asked.

"When Phillip got tired and asked you to take a turn, you started drawing your sword, but stopped. You then claimed your hand was hurting from accidently firing your gun. But that wasn't true." Jason leaned in close and whispered. "You couldn't draw your sword because there was still blood on it from the night before."

Nicholas squeezed his eyes shut. "You noticed that, did you? I must say, you're a very observant man, Jason. A good detective."

"You know that," Jason said. "That's why when the detectives came to the house, you were acting tired. Your hands were trembling. But that was just an act. You were playing up the fake injury just in case I caught on, because you knew I was smart enough that I just might." Jason gestured to Nicholas' body. "You're actually in great health, for your age. Everyone assumes you're old and weak, and you let them think that, don't you?"

"I am a knight," Nicholas said. "I am always underestimated."

"But even if I did find blood on your sword," Jason went on. "That wouldn't hold up in court. Even if I did a lab test and matched DNA to Samantha, you could just claim someone used your sword. It would not get a conviction. But you know what would get a conviction?" He gestured to Nicholas in his chair. "Being accused of a murder, and responding with, 'how did you know?' To a cop, that's as good as a confession."

Nicholas leaned back in his chair. "Ah. Very clever. I assumed you knew for a fact. You just seemed so certain …" he trailed off. "That was well done. The real question is, are you planning to arrest me, my son?"

"*Don't* call me son!" Jason hissed. Nicholas's mouth fell open. His eyes showed the pain he felt. But Jason didn't care. "I can't believe you would do that. Just because I spoke to someone who hates the Imperium, you would take it on yourself to kill them. Are you insane? You couldn't just come and talk to me about it?"

"I couldn't take that risk," Nicholas pleaded.

"You bastard," Jason cried, hot tears springing to his eyes as he spoke. "Don't you understand? I love you, Nicholas. You were the father I always wanted."

"And you're the son I always wanted."

"But you're a murderer!" Jason growled. "Just like my real dad. You're no better than him, and he's a low life piece of shit. A lady killer."

"Jason," Nicholas groaned and squeezed his eyes shut. "That's completely different. Your father tormented a woman he was sworn to protect. Tormented her for years and years. I killed a wizard in a moment. She barely suffered."

"You have *no idea* how much she suffered!" Jason struggled to keep his voice down. He forced himself to speak softer. "Just tell me why. Why'd you do it? Was this the law of coexistence? Or were you ordered to do it by the High King? Don't tell me you were just following orders."

Nicholas waved his hand back and forth. He had a single tear trapped in the bottom of his eye. "Jason, my s..." he stopped himself. "It's not like that."

"Then tell me the truth!"

"I did it to protect you. To protect this family. And most of all, to protect Silvana."

"Bullshit," Jason growled. "Don't give me that self-righteous crap. You murdered a woman in cold blood. How does that help us?"

"She was an idealist, wasn't she?" Nicholas's voice was cold. "I know the type. They befriend people new to the international community, put ideas in your head, and before you know it they invite you to join a rebellion against the Imperium. We've seen it a dozen times before. There's always a rebellion against the High Kings. That's how both World Wars started. But the Imperium has stood for thousands of years. No rebellion is ever going to dislodge them."

"You don't know that for certain."

Nicholas went on, "I couldn't risk letting you and Silvana get swept up in their delusion. So I killed her. When the explosion happened, I saw my chance. I struck from behind and cut her throat, so she couldn't breathe and throw a spell at me." He waved his hands outward in invitation. "I'm an eighty-four-year-old mortal, and I took down a fully trained wizard on my own. You say it was cold blood. I say it was David versus Goliath. I did a deed worthy of a hero's song. I am a Mortal Knight as great as Saint George."

Jason shook his head. "Then why couldn't you just *talk* to me about it? You're my teacher! Why not *teach* me?"

"Because I know you, Jason. You wouldn't have listened to me. You knew Ms Al Khalifa wanted rebellion, yet you came back home the next day and tried to convince us to work with her. You had no concept of the risks involved. I love you, but you're too short-sighted. You weren't ready for this lesson."

"I can't believe you're trying to justify this to me," Jason said. "You're…you're despicable!"

Nicholas still had the tears in his eyes, but he hardened his jaw and raised his head. "I am the son of kings. I will be hard when I need to be. Just as you were when you killed Peter Erikson."

"Don't you dare compare yourself to me. Peter was about to kill Silvana, and there were no other options."

"Just as there were no options with Samantha Kennedy."

Jason felt his temper rising. "There were plenty of options! And there was no immediate risk. You should have thought it through and talked with us. But you treated both me and Silvana as children! You didn't even try to treat us like equals."

"Jason, this isn't a perfect world. I'm sorry I've disappointed you, I truly am. But the Immortal world is not like the mortal one. If someone commits a mortal crime, you go lock them up. But with Immortals, it doesn't matter who's right or wrong. It only matters who has more power. The High Kings have the most power. You don't understand, because you've lived all your life under governments. You have democracies and elections. If someone is a bad ruler, you vote them out."

Jason rolled his eyes. "Clearly, you haven't followed politics in a while."

"It's completely different in a monarchy. A king has the divine right of rule. No one can question them. No one can challenge them."

"Really? Then what happened to your namesake, Nicholas the Second, Tsar of Russia? The Romanovs were famously disposed."

"He was a mortal king. Would you compare him to Reynold?" Nicholas twisted his lip, a glimpse of anger showing on his face. "You know why Nicholas was removed from power? Look it up. It's called the Khodynka tragedy. He served food at his coronation to thousands of starving peasants, expecting them to praise him. He had no idea the poverty they lived in. They were all so desperate for food that they stampeded, and thirteen hundred people were crushed to death."

Jason blinked. "Thirteen hundred? Holy shit."

"Exactly. Nicholas the Second was a fool. He pissed off too many people all at the same time. But the High Kings don't do that. They don't piss off everyone. They just piss off one or two. Cause they know from watching the mortal kings fail that there is a risk of revolution. It's the only thing that truly threatens their power. So they don't make big mistakes." Nicholas pointed to the far wall. "You think your rebels have a just cause? They'll never have the numbers they need to make a difference. The Imperium are too strong. The High Kings are essentially gods. In all of history, a High King has never been defeated. Not even *once*. It's impossible."

Jason thought of Chaitan being crushed in a ball, and Mikeru being ripped apart, and he couldn't help see the truth of what Nicholas was saying.

"So the best way you can protect your family is to serve the Imperium. Remove the Imperium's enemies for them. Keep yourself in their good graces. We must all serve the High Kings."

Jason stood up and turned away. Nicholas talked at his back. "I know it's awful, and believe me, however much you think you hate it, I hate it more. My hands are filthy. Samantha wasn't the first I've killed in service to the Imperium. But I'd do it again if it keeps my family safe. And I guarantee you, Jason, there is no better option out there. You must realise this. To be a Knight Templar is to serve the High Kings."

Jason leaned over his shoulder. "I can't even look at you," he whispered.

"Jason, please. I know it's hard to accept. But we can't let ourselves be destroyed like the old Knight Templar."

"No," Jason whispered. He turned around and looked at Nicholas once more. He saw the sorrow on the old man's face, but he made his heart rock hard in response. "We solved the case for Khadija, and in a few days she'll pay us five million pounds. You can use it to pay off Silvana's bank loan and retain your family fortune. Silvana and I saved House Romanov."

"What?" Nicholas took a moment to process this, before he

softened his voice and smiled. "Oh Jason, that's wonderful. This is such good news. You can still inherit the fortune after all…"

"I don't want it."

Nicholas recoiled as if he'd been slapped in the face.

"I'm not your son," Jason said in a flat voice. "I'm not your heir. I don't want a cent of your blood money. And I'll do everything I can to keep Silvana away from you. I think that's a fair exchange for not trying to arrest you."

Then he turned around and walked to the door. He didn't let himself look back once. Even when he heard Nicholas let out a pained sob. Jason closed the door behind him. He walked down the hallway with his vision blurring, but within a few steps, he was shaking with silent sobs. He pressed his face into his hands and clenched his teeth to keep from making noise. He let himself cry, knowing there was nothing he could do to stop it now.

By the time he reached Silvana's room, he had wiped his eyes dry. He found her waiting for him at the foot of the bed.

"Everything ok?" she asked.

He nodded. "Yes," his voice came out steady. "I'm ready to leave this place."

They walked together silently through the house towards the front door. Jason half hoped to see Nicholas chasing after him, or even the vampire aunts running downstairs to see what was making noise. But no one was coming, and no one heard them pass through the house. Silvana opened the large front door without letting it squeak. They stepped through with one last look at the inside of their home. Then they closed the door behind them.

Chapter 34

Jason went to work the next day.

It felt absurd to be back in a normal place as if nothing had occurred. Everyone in the precinct was a bit hesitant to talk to him. He could understand. They had last seen a wizard appear beside him and teleport him away. He just focused on writing down everything that had happened in the Immortal Investigations.

Around midday, Lynch and Cole came over to his desk. "Hey rookie," Lynch said in his normal chipper voice as if nothing had happened. "Good news. The auditors were looking into your embezzlement angle, and they said they found something."

"Oh yeah?"

"They said the discrepancy wasn't tax fraud at all. It seems someone deposited five million pounds into the account at the exact second that five million was taken out. So there was no change. Then the records were scrubbed."

Of course. Reynold put the money in, and Mikeru took it out.

Lynch gave him a pat on the shoulder. "Hey, don't look so glum. You were completely right. Looks like you solved your first case, rookie."

Jason blinked. "Really?"

"Don't lay it on too thick," Cole said with a shaking head.

Lynch shrugged her off. "I'm just relieved. This means we can get your girl back all her money! She can pay off that debt to the bank. Just advise her to be a bit smarter with it this time, and she'll be fine. Hopefully, she has no hard feelings, yeah?" Jason nodded in agreement.

"You showed good instincts," Cole said. "We still don't know where the money came from or went. Likely it was in off-shore accounts."

"And probably untraceable," Jason said. "If they were from Immortal sources." The detectives shuffled on their feet and avoided his eye contact. "Sorry. So what does this mean for Kennedy and sons?"

Cole rolled her eyes. "They'll get an infringement notice. It's a slap on a wrist, but it's about all we can do."

"Sorry, mate," Lynch said. "We can't arrest Gene Conroy today. But if we ever do, I'll let you slap on the cuffs, hey?"

Jason couldn't help a wide grin. "Thanks guys. I learnt a lot from this."

"Yeah," Lynch muttered, sounding unconvinced. "Guess you'll have to consult with us again sometime." He patted Jason's arm again and left without another word. Cole offered a quick nod before following.

Jason finished up his report on all his recent activities. He hit save on the document. A moment later, Captain Kader came up as 'viewed'. He waited a few minutes before going into the captain's office to discuss it with her.

"So," Kader said as he entered. "Nicholas the Third was the killer after all."

"Yeah," Jason said with a groan.

"And you don't want to bring him to justice?"

Jason just sighed. "At this point, I don't think we'd ever get a conviction. Samantha is alive again and locked up in some asylum.

There is no evidence of her being murdered by a sword. And I'm sure the Vigiles would show up to interfere if I tried to gather evidence. It's just…pointless."

"I agree." Kader was eyeing him strangely. "How do you feel about Nicholas right now?"

"I'm furious. I never want to see him again."

"Really? Cause up till now, he's been your friend and mentor."

"Yeah, well, that was before I knew the real Nicholas. Turns out, he's just as bad as my real father."

Kader seemed to find that idea amusing. "Jason, I may be out of line for saying this. But do you realise Nicholas is not your father?"

Jason looked up sharply, and felt his temper flare. He quickly put it in check and took a deep breath. "What do you mean, captain?"

"Your father made many evil choices over and over again, and no one ever made him do it. He also had almost no redeeming traits. That's very different to someone who has been – up to this point – a good person, but felt compelled to do one bad act because of tough circumstances."

Jason stopped and thought about it. Maybe there was some truth to what she said. Nicholas had been a father to Jason till now. But he hated that Nicholas had killed a woman. It felt too similar to losing his mother.

"I'm going to tell you something," Kader said. "But you have to swear not to disclose this to anyone else. Do you understand?"

"Of course."

"You know my terrible secret?"

Jason sat up straighter. He remembered Kader in a hall with a telepath, crying that she couldn't save 'him', and pointing a gun at her own head. He had wondered about that for months now. "Yes, captain?"

"Well, you need to know the truth." Kader shut her eyes and took a long breath. Her eyes opened, and they were hard. "I was married to my children's father for ten years. He was a man very much like your father, Jason. I was abused by him for that entire time."

"I'm so sorry."

She waved a hand at him. "When I finally had the courage to leave him, I was afraid that he would try to kill me and the two boys. So I left in secret. I came to England without any possessions. I came here with no money, no proof of education, and no qualifications. Also, I had two boys, aged four and two."

She went quiet for some time. Jason could sense that she wasn't done talking, but something was hard to say. She inhaled, and the words came out in a rush.

"I was also pregnant."

Jason understood immediately where this was going. "Captain, that must have been horrible."

She nodded. "I couldn't care for my two boys. I couldn't even get a job while caring for them. And somehow, I was trying to keep my unborn baby healthy." She shook her head. "I was homeless for three weeks. I slept on the streets of London with my two babies. Every night I was terrified for my life. In a new country with a new language…you can never imagine what that's like until you've immigrated somewhere."

"Of course."

"So, I did what I had to do." She offered Jason a smile. "I had an abortion."

"Captain…"

She waved him down again. "I know what you're going to say, Jason. I've heard it before. I know I had every right to do it. I had good reason to do it. And I totally believe every woman should have that choice." She shook her head. "But it was the wrong choice for me."

Kader took a tissue off her desk and wiped her eyes. "It was only a few days after this when I was taken in by social workers. They set me up in a shelter and put me in a work placement program. I worked my ass off to get where I am today. Nearly 10 years later, a police captain." She shrugged. "But I have to live with that choice every day."

"Captain, if anyone had good cause, it was you. I mean, not that you need a 'good cause'. It's your choice. It's no one else's business."

"You don't understand, Jason. I love my two boys. They are the greatest joy in my life. And it breaks my heart every day to know there might have been one more like them." She wiped her eyes with the tissue and sighed. "I ask myself over and over, did I really *have* to do it? Could I have tried just a little harder, waited just a little longer? Did I really give it my best shot, or did I give up too easily? These are questions I can't answer."

"That's why the telepath hurt you," Jason said. "Your words were, 'I couldn't save him'. I thought you lost someone…" he trailed off, unsure how to word it correctly.

"I did lose someone. And I couldn't save him."

Jason understood now. The few times this issue had come up again, it's because he was facing something dangerous. Seeing Jason at risk reminded Kader of losing her child. Because she cared about him in a similar way.

Kader cleared her throat, and spoke with her usual sternness. "Now Jason, do you think less of me for this?"

"What? No, of course not."

"Why not?"

"Because you did what you had to do. You made a tough choice. No one has the right to judge you unless they've been in the same position."

"But some might say I committed murder."

Jason shrugged. "Screw those people. You made the hardest decision ever. I would never judge you for it."

"But you judge Nicholas."

Jason stopped. All at once, he understood what Kader was trying to show him. He wanted to insist that she was wrong, and she didn't understand, but he didn't have the heart to do it. She made sense.

"Nicholas was in an extremely tough situation," Kader said. "He felt he had no other choice. He did something that was morally questionable, and he did it for his own reasons. Hell, maybe his reasons are better than we can understand as police officers. He knows the Imperium better than we do. Maybe he's right, and the only way to survive with such powerful rulers is to do what they want. Submit to them and live within the broken system."

"But it's still murder," Jason said. "You had an operation. He slashed a woman's throat."

"Yes, but that woman could also wield the power of creation and create earthquakes and tornados and firestorms." Kader shrugged. "Maybe it was the wrong choice. Or maybe he was making an impossible choice. I don't know. All I know is, he loves you, Jason. And I would hate to see you walk away from him because of this." She sat back in her chair and shrugged. "Just keep an open mind. That's all I ask. Maybe one day, you'll understand him better."

Jason's stomach churned uncomfortably at the thought. But he nodded. "I'll try."

Kader nodded. "Good. Now. What are you going to do about these enemies you've made? Glucksburg, Yamato, and Reynold?"

"Ugh, don't remind me." He tried to laugh, but she didn't join in. "Right. Well, I guess I also have some allies now. Khadija and Edward. Maybe Samantha, though she's unavailable. Plus I think the Vigile Portia is beginning to trust me."

"You may need more allies than that. I appreciate Nicholas's idea of coexisting, but I think it's better to have multiple options. A good approach is to simply have lots of friends."

"I know. But I got all of these enemies while *trying* to make friends. A lot of these Immortals are just assholes, you know."

That got a laugh from Kader. "Good point. But all the same, let's make that your goal for the next little while."

"Good idea."

The chat with the captain had gone well, overall. Yet he wondered if he should have included Silvana's strange behaviour in his report.

Jason went home at the end of the day with a smile on his face. Things were looking up. He had solved his first case, and escaped the danger of the Immortal world, for now. He even found himself slightly happy at the idea of reconciling with Nicholas one day, even though he could barely admit the idea to himself.

He arrived home, and Silvana practically leapt straight into his arms.

"Khadija paid me!" she screamed right into his ear.

"Christ, Silvy!"

"Look in my account. Five million pounds!" She shoved her phone in his face. "I've thought long and hard about it, and you know what? I want to pay off my loan, straight away. So we don't have to pay any interest. What do you think about that?"

"Hey Jase," Freddie said from the couch. "I've got you a cold beer already, mate."

He chuckled at Freddie's total nonchalance, as if five million was an everyday occurrence. "Yes, absolutely pay off the loan. But keep in mind. The detectives solved the case. So what are you gonna do when you get your...*other* five million pounds back from the cops?"

She let out a laugh. "I've already thought of it!" Then she put on a serious face. "Well the first thing I'll do is make sure it's completely withdrawn from Kennedy and Sons. I don't want Hana getting access to it. Then I'll probably give most of it back to the family. They can use it to repair their mansion, finally, and have a financial buffer once again. There should be some left over for us. Oh, and Jason?" She clearly didn't want to say this next part. "I just want to say again how sorry I am that I didn't tell you about the loan. I'm sorry I kept that from you."

Jason suddenly pictured Silvana, standing over Hana with a crazed demonic look in her eyes, blood coating her teeth. *Silvana's not here.* Jason wanted to shudder. He was keeping a secret from her in the same way she had. He should tell her the truth.

Not to mention, Nicholas. The truth about him. He should tell her that too. He opened his mouth, and found himself saying, "Don't worry, I'm not mad."

Silvana had such a look of relief. "Thank you. And Jason, this money means we could buy a house together." She stopped short. "I mean, if you want. I know we've been putting off getting married so I can get to know myself. But I'd like to take one step to being closer. I'd like to move in with you."

"And leave me?" Freddie moaned. "I just got used to having the two of you here."

Silvana laughed, yet didn't look away from Jason. "What do you think? Cause I really don't want to move back in with my family. I've been out three days, and I'm already feeling so free. How about it?"

Jason smiled. "Sure. I would love to. You know it might take a while until you get that money back from the cops though. And buying a house is not simple."

"Hey, I'm happy for once. Just let me have this."

"Alright! We'll deal with that step later." Silvana laughed and kissed him on the lips.

They sat down on the couch together. Freddie handed Jason the beer and they clinked glasses. They were watching reruns of *Peep Show*. Jason sat with his arm around Silvana and found himself smiling.

"You know," he said. "There is one thing we didn't solve. We never found out who that Dorin guy was. The one who claimed to know you."

Silvana nodded. "I was thinking about that today, actually. You remember when we were fighting Hana and Mikeru, and you got stabbed?"

"You got stabbed?" Freddie cried.

Jason rolled his eyes. "Honestly, it was less stabbed, and more impaled."

"You got *impaled?!*"

"And yes, Silvy, I remember it pretty clearly."

"Well…I don't really remember much after that."

Jason went quiet. He wanted to avoid this topic. But here she was, bringing it up organically. He was going to have to tell her the truth about her alter ego, and what he knew of her past. But would it change things between them if he did?

"Anyway," she went on. "It was a weird experience. It felt like my mind snapped on its own. Now I feel like…I don't know. Like I don't know myself as well as I thought. So maybe I would like to know more about my past after all. How would you feel about starting another investigation?"

"Into your past?"

"Yeah. I was thinking, could we track down Dorin? See what he knows?"

Jason hummed in thought. "I don't know. Aakriti told us that Dorin was a leader among the Royalists. I'm not sure if he's someone we want to get close to."

"I know. It's probably risky. But I think I'm ready. I want to know where I come from."

Jason nodded. "Ok. That'll be our next investigation. Finding out where you came from. Starting with finding Dorin."

"Thank you, Jason. I love you."

"I love you too."

"And I love me!" Freddie shouted. They all laughed and clapped Freddie on the shoulders.

"We love you too, Freddie!" Silvana said.

"Hey I was thinking," Freddie said. "Finding Dorin. Isn't that a movie already?"

"Shut it, Freddie," Jason growled as the other two laughed.

They settled in to watch TV and drink on the couch. Jason leaned back in his chair while Silvana nuzzled in to his shoulder. Life was good. He couldn't bear to interrupt the good times they were having. They deserved to be happy today.

He would tell her everything tomorrow.

Epilogue

Portia looked up from her computer screen.

Desdemona had just entered their office space in the old stone castle. *She's up early.* Portia straightened her suit jacket and stood to attention. "Good morning, Mistress. I was just getting an early start on my research."

Desdemona was still in her white sleeping shift with thin straps on the shoulders and no sleeves. "Hast thou found anything, my dear?"

"Yes. My research has confirmed your suspicion. Mikeru was moving money around, before his death."

Desdemona crossed the room and leaned over Portia's shoulder to look at her screen. It made Portia shiver. It had been three days since she'd run off without her mistress's permission and tried to take down the Yamatos alone, yet Desdemona still hadn't acknowledged it. She hadn't even mentioned Portia's freak-out at seeing the High King again. She was just being quiet. And Portia hated it. *Say something already.*

"Where's the money coming from?" Desdemona asked.

"Multiple sources. I've confirmed the five million that came from Reynold, but that was just the tip of the iceberg, where Mikeru was concerned. I've found charitable donations, investments, and definitely a lot of theft. He was pooling resources. The Glucksburgs were involved too. And probably more sources than that."

"The Royalists are pooling their money. But where is it all going?"

"That's the problem. I don't think I can find out." Portia sighed and stepped back from her screen. "The Royalists are up to something, and they have hundreds of millions of dollars backing them. We need to find out what they're planning."

"What art thou suggesting, my dear?"

Portia looked her mistress in the eye. "This is something big. If these Royalists want to remove the High Kings, they may be genuinely taking steps towards that. But they cannot be acting alone."

"I agree," Desdemona said and actually sighed, a rare show of emotion. "I was hoping thou wouldst find a different answer. Yet my suspicions have been confirmed." She leaned towards Portia, and whispered even though they were alone, as if the very thought was almost sacrilegious.

"The Royalists must be collaborating with one of the High Kings. Someone is about to make a bid for power."

"Another High King?" Portia gasped. "That could change the Imperium."

"Nay, my dear. It could change the world itself."

Acknowledgements

This book was published at the same time as The Immortal Investigation and A King in Waiting, which means many of the same people worked on all three books. But each one is worth acknowledging as many times as it takes. So once more…

Thanks to my wife, Kit, who told me, "Don't you dare do [this] in your second book! It would be the most emotionally devastating thing possible!" Which is the worst thing you can ever say to a writer, so naturally, I wrote the entire book around this one idea. Thanks sweetheart! Love you!

To the same early readers Sam, Nick, and Kit (again), for once more giving brilliant ideas.

To Kirsty Inic, for editing the crap out of this, crushing my soul, and overall pushing me to even further heights.

To Wouter K, for proofreading this one even more extensively than the last. Sorry for all the typos, my cats like to walk on the keyboard. That's my excuse and I'm sticking to it.

To Anna, for sensitivity reading and crucial character development. Everyone's going to think I'm so clever and I literally just copied your advice, so thanks for that.

To Michael R Miller, for ongoing guidance and wisdom on Indie publishing, and showing me that success if possible.

To every single person in the YouTube community who liked, commented, and subscribed. I know it's a cliché of YouTube terms, but the support really did help me achieve my dreams. I appreciate the hell out of each and every one of you.

Finally, to Kit (again, again). For reminding me to drink water, stop for meals, and take time off for rest. But most of all, thank you for initiating coffee runs. Even if they were only because you wanted me to drive you there. That still counts.

www.ingramcontent.com/pod-product-compliance
Lightning Source LLC
Chambersburg PA
CBHW050845210726
48290CB00004B/1092